Bayard Taylor, Marie Hansen Taylor

Life and letters of Bayard Taylor

Vol. II.

Bayard Taylor, Marie Hansen Taylor

Life and letters of Bayard Taylor
Vol. II.

ISBN/EAN: 9783337021627

Printed in Europe, USA, Canada, Australia, Japan

Cover: Foto ©Raphael Reischuk / pixelio.de

More available books at **www.hansebooks.com**

From a photograph by Sarony, taken in 1862.

LIFE AND LETTERS OF
BAYARD TAYLOR

EDITED BY

MARIE HANSEN-TAYLOR

AND

HORACE E. SCUDDER

IN TWO VOLUMES

VOL. II.

FIFTH EDITION.

BOSTON
HOUGHTON, MIFFLIN AND COMPANY
New York: 11 East Seventeenth Street
𝕮𝖍𝖊 𝕽𝖎𝖛𝖊𝖗𝖘𝖎𝖉𝖊 𝕻𝖗𝖊𝖘𝖘, 𝕮𝖆𝖒𝖇𝖗𝖎𝖉𝖌𝖊
1895

Poet! Thou whose latest verse
Was a garland on thy hearse;
Thou hast sung with organ tone,
In Deukalion's life thine own.

H. W. Longfellow.

I am a voice, and cannot more be still
Than some high tree that takes the whirlwind's stress
Upon the summit of a lonely hill. . . .
Such voices were, and such must ever be,
Omnipotent as love, unforced as prayer,
And poured round Life as round its isles the sea!

Prince Deukalion.

CONTENTS OF VOLUME II.

vi   *CONTENTS OF VOLUME II.*

CHAPTER XXVII.

CHAPTER XXVIII.

CHAPTER XXIX.

CHAPTER XXX.

CHAPTER XXXI.

ILLUSTRATIONS.

Cedarcroft.

CHAPTER XVIII.

NOVEL-WRITING.

1863–1865.

The Poet's leaves are gathered one by one,
In the slow process of the doutful years.
Who seeks too eagerly, he shall not find :
Who, seeking not, pursues with single mind
Art's lofty aim, to him will she accord,
At her appointed time, the sure reward.
The Poet's Journal.

" HANNAH THURSTON " was published a few weeks
after Bayard Taylor's return to America. It was ded-
icated to Mr. Putnam, in a letter which acknowledged
gratefully the kindness which the publisher had shown
the author ever since the day when they met in London, and bore testimony to the unselfish nature of a
man who holds an honorable place among American

publishers, and whose own failure to achieve lasting success was never embittered by the reproaches of the authors to whose interests he gave himself unreservedly. Mr. Putnam, to whom the dedication was a pleasant surprise, wrote in reply a frank, manly letter, in which he says, " As for exemption from the ordinary share of human selfishness, I don't claim it and never have, and I don't pretend to have acted at any time by you on any higher principles than mere justice and mutual benefit, except that I have had the satisfaction of feeling that confidence and good-will were also mutual between us; and that if I had been able to do a good deal more for your interests the service would have been most worthily rendered if rendered to you, and would have been equally for my advantage too. In fact, antagonism between author and publisher, even outside of personal relations, has always seemed to me impolitic and absurd."

The dedication also contains some passages which indicate the attitude which the author took toward his first novel. " I do not," he says, " rest the interest of the book on its slender plot, but on the fidelity with which it represents certain types of character and phases of society. That in it which most resembles caricature is oftenest the transcript of actual fact, and there are none of the opinions uttered by the various characters which may not now and then be heard in almost any country community of the Northern and Western States."

The defense which an author sets up beforehand for his work is pretty sure to indicate not necessarily its weakness but the point most likely to be attacked. The class of people satirized in the novel were loud in their denial of its truthfulness, but the author had the satisfaction of seeing the book diligently read in circles most qualified to pass upon its faithfulness to nature, and of hearing both willing and unwilling testimony of its accuracy. Indeed, the success of the book was most emphatically with the people who read a novel for what it may betray of human life. The critics and those who look more narrowly to the artistic plan were divided in their judgment. The very carefulness of the novelist not to allow his characters to become caricatures exposed him to the peril of a too level portraiture, and the fact that the phase of life which he depicted had its presentation in Kennett made him rely often upon actual circumstances and words which he reported with fidelity. The form of the novel was an experiment with him, although he had tried his hand at short stories, and a certain caution in movement followed from the unfamiliarity of the exercise. Nevertheless, the thing in "Hannah Thurston" which he was aiming at he reached, and it was a pleasure to him to find this recognized by others and by those who had the best right to know whether or no he had succeeded. Hawthorne, for example, wrote to him, "The book is an admirable one, new, true, and striking, — worthy of such a world-wide observer as yourself, and with a kind of thought in it which does not lie scattered about the world's highways."

The fall of 1863 was spent at Cedarcroft, whence Bayard Taylor made occasional journeys to Canada to secure an English copyright for "Hannah Thurston," and to various places to meet lecture engagements. He wrote a lecture on "Russia and her People," but gave most of his leisure to poetry. At the request of Ticknor & Fields he prepared a revised edition of his poems to be put in the series then very popular, known

from its binding as the " Blue and Gold " editions.
He also worked from time to time on his poem, "The
Picture of St. John," and he carried forward the work,
which he had conceived nearly fifteen years before, of
a translation of Goethe's " Faust." The experiments
which he had made in translating Rückert, Hebel, and
other German poets disclosed to him his facility in reproducing both the rhythm of the original and the poetic sense.   He began with rendering the lyrical portions.   The more he tried the work and the better
acquaintance he had with previous translations, the
more confidence he felt in undertaking a complete
translation.

Immediately after the new year opened he removed
his family to New York for the winter, and was off and
on lecturing until the spring.   He only needed to
finish his series of engagements to begin eagerly upon
his second novel, " John Godfrey's Fortunes," which
had long been outlined in his mind.

TO GEORGE H. BOKER.

156 East 14th St., New York, *Friday, March* 11, 1864.

Congratulate me ! I gave my last lecture on Wednesday
night.   This makes about fifty for the winter.   I had an attack
of fever in Michigan ten days ago, brought on by fatigue and ex-
posure, and am still a little weak, but in capital spirits.   I shall
commence work on my new novel this afternoon or to-morrow.
Putnam is now printing the thirteenth and fourteenth thousands
of " Hannah," and the sale keeps up finely.   I have just had a
remittance of one hundred pounds from London.   In pecuniary
matters I consider myself pretty well out of the woods. . . . Graham has presented me with a splendid library table, and I want to
have the library finished for occupation this year.   All this is encouraging, and takes a great strain off my mind for the future,
though not for my sake.

We shall be here until April 1st.   Why can't you come on for
a day or two, at least, and let us all be together once more ?

. . . I have read " Sordello " ! and retain (though with some
effort) my reason.

Cedarcroft, with every addition that was made and every new growth of the rich nature in the midst of which it was planted, became dearer to its owner and more exacting in its demands. He asked for short winters in the city, much as he enjoyed the society and pleasures which winter life in town brought, and long summers at Cedarcroft, where he kept open house and led the ideal life of a poet who was country-gentleman as well. There were a stable to be built, a well to be dug, trees and hedges to be planted, a terrace raised, and an infinite diversity of labor to be expended upon an estate which could yield fruits for the market and table and pleasures untold to the eye and ear.

In his library he worked at "John Godfrey's Fortunes," "The Picture of St. John," and "Faust." He had not yet, indeed, absolute leisure of mind. He must needs drop pen and hasten off to fulfill lecture engagements for the money which they brought in; and in spite of his buoyant mind, the care of providing for the expenses of an estate vexed him at times, and set him upon plans which interfered sadly with poetry. Nevertheless it was a time of exhilaration with him, and he was quickly absorbed in his literary work after each interruption. His hospitality and frank welcome involved him also in constant toils. In vain would he make iron rules by which his hours of work were to be regulated; in vain sentinels posted themselves to guard his library door. When he heard the voice of friends without, his rules were scattered to the winds, and he had jumped up to give a prompt welcome.

TO JAMES T. FIELDS.

CEDARCROFT, KENNETT SQUARE, PA., *April* 25, 1864.

The new novel is my first care, and it goes on but slowly as yet, owing to my out-door duties. It is almost impossible to get laborers, and I am obliged to dig, plant, and water myself, in order to be sure of any increase. I have a crick in my back from digging, ten scratches and four blisters on one hand, a burnt face, and dirty boots. I have three hundred and sixty-three fruit trees to take care of, and any quantity of onions, beets, parsnips, and celery to plant. We make our own butter, lay our own eggs, and have already our own salad, radishes, and rhubarb. At night I am generally so tired that I can't accomplish more than four or five pages of MS. As for letters, I can only answer them by accident, — as to-day, for instance, while it rains and nothing can be done out-of-doors.

This novel bids fair to be entertaining, if not quite so original in design as " Hannah." I enjoy writing it quite as well, which is at least a good sign. There is n't a single " reformer " in it.

Good-by ! There are signs of the sky clearing, and I must air my hot-beds.

TO E. C. STEDMAN.

CEDARCROFT, KENNETT SQUARE, PA., *May* 6, 1864.

Dick writes to me that you have been sick again. Now I want you to come on and do your convalescing at Cedarcroft. In order that you may feel perfectly free to come at once, I will frankly say that we are short of help in house and garden, and live in a wild, rough, hand-to-mouth way. We shall not attempt to make things better for you. My out-of-doors is so fine that you must be content with daily pot-luck in the house. You will get neither wine nor much whisky ("Woe ! woe ! the whisky's low !"), neither *filet-aux-champignons*, lamb and mint, green peas (until *we* grow them), nor any of the usual delicacies of the season ; but usually a country steak or cutlet, ham, frizzled hung beef, potatoes, macaroni, and bread ; also young onions, raw, and "poke " boiled for greens. My cigars are not only " of the period," but also " of the province, " — three cents apiece, and bitter, but tolerable in a high wind. You shall loaf as much as you like, for M. and I have our hands pretty full, and no time for ceremonious attention. But our air is dry, pure, and full of vitality, our trees old and grand, our lawn green, our birds new-tuned, and we shall be delighted to have you literally as " one of the family." Come, then, and take a rest here ; it will do you good, I know.

If you write to me by what train you come (they leave Philadelphia, corner of Market and Thirty-first streets, at 8 A. M. and 4.30 P. M.), I will meet you at the station.

M. and I send our kindest remembrances to Mrs. Stedman.

TO T. B. ALDRICH.

CEDARCROFT, KENNETT SQUARE, PA., *May* 11, 1864.

The sight of your well-known " back-hand " on the envelope told me two pleasant things,— that you think of me now and then, and that there is no danger of your becoming Homeric or Miltonic ; the latter, of course, in the visual sense. I have no objection to your rivaling either as a poet, because then I should be sure to be represented, three hundred years hence, in the pictures of " Aldrich and his Contemporaries." We have thus a side-chance for immortality in each other's fames.

For my part, I suppose I have had as much popularity as falls to the average. I don't expect ever to be a classic proper, but I want to write clearly, elegantly, and picturesquely. . . .

I am gardening, managing, scolding, and writing by turns. You should have added " Gardener " to your list of titles. I may say, modifying Marvell, —

> What wondrous life is this I lead !
> My hands are full of turnip seed ;
> The onion and the curious corn
> Drop from my fingers every morn ;
> The cabbage and the sallow squash
> Do force me oft my hands to wash ;
> I watch the sprouting of the beet,
> The scarlet radish I do eat ;
> And often in my daily walk
> Do pull the giant rhubarb stalk,
> The which my spouse, neat-handed, takes,
> And in a pie serenely bakes.

Cedarcroft is superb just now ; the country is really like a vision of Paradise, in its mixture of greenness and blossom, all covered with a delicious purple haze of heat. Our great trouble is the impossibility of getting labor, — hence my out-door occupation. I must literally plant in order to have my own table supplied, — help can't be had at any price. But Grant is victorious, and God is over us, and we rejoice. I write this in my shirt-sleeves, — temperature 80°, and my own melons and cucumbers well out of the ground. I have lost ten pounds of flesh, and am as brown as a berry. All send their love to you, and hope to see you here again.

TO R. II. STODDARD.

CEDARCROFT, *Wednesday, May* 14, 1864.

I propose that you come on Saturday, the 28th. You will thus
have Sunday and the week together here. I am going *via* New
York to my lectures, and will return with you on Saturday, Sunday, or Monday, as you are bound to do. The country is just
now at its loveliest, and I'm only afraid the new splendor of the
green will be gone before you can see it. I'm delighted that you
are coming : the rest and change of air will do you good. We
have thunder-showers every day, with intervals of summer heat ;
but it's just the temperature when you don't have to hoe or dig.
I have Little & Brown's "British Poets" complete now, so
you'll have wherewithal to mouse over. . . .

TO JAMES T. FIELDS.

CEDARCROFT, *May* 20, 1864.

Yours of yesterday is at hand. I expect the package by to-
night's train, and will lose no time in examining and returning.

I am shocked to hear, an hour ago, that we have lost Hawthorne. Good God ! Are all the choice spirits leaving us ?
Dear, good old Ticknor, — I don't think I wrote to you how
much I felt his sudden calling away ; how cordially I liked and
respected him, and feel the edges of the gap he has left reaching
even to myself. And now his friend, and ours, and our pride, —
the matchless master ! What shall we do without him ? Who
can ever hope to fill his place ? When such a man dies, I feel
as if I should like to sit down in a lonely place, and throw ashes
upon my head.

You should have had the prose article before this, but I have
somehow mislaid the commencement, and am in half-despair
about it. Well begun, with me, is more than half done, and I
shrink back with dread from the thought of re-writing it. Then,
too much work in the hot sun has given me headaches, and I
have really not felt in the mood to make an extra exertion.
Don't count upon much more than this article from me before
September. I am very glad that "Lake Ladoga" gives satisfaction. In point of style, it is one of my best prose articles. I
want to make the "Europe and Asia" equal or superior to it,
so don't swear over the delay.

TO R. H. STODDARD.

CEDARCROFT, *August* 11, 1864.

Last night at ten o'clock, mercury at 85°, I wrote the last lines of "John Godfrey." I began about the 15th of March, and in spite of interruptions and the languor of this African summer have produced five hundred and ninety-four pages of MS. (letter sheet). Don't you think I deserve a holiday? To-day I loaf and invite my soul. The mercury is 95° in the shade, and so it has been for days. Everything is burning up, the wells are drying, cooking is nearly an impossible performance, and what shall I do? I know not. . . . Low has gained his case in London, so the Canada dodge holds, and I shall probably have to try it again in the fall. I want to get £200 for the advance sheets and copyright. If I do, or even £150, I'll take you with me to Niagara, if you'll go, old fellow, and we'll get Graham to go with us on publication day, — about October 15th.

We are existing here as best we can. There is no hour of the day or night when one can walk a hundred paces without sweating. . . . I have two men digging a well : three times a day a blast goes off and shakes the house. They have struck water, but not enough, and it threatens to be a frightful expense ; but without it my stable can't go up.

Tell me how you like "E. Arden," etc. I've been reading Swift, and find that Hood took hints from him, in comic poetry. Also Donne : did you ever read his "Progress of a Soul"? — immensely queer. I want very much to go to Mattapoisett with you the end of this month, but M. seems despondent about the prospect. We have no end of trouble in getting along with our kitchen help : we are, verily, the slaves of our servants. Either they are all bad and fraternize, or they are passably good and fight. I hope order will come out of this chaos, and we shall get off. I don't want to go without M., for she needs a holiday worse than I do.

TO JAMES T. FIELDS.

CEDARCROFT, KENNETT SQUARE, PA., *September* 26, 1864.

Who *wills* may hear Sordello's story told
By Robert Browning ; warm ? (you ask) or cold ?
But just so much as seemeth to enhance —
The start being granted, onward goes the dance
To its own music — the poem's inward sense ;
So, by its verity . . . nay, no pretense

Avails your self-created bards, and thus
By just the chance of half a hair to us,
If understood — but what's the odds to you,
Who with no obligation to pursue
Scant tracks of thought, if such, indeed, there be
In this one poem . . . stay, my friend, and see
Whether you note that creamy tint of flesh
Softer than bivalve pink, impearled and fresh,
Just where the small o' th' back goes curving down
To the full buttock — ay, but that's the crown
Protos, incumbered, cast before the feet
Of Grecian women . . . ah! you hear me, sweet!

And so on, and so on. . . .

And now, my dear J. T. F., I must congratulate you on the October " Atlantic," which is an admirable number. Whoever wrote " Communication " [1] is a trump, if his diction *is* modeled on Emerson's ; he knows what's what. The political article made me swear. The fellow has stolen *whole chunks* out of my new, unwritten lecture ; what shall I do ? The poem " Service " is refreshing. Who wrote it ? [2] " Madame Récamier " is so-so, but will interest " the masses." Are the Lamb articles yours ? They're delightful, whencever they come.[3] The reviews puzzle me, — such a singular mixture of shallowness and smartness. Whoever the man is, he lacks objective vision. He lets his own pet notions of the *subjects* of the books stick out a little too plainly ; on the whole, he is not the ideal critic. Some things in the articles suggest ——, and yet other things in them he could not possibly write. Who is it ? Do you tell ?

However, my main object is to say that my Russian article is half written. I am busy with my " St. John," and feel inclined to " leave all meaner things."

I have a poetic fit on me, but it does n't run into lyrics. I shall finish the prose sketch this week, and send it to you. It brings me more bother than it will value, and I shall burn six wax candles before the shrine of St. Goethe when it 's off my hands.

. . . My hands are full, what with lectures, gardening, building a stable, governing my family, keeping the run of politics, in order to stump, if necessary, and reading the proofs of " John Godfrey's Fortunes." It 's only by chance that I have an hour loose this afternoon.

[1] D. A. Wasson was the author.
[2] J. T. Trowbridge.
[3] *Charles Lamb's Uncollected Writings*, by J. E. Babson.

October 5, 1864.

Here you have the article,[1] which I should have sent three days sooner but for the visit of a friend from Indiana, who interrupted my writing. It is not so good as I could wish ; losing the original commencement took away all my satisfaction in the work. It was not written *senza*, exactly, but neither *con* the proper *amore*. But perhaps it may help to diversify and relieve your Cullets and Cadmean madnesses. I hope so.

I've been thinking about the other articles, and if the proper vein can be opened will try one. But "John Godfrey" has driven me into poetry, and I have been hammering away at " St. John " for nearly two months. Two books are finished, — half the poem. I'd like to show you parts of it, but can't trust the MS. out of my hands yet. It is much the best thing I've done, so far. I have also another important project on hand, which cannot be completed in less than a year or two, to say nothing of plans (old ones) for two additional novels. You shall have J. G. as soon as he can be seen by anybody. . . .

TO MRS. MARIE BLOEDE.[2]

CEDARCROFT, KENNETT SQUARE, PA., *October* 11, 1864.

Many thanks for your very welcome letter of the 6th. I have written to Mr. Butz, accepting his offer [3] in case the publication in Germany is assured, that being our main object. The publication of the translation here is a subordinate matter, and I am willing to give it to him only in order that the work may appear in Germany. Through my English copyright I acquire also the right of German or French translation, so that I can secure the copyright in either country. The book will not appear here before November 15th, on account of the London edition appearing at the same time, and I must spend the previous ten days in Canada, — a great bore. I am glad you are interested in the book. The interest of the story properly commences afterwards, and increases towards the end.

[1] " Between Europe and Asia."

[2] Mrs. Bloede was half sister of the poet Friederich von Sallet, and wife of Dr. Gustav Bloede, a physician and journalist, who was implicated in the revolutionary movement in Germany in 1848, and escaped at that time to America. Mrs. Bloede was herself a writer of no mean ability, and Bayard Taylor had great respect for her critical judgment. She died in 1870.

[3] To publish a translation of " John Godfrey's Fortunes " in his monthly, *Westliche Monatshefte.*

I have finished the Second Book of my " St. John," and commenced the Third, having written about six hundred lines since you were here. But the poem will hardly be finished before next spring. I have also another important literary task on hand, about which I wish to consult you when we meet in December. In fact, it is perhaps well that I am forced at present to attend to the building of a stable, the preparation of a garden, and other out-door matters, for I am so fascinated by my poetic labors that I should otherwise overtask my powers. I wish, sometimes, that my brain were less prolific in plans. I pick up everywhere suggestions of poems, novels, and works in every branch of literature, nine tenths of which must be rejected. . . .

TO JAMES T. FIELDS.

KENNETT SQUARE, PA., *October* 13, 1864.

The books [1] are here, and they are charming ! My wife, mother, sister, and daughter pronounce the portrait admirable, and *I* am entirely satisfied with it.

I think I never had so much pleasure in looking at a book of mine as just this one. Each separate poem seems to read better than it ever did before.

I 'll try to do another article for you in the course of the month. But I have also a lecture to write and a stable to build in the mean time. The check came safely to hand, and is already cashed. Many thanks.

Please send me, by mail, at once, Hayward's " Faust."

TO DONALD G. MITCHELL.

TREMONT HOUSE, CHICAGO, *November* 29, 1864.

I have this moment received and read your very kind and gratifying note, and reply at once, not only to thank you heartily for that cordial sympathy which an author expects (but does not always receive) from a brother author, but also to disabuse your mind of any possible suspicion that I objected to your notice of " Hannah Thurston."

I read the notice with pleasure as a candid criticism; not feeling myself bound to agree with it in all points, but admitting that, in one or two instances, you had censured me justly. I never care to read a notice which is unmitigated praise, and find that I always learn more from condemnation than from eulogium.

[1] Copies of the Blue and Gold edition of Bayard Taylor's Poems.

Your notice, I felt, was honest, and that is all I ask. Perhaps I now see more faults in the book than many of my friends. It was a first attempt in a new field, and I wrote under a constraining sense of experiment which was absent when I wrote "John Godfrey." My own private opinion is that the latter book is much the better literary performance, and I will not conceal the pleasure it gives me to receive your accordant judgment, — the very first which I have heard.

Pray remember me very kindly to Mrs. Mitchell. My wife, little girl, and myself will be in New York for the winter, at 139 East Eighth Street, opposite Clinton Hall, and you must let me know when you come down, that we may neutralize each other's country rust.

"Bayard Taylor's fortieth birthday, January 11, 1865, was the occasion of a frolic with his friends, who prepared for it beforehand," writes Mr. Stoddard, "each thinking what would be most appropriate (or inappropriate) to present him, and all keeping their own counsel, ransacking invention for preposterous mementoes. It fell to my lot to act as the scribe, and . . . I imagined the decoration of Bayard Taylor's chamber, the gathering of his friends, and wrote letters of regret from those who could not be present, but who somehow happened to be present in spite of their letters. The reading of these missives and sundry copies of verse and the bestowal of our mementoes provoked more fun than had ever before, or has ever since, distinguished our Taylor nights. It was not so much that they were comical in themselves (though they were) as that we were willing to fool and be fooled to the top of our bent."

The intervals between lecture tours were passed with his family in New York, and his house was the centre of a most agreeable literary and artistic circle. Sunday evenings Bayard Taylor and his wife were at home, and he was a welcome guest in many houses.

The Century Club was a favorite resort, and the Travellers, a small club composed of gentlemen who had seen much of the world's surface, was a congenial society. "If you intend coming to the city soon," Bayard Taylor writes to Mr. Donald G. Mitchell, "pray come next Monday. A 'close corporation,' called the *Travellers*, meets here on that evening, and I, as host, have the right of invitation. Among the members are Church, Bierstadt, Blodgett, Cyrus Field, Bristed, Darley, Bellows, Palmer the sculptor, and Hunt. We simply talk, smoke, and take frugal refreshments, but the evenings so far have been very pleasant. I shall also ask Curtis and Herman Melville. Do pray come out of your solitude and the pleasant society of 'Dr. Johns' for one evening." He amused himself also with a pretty diligent attention to his delightful diversion of water-color painting. His friends took a lively interest in this occupation, for the amateur artist was good-natured in distributing his pictures as souvenirs. He did not set an extravagant estimate on their value, but they gave him unfailing pleasure. They were copies, for the most part, of sketches which he had made in his travels, and had thus a peculiar personal value.

The winter of 1865 saw the war nearing its close; it saw also that steady rise in prices which played havoc with the fortunes of men living on salaries or incomes which did not enjoy a corresponding rise. The following letter, written to a friend who had asked his advice in a question of publishing, is introduced for its illustration of the business side of an author's life : —

No. 139 East Eighth Street,
New York, *February* 14, 1865.

My engagements (I am still forced to lecture) have prevented my immediate reply to your note. I have often wished that there could be a general understanding among American authors in regard to the value of copyright and the amount of percentage proper to be paid by publishers. As it is, each one must now make the best terms he can. The publishers seem to consider ten per cent. on the retail price as a sort of *par*, above which they only allow an author to rise when he is sufficiently popular to enforce better terms. This, of course, is considerably less than half profits (in ordinary times), which ought to be the standard. Mr. Putnam estimated that twelve and one half per cent. is about equivalent to half profits, and Mr. Irving and myself accepted this estimate, the publisher paying for the plates and owning them. Afterwards, when Putnam became embarrassed, we arranged to purchase the plates, and a new contract was made, by which I received twenty-five cents per volume, the retail price being $1.50. Afterwards, Mr. P. thinking this too high, I voluntarily reduced it to twenty cents, until last summer. In July I made a new contract, when Hurd & Houghton undertook the details of publication, and the price of the volumes was raised to $1.75. By this contract I get twenty-five cents on each volume, except "John Godfrey," for which I receive thirty cents, the retail price being $2.25. This is an average of about fourteen per cent. But as I own the plates, engravings, etc., — a dead capital of about $8,000, the interest of which should be deducted from my receipts, — it is almost equivalent to the old arrangement of twelve and one half per cent. You do not state whether you pay for your own plates, which is a point of some importance. I think the scale of half profits is a fair one, provided the estimate is fairly made. For instance, some publishers, I know, take their lowest rate of discount to the trade (forty per cent. off) as the basis of the calculation, when the usual rate is thirty-three and one third per cent, and when, moreover, they sell hundreds or thousands of volumes at the retail price.

My experience with —— —— is similar to your own. They actually insist on reducing the copyright to *seven per cent.* on the retail price. This *I* have not submitted to, although they assure me that L——, H——, and W—— have accepted. I am not of the opinion that coffee, tin, turpentine, and whiskey should go up, and an author's copyright go down, at the same time. I believe, however, that publishers are earning less now than formerly, because they have so long delayed increasing the price of books. But that is their business, and an author should not be made to suffer for it.

With regard to advertising, I have always insisted that the statement of the sale of a volume should be correct, and therefore returned in the account; and thus far I have been paid according to the advertised number. I am sure that a publisher could be legally held to pay the author the copyright on the number of volumes which he advertises as having been sold.

We now have to depend entirely on the publisher's returns, which we cannot verify without seeming to doubt his honesty. I am fortunately situated in this respect, and I believe you are, so far as Mr. S—— is concerned; but the plan is bad, for all that. I wish some arrangement could be devised by which the author could have control over, or at least cognizance of, the exact number of copies printed and bound. If we could do this, and then ascertain the exact percentage which represents the actual half profit, our interests would stand on a much more satisfactory basis. First of all, there should be a full and free comparison of experiences among authors, and to this end I have sent you mine. If it is not as complete as you need, pray let me know. I have written hastily, and may have overlooked some points.

TO MRS. JAMES T. FIELDS.

NEW YORK, *March* 27, 1865.

I send you the first thing which I can spare, — a rough little sketch of the Falls of Badimanta (among the Cebralian hills), — which I hope may answer your purpose. Remember, however, that it does n't in the least invalidate your claim to a bigger and better artistic (?) production from my pencil. The reason why I have delayed with the latter is one which works to your advantage in the end, simply this : that I have been haunting the studios this winter, picking up hints here and there, and learning how to remedy some of my many deficiencies. The result is, your picture is a hundred per cent. better now than it would have been a year ago.

As soon as April came the family flitted back to Cedarcroft, where the summer life began with the marriage of Bayard Taylor's youngest sister, on the eve of the day when the tragedy of President Lincoln's assassination stopped all rejoicing, and turned back the lengthening days of hope into the darkest of nights. The correspondence of Bayard Taylor and his friends at this time recalls vividly the intense feeling which the event inspired and the subtle side-current of sympathy and affection for one of their own number who was drawn suddenly and terribly into the tragedy. As summer drew on the sweet country life seemed to throw a charm over existence. The angry world was shut out, friends gathered in the hospitable house, poetry again flowed freely, and a new novel, " The Story of Kennett," was set up. The worries of farm work also gave way before the advent of a trained superintendent and the colonizing of his laborers, and so the place grew and flourished under the owner's eye.

One of the pleasant episodes of the summer was a picnic on the Brandywine, when Mr. and Mrs. Stedman were guests at Cedarcroft. It was a perfect June day, and the company consisted only of the family and these two guests. A drive of five or six miles brought them to an enchanting meadow on the banks of the historic stream. Not a house was in sight. The Brandywine rippled past, and curved around the narrow edge of the meadow. On one side was the creek and the wooded heights past which it flowed; on the other groves of stately oaks, and the vista stretched for a mile up the stream. The party had spread its feast and was in full enjoyment of the scene, when they saw in the distance a herd of cattle coming slowly down the meadow. It was at least a hundred strong, and seemed to be attracted by the intruders. Nearer came the herd, and at last, halting, formed itself into a line of battle, reaching from one side of the meadow to the other. For a moment it looked as if this formidable host was about to charge, and the little party began to consider if discretion might not be the better part of valor. The gentlemen had been wading in the creek, with long staffs in their hands, and a hurried council of war considered the expediency of their becoming pack animals to carry the ladies across the stream to safety on the wooded heights. Meanwhile the cattle also seemed to have been taking council, and an advance party of eighteen or twenty moved forward for a reconnaissance. It was a slight sign of weakness or conciliation, and the two poets were suddenly inspired with daring and fun. Mr. Stedman, in great glee, flung himself upon the back of a fine, short-horned steer, and Bayard Taylor, like a sacrificial priest, took hold of one of the horns, and swinging his staff led the astonished animal and his rider about in triumphal procession. It is to this that he refers in his sonnet to E. C. S., at Christmas, in the same year: —

> When days were long, and o'er that farm of mine,
> Green Cedarcroft, the summer breezes blew,
> And from the walnut shadows I and you,
> Dear Edmund, saw the red lawn-roses shine,
> Or followed our idyllic Brandywine
> Through meadows flecked with many a flowery hue,
> To where with wild Arcadian pomp I drew
> Your Bacchic march among the startled kine,
> You gave me, linked with old Mæonides,
> Your loving sonnet,[1] — record dear and true
> Of days as dear : and now, when suns are brief,
> And Christmas snows are on the naked trees,
> I give you this, — a withered winter leaf,
> Yet with your blossom from one root it grew.

[1] See Mr. Stedman's sonnet, "To Bayard Taylor, with a Copy of the Iliad."

TO JERVIS MCENTEE.

CEDARCROFT, KENNETT SQUARE, PA., *June* 3, 1865.

I was very glad to get your letter from Rondout, and felt, per-haps, a little unchristian pleasure on learning that artists, as well as authors, have their petty daily household jobs to interfere with the work of hand and brain. Such have I, and I never shall get used to them. Habit does not soften their asperity, and it re-quires a forty-horse-power sense of duty to discharge them. If our food would only cook itself, our rooms do their own sweep-ing, and our gardens bring forth prime vegetables without weeds, what fine lives we should lead !

At present I pay enormous sums to get about half the work done which needs to be done. A "country-place" is no economy, but it is a vast delight. The gardening this year satisfies us tol-erably. We have had cucumbers for six weeks past, and to-day pull our first peas. Cantaloupes are in blossom, ditto tomatoes, and cherries are ripe. The country here never was lovelier, and the best thing you can do is to come down to us for a week or two. We will try to see you at Rondout some time this summer, but cannot possibly leave home this month.

I was in Washington to see the grand reviews, which *were* grand. The day after my return, Launt Thompson called here on his way back to New York, and I persuaded him to stay two days with me. On Monday came Stedman and wife, and re-mained until this morning. Yesterday was my wife's birthday, and we had a picnic on the banks of the Brandywine. You should have seen us mounted on grazing oxen and riding over the meadows, or wading the swift stream in water to the knees. We all wished for your presence. Stedman agreed with me that the scenery just suits your pencil. For the past six days the country is wrapped in a wonderful pale-blue haze, which makes the commonest landscape seem Arcadian. Your not coming this spring is a great disappointment to all of us, and we insist upon having you before we all go back to New York for the winter. September is a pleasant month here, and will be especially so this year on account of our large crop of peaches.

We have been buried in roses for a week past, and the atmos-phere for a hundred yards round about the house is tinctured with the fragrance thereof. It is just the season for a sleepy, epi-curean, loafing spell. Why can't you come and try it ? . . .

I have commenced another novel, but am not yet through with the first chapter. This will claim me at home, for I cannot write elsewhere until after a residence of a week or two. If we come to Rondout I will only bring a sketch-book and water-colors. My wife sends best love, and repeats with me the old invitation, which we by no means intend to let drop, in spite of our bad luck so far.

I must now close to catch this afternoon's mail. Pray send us your *cartes*, if you have 'em. At any rate, let me hear from you whenever those hands are not too much "bunged" with hoeing. I promise to respond as promptly as could be expected from one of our profession.

TO E. C. STEDMAN.

CEDARCROFT, KENNETT SQUARE, PA., *June* 16, 1865.

The wind was blowing from *nothe*-east, direct from Schooley's Mountain, when I opened your letterful of pure oxygen into our opulent, indolent, summer atmosphere. I finished an article for the "Atlantic" that day. As if I were not "a tool of the elements"! "*And how?*" as the Germans say. (Americanicé, "You'd better believe it!") Why, I am physically so condemnably thin-skinned that my cerebral productivity depends entirely on certain delicate conditions of the surface-nerves. The touch of dry sand or earth makes me shudder with horror; the smell of wild grape-blossoms inebriates me with an unspeakable sense of luxury; to feel velvet under my bare soles is a heavenly delight. So of the winds, clouds, and all other elemental influences. I have steadfastly turned my face away from the expression of sensation, because it is my strong (*i. e.*, weak) point. What your lungs are to you the skin of my whole body is to me. The animal (not always in the grosser sense) and the spiritual renew their battle in me every morning. They are so evenly balanced that the strife is never decided. Health has its inconveniences as well as disease; sometimes I am in doubt which is best.

Would that we could go up into an high mountain apart and drink the milk-punch of human kindness with you! But much I fear me that it is not to be. If we go to Cape May in August we must stay at home meanwhile, — I to write and inspect my cauliflowers, and M. to get ahead of the German printers. Moreover, we have just rigged up my tenant house, and installed an old woman therein, who boardeth the male retainers, and who still needeth our counsel and assistance in this (for the country) unusual arrangement. Half the household bother is thus transferred from M.'s shoulders to those of the said old woman, and a new content descends upon Cedarcroft. Garrison and George Thompson spent Sunday afternoon with us, — both agreeable gentlemen, in spite of the "World" and Copperheads. The annual meeting of the Progressives was very funny. G. and G. T. spoke admirable sense, but most of the others belched out bosh and rant. Some of them attacked me virulently *à propos* of "Hannah Thurston," so on Sunday morning I went over and gave them a blast in return. I was sweetly cool and composed, and stirred them up with pleasant irony. Such a writhing and groaning and howling as followed! It was like sticking a pole into a cage of animals. G. T. was immensely diverted ; he whispered to me afterwards that he had never heard anything better. The meeting adjourned in haste to prevent a row. This thing has given me a little popularity, even among the reformers, — the first I have ever received at home. I like to make studies in *corpore vili*, and this has been a good one.

By the bye, you came near losing a friend ten days ago, and in the most singular way ; for I never yet heard of a man being killed by his brother's tombstone. The monument for poor Fred came out from Philadelphia, and I summoned fifteen or twenty of his old soldiers to help transport it to the cemetery. At the station three or four of us were engaged in turning over the largest block, weighing perhaps 1,500 pounds, when the platform broke under the weight, and three of us went down in a heap upon the railroad track, eight or ten feet below. I was in front of the block. How I escaped I don't know ; but I found myself after a moment of bewilderment standing on the track, with torn trousers, bleeding knees, and various contusions about the body. One other man was slightly bruised. . . .

Tell L. that my sketch of the Brandywine meadows has succeeded admirably. She shall see it next winter.

Now, why won't you send me now and then a MS. poem as you write it ? I like that sort of literary interchange. The old fellows used to do it, and they were right. Don't let us of our generation be so incorrigibly glued to our own bottoms, but be upper and nether millstones to each other.

Well, this is enough for one day. It is cloudy, the house is still, the seclusion wraps me about like a mantle, and I am i' the vein for a talk with a friend. Though reading may be no pulmonary strain upon you, I remember in time that you have a semi-fear of my vitality, and know not how much of it I may have pitched upon these leaves.

M. sends love to you and L. ; so does all Cedarcroft, in fact, including Jack, Picket, and the blind mare. Do write again ; you have now nothing else to do.

TO JERVIS M^CENTEE.

CEDARCROFT, KENNETT SQUARE, PA., *June* 17, 1865.

I am glad to find, from your welcome letter, that there are so many points of sympathy between us. Your honest confessions are just such as I continually make to myself, and sometimes to others. I don't think the artist nature incapable of attending to any of the practical details of life, — on the contrary, I think an artist or author might always be a superior business man if he chose, as the greater always includes the less, — but the search for beauty brings a distaste for everything material and mechanical. I have recently been occupied in cleaning and fitting up a tenant house (that is, directing, not doing the dirty work myself) for an old woman, who now boards all my male retainers, and so takes a vast deal of work and worry out of my own house and off my wife's shoulders. A very happy change, now that it is accomplished, but how irksome while under way ! Little by little I hope so to organize the operations here that I shall be left tolerably free to my own devices. I enjoy the quiet and seclusion of this lovely pastoral region ; my mind works easily and pleasantly here, and there are no serious drawbacks except the possibility of being called from my sanctum at any moment, to have the coal-bin replenished, or to select trees to be felled for firewood, or to decide whether potatoes or corn first need attention, or to pay the butcher, or to drive the pigs out of the cabbages, or to nail a pale on the chicken-yard, or to blow up a lazy darkey for being slack in his hoeing. I can sit at my table, as I do now, with the windows open before me, and look out on the sloping, cedared lawn, the immense oaks on either side, the blossoming magnolias and the geranium-beds ; and all that I see harmonizes with the productive mood, — gently stimulates and refreshes me at my work. The wind in the leaves makes a soft, mellow accompaniment to the scratching of my pen, and the distant forms and tints of the clouds excite my imagination. Perhaps this end of the scale would go too high, and kick a beam somewhere out of sight, but for the hard, commonplace duties which balance it. I guess " things " are about right, after all. When I compare my life with that of my neighbors round about, I am very well satisfied. I am veritably richer than our two or three semi-millionaires, because, although I save less, I spend more, and have no anxiety from precarious investments. Besides, I am insensible to the gossip and the narrow prejudices of a country community, and make fun out of everything intended to annoy me. By following this course I have not only secured my independence, but also a certain amount of respect.

My pen has run on, unconsciously, until the sight of this fourth page warns me not to bore you. We are all in good spirits, now that our household is so arranged that we can receive a friend or friends at any time. We do not yet give up the hope of seeing you here before the winter. If you can't come for one week, can't you for *three?* I'll give you a studio, and you can paint as much as you like. Besides, I'll order a small picture, if that will be any inducement. M. and I want to have our place enriched by the presence of all our friends, and your presences have been sorely lacking to us. . . .

We have green tomatoes and cantaloupes on our vines, and the Latakia tobacco (the only plants in the United States) are coming into blossom.

The reference at the close of this letter is to a curious contribution to American crops which Bayard Taylor made from his traveling experience. The Latakia tobacco is indigenous to Egypt, where he had known its agreeable qualities. A friend had brought some seed from Egypt, and the experiment was made of raising plants from it at Cedarcroft. The result was so successful that the poet entered into arrangements with a seedsman, who sold the seed with profit. At Nijni Novgorod, also, a melon from the Caspian had so pleased Bayard Taylor and his wife that they saved the seed, planted it at Cedarcroft, mixed it with the variety of Mountain Sweet, and produced a new and very fine watermelon, the seed of which they also made popular.

TO E. C. STEDMAN.

CEDARCROFT, KENNETT SQUARE, PA., *July* 19, 1865.

. . . I am very jolly these days. The "Tribune" declared a dividend of $500 a share, besides laying aside a surplus of $60,000. This gives me $2,500 where I expected only $500 ; and from Putnam I get for three months' copyright $520, where my estimate (on account of the dull trade) was only $250. Moreover, Fields has just sent me checks of $200 for a singular story called "Beauty and the Beast," $100 for a paper on the "Author of 'Saul,'" and $50 for a poem, "The Sleeper." (I'll send you the last with this, if I can find time to copy it.) Thus I am unexpectedly rich, and the fact so stimulates my mental activity that I am writing every day, both on my novel and the "St. John." Prose by daylight, and poetry by night! — a new tandem, which I never drove before, but it goes smoothly and well. Freedom from pecuniary anxiety gives my brain a genial glow, a nimble ease, a procreative power, which I never feel at other times. I sing better after the thorn is pulled out of my breast. Nature designed some men to be rich, — you and me, for instance. Nothing but the accident of ill-health has prevented you from paying an income-tax of $1,000 a year. . . .

. . . I quite agree with what you say of Niagara. I have been there a dozen times, and know every phase of the creature ; yet "awe" is an emotion I never felt. I was never overpowered and crushed — neither was ever any sensible person — by the plunge and roar ; but I reveled in the endless motion, the blossoming spray, and the splendid emerald along the curving brink. The fall fascinated me, but didn't overwhelm me in any sense. The ocean has ten bushels of mystery and suggestiveness where the fall has a quart. Still, the latter is a wonderful thing, and I like it.

CHAPTER XIX.

THE PICTURE OF ST. JOHN.

1865–1867.

> The sober hermit I,
> Whose evening songs but few approach to hear, —
> Who, if those few should cease to lend an ear,
> Would sing them to the forest and the sky
> Contented : singing for myself alone.
>
> *The Poet's Journal.*

THE field of profitable work which his novels had opened gave Bayard Taylor hope that he could relinquish lecturing except in places so near to New York as to rid the labor of its greatest evil. He hailed the prospect of this freedom with rejoicing as holding out the promise of greater leisure of mind and body for the writing of poetry. "The Picture of St. John" had now come to absorb his thought. At first working at it alternately with the "Story of Kennett," he became so fascinated by the poem that he pushed aside his novel, and everything else which stood in the way, and abandoned himself to the luxury of composition.

TO T. B. ALDRICH.

CEDARCROFT, KENNETT SQUARE, PA., *August* 16, 1865.

. . . I have been hard at work this summer, my "St. John" having suddenly "hopped up revived" (in the classical phrase of Olympus Pump), and demanded to be written. So I wrote : and behold ! the Third Book is finished, and I commence the Fourth and Last to-night. Moreover, I have written for the "Atlantic" a poem ("The Sleeper"), — *not* a reminiscence of the N. Y. and N. H. R. R. ! — a critical paper ("The Author of

'Saul'"), and a long and very queer Russian story ("Beauty and the Beast"), all of which you will find in the coming numbers. I shall look out expectantly for your sonnet. My novel has only advanced to the second chapter, but "St. John" has precedence over all other guests of the brain. He is my private luxury, — from head to tail of my own solitary begetting, — and I drop everything when he comes. The poem is one of the great delights of my life, and I do not intend to care a D. whether or not it is popular. It is mine : that's enough. I shall have it finished, the Lord willing, in another month. My lecturing this year will be done in October and November, and I shall have the winter free in New York. Then we can consult, and revise, and prepare. I congratulate you on your most agreeable summer programme. If it were not that I shall be absent, I should insist on your spending your October in Cedarcroft. But I must be away then, — just our loveliest season, — in order that I may have a full, free winter in New York, for the first time since 1851. I have recently been summing up my labors for the last seven years, and they are almost incredible. I need and must have *rest*, and will have complete rest of mind and body as soon as "St. John" and the novel are finished.

"The Author of 'Saul,'" referred to in the last letter, is the title of a biographical and critical paper which Bayard Taylor contributed to the "Atlantic Monthly," with a view to directing attention to the drama of "Saul," which had been published anonymously at Montreal, and had not yet received the public recognition which he conceived was its due. His article was influential in leading to its re-issue in the United States, and Mr. Charles Heavysege, the author of the drama, wrote to his sympathetic reviewer, "Your good opinion and that of several of your most eminently gifted countrymen goes far to repay me for that deferring of hope which to the strongest of us is apt to make the heart sick. Your qualified yet generous commendation is more grateful to me and more highly valued than would be a loud and general huzza proceeding from a vulgar popular vanity, or any premature outburst of ignorant admiration and applause."

TO GEORGE H. BOKER.

CEDARCROFT, KENNETT SQUARE, PA., *August* 21, 1865.

. . . I am working hard at my " St. John," and if I were sure of three weeks without any "worry" (of the low, sneaking, material sort) would see the end. I am now writing on the Fourth and Last Book. The subject possesses me most vitally, and what I have done this summer is not the worst part of the poem. It will make about 3,200 lines, of which I have written some 2,600 already. I am now impatient to finish, as further delay will not improve the work, but rather the contrary. I feel the first wave of a current which may drift me away from the poetical stage which this poem represents. When I close it, I stand squarely upon tolerably matured powers, with all tasks finished, and a clear, fresh field before me. Do you feel these transitions ? This is my third, and in all probability the last. But come, and we will regulate all things in our talk.

CEDARCROFT, *Sunday, August* 27, 1865.

To-day I have finished my "St. John"! That you may know the bulk of this poem, conceived fifteen years ago, but chiefly written since March, 1863, let me give you this *material* statement : Book I., The Artist, 98 stanzas ; Book II., The Woman, 103 stanzas ; Book III., The Child, 102 stanzas ; Book IV., The Picture, 94 stanzas. Total, 397 stanzas, or 3,176 lines ! You have seen (and may or may not remember something of) Book I. I can only say that Book II. is better than I., III. better than II., and IV. better than III. Of the poem as a whole you must judge when you come out, which I hope will be within the next ten days. Graham does not write to me very positively about coming, but I shall send him another missive to-morrow morning, of a more threatening and persuasive character. Now that I have done my task I am impatient to have a poet's impression. The thing is mine, mine alone, from beginning to end, and will either make or unmake forever my title of poet. I am possessed, mastered by it ; and the impetus which carried me so swiftly to the end still drives me, though now towards no end. I am at the same time exhausted, and unable to rest.

We have lovely weather, and Cedarcroft was never more en-

joyable. I really must see you here before I go westward; I
shall insist on Graham coming by the end of this week, and will
duly inform you, so that you may come with him : though I hope
that your movements will not wait upon his, but that you will
come in any case.

My mood is a reflection from our old days of '49 and '50. Do
you remember those days?

The concentration of mind which saw the completion of " The Picture of St. John " obtains expression
in these almost overwrought words. A more definite
record of the mood in which he found himself when
the last line was written appears in a note appended
to the first draft of the poem, and bearing the same
date as the last quoted letter to Mr. Boker : —

" Cedarcroft, August 27, 1865. Sunday, 12.30 P. M.
I commenced 'The Picture of St. John' in June,
1850, with no very clear conception, and no more serious purpose than to write a narrative poem of love
and sorrow, with an artist as the hero. Its only relation to art, as nearly as I can recall my idea, was
this : that the artist should seek his subject in nature,
and in his own experience of life. The picture of the
young St. John, painted from his child, was to be
the basis of his fame and success. My conception of
the poem was wholly and intensely subjective. Some
providential instinct held me from writing more than
twenty-two stanzas, and even when, in 1854, I recommenced, a vague feeling that the theme contained material which I was not mature enough to use made me
desist. But I never gave up the idea of completing
the poem at some future time. I carried this book
with me, everywhere, upon my travels, — to Sweden,
Germany, Italy, Greece; to Germany again; even
upon lecturing tours through our Western States, —
but never seriously took up the pen until after com-

pleting ' Hannah Thurston,' in St. Petersburg, about
the end of March, 1863; and feeling the urgent need
of some further creative exercise of what faculties I
have, I resumed this poem rather as an experiment.
I soon discovered, by the new and more important
shape which it assumed in my mind, that the time had
come when, if ever, it should be written. Since then,
for nearly two years and a half, it has been constantly
present to my imagination; and, with little variation
from the original outline of the story, the whole character and purpose of the poem has changed. Such as
it now is, it has grown naturally through the growth
of my own mind. Whatever faults or merits the poem
may have, it is *my own,* unsuggested by any circumstance, and uninfluenced by any creation of others.
It closes the second stage of my development as a
poet, and is already colored, towards the end, by the
growth of what I feel to be a new (and probably the
last) stage of my poetic faculty. I have written only
as the desire and the need impelled me, — never as a
task, but always as a vital joy. Whatever verdict may
be pronounced upon it, I feel and know that it is beyond all comparison the one good thing which I have
produced. I lay down the pen with sorrow, but the
end is reached and I dare not go beyond it."

The poem was laid aside to wait for a final revision
before printing, and work resumed on the novel. A
proposition had been made and accepted by which
Bayard Taylor was to give a series of lectures at the
West, under charge of a business firm, to be free from
all responsibility and risk, and receive a fixed sum for
the course. As the following letter will show, the arrangement fell through, and he returned to his old
method for a while in the fall, before settling in New

York for the winter. The reference to an outing is to a journey which Bayard Taylor and his wife took in August, to the northward, in the course of which they visited Mr. and Mrs. McEntee at Rondout.

TO JERVIS M^CENTEE.

CEDARCROFT, KENNETT SQUARE, PA., *August* 30, 1865.

I intended to have reported to you long before this, seeing that we reached home on the 15th ; but you will understand my delay, and pardon it at once, when I tell you that I have been possessed, soul and body, with my poem. And now — just fifteen years after I wrote the first stanza — the work is done — DONE ! I have been almost crazy over it, — unable to drop the pen, — and in these fifteen days since my return have written a thousand lines. My " Picture of St. John " is painted at last, — a large canvas, but with few figures, — completely painted, in all its parts, and only lacks the final varnishing. I am now plunged in a mingled sensation of delight, relief, and regret, which you, an artist, will not require me to explain. This poem is the one good thing I have done ; but I care very little whether the public will think so, or not, when it is published. I have written it for myself, and a few others, of whom you are one. It gives the inner life of an artist, and his growth, with all the power of poetry which I possess, and is, so far, a new thing in literature.

Now I must buckle to work on my new novel, and when that is finished I shall consider myself entitled to a year's rest, at least. I shall have much more time than I anticipated, for the beautiful arrangement for lecturing in the West (of which I believe I told you) has fallen to pieces. I learned yesterday that the parties with whom I made the contract are bankrupt, and so the delightful sum of four thousand dollars upon which I counted does not and will not exist. My new barn and outbuildings, and various other improvements, thus tumble down before they are built ; but I am jolly, for all that. It is the height of folly to blubber over what can't be helped : life is too precious for unavailing lamentation. We have already sketched a simpler programme for the fall and winter, — or, rather, returned to the old plan, before the flattering offer was made and accepted. We live on the freshest and most succulent vegetables, the most aromatic peaches, and hugest sugary melons this earth produces, and are happy. I sell my surplus at good prices, and find such a satisfaction therein that I intend planting eight hundred additional peach-trees this fall ! My grapes are already ripe, and are admirable in bloom and flavor. Moreover, I have just purchased six hundred bushels of lime, a pyramid of manure, and two tons of phosphate, determined to make my picturesque acres pay for their keep. I wish you could come here this fall, and help me arrange and decide how best to use Nature without spoiling her looks.

We had a most agreeable visit at Springfield, and reached Boston on the Friday night after leaving you. Making our headquarters there, we spent Saturday with Whittier at Amesbury, and on Sunday drove to Nahant, and passed the afternoon with Longfellow. The weather was perfection, and the coast scenery more charming than I ever saw it before. The Atlantic was as blue as the Mediterranean. I met Suydam, who told me that he and Gifford[1] were at Newburyport, and Whittredge at Portsmouth. We left Boston on Monday evening, and came directly home by the Newport way. So ended the short but delightful summer vacation. It is pleasant to know your Rondout nook, and to put you, in memory, among your proper surroundings.

I expect Graham and Boker (if they don't disappoint me) in a few days. With that exception my autumn will be lonely. Perhaps, if my funds run low, I shall go out to Iowa and Kansas in October, and pick up a few lectures. I have still this good staff (though a tiresome crutch) upon which to lean at need. But next winter I shall and must have free in New York, even if I have to borrow my expenses. And next summer, D. V., we shall all go to Italy !

TO E. C. STEDMAN.

CEDARCROFT, KENNETT SQUARE, PA., *September* 1, 1865.

Your Sunday message from the Adirondacks was welcome in every way. It had a healthy, resinous twang, which, without your assurance of the same, would have told me of your physical improvement. Stay as long as you can, therefore, and bring back to us a double portion of strength from the hills. Your fare and surroundings make a profound impression both upon M. and myself ; but since we can't share them, we take up our bas-

[1] The late Sanford R. Gifford.

kets, go out-of-doors, and gather a bushel of the loveliest peaches — in flavor, color, and aromatic breath — ever grown. Then we pluck bunches of the pink Delaware, the misty blue Isabella, and the black Concord grape. Then we press upon huge melons to see which, by a soft, crisp crack of the heart, gives sign of sugary ripeness. Then we gather the rotund Duc d'Angoulême and the honey-blooded Doyenne d'Eté, and dress our spoils for the table with Bacchic vine-leaves. The butcher has left a quarter of succulent lamb, there is okra fresh pulled for our gumbo soup, great egg-plants tumble about the kitchen floor, and the cellar is heaped with tomatoes, squashes, green corn, Lima beans, and fresh celery, matured by a wonderful invention of my own. Moreover, the last bottle of sparkling Moselle is in ice, and will be drunk at dinner, to commemorate — what ?

This brings me to a piece of news which I am vain enough, selfish enough, and ridiculous enough to communicate to you, O my friend, without loss of time, in the hallucination that you will experience a mild thrill of sympathetic interest. I have finished my " Picture of St. John " ! Soon after writing to you last, I found that the leading horse of my tandem was running away with me, so I cut loose from the prose animal in the thills, jumped upon Pegasus just as the wings were growing out of his shoulders and flanks, and off we went ! I was possessed, as I have not been for years, — utterly absorbed, *distrait*, and lost for the material aspects of life. So, by August 1st, the Third Book — which was barely commenced, you may remember — was finished. Then M. and I went on a ten days' trip to Rondout (McEntees) and Massachusetts, spending a day with dear old Whittier at Amesbury and a day with Longfellow at Nahaut. We had a charming little journey, but I was pursued by " St. John," and no sooner had I returned home than I recommenced, with the same overpowering possession. One day I wrote nineteen stanzas ! not because I was hurried, but because it was impossible to drop the pen. So, a week ago, the Fourth and last Book was finished. Then, still unsatisfied, I turned back and re-wrote the first third of Book First, rounding and completing the poem ; then the introductory Proem ; and now, everything being completed at last and laid aside to cool for the final revision, behold the explanation of the Moselle ! You cannot conceive how I rejoice at having thus been forced to finish my task, the last half of which is much better than the first. The

poem is the one good thing I have done, but I don't know
whether relief or regret is my predominant feeling now. For
the first time in many years I feel my physical nature completely
bound and trodden under foot by the intellectual. But it is not
altogether agreeable. I was fast losing my appetite, my healthy
sleep, and my delight in air and sunshine.

A four weeks' lecturing tour in the West broke into
the autumn and interrupted work on "Kennett," but
after a rest at Cedarcroft, where he lingered until the
winter snows came, Bayard Taylor went, with his family, into winter quarters in New York, and settled
down to work on his novel. He looked forward to a
quiet winter of social pleasures and freedom from work
as soon as his novel should be completed ; to the old
delights of painting, and then to poetry and a revision
of "St. John." He had reached one of those stages
where he was minded to halt, look about him leisurely,
and wait for the next impulse which should send him
forward. Idle he could never be : if he did not work
in earnest, he worked in fun ; if poetry did not inspire
him, he played with the muse and teased her into giving out quips and oddities. But there were tides in
his life, and it was one thing to work as under possession, another to work from sheer inability of his mind
to remain inactive. He had, besides, so far disposed
of schemes and fancies that now he looked rather to
the large movements of his mind than to merely busy
occupation. The writing of a sustained poem had
made him indifferent to lesser *motifs ;* the carrying
forward of a plot in a substantial novel had accustomed him to full measure in intellectual effort; and
perhaps it is not insignificant that he should, at this
time, have found satisfaction in the sonnet, as if even
in the briefer expressions of poetry he chose a form

which to the poetic soul is like a planet, — a brilliant gleam in appearance, a vast world in reality.

He did not lack opportunities for literary occupation. His position invited proposals from publishers and editors, but he knew his own powers well by this time, and he was not to be diverted from the plan of his life, — though, to be sure, a new barn or greenhouse was a tolerably potent engine to draw him off his conscious course. An enthusiastic admirer, plotting great things for himself and his idol, proposed a new monthly magazine, to be called " Bayard Taylor's Journal," and received the following reply : —

NEW YORK, *December* 16, 1865.

DEAR SIR, — The undertaking you suggest never entered my mind, for the simple reason that, as I am individually constituted, it is utterly impracticable.

1. I never would give my own name to a periodical. That is a thing which *publishers* do (Chambers, Blackwood, etc.), not *authors*.

2. I never would allow my name to be responsible before the public for the conduct of a journal, unless I actually assumed the responsibility, not even if my best literary friend were the editor. There is no satisfaction in even a pint of hot water which has been heated by somebody else.

3. Nothing is a more precarious venture than the establishment of a new journal. It is just one of those things wherein Ned Buntline might succeed, and the angel Gabriel fail.

4. In any case, this is not the time for such a venture. Several dozens of new periodicals have been started within the year, more are announced, and there will soon be a surfeit.

With regard to Mr. Dickens, I happen to know that there is not a better man of business in all England. He is his own publisher, editor, and man-of-all-work. Not even an advertisement goes upon the covers of his magazine without having passed through his hands. He directs, personally, all the details of the business, and is found daily at his working desk in the office.

Finally, I once allowed my name to be used as simply co-editor of "Graham's Magazine," to my lasting regret and disgust.

Henceforward I put my name to nothing that is not wholly and solely my own, and the most brilliant pecuniary glitter will not change my mind.   Very truly yours,

BAYARD TAYLOR.

Bayard Taylor found his relief from the work and care of the day in the social diversions of the evening. His house had come to be the meeting-place of a group of artists, men of letters, and cultivated people who liked best such associates. Among these, the tired poet was like a boy, and his own contagious cheerfulness was so genuine that no one was surprised at it, or imagined that it was not the habitual temper of his days. The charm of these evenings was in their unconventionality, their hearty yet refined devotion to fun and frolic, and the impromptu wit which turned the shop even into merry-making. Among the *habitués* were the Stoddards, Stedmans, McEntees, Mr. S. R. Gifford, Mr. Launt Thompson, Mr. Macdonough, Mr. Aldrich, Mr. Whitelaw Reid, Mr. Eastman Johnson, as well as some unknown to fame, but welcomed for their wit and geniality. One would occasionally see Horace Greeley open the door a crack, squeeze in like a bashful boy, and seat himself in a chair nearest the door. "Once I remember," writes an artist of these evenings, "when the Taylors had rooms in Eighth Street, and a number of us, among whom I recall Gifford, Cranch, Launt Thompson, the Stoddards, and McEntees, had been celebrating some anniversary, — a birthday, perhaps. Towards evening it was proposed to go to my studio. We gathered up the salads and remaining dishes, and hiding them under cloaks and shawls adjourned to my rooms and spent the evening. Some of the other artists came in, and at last they lighted up their studios, and we went from one to the other, dressing up in any fantastic thing we found in the studios, — Arctic dresses from Bradford's and Indian toggery from Bierstadt's."

If art was turned into sport, so was literature. One favorite entertainment was the writing of impromptu verses upon some subject, the poets being furnished with tags of rhymes ; or parodies were perpetrated on the spur of the moment. Here is one of Bayard Taylor's bits of nonsense : —

THE VALE OF AUREA.

There 's not in this wide world a color so sweet
As that hill where the ochre and indigo meet ;
Where the shadows are umber, the lights are gamboge,
And the clouds in the distance are tinted with rouge.

Oh, the last drop of varnish and oil shall depart
Ere the hue of the pigments shall fade from my heart ;
Ere the glow of sienna shall fall to decay,
And the gloom of asphaltum shall vanish away.

It is not that Nature hath spread o'er the scene
The olive and lake and Veronese green ;
'T is not the soft magic of madder and blue,
Nor the glitter of cadmium shining all through.

Oh, no ! 'T is that purchasers eager are near,
And the price shall be higher, for the colors are dear.
If the frame is expensive the picture will sell,
And at least for two weeks I shall eat and drink well.

"Trying to analyze my own delight in these gatherings," writes the artist whose letter is quoted above, "it seems to me that it came from the feeling of freedom from restraint and criticism. These bright men and women were sufficient unto each other. The unostentatious hospitality was so cheerily dispensed ; the ignoring and forgetting all vexing and disturbing affairs in his home being one of the marked features in Taylor's .character. Busy, hard-working man as he was, he must have had many trials and annoyances, as we all have, but the friends who were always ready to go to his house never wondered why Taylor was particularly cheerful, for he was that always as a matter of course."

The "Story of Kennett" was finished in January and published early in April. While engaged upon it the author had a letter from an old friend, criticising the two novels already published, and his reply intimates something of the attitude which he took toward his works of fiction.

TO JOHN B. PHILLIPS.

NEW YORK, *January* 6, 1866.

. . . "Hannah" is not my "pet child" (no prose work of mine is, or can be), but the book has certain positive merits which I can see, although I be its author. Artistically, it is not a failure. To be sure, it has serious faults : it lacks movement, especially in the first half ; there is much unnecessary detail, frequently a want of relief, and some of the characters are imperfectly developed. But Hannah Thurston, the woman, is a successful creation ; the scope and plan of the book are correct. Were I to write it again, I would retain these as they are. . . . As to "John Godfrey," it is greatly superior to "Hannah Thurston " in execution. It is livelier, more entertaining to the general reader, and written in a more fresh and vigorous style, but the subject is less original. Both books have had a great sale, and are still selling at a surprising rate, considering they are already old. I am glad you like John, — men generally do ; while the women still prefer Hannah. My pet novel is one upon which I am now engaged, and which will be published in about two months. It is totally different from the others, — altogether objective in subject and treatment, — and I know it will greatly interest you, whether you may like it or not.

Some details of defense of "Hannah Thurston" were added, and brought later a second letter from his friend, in which the impressions received upon a second reading were given. The letter came just as Bayard Taylor was returning with his family to Cedarcroft. The answer to this letter gives further history of his ventures in fiction.

TO JOHN B. PHILLIPS.

KENNETT SQUARE, PA., *April* 2, 1866.

. . . My new novel, "The Story of Kennett," promises to be a marked success, so far as present indications go. Although the publishing business is as flat as possible, more than six thousand copies have been ordered in advance of publication, and the few who have read the book are unanimous as to its interest. I am curious to hear your verdict.

I have not your second letter at hand to-day ; it is among some papers yet unpacked. (We only returned from New York day before yesterday.) But I was a little amused at the new aspects which "Hannah Thurston" presented to you on a second reading. The same thing has happened in this neighborhood. Several of those who were at first most indignant have since confessed that they had overlooked or misinterpreted many important points, and are now much better satisfied. I probably could not have entered upon a new literary field with a better subject, because the very difference of opinion was an advantage. For this reason I deliberately chose it, not wishing to venture either "John Godfrey" or the "Story of Kennett" (both of which were *first* conceived, years ago) upon an experiment. Each work has taught me much that I could not have known without writing it, and, whatever may be individual opinions, has upon the whole advanced my position as an author. I am entirely satisfied, — not with the works themselves, God forbid ! but with the result of the experiment, — and am now sure that I can write a good and characteristic American novel. My mind is now so trained by twenty years' work that I cannot rest without production, and as my standard of literary art recedes just in proportion as I approach it I am all the time kept in good heart. I began ten years, in development, behind almost every other author whom I know, and therefore shall continue to grow when many of them have reached their full stature. Whatever may be the faults of " H. T." (and I confess to a great many), the booksellers tell me that it already has the character of a standard work. Now, two and a half years after publication, there is a steady, permanent demand for it. The same people also say (looking at the thing solely as a matter of business) that I am entirely successful as a novelist. But I know my own deficiencies, and attribute what success I have to want of satisfaction in former works, — the spur that drives me onward. I have never before worked so steadily and untiringly with the pen as last year, and I shall work harder this year than the last. There is no lack of material. So long as the faculty does not flag I shall labor, finding a joy in solid, conscientious work which I never found in the youthful glow and formless excitement of a very undeveloped brain.

The " Story of Kennett " was received, not only by a larger public, but also by a more unanimous press. The idyllic character of the work, its freedom from burning questions, and its objectivity gave it great popularity. The people conversant with the locality of the tale were especially eager to read it. Only one passage received condemnation, and as the fullest criticism of it was from the pen of his old Kennett friend, John B. Phillips, we reproduce it here, with the author's defense : —

" L. has just finished reading me the ' Story of Kennett,' " writes Mr. Phillips, " with which, in the main, we were very much delighted. With one solitary exception I think it admirable ! We drove on through it at a rapid pace. The chase, the raising, the corn-husking, the journey to Chester, the robbery, the flood at Chad's Ford, the peril, the rescue, the daring Sandy Flash and Deb Smith, all throw a glamour of romance over the whole thing. The wanderings of Sandy and Deb, the final capture of the former on the

Brandywine, are admirable. The love is all right, too ; Martha Deane capital. Indeed, the whole thing was sweeping toward a complete and perfect success, without slip, halt, flaw, or blemish. We stopped again and again to praise. L. said twenty times, ' I want to write to him and tell him how much I admire it.' I noticed nothing that jarred at all until we came to the funeral of old Barton. Mary Potter's course began to grate on my feelings then, and kept on doing it all through. I stopped the reading and made my first objection there, almost at the end of the book. As this is the very climax of the whole thing, you have of course well considered what you were about, and my objections will not change your own ideas. But I am bound to give my real opinion, if I give any opinion of the book at all. It seemed to me like a ship grating on sunken rocks, in sight of the harbor. Mary Potter announces before she leaves home that that is to be ' her day,' and she makes a field day of it for certain. I am sorry to think that she damages herself seriously by her course. I am disposed to deny to her altogether the right to call it *her* day. It was a day set apart for a funeral, at which all people, civilized and savage, feel bound to act with more than ordinary decorum, to suppress their passions and postpone their private rights, wrongs, and grievances. The relatives and neighbors of the old man, it is to be presumed, honestly meant to give him a decent burial. They had a right to do it without molestation from Mary Potter or any one else. They had never harmed her, the other relations never harmed her ; the old man had left her twenty thousand dollars, and she knew it, or at least that she was left something. Why not allow him a decent burial ? What had the funeral party to do

with the fact of her having been married to Alfred for
twenty-five years? What had that to do with the funeral? What had her triumph or her justification to
do with it? What right had she to make the old
man's coffin a platform on which to exhibit her triumph or her justification, and, to use her own words,
to make it her day? She suffered so much! Everybody suffers or has suffered. But she had a right as
wife to do it! Technically, she had. I have a right
to break a funeral procession in the street, — the street
is as much mine as anybody's: but I don't do it. The
rule in short is, You are bound to postpone the exercise of your rights at a funeral if it should mar the
solemnity or propriety of the occasion. . . . But the
principal person who has my sympathy on that occasion is Gilbert Potter. He is the man that is pilloried.
For him the thing must have been perfectly awful. I
can't imagine how his worst or meanest enemy, by the
utmost stretch of malice, could have by any possibility contrived a more harrowing way of breaking to
him a most loathsome fact. His humiliation is perfect
and complete. I agree with him that Sandy Flash
were a much better father. I fail to see much triumph in Mary's hanging on to Alf's rotten carcass.
The funeral becomes a rabble not pleasant to contemplate. The procession is broken, and men lash their
horses to get ahead and gloat their greedy eyes on the
pilloried Alf and Potter and the triumphant Mary
Potter."

To this Bayard Taylor replied : —

" Your criticism of ' Kennett ' astounded me quite
as much as your rage about ' Hannah.' That you
should have picked out the most powerful, most dramatic, most (by all the principles of art and life) jus-

tifiable chapter in the book for condemnation almost takes the breath out of me. You must remember that Mary Potter is both proud and stubborn; a merely good woman could never have exhibited her energy and determination. She had fixed, for years, just this justification in her mind; there is a vein of superstition about her; she sees simply what she believes the Lord has directed her to do, and she does it. What you say of the order of funerals in Kennett is quite true. Such an incident as I have described probably never occurred, but that makes no difference whatever. It is natural for Mary to do it; there could be no other culmination to her history. I was a year studying out the plot before I began to write, and the idea of the *dénouement* at the funeral came to me like an inspiration."

As soon as the novel was finished Bayard Taylor took up again " The Picture of St. John," and had revised it for publication by the time " Kennett " was fairly launched. The novel was coming back to him in a hundred ways in the congratulation of friends and notices of the press, but his mind was set on his poem and its final form far more intently. A thing done had not the charm of a thing doing. His translation of " Faust " also was resumed.

TO E. C. STEDMAN.

CEDARCROFT, KENNETT SQUARE, PA., *April* 15 (*Sunday*), 1866.

I wish you could be here to-day to smell the blossoming hyacinths on our terrace, and to go out with us and gather the first wild-wood flowers. It throws me into an incredulous ecstasy to see budding, growing, and greening all over the land. Moreover, in spite of various worries (inevitable, I suppose) with my retainers, I am in the jolliest mood. On Friday I received letters from Tennyson, Whittier, and Howells. Tennyson praises my blue-and-gold poems, and cordially invites me to revisit him

in England. Whittier is enthusiastic about "Kennett;" ditto
Howells. The former says it contains "as good things as there
are in the English language;" the latter, "it is the best historical (historical in the sense of retrospective) novel ever written in
America." Curtis said very nearly the same thing to me at our
dinner. So, you see, my hope and your prophecy are in a way to
be fulfilled. The people in this county are buying it like mad.
I was in the West Chester book-store yesterday, and found three
men walking out with it in their pockets and two buying it at the
counter. I am refreshed, encouraged, stimulated, delighted, —
and I don't care who knows it !

Yesterday came the proof of the first eighty pages of "St.
John." The page is altogether lovely ; and the poem (an unusual experience with me) looks better in type than in MS. I am
going to order two revises, and send one to you and Dick. I
want, by the bye, to tell you that your denunciation of a certain
prosaic stanza in Book III. produced its effect. It ran this
way : —

> But on the pier a messenger I found
> From Como, hasty with intelligence
> Of orders waiting me in Milan, whence
> The summons came. My work had grown renowned,
> He said, and certain frescoes might be mine
> If I but claimed them : here a field divine
> Offered : he saw my brows already crowned,
> For who would shrink occasion so benign?

Now it reads thus : —

> But on the pier a messenger I found
> From Milan, where the borrowed name I bore
> Was known, he said, and more than half-renowned ;
> And now a bright occasion offered me
> A fairer crown than yet my forehead wore, —
> A range of palace-chambers to adorn
> With sportive frescoes, nymphs of earth and sea,
> Pursuing Hours, and marches of the Morn !

You thus see that a criticism strongly expressed sometimes
does good. I find, however, that I cannot make many additional
changes in the proof, not so much from want of desire or
ability as because the subject, once expressed, is losing its hold
on my imagination, — passing from me. You will understand
this, I think. . . .

Would that you could breathe this soft, sweet air with us !
We have cucumbers to-day for dinner, and the house is filled

with delicate bouquets from flowers blooming in the open air. I
have a fine promise of fruit, in spite of the severe winter ; and as
for the repose and seclusion of the place, it is simply heavenly.
When the ferment of the winter has subsided a little more, 1
shall produce lots of poems "and things." Love from M. (and
me) to you and L. and the boys.

TO T. B. ALDRICH.

CEDARCROFT, KENNETT SQUARE, PA., *April* 16, 1866.

. . . I had bestowed much preliminary thought upon the book,
["Kennett"], and I worked out the idea with the most conscientious care, hoping to make a stride in advance. It is a great joy
and a great encouragement to be so unanimously assured that I
have not failed in my aim. The moral is that labor pays, in a
literary sense.

As for the poem, I hope also that it shows equal growth. Certainly, it is the result of long and patient study. I have written
to Fields, asking that one revised proof be furnished conjointly
to yourself and Howells, and I want to ask you both to read it
critically as you have time, and make any suggestion to me that
you may think needful. The plan of the poem cannot be changed,
of course, but it will always be possible to make verbal or poet-
ically technical corrections. I need not say that the proof is only
for the private eyes of you two. I don't want anything in relation to the poem to get into the papers before it appears. . . .

CEDARCROFT, KENNETT SQUARE, PA., *May* 18, 1866.

. . . Such time as I can spare from gardening, making pumps,
sowing phosphates, and hauling manure is devoted to my translation of "Faust"—a heart-rending yet intensely fascinating labor.
I design nothing less than to produce *the* English "Faust;" it can
be done, I know, and pray Heaven that I may be the chosen man
to do it. When I look into the other translations, I am encouraged and comforted. Yesterday I put thirty-nine two-footed
dactylic double-rhymed lines of Goethe into thirty-nine do. do. do.
of my own, preserving the exact order of rhyme, and translating
the sense nearly literally. Good God, what a job it was! But
I enjoy it, withal. My great delight in the labor gives me hope ;
for that which I do with a real luxurious satisfaction, with a
sense like the gratification of a carnal appetite, is almost sure
(so I have learned by experience) to be pronounced good by

others. Let me hear from you before the 1st of June, because
I fully expect to set out then on a six weeks' trip to Colorado,
with Beard and Whittredge. I'll lecture a little, write letters,
and make sketches.

TO E. C. STEDMAN.

CEDARCROFT, KENNETT SQUARE, PA., *May* 21, 1866.

. . . If you see Church, I wish you'd be kind enough to sound
him about a translation of Mügge's Norwegian romance of
" Arvor Spang " as a serial for the " Galaxy." (Mügge, you know,
is the author of " Afraja.") It would make twenty-five pages a
month for six months, about, and I'd do the whole thing, with a
prefatory sketch of the author, for a thousand dollars. I want
to go to Germany in the fall, on M.'s account (her mother
complains of ill-health), and must therefore earn some money.
Moreover, I don't want to commence another novel at once.

I'll be in New York in about a week from now, and will
then see you. I can also bring you the first three books of " St.
John." . . .

The months of June and July were spent in the trip
to Colorado, where the party roughed it, and Bayard
Taylor occupied himself besides in occasional lectures
and in frequent letters to the "Tribune." He summed
up his experience in a letter to Mr. Phillips, just after
his return, when he wrote, "My trip to the Rocky
Mountains was very fatiguing, perhaps as much so as
any short journey I ever made; but it has refreshed
me greatly, both physically and mentally. I needed a
little 'let up' after finishing both 'Kennett' and 'The
Picture of St. John' within the same year. In addition I shall take some further rest before commencing
any work of importance." It was a pleasure to him to
renew acquaintance with the most intimate friend of
his boyhood, and he wished greatly that they might
meet after the lapse of years, to compare notes of experience. Of himself he says in the same letter:
"My studies now are changed from what they once

were. I read first of all Goethe, then Montaigne, Burton, Mill, Buckle, Matthew Arnold, and the old English poets; of the modern, chiefly Wordsworth, Tennyson, and Clough. Ruskin and Carlyle serve as *entrées.* I abhor everything spasmodic and sensational, and aim at the purest, simplest, quietest style in whatever I write. My ideal is as far off as ever, but it has at least taken a clear, definite shape. Instead of mist, I see form. I have lost something of lyrical heat and passion, but gained in feeling of proportion and construction. You can easily understand how this change has come about."

TO E. C. STEDMAN.

CEDARCROFT, *August* 13, 1866.

. . . Howells and Aldrich are the only ones who have read the proof, and the combined reports will be a useful guide to me. Of course I can't change the plan of the poem or its process of development, but the minor features of a poem of this length are hardly less important, and therein you may do me friendly service.

I doubt whether I shall begin any serious work this fall, though, physically, I feel capable of anything. I have lost seventeen pounds of my weight, am very brown, and have gone through such a rough and tough experience that now it seems as if I had put on a complete suit of new flesh. M. superintended all the building while I was away, and now the work is almost done. We have no peaches this year, but melons every day. The place is wonderfully improved, in an agricultural sense, and the fields yield fine crops. I begin, at last, to see the result of my experiment in culture, and am both vain and proud of my success. When will you come to us? The fall will soon be here, and I suggest that you come before returning to your house. While you are on the wing it will be easier for you to take an additional flight hitherwards than to leave your perch afterwards.

Let me hear from you soon, in any case. I am hungry for words from all who are both friends and poets. It seems as if I had been absent a year.

KENNETT SQUARE, PA., *September* 17, 1866.

Ever since I got back from the Rocky Mountains (now more than six weeks) I have been intending to write to you ; but I did n't know your address until Madam Gertrude's letter came, and since then I have been exceedingly busy, my three or four days of leisure having been devoted to attending the Loyal Southern Convention at Philadelphia, which, I know, you won't think was time ill-spent. Beard and I had the roughest, wildest, grandest, jolliest time among the great mountains, and there was n't a day when we did n't wish for you and Gifford. We did n't make a great many sketches, being too much demoralized by fatigue. I had the skin burned off my face twice, every bone in my body broken (as it seemed by my sensations), and lost seventeen pounds of flesh. But I am all the better for it ; came back physically refreshed, and with a store of wonderful pictures in my memory.

Soon after my return M.'s brother came to spend a month with us. The young man had taken up landscape-painting as a private hobby, and brought a lot of oils with him. I seized on them instantly, and made a Rocky Mountain scene from memory. I was so fascinated by the ability to work slowly and correct mistakes, that I procured a twelve-dollar tin box from Goupil's, with a few mill-boards, four of which I have already covered. I am so fascinated by the delight of working in this new and delightful material that I hardly know how to stop, and must, perforce, limit my indulgence to Sundays, in order not to neglect my legitimate business. My brother-in-law knows no more about the manipulation than I do, and so we blunder away, but with all blundering, I find I can produce effects utterly impossible to me in water-colors. I have half a mind to send you a specimen after I know that you are back in Rondout.

Do let me hear what you have done and where you have been, and what are your plans for the winter, etc., etc. We did n't meet Whittredge in Colorado. I hear through Stedman that Gifford has been with you this summer. We hope to go to Europe, for fifteen or eighteen months, in February. I must have rest. Although not wholly out of debt, I have been prospering, and will take a release from drudgery, because I think I deserve it.

The "St. John" will be given to the public the first week in November. The type is very handsome, and Fields promised to have it printed and bound in sumptuous style. So you will soon be able to read the thing at your cool, critical leisure. Have you seen any of my "Tribune" letters? I've half a mind to make a little volume of them, merely for temporary sale, while the curiosity about Colorado is active.

I'm called to dinner, and must close. I wish you were here to help eat our splendid melons and pears. Say you'll come for a fortnight. I'll give you a studio, and we'll all be happy!

As appears from the correspondence, Bayard Taylor was forming plans for another visit to Europe and a leisurely stay there. He was tired; he was reluctant to enter upon any new and considerable work at present beside his "Faust;" he saw that by living in Europe he could avoid some expenses, and could more easily find abundant material for single sketches than he could at home; and his family connections in Germany made that place very much of a home to him. So he began arranging his work and schemes with reference to leaving in the winter. "St. John" would then be published, and he would have cleared away the odds and ends of his engagements.

TO JAMES T. FIELDS.

CEDARCROFT, KENNETT SQUARE, PA., *September* 17, 1866.

We won't give up the hope of your coming yet. There are still six weeks here of the loveliest autumn weather.

Your proposal chimes in very well with my own plans, so I should not wonder if we could come to an agreement. In return I also have a proposal to make, and the whole matter will be clearer if I simply tell you exactly how I am situated and what my plans are, the Lord willing, for the next two years.

I have been working very hard for some years past to acquire enough property to give me a tolerably certain income, sufficient for both needs and tastes, and an ample provision for both wife and child in case of my death. The war set me back, but I have got on fortunately, on the whole, and hope to come out fair and square, with a light heart and a clear conscience, on the 31st of December, 1866. My great ambition has been to give up lecturing entirely, and only write the things which I feel I can best do. I don't need the pecuniary spur, and can always accomplish more when I don't feel it. Now, I propose first to take a year's holiday, going to Europe next February, and returning in the spring of 1868. I intend, also, to accomplish a long-cherished desire, and visit a number of the most picturesque and least known corners and by-ways of Europe. What do you say to a series of articles for the "Atlantic," similar in manner to the Russian sketches? *Sub rosa,* these are some of the places in my mind : Friesland (Peasant Life) ; Castle Kyffhäuser (Barbarossa) ; Auvergne ; the Republic of Andorre (Pyrenees) ; Majorca ; the Monastery of Montserrat ; Gruyère and the other Cheese Valleys of Switzerland ; Elba ; Girgenti (Sicily) ; Upper Campagna and Volscian Mountains ; Brittany.

The series would commence in July or August next. I want to make some arrangement anent them this fall.

Now as to the novel. I have two good subjects, one of which bothers me in regard to construction, and will require a good year to work over in my head before I begin to write. About the end of 1868 was the time I set (mentally) to have it written and printed. It must be completed from end to end before any part of it goes out of my hands. If I publish serially, at least I won't write serially. I understand that the sum you offer is for the publication in the "Atlantic," the privilege of issuing the book not covering the copyright thereon. The reverse would be simply asking me to lose money, which of course you can't mean. The question of copyright for the book, and arrangements for adding it, *during the five years* (an important particular), to the complete series of my prose works, remain to be settled. With regard to the novel, I expect to have one ready in two years from now ; a work illustrating a phase of American life which interests me profoundly, and which I want to make better than the former ones. Your offer, as I understand it, is what has been offered and accepted in other cases, and therefore we should not quarrel over that point.

I must have my rest and recreation first, after nearly four years of unremitting labor, and then I shall take hold with fresh spirit, all serious worries being left behind me. My ruling passion, as an author, is to do something better, — to overcome, by

hard work and honest study, the disadvantages of early senti-
mentality and shallowness. I am just beginning to "feel my
oats."

By the bye, while in Germany I shall go on with the translation of "Faust." My wife is acquainted with Frau von Goethe,
whom we shall visit, and I expect to gather together a deal of
interesting material about Part II. I have already done nearly
half of Part I. I want to do for friendship ("Faust") what
Petrarch (Longfellow) has done for love (Dante). Will you
give me three volumes in 4to when the work is completed?

Now, what do you say to my programme? I suppose the
sketches will make fifteen or twenty pages apiece, and there may
be twelve or fifteen of 'em. Will that be too much of a good
thing? Also, as to arranging to include the novel in my series
of works, because there is a steady sale of *sets* of the latter.

This is as much as you can read at one pull, so good-by.

TO JERVIS McENTEE.

KENNETT SQUARE, PA., *September* 25, 1866.

I was delighted to get your letter yesterday, and, to prove
the interest I take in your plans, I reply without delay. We
are going to New York about the middle of October, but if we
can manage to run up to Rondout for one evening it will hardly
be before the 15th. Don't count on it too positively, and carry
out your own sketching tour without reference to us.

My plans for the European tour are tolerably well fixed, and
I hope the Lord will graciously permit me to carry them into
execution; for, as proposed, they will give me rest, refreshment,
and enjoyment. We want to leave in February, so as to reach
Gotha by the 10th of March, at the latest. In April we shall
make a leisurely journey southward through the Tyrol, spend a
month in Venice, and then go to my sister in Lausanne for another month. After running over to Paris to see the exhibition,
we shall be back in Gotha towards the end of June. We have
already written to engage our former cottage in the mountains
for the months of July and August. In September we 'll go
by way of Switzerland to Italy, spend the fall in Florence, the
winter in Naples, and the spring in Rome. Towards the end of
summer (1868) we shall return to America. I have made a literary engagement for detached sketches of out-o'-the-way corners of Europe, and must therefore make a number of brief

and picturesque excursions. This engagement will pay half my expenses, and is therefore not to be slighted. Moreover, I shall sketch as much as possible, one article a month taking up very little of my time. I hope to have a good long holiday, doing only what I like best to do. It will not be idleness, but a cessation of active, steady work, in which I shall insensibly accumulate a deal of material. You understand this.

TO JAMES T. FIELDS.

CEDARCROFT, *October* 4, 1866.

All unexpectedly to-day came a dozen "Pictures." I want simply to say how delighted I am with the whole — what d' you call it ? — *mise en scène ?* "Getting up" is too commonplace and prosy an expression for this (externally) delicious book. It can't be improved except in one slight particular, — the lettering of the title on the back ; and that is a matter of personal taste. The paper is of the right quality, has the right tint, and the type is supreme.

TO HENRY W. LONGFELLOW.

CEDARCROFT, KENNETT SQUARE, *Sunday, December* 30, 1866.

It has always been my rule to obey a genuine impulse, and I so strongly feel the desire to say a few words to you that I do not ask myself whether you will care to hear them. I could not tell you when I was at Cambridge how much, how very much, I was cheered and strengthened by your praise of my poem ; nor could you well understand the value of your words to me at this time, without a little confession of my own. In the first place, then, let me say that nearly everything which I have published, up to last year, seems to me more or less crude and unsatisfactory. My former works are simply so many phases of an education which circumstances have compelled me to acquire in the sight of the public. I had in, fact, very little early education, except that of travel ; I began to publish (it was inevitable) much too soon ; and moreover, I am descended from two hundred years of Quaker farmers, whose transmitted slowness of maturity I have hardly yet overcome. The artistic sense was long dormant, and is only at present becoming fairly active : I am, perhaps, ten years behind a man who has had more favorable antecedents and opportunities. I have worked earnestly and faithfully during the past three or four years, and finally come to look upon the ventures of this year (my "Story of Kennett" and " Picture of St. John ") as being destined to decide the question whether I was to have any place in our literature. The poem, I knew, could not be popular, and so I looked only to the verdict of the poets who should read it. I can write for myself alone, and should probably always write, though no one should read ; but I feel a thoroughly joyous activity of mind, and know that I do better things when I am encouraged by the " well done ! " of brother authors. Never before in my life have I received such hearty, substantial cheer as during my recent visit to Boston. I feel now as if I had, at last, a little solid ground under my feet, — as if the long *Wanderjahre* were past, and I could begin to build a house. I have always estimated my former successes (or what were considered such) at their true value, and have waited patiently for twenty years for the welcome of the masters. When you praised the poem for the very qualities I aimed to reach, you confirmed the hopes of my life. There is no very serene literary atmosphere in New York, as you doubtless know, and I get little help or encouragement there ; but I do not need it now.

I shall try to do better things in the future, taking a new departure from this point. There is still time, with life and health, to atone for the imperfections of the past. I shall never forget how much I owe to you (and to Lowell also) in this self-appointed crisis. But enough of this ; I am presuming a good deal on your friendship to write so much. I kept your book for the Christmas-tree, where my wife had a surprise as well as a delight on finding it. She bids me thank you most heartily for your kind remembrance of her. A Happy New Year to you all !

TO J. B. PHILLIPS.

CEDARCROFT, *January* 30, 1867.

I only reached home last night after two weeks among the snow-drifts [on a lecturing tour], and write immediately, because I am not sure that I shall again have time, in the hurry and rush of preparation for departure. We sail on the 9th of February, and shall be absent a year and a half, mostly in Italy. I am somewhat fagged and worn from my labors during the past five or six years, and must have a holiday before undertaking the more important literary labors which I have proposed to myself.

I am very glad you like the " St. John." It has done more

for me with the authors than anything I ever wrote. Longfellow said to me, "You have written a great poem, — noble, sustained, and beautiful from beginning to end." Bryant wrote me the most charming letter about it. Lowell says that no American poem except the "Golden Legend" can match it in finish and sustained power. The "London Athenæum" says about the same thing. In fact, it has at last procured me admission into the small company of American poets who have some chance of life. It never can be popular (in the ordinary sense), but it will be always liked, I think, by the few who make fame for an author. I feel deeply, profoundly satisfied, but not elated. I have now a little solid ground under my feet, and can take a fresh departure, having left the crude, educational phase (to which nearly all my former works belong) behind me. Hence the need of rest before I do any more serious work.

The recognition by his fellow-poets was all that Bayard Taylor asked. He wished to be judged by his peers, and the hearty, unequivocal verdict by his elders was exceedingly grateful to him. "It very rarely happens," wrote Mr. Bryant, "that I finish a book at a sitting, but I did it with yours. You may judge, therefore, of the degree to which it interested me. I congratulate you on having produced the best of your longer poems, and that is no small praise. Your success has been such as to justify all the pains which, as you intimate, you have bestowed upon the work. The Proem it would be injurious to the rest of the volume to call the best part of it, — and I do not call it so, — but it is so charmingly written that I have recurred to it several times after having finished the reading of the other cantos. Proems are generally just a little dull, but this has the good fortune to be an exception."

He had secured a repute as a traveler and popularity as a novelist. To be known as a poet by poets was far sweeter to him, and joined with it was the consciousness that he was fulfilling his destiny, expressing his power. " I think it must be an American gift," writes Dr. Holmes, " to unite such different powers as those which belong to the traveler and the poet, and you are one of the most American of Americans, as it seems to me." Another poet was then just bringing out one of his group of poems. " I must beg Fields," he writes, " to send thee the proof-sheets of ' The Tent on the Beach.' And I here beg pardon for the friendly license of using thee as one of the imaginary trio on the sea-shore. . . . The 'St. John' is a poem which grows upon me more and more. I marvel at its exquisite finish and beauty. It is a poem for poets and painters." On the same sheet, Mr. Whittier copied a stanza from an earlier poem, " The Last Walk in Autumn," in which he had already enshrined his friend : —

" Here, too, of answering love secure,
    Have I not welcomed to my hearth
The gentle pilgrim troubadour,
    Whose songs have girdled half the earth ;
Whose pages, like the magic mat
Whereon the Eastern lover sat,
Have borne me over Rhine-land's purple vines,
And Nubia's tawny sands, and Phrygia's mountain pines ! "

CHAPTER XX.

> Returned to warm existence, — even as one
> Sentenced, then blotted from the headsman's book,
> Accepts with doubt the life again begun,—
> I leave the duress of my couch, and look
> Through Casa Guidi windows to the sun.
>
> *Casa Guidi Windows.*

BAYARD TAYLOR had been looking forward with feverish impatience to the holiday which he felt he had earned and knew he needed. "Oh, how I long," he writes on the eve of sailing, "for the rest and recreation of Europe! My Russian trip was only substituting one kind of labor and anxiety for another. I have really had no holiday since I came home in 1858, and since then I have published nine volumes, lectured exactly six hundred times, built a house, barn, stable, and other out-buildings, and paid off nearly all my debts. But for a hopeful and elastic temperament, a gift of God, I could n't have done it. I confess to feeling fagged and weary, to a mighty craving for fresh woods and pastures new. My blood is thick and sluggish; I sleep badly, for the first time in my life, and have a general sense of discomfort, though I can't put my finger on one ailing spot."

For the first time, also, he found writing irksome. Work which before had been easy now lay upon his mind as a weight, and he dragged through a few lectures and toiled with difficulty over a simple article, struggling to leave no engagement unfulfilled. His letters to the "Tribune" from Colorado were published in a thin volume by Mr. Putnam at the end of January, and at last, on the 9th of February, 1867, he sailed for England with his wife and daughter and a lady friend who accompanied them. Once more he tasted the freedom and luxurious rest of an ocean voyage. He needed only this to give him a return of hopefulness, although he knew better at a later date that he could not so easily recover a strength which had been overtasked. He called his proposed sojourn in Europe a holiday, and such he intended it to be; meaning to give his time to his friends in Gotha and elsewhere, to amuse himself with his painting, and to ramble into corners of the continent which he had not yet visited. He could not be absolutely free, however. Those debts which he had *nearly* paid still hung over him, and though he had made as careful provision for his absence as he could his establishment at Cedarcroft followed him in waking hours and dreams. He felt the necessity, also, of turning his journey into papers which should partly provide his traveling expenses. So he had planned letters to the "Tribune," and the series of papers for the "Atlantic" which he had outlined to Mr. Fields.

Labor and worries aside, he anticipated great pleasure from his stay abroad, and could not help knowing that he was in better condition than ever for enjoying Europe. Since his last visit, when he had made good friends amongst people whom he valued, he had shown that he was himself a man well worth knowing and valuing. His literary work had set him steadily forward, and his "Picture of St. John," especially, had been his announcement of his own conscious position in literature. He had not long to wait to discover how large a welcome he had earned. His short stay in England was crowded with pleasures which the best English hospitality afforded him, so that he had scarcely an opportunity to record his experience until he was once more in his German home.

TO E. C. STEDMAN.

GOTHA, GERMANY, *March* 11, 1867.

No chance to write a word to you sooner, but as no letter has yet arrived from you I may still be beforehand. I have a great deal to say, and scarcely know whether I can tell you everything in this letter. . . . We landed at Southampton in heavenly May weather, and I determined to visit Farringford before going on to London. So I wrote at once to Tennyson, proposing a visit of an hour or two. Next morning came a friendly reply from Mrs. T., saying that there was a room ready for us, and we must make a longer visit. M. and I crossed to Cowes and Newport, and took a "fly" to Farringford, distant twelve miles ; a glorious drive across the Isle of Wight, between ivied hedges and past gardens of laurel and lauristinus in blossom. Green meadows, cowslips, daisies, and hyacinths, — think of that for February 21st ! I found Farringford wonderfully improved : the little park is a gem of gardening art. The magnificent Roman ilexes in front of the house are finer than any I saw in Italy. We arrived about three o'clock, and were ushered into the drawing-room. The house has been refurnished, and a great many pictures and statues added since I was there. In a minute in came Tennyson, cordial as an old friend, followed by his wife. In Tennyson himself I could see no particular change. He did not seem older than when I saw him last. We walked through the park and garden ; then M. returned to the house, while he and I went up on the downs, and walked for miles along the chalk cliffs above the sea. He was delightfully free and confidential, and I wish I could write to you much of what he said ; but it was so inwrought with high philosophy and broad views of life that a fragment here and there would not fairly represent him. He showed me all his newly acquired territory ; among the rest, a

great stretch of wheat-fields bought for him by "Enoch Arden."
We dined at six in a quaint room hung with pictures, and then
went to the drawing-room for dessert. Tennyson and I retired
to his study at the top of the house, lit pipes, and talked of poetry. He asked me if I could read his "Boadicea." I thought
I could. "Read it, and let me see!" said he. "I would rather
hear you read it!" I answered. Thereupon he did so, chanting
the lumbering lines with great unction. I spoke of the idyl of
Guinevere as being perhaps his finest poem, and said that I
could not read it aloud without my voice breaking down at certain passages. "Why, I can read it, and keep my voice!" he
exclaimed triumphantly. This I doubted, and he agreed to try,
after we went down to our wives. But the first thing he did was
to produce a magnum of wonderful sherry, thirty years old,
which had been sent him by a poetic wine-dealer. Such wine I
never tasted. "It was meant to be drunk by Cleopatra, or Cath-
arine of Russia," said Tennyson. We had two glasses apiece,
when he said, "To-night you shall help me drink one of the few
bottles of my Waterloo, — 1815." The bottle was brought, and
after another glass all around Tennyson took up the "Idyls of
the King." His reading is a strange, monotonous chant, with unexpected falling inflections, which I cannot describe, but can imi-
tate exactly. It is very impressive. In spite of myself I became very much excited as he went on. Finally, when Arthur
forgives the Queen, Tennyson's voice fairly broke. I found
tears on my cheeks, and M. and Mrs. Tennyson were crying, one
on either side of me. He made an effort and went on to the
end, closing grandly. "How can you say," I asked (referring
to previous conversation), "that you have no surety of permanent
fame? This poem will only die with the language in which it
is written." Mrs. Tennyson started up from her couch. "It is
true!" she exclaimed. "I have told Alfred the same thing."

After that we went up to the garret to smoke and talk.
Tennyson read the "Hylas" of Theocritus in Greek, his own
"Northern Farmer," and Andrew Marvell's "Coy Mistress." . . .
We parted at two o'clock, and met again at nine in the breakfast
room. I had arranged to leave at noon, so there were only three
hours left, but I had them with him on the lawn and in the nook
under the roof. . . . Tennyson said at parting, "The gates are
always open to you." His manner was altogether more cordial
and intimate than at my first visit. He took up the acquaintance

where it first broke off, and had forgotten no word (neither had I) of our conversation ten years ago. When I spoke of certain things in his poetry which I specially valued, he said more than once, "But the critics blame me for just that. It is only now and then a man like yourself who sees what I meant to do." He is very sensitive to criticism, I find, but perhaps not more than the rest of us; only one sees it more clearly in another. Our talk was to me delightful; it was as free and frank as if you had been in his place. . . . I felt, when I left Farringford, that I had a friend's right to return again.

Soon after reaching London, I called on dear old Barry Cornwall, who has taken a great liking to Lorry Graham. Mrs. Procter invited both of us and our wives to a literary *soirée* at their house. In the mean time Lorry took me with him to call on Matthew Arnold. He is a man to like, if not love, at first sight. His resemblance to George Curtis struck both of us. A little more stoutly built, more irregularly masculine features, but the same general character of man, with the same full, mellow voice. After Thackeray, I think I should soon come to like him better than any other Englishman. His eyes sparkled when I told him that I always kept his poems on my library table. He said they were not popular, and he was always a little surprised when any one expressed a particular liking for them. I did not make a long visit, knowing that he was run down with government work.

Then I went to Browning, who had sent me a pleasant note of invitation. He has gray hair and beard, but has lost none of his vigorous life. He had "St. John" on the table. He has a long poem on the stocks, — an Italian subject, told in I don't know how many thousand lines. He called up his boy, who was hard at work with a tutor, reading up for Oxford, to shake hands with me, — a lusty young fellow, I was glad to see, a good rower, horseman, and swimmer. In the evening, at Procter's, we met Browning again, and Arnold, Lord Houghton (Milnes), Dante Rossetti, and many others. Browning professed to remember M. from Rome. It was a lively, crowded, pleasant party.

Lorry and I were to breakfast the next morning with Lord Houghton. When we arrived we found our host in conversation with a plain, red-haired, farmer-like individual whom he introduced to us as the Duke of Argyll. The latter said to me, "Do you know that *you* were the cause of Tennyson's visit to Norway? After he read your book he could not rest until he went there himself." Then entered, in succession, Froude, the historian, the Bishop of Oxford (Wilberforce), Lord Wentworth, the grandson of Byron, with a Byronic profile (a nice young man, whom I liked exceedingly), the Bishop of St. Davids, Venables (the lawyer and publicist), and Sir William Stirling Maxwell, author of the " Cloister Life of Charles V." It was a charming breakfast : only an old butler and a page waited, the guests helping each other, — the conversation a mosaic of cheerful, cordial chat. I sat between the Duke and the Bishop of Oxford, and the latter kept my plate constantly supplied with butter and salt. Froude told us of his researches in the Spanish archives, and the Duke discussed Dixon's book on America.

I had to tear myself away from *entrées* to clubs and invitations to dinner, and leave London. I might have floated for a month or so (with money and inclination) on the top wave of London society, but after the poets it would have been a descent. One thing, however, does pleasantly tickle my vanity : I am weak enough to feel it, yet frank enough to confess it. That is, that I have made myself a footing in England, in the last four or five years. Trübner told me that " St. John " has been greatly praised in all the reviews ; his stock of the poem was immediately sold, and he had ordered a fresh supply from Boston. He considers it one of the most successful of recent American books. Hotten (the publisher) told me the same thing. From the authors I had the kindest and most cheering words. I need not tell you how grateful is this knowledge to me, for you can easily guess it.

We went one night to hear Dickens read " David Copperfield." Sothern gave us a box for his " Dundreary " another night, and again we dined with Anne Thackeray and her sister. A. T. is one of the dearest and best girls in the world. It was like old times to see her again. She gave me a fine portrait of her father. She stands by " Hannah Thurston," which she says she knows by heart. On the whole, I never had a richer eight days than those in London. Remember, all this is private. I write to you instead of in a journal. These are things that I can't publish, yet wish to note as I go along.[1]

[1] By a sorry mischance this letter did get published. It fell into the hands of a newspaper correspondent, who kept it long enough to copy the portion relating to Mr. Tennyson, and then, without asking leave of the author, the recipient, or conscience, printed it as a lively piece of literary

We came hither by way of Brussels and Cologne, stopping a day at each place. It was spring as far as the Rhine, then snow commenced, and we came here in midwinter. . . . To-day the snows have nearly disappeared, and we begin to see the green plains. . . . M.'s family are well, and delighted to have us back, and I think we shall get through this dismal month agreeably. I begin to feel quite rejuvenated, although longing for movement in the open air.

M. joins me in dearest love to you and L. Would you could be here a while to rest your busy brain! It is late at night, and I must close. Pray write to me some quiet Sunday morning, when you have leisure, and write me all the news. Recollect, I am absent and you are at home, so your letters are worth the most. Vale!

A month was spent at Gotha and then the party went to Lausanne to visit Bayard Taylor's oldest sister who was married to a Swiss gentleman and living there. The journey thither by way of Nürnberg and Munich gave Bayard Taylor an opportunity to revive and revise former impressions. European life, in many of its aspects, was now so familiar to him, that he enjoyed a new pleasure in a study which rested on the comparison of changes, not only in external objects, but in his own attitude toward them. "I am more than ever convinced," he wrote in one of his "Random Letters" to the "Tribune," at this time, "that the best pleasures and most lasting advantages of travel belong not to the first or second, but to the fourth or fifth visit to foreign lands. If one misses the enthusiasm, the exhilaration, the capacity for thoughtless enjoyment, and the delightful ignorance of youth, on

gossip. Bayard Taylor heard nothing of the publication until he learned it in a roundabout way from Mr. Tennyson himself, who was naturally annoyed. But Mr. Tennyson's cause for annoyance was momentary beside the rage which possessed Bayard Taylor at the cruelly false position in which he was placed. He received an abject apology from the correspondent, and he made an explicit statement to Mr. Tennyson, but these things could not give his wounded pride much solace.

the other hand, one has less of uncertainty, of perplexing questions to solve; a keener, closer, more intelligent appreciation; a far wider and more fruitful field of interest, and a cultivated perception of beauty, which is gratified at every turn. Let the years go by unlamented! They bring more than they take away. I prefer the tender, familiar interest which comes from old acquaintance, to the pleasant shock of love at first sight, in this matter of travel. What if some celestial quality has vanished from the azure of the sky, or the fluid gold of the sunshine? What if the cuckoo's call now says no more to one than the coo of our American rain-dove? . . . It is a weak affectation to regret the *illusions perdues.* There is enough in Europe that — brush, and whitewash, and deodorize it as we may — retains the full flavor and character of the Past; there are influences, enriched by centuries of transmission, which we cannot escape. Quite sufficient remains to satisfy any one who has learned where the true work of the world lies."

Lausanne was a convenient point from which to make excursions, and offered good opportunities for sketching. Indeed the zest with which Bayard Taylor applied himself to painting at this time could scarcely have been more intense if he had purposed to drop literature and betake himself to the other art. He painted and sketched as if it were his business, not his pastime. He took a special jaunt, which is reproduced in the first of his series in the " Atlantic," the very agreeable and popular sketch of " The Little Land of Appenzell." Back again in Lausanne after this journey, which was one of great refreshment, he was able to write to a friend: "I am slowly recovering my freshness and elasticity of mind and body, and begin again to feel the old sensation of rest in work; but I intend to lie fallow as much as possible while away."

He spent a week with his wife in Paris. It was the year of the Exhibition and he made the art-collection the theme of a letter to the "Tribune," in which he wrote with frankness and hearty interest of the American contributions. He visited the Pyrenees and Majorca for material for further "By-Ways," and then joined his wife and daughter, who had gone on to Gotha, and spent the rest of the summer in a cottage at Friedrichroda near Gotha, where he busied himself with putting his material into shape.

TO JAMES T. FIELDS.

LAUSANNE, *June* 26, 1867.

Your welcome letter came a month ago or more, as I was setting out on my southern trip, whence I have but just returned. This trip has been in the highest degree successful. I have visited Majorca, Minorca, Montserrat, crossed Catalonia by difficult bridle-roads, saw the little republic of Andorre (the first American who ever did see it), went over the Pyrenees, and returned hither by way of the Grande Chartreuse and the Château Bayard. I devoted myself, you see, entirely to out - of - the - way corners of Europe, and have been well repaid. I come back with material for five or six papers for the "Atlantic Monthly," and shall commence work at once. In four or five days from now we shall be installed in our mountain cottage near Gotha for the rest of the summer, where I shall have quiet for work, so you may expect an article very soon after this reaches you. I hope the "Appenzell" (forwarded from Paris May 10th) reached you safely.

I do not expect to reach home before next summer (1868), and would be glad if this could be said in the newspapers, in order to prevent invitations for lectures being sent across the water. Won't you please send one of your boys to the Secretary of the Boston Mercantile Library Association to say that I can't lecture for them next winter, and thus save me a letter and postage?

Other invitations come, and the thing is a nuisance. I feel already much improved by my holiday, but needed it even more than I thought, and therefore want to be fully rejuvenated before I return. I make good use of my time, having already forty sketches of scenery, in addition to the literary material. I intend also writing some poems this summer.

I 'm glad you think the "St. John" something of a success as a publication. I think it will repay me some years hence better than now, but I am very well satisfied. Whittier's success [1] is delightful to hear : I 'm as glad of it as if the book were mine own. Time is just, after all ; he has had to wait for a long time, but now the recognition comes in ample measure. The "Dante," I am sure, will be a grand literary success, whatever may be the sale of the work. We Americans make better translators than the English, and we shall drive the latter out of the field. In the coming years, Longfellow's "Dante" will be the classic, and Cary's the curiosity. By the bye, what an exquisite poem of Lowell to Longfellow on his birthday! I never saw anything finer of the kind. I wish I could get an "Atlantic" occasionally. Could it be sent through Barings without ruinous postage ?

We expect to be joined by the Grahams next week in our cottage ; they are now in Sweden. Until September I shall have a rest in the green Thüringian land. Ah, could the trio of the "Tent on the Beach" be together there ! How pleasantly you and I will float down to posterity, each holding on to the strong swimmer, J. G. W.!

M. is waiting for me in Gotha, and I leave here to-morrow. . . . I find that with every time I go abroad more and more of me remains at home. I shall not keep up this rôle of a *traveler* much longer.

TO E. C. STEDMAN.

FRIEDRICHRODA (IN THE THÜRINGIAN FOREST),
July 30, 1867.

. . . The Grahams have been living with us since the 3d, and will stay four weeks longer, so we have half our American atmosphere here in this green region of mountains and meadows, of tinkling herds and fairy lore. Our cottage has a flag-staff, and on that staff floats the American flag ; inside we have German lessons, exercises in art, beer, wine, occasional trout, visitors

[1] *The Tent on the Beach* had recently been published.

from Gotha, chess, and my papers for the "Atlantic," — the which I am now working upon, to the delay of "Faust."

. . . I had a very fatiguing, but wonderfully fresh and interesting trip to the Balearic Islands and the Pyrenees. Three papers thereanent have already gone to Fields, and two more are to follow. I don't know how they will strike you, but they are certainly better than my "Tribune" letters. The latter are simply written to keep a little more fire under the pot, and will never be used again. Therefore I cannot put much "life-blood" into them, but I don't think they are so very poor as to affect my reputation as a writer. They are plain, easy talks about certain little matters which I may observe from time to time, and some of them, I think, will interest country readers of the "Tribune." In fact, I intend them chiefly for these latter. I wish you would read my "Atlantic" articles when they appear, and then tell me honestly what you think of them. I must naturally save my best things for the "Atlantic Monthly," not only because it pays me much better, but because a detached sketch, complete in itself, is more agreeable work than newspaper letters. The latter are always stamped *ephemera*, no matter who writes them.

How delighted I am with Whittier's success! Fields writes that his "Tent" has already sold 20,000 copies. Here is a man who has waited twenty-five years to be generally appreciated. I remember when his name was never mentioned without a sneer, except by the small Abolition clique. In England, too, they are now beginning to read him for the first time. In fact, the experience of most authors — of Tennyson, Browning, Emerson, Hawthorne, as well — of Matthew Arnold yet — ought to encourage you and me. What endures is of slow growth. I think a man should be satisfied to let the first twenty years of his literary activity go for foundation-walls, if they will only support a pillar or two above ground afterwards. . . .

When the summer was past Bayard Taylor set his face toward Italy, purposing to spend the winter there with his family. They went to Munich, over the Brenner Pass, and after lingering a day or two kept on to Verona. On the last day of September they were in Venice. Here they stayed nearly the whole month.   They formed new acquaintances among the artists in Mr. Yewell and Mr. Loop, who had studios there, and Bayard Taylor devoted himself to painting with increased ardor.

TO JERVIS McENTEE.

VENICE, *Sunday, October* 20, 1867.

How is it that I have not written to you before ?   Not from lack of thinking of you and talking about you, and resolving, over and over again, to sit and talk with you across the ocean : but somehow writing duties and sketching enthusiasms and movements to and fro came between the purpose and the deed. So here I am, in the same position before you as Emperor Barbarossa was six hundred years ago, around in St. Mark's, before Pope Alexander, — on my knees, waiting for you to put your foot on my neck.   Hang explanations and apologies !   If you imagine that I have in any way forgotten you, it only proves that you don't thoroughly know me.   I did appoint an evening in Paris to tell you how your pictures were hung, and would have done so but for a visit which came just as the portfolio was opened and the pen on its way to the inkstand.   Six months later, — no, five, — I resume the suspended duty.

First, about the pictures.   The " Virginia " was in the avenue, outside the gallery, — on the line, but with hardly space enough to look at it properly.   I did n't think that a very good place for it.   The " October " was a little above the line, in the gallery, with a good light coming from the right hand.   The " Woods of — Ass " — something was below the line, under Church's rainbow, and beside Gifford's twilight picture, in a good light, but the two neighbors made it look a little pale and cold. On the whole, however, you fared tolerably well.   The two latter pictures were where everybody would be sure to see them, and I saw lots of people looking at them.   In point of harmony, you and Gifford and Kensett (in my opinion) beat all the landscapes in the Exposition.   I remarked, however, in all American pictures, a lack of something, — not exactly boldness or force of color, but something of the kind.   The forms have not the same plastic strength as those of the European artists.   They stand in a sweet, poetic, Arcadian atmosphere, which lulls and delights you, but does not brace and invigorate like some things I saw.

There was the edge of a forest by Rousseau, in which the shadows appeared almost black at first sight ; yet they were perfectly transparent and full of wonderful perspective. I don't mean that this sort of thing would do for your autumn landscapes (it would n't at all), —indeed I am not writing with reference to your pictures, or G.'s, or K.'s, which belong to a different class, but it seems to me that here is a field which our artists have neglected. Our part of the exhibition was very creditable : I think we made a much better show than the English, who showed the most astonishing contortions.

. . . Yewell (whom I think you know) and Loop are living here, and I see them occasionally. They, their wives, and the consul and his wife, are our only acquaintances. A great many Americans come here for a few days, but we don't see them. We have four delightful rooms, near the Doge's Palace, with a magnificent view over the waters, for eight francs a day, including attendance. Our living costs us fifteen francs a day, for four persons. This will give you an idea of Venetian expenses. A gondola costs one franc for the first hour, and half that the next. Grapes are four cents per pound, cigars one and a half cents, wine as little as you choose to pay. If you order a dinner for two and one half francs you get four courses and a bottle of wine thrown in. If you sketch in the streets, somebody brings you a chair, and keeps the small boys off. Beggars and flower-girls are the only trouble.

Now I ought not to send a blank page so far, but I must stop to-night for three reasons, — it is late, I am very tired with running errands for my convalescents (being myself only a convalescent), and my head is thick with a cold, a sort of after-clap to the more serious ailment. My next letter, and soon, will be to Launt Thompson, to whom, and Gifford, and Eastman Johnson, and all other good and faithfully-remembered friends, my love. . . .

This letter gives intimation of an illness from which the writer had suffered, a bilious fever and inflammation of the throat. Long hours spent by the canal-side in the chill October air, often in the heavy shade of palaces, added to the low tone of his system, of which he had been more or less conscious all the sum-

mer, brought about the first serious illness from which
he had ever suffered, and it was very serious. The
party left Venice October 27th, and stopping successively at Padua and Bologna reached Florence, where,
on the last day of the month, they found lodgings in
Casa Guidi. The fever which had been rendering
Bayard Taylor wretched now burst into a flame, and
for four weeks he hovered between life and death.
He was fortunate in having admirable medical attendance in the services of Dr. Wilson, an English physician living in Florence, but his own resolution was
an efficient aid. Even while he was passing through a
violent phase of the disease, the old will, which was
stronger than his body, asserted itself, and he insisted
upon some show of activity every day, if it were only
to rise and be moved from one room to another. Indeed, sickness to him was an offense against nature,
to be fought and conquered. It was almost intolera-
ble to him to witness sickness; it was a humiliation
to endure it. All his healthy sense revolted at it. He
had a singular experience during his illness. He was
housed where Mrs. Browning had lived and died, and
in one of his wandering hours —

> She came, whom Casa Guidi's chambers knew
> And know more proudly, an Immortal, now;
> The air without a star, was shivered through
> With the resistless radiance of her brow,
> And glimmering landscapes from the darkness grew.
>
> Thin, phantom-like; and yet she brought me rest.
> Unspoken words, an understood command
> Sealed weary lids with sleep, together pressed
> In clasping quiet wandering hand to hand,
> And smoothed the folded cloth above the breast.[1]

[1] Bayard Taylor sent the poem of "Casa Guidi Windows," from which
these stanzas are taken, to Robert Browning, when writing to him, and

The physician enjoined the strictest seclusion and freedom from mental exercise. The convalescent saw no letters, received no visitors, and was kept as near to a merely animal existence as was possible. With returning strength he gradually resumed something of his old life, and when he could once more go out, think, write, and see his friends, he was aware that he had passed not only through a physical crisis, but through a mental and spiritual one as well. He did not often speak of this except to those closest to him, but he was wont to note the change as if a veil had fallen from his eyes, and he saw all things clearly. The world came back to him in papers and letters. There had been time in his long illness for the news to go to America, and for letters of sympathy to come back and greet him as he awoke out of his enforced obscuration.

TO HIS MOTHER.

FLORENCE, *December* 1, 1867.

The doctor has just given me permission to write *a little*, and I make use of it to let you know directly from myself how I am getting along. Up to Monday last, — six days ago, — my progress was so slow that I felt discouraged ; then, all at once, I seemed to turn a corner, and got better so rapidly that I can scarcely believe it. Two or three weeks ago I was really in a very serious state, entirely prostrated by violent fever, my stomach in such a condition that it generated only carbonic acid gas, and my lungs congested. The doctor said I would probably have to be in bed for a month to come. Now I get up at nine o'clock, wash and dress myself, eat ravenously, read a little, paint a little, walk the room for exercise, and don't go to bed till eight in the evening ! If the weather is fine to-morrow, I am

received a warm letter in reply, in which the poet says : " There used to be healing once in a shadow, and there is all the interest in the world to me in shadows, were they far fainter than this one you describe, which come from what is real and present to me at all times. Thank you very heartily and affectionately."

to ride out in a carriage. I feel very bright and fresh and hopeful. I am truly grateful for this fortunate change in my condition, and hope that you will have no further anxiety about me.
Even if I should happen to have a slight relapse, I have now
gained so much strength that it would not be dangerous. I can
tell you now that the illness has been most serious, but Dr. Wilson's great skill and care have brought me through it. . . .
Well, we 'll say no more about this subject now. The doctor
says it has been slowly coming on me for months past, and I
think he 's right. I trust I shall be better and stronger than
before, after I get entirely well.

TO E. C. STEDMAN.

CASA GUIDI, FLORENCE, *December* 18, 1867.

I can't tell you how much good your letter did me. It came
like a providence, on the very day when I was first allowed to
read a letter; and although M. was almost afraid to let me go
through with the copied sheets, in addition, I did so and was all
the cheerier for it. I was just turning the corner between weakness and strength, and the livelier motion that came into my
blood with your welcome words was very different from the excitement of fever.

Of course you know what a gulf I have been hanging over,
and how fortunately the danger has been passed. Nature kindly
threw me into a state of mental apathy (so far as my own consciousness was concerned) which made me ignorant of my worst
troubles, and it is only little by little that M. has ventured to
describe them. I had spells of delirium during eight or ten
days, and supposed that I slept! Then my lungs were badly
congested, — half of the right lung being solid and without action, — and I had not the least suspicion of the fact. The doctor
gave me another month in bed, and was one of the most surprised at the pace with which I rushed back into health. I now
feel better than at any time during the past three or four years,
— in fact, very much as if I had been completely ground over
and come out new. I must still be a little careful of my lungs,
which, although perfectly well again, are still just a little bit
sensitive. But does n't it seem absurd? I had always supposed that, whatever organ might get out of gear, my lungs were
safe. Twenty times a day I draw in a breath containing some
forty cubic feet of air, and as every cell of the machinery ex-

pands clearly and smoothly to its utmost capacity, without ache or strain, I doubt the doctor's assurances of my recent condition. However, there is a vast space on my back, reaching from the shoulder-blades to the reins, whence the skin has been burnt by fires of mustard, and that convinces me that something must have been the matter.

I can now thank God not only for my recovery, but for my illness. For two years I have felt that my vital power was lowered, without being able to point to any symptom of disease, and a crisis like this was necessary. In mind and moral temperament a corresponding process has taken place, and I look forth into the re-bestowed world with younger, more hopeful, and more courageous eyes. I take a fresh departure from this point, and believe that it may be toward better things. Your pluck and patience and cheerfulness under most discouraging circumstances came to me like a cry of "Shame on your shallow, miserable worries!" I had taken up the question already, while I lay on my back, pondered, and settled it. One should never doubt God, nor defy what we call Chance. I am going to have, henceforth, more calm and moral poise, — perhaps you don't know my previous restlessness, because I did my best to conceal it. A whisper comes to me as I write that I should make no promises for the future, so I will only say that I am happier now than for many, many a month.

. . . My fancy stirs now with health, as if a dozen new wings had sprouted, — whence, I foresee, there will be much consumption of cream-laid paper (enormously dear here, but I prefer it for poetry) in the next two or three months. I 'm very glad that you liked my Pyrenean article, — but those now to come are better, I think. I 'm not allowed to sketch, however, mainly because my studies in the back streets of Venice gave me the malaria, which brought on the whole complication of ills. But when we get to Naples, in a fortnight from now, I 'll brave banditti and doctors, and bring you something from the *Terra di Lavoro.*

This is not much of a letter, in answer to your rich package of sheets, but all the delayed work and correspondence of two months is upon me, and I must therefore ask you to take this as a sign of life and love until I can do better. . . .

TO GEORGE H. YEWELL.

FLORENCE, *Wednesday, December* 18, 1867.

Your welcome letter arrived on Saturday, and you may be sure that we are all glad to hear that you are so pleasantly situated. Indeed, your account (notwithstanding the one hundred and six steps to the studio) makes me almost regret that we are not going to Rome at once. My plans, however, depend considerably upon certain things which are to be written, and so we must needs go to Naples first. We hope to reach there on the 31st of this month, and come back to Rome by the first of March. But we shall certainly find you there then, and I hope we shall be able to find quarters in your neighborhood.

. . . There are at least two hundred Americans (so Mr. Marsh tells me) here at present, and I presume the most of them are bound for Rome. Dr. Bellows is the only New Yorker whom I have met. I have been visiting the sculptors here during the last few days, and have run through the galleries once. We have gone out to Fiesole and to Galileo's Tower, during the half-dozen days of fine weather, trying, as much as possible, to make up for lost time, — but, with the best will, we shall have to leave a great many things unseen. The months of November and December, thus far, have been unusually cold for Florence ; you have it a great deal milder at Rome. . . .

It is comforting to know that rent is so moderate in Rome. I can't travel yet without counting the cost, and am therefore interested in such matters. We live here more cheaply than in Venice, but expensively, compared with ten years ago. Some things are very cheap, but apartments have doubled in price. We shall want just such a household arrangement as yours in Rome, and if we can get as good quarters at the same price, I think I shall take a studio in addition, and play the amateur at a great rate. (I give you leave to laugh at my presumption.)

My Naples address is "care of Frères Forquet," and I hope you won't forget it. It will be hard to go past Rome, seeing the Campagna and the dome of St. Peter's, without stopping ; but the convenience of a through journey, without frontier examinations, will oblige us to do it. Give my friendliest greetings to Vedder, Loops, and all other friends. T. B. Read is in Rome : if you don't know him, and want to, use my name. I hope you will stay during all the three spring months, as we will.

On the last day of the year Bayard Taylor and his party were in Naples, where they spent three or four weeks, and then went to Sorrento, spending a week meanwhile at Capri. They returned to Naples for a month, and in the middle of March went to Rome. During the stay at Sorrento he wrote two more of his " Atlantic " papers, " A Week on Capri " and " A Trip to Ischia."

TO JERVIS M^CENTEE.

SORRENTO, *February* 3, 1868.

It was a joyous day for us, three weeks ago, when we came down from Vesuvius, and found seven letters (one of which was from you) awaiting us. I should have written to you sooner, in answer to your first ; but I presume you know all about my illness by this time, and will understand and admit the delay. In fact, I am only just now venturing to do my usual amount of work. Although my recovery from the critical stage of the disease was wonderfully rapid, I have remained weak, and (though you will scarcely believe it) with delicate lungs until within a few days. My literary work, my business letters, all the external machinery of my life, indeed, have had to wait, — and so it has been with my correspondence. The first intoxication of convalescence was followed by a severe cold and cough after arriving at Naples, — perhaps the climbing of Vesuvius a little too soon for my strength had something to do with it, — and it has required a week on Capri to fully reëstablish me. We came over from the island last night in a sail-boat, and are now settled at Sorrento for four or five weeks to come. Within the last three days we have heard of another wonderful escape. While in Naples we took rooms in a house on the quay of Santa Lucia, facing Vesuvius, and stayed there four weeks. We had not left the quarters four days before the great rock of Pizzofalcone, behind the quay, fell down and buried the houses, ours among them. We hear that eighty lives are lost. Had we remained another week, we should all have been lost, as the slide happened at an hour when we were sure to have been at home. Graham, who has been to Naples since, says that not one stone of our house is left upon the other. What a wonderful chance ! Moreover, the mountain road from Castellamare to this place was covered and destroyed by a tremendous slide of rocks a few hours after we passed over it. Graham and his wife, who came after us, had the narrowest escape. My confidence in the stability of the earth is considerably shaken, after these experiences. Death has reached after me three times, and missed, in the last two months; I hope he will now let me live a while longer.

TO E. C. STEDMAN.

SORRENTO, *March* 3, 1868.

. . . We have been here four or five weeks already, and are beginning to pack up for Rome. A great deal has transpired since I last wrote to you, and I hardly know where to begin or what to say first. I think I have at last my full, normal strength again, but only since our week on Capri, where the brisk sea air, the excitement of the rocky rambles, and the good fare we had in the artists' hotel, seemed to make a new man of me at once. Last week I went to Ischia for two or three days, returning by way of Naples, where I stopped to look at the pile of rocks which covers the spot where we lived. You have heard of the great land-slide by telegraph, I presume. The rock of Pizzofalcone fell down on the quay of Santa Lucia, only three days after we left our quarters there. I had a providential cold and soreness in the lungs, which made us leave for Capri, and so we narrowly escaped a fearful death. Grahams and Bierstadts were wont to take tea with us there, and we might all have perished together; for it seems that the rock had been suspended, like the sword of Damocles, for weeks before it fell. Chance (which is another name for God's mercy) saved us. Sixty persons were killed. . . . I wish you could breathe this air, see this splendid sapphire of the sea, walk as we do under budding orange and blossoming almond trees, and dine on sardines fresh from the water, cuttle-fish (the *pieuvre* of Victor Hugo), roast kid, woodcock, and grapes dried with aniseed in fig-leaves. We live in an old Jesuit monastery, about a mile from Sorrento, — a charming, picturesque old pile, the cellars of which are supposed to have belonged to a Roman temple of the Sirens. From the broad, vine-covered terrace we can see Vesuvius, Naples, Posilipo, Baiæ, and Ischia. Here we have three large rooms, a capital table (private), and the best of attendance, for six francs a day apiece. Grahams are at a villa three quarters of a mile from us, and we see them every day. We have donkey-rides on the mountains, carriage-drives along this magnificent shore, and sometimes, as a diversion, fishermen to dance the tarantella of an evening. I could stay for months and be happy, yet we must go to Rome next week, to make the most of our remaining time in Italy. The greatest day I have had — one of the white days of my life, in fact — was that spent in Pompeii. How I wished for you ! We read Overbeck's admirable work first, so that everything was clear and familiar, — and such an insight into the life of the ancients ! But, alas ! the way people see Pompeii is enough to disgust one. Of all the multitude of Americans who are in this region (three hundred at one time), scarcely ten have a real, intelligent interest in what they see. On the rocks about here the asphodels are now in blossom. Do you suppose the tourists know what an asphodel is, when I point it out to them ? No, indeed. We purposely live secluded (seeing only the Grahams and their friends), and very few of the crowd have found us out.

. . . I had a letter from Brockhaus, of Leipzig, the other day, wanting my biography for his "Conversations-Lexicon." That seems almost like fame, does n't it ? But ah, how much is there yet to be achieved, before I have any right to a name that will last even fifty years ! After all, literature is and must be its own reward. I would not give up my calling though everything I have done should die with me.

We already begin to turn our thoughts homeward, and I assure you there are frequent times when I long to be back again, and quietly at work in my own room on my suspended plans. The few years at Cedarcroft have injured my capacity for writing while on the wing. I can work best in quarters to which I am accustomed. I brought along my "Faust," expecting to do something considerable at the translation, but devil a line shall I write until we are back again. However, I have got upon the track of the almost endless Faust literature, and shall be able to examine everything of importance that has been written about the poem, before publishing.

M. has been unwell for a week, and is only now getting about again. This has delayed (and may possibly prevent) our trip to Amalfi and Pæstum, and we want to get to Rome next week. The change in the season is like heaven to me. That and the Capri and Falernian wines have restored all my lost flesh, and M. says my cheeks are now as full-blown as those of one of the

judgment-trumpeting angels. I hope you have not waited for
this, but that it may cross one of yours on the Atlantic.

TO HIS MOTHER.

ROME, *March* 16, 1868.

I take the first chance we have after getting to Rome to write
to you. We left Naples last Friday morning, the 13th, and reached
here the same evening. Saturday and yesterday were devoted
to hunting for rooms, as the hotel was enormously expensive,
and, moreover, very uncomfortable ; but we have been lucky in
getting pleasant quarters at last. We have taken furnished
rooms at a rent of sixty francs per month, which would be dear
in ordinary times, but now, when there are twelve hundred
Americans in Rome, it is considered very cheap. We have five
rooms on the second floor, in a pleasant street, and keep house
ourselves, which is the most independent and agreeable plan.
The weather is so warm and delightful, and the spring so far
advanced, that we scarcely need any fire, except a little in the
evening. We are all in the best of health and spirits, and are
determined to enjoy our stay as fully as possible.

The two months' stay in Rome was full of agreeable
occupation. There were many friends near at hand,
the Yewells and Loops, the Bierstadts, Reads, and
others, and Bayard Taylor had besides allowed his
passion for painting to transform him into a very
close likeness to a professional artist, for he hired a
studio where he secreted himself every forenoon. He
did not disclose its situation to his friends, but worked
industriously in it, without fear of interruption, taking up figure painting. He felt the vigor of a returning health, but he was made aware, also, that he was
more sensitive than formerly to atmospheric changes.

TO HIS MOTHER.

ROME, *April* 21, 1868.

. . . Since we came to Rome I have been very busy, trying to
learn to paint a little. Yewell, an American artist, has given me
some instruction, and I am getting on tolerably well. I work

three or four hours every morning, spend the afternoons in seeing sights, and the evenings in visiting, receiving visits, or writing. The time goes very fast, but I don't object to that, as I
have a real longing to get home again. I have seen no place,
even in Italy, that I like so well. Nevertheless, there is a great
deal here that we want to see, and we shall probably leave before we can do all we want. Rome has been so crowded with
Americans that in spite of all our endeavors to keep out of society we have been drawn into it. Since Easter week is over
they have nearly all left, and we can now begin to enjoy Rome.
The weather has been raw, rainy, and windy until to-day, when
the moon changes and the day is fine, giving us a promise of
better days. The spring is not much more advanced there than
it sometimes is with us. The oaks are just coming into leaf, but
locusts and mulberries are still bare. Strawberries are in the
market, but they ask five francs a basket. Lilacs are just beginning to bloom. To-day is the first really warm day we have had
in Rome.

TO E. C. STEDMAN.

ROME, *April* 27, 1868.

. . . I must write to you from Rome, if only to tell you that
we are thus far on the way homeward, Sorrento having been the
turning-point. We have now been here six weeks, and in three
more will move forward another stage, — nor reluctantly, much
as we enjoy being in Rome. I have now been seven months in
Italy, and am (let me confess to you) a little *desillusionné*. I
presume the old longing will return again after I leave, but
there is less of the " light that never was on sea or land " than
there used to be. I want to work, I am bursting with fresh
plans, and this delightful atmosphere is like a narcotic which
benumbs one's executive faculties while stimulating the imagination. The past is too powerful here : it draws us constantly
away from the work intended for us. A singular indifference to
the movements of this present and grand world creeps over us,
and we end by becoming idle, Epicurean dreamers. I am satisfied that Rome is no place for a poet, however it may be with
artists. I have written five or six short poems, but postpone all
more important plans until I get home again. Being here,
where models are plentiful and color is part of the atmosphere, I
have taken a little studio for two months, and paint three or four

hours every day from the living figure. It is most instructive, and at the same time not a little amusing. The studio is strictly private ; I tell nobody where it is, and hence many would like to know. My beginnings were in the style of the early Christian mosaics, but I have already advanced about five centuries since then, and am now painting in the style of the Venetian genera-' tion before Titian. I don't presume to hope that I could ever be mistaken for one of the contemporaries of the latter, but, with time, I might skip over the intervening centuries and emulate such moderns as —— and ——. I find that the hard work and study necessary in order to be something more than a contemptible amateur is a good discipline. I have held myself forcibly to the task, through disgust and despair, and am rewarded by learning a little at last. It seems to me that one cannot grow old so long as one is capable of undertaking a new study. I have made one hundred and forty sketches since leaving home, and have therefore plenty of material on which to expend my technical gains when I return. (You are free to laugh at this wanity). . . .

Florence again received the travelers, on their homeward way, and Bayard Taylor and his wife made an excursion to Corsica which bore fruit in the two papers, " The Land of Paoli " and " The Island of Maddalena, with a Distant View of Caprera ; " continuing the series of " By-Ways " which he had engaged to contribute during his absence to the " Atlantic Monthly." Mr. Fields in writing to him urged him to send also short stories.

TO JAMES T. FIELDS.

FLORENCE, *May* 25, 1868.

. . . About a short story. You will easily comprehend that here, where my mind is occupied with quite other subjects, — where I am making studies, gathering materials, bridging over many chasms of uncompleted knowledge in literature and art, — it would be nearly impossible to do what you want. I must leave it until I get home, which will be in August. If I had twenty short stories on hand I could dispose of them at once, the demand seems to be so great. But I shall undertake none until the roof of Cedarcroft shelters me.

I should have been in Corsica this week but for a most provoking circumstance. There was much small-pox in Rome, and I was vaccinated again. It did not take, but the vaccine matter acted as a sort of poison to my system. Since coming here I have had a terribly inflamed left arm, with fever, and the doctor was quite anxious for a day or two. I am now better, but am bandaged and poulticed as I write.

In June the party returned to Gotha, spending a week on the way at Lausanne.

TO HIS MOTHER.

Gotha, *June* 21, 1868.

. . . We left Lausanne last Tuesday noon, the 16th, traveled all night, and reached here on Wednesday afternoon. All are well, and the weather is superb. I am delighted that our journeys are so nearly over. When we move again it will be to go homeward. I have still to write four articles on German out-of-the-way places, which will take the month of July, and then we shall be ready to start. Since I came back to Gotha I really learn for the first time how much better and stronger I am than last year. The difference is wonderful and everybody notices it. I hope, now, that I shall be able to keep what I have gained.

Bayard Taylor made excursions from Gotha which resulted in the final papers of " By-Ways," " In the Teutoburger Forest" and " The Suabian Alb." Much of his time, however, was occupied with social pleasures, and with the accumulation of material for his study of " Faust." He visited Hirzel, the publisher, in Leipzig, who had made a specialty of collecting Faust literature, and used every opportunity to consult German scholars and poets, who entered heartily into his schemes.

GOTHA, *August* 9, 1868.

Yesterday came your very welcome note of July 23d. I am glad that the articles find favor in your sight. I did not get to the Carpathians, on account of the weather, but visited two little-known corners of Germany — the Teutoburger Forest and the Suabian Alb. My Corsican article is half written, but for the life of me I can't find time (in this season of packing and farewell dinner and supper parties) to finish. I must e'en throw myself on your grace, take the thing home with me, and finish it as soon as may be after arrival, in season for the November "Atlantic." When I am once more settled at Cedarcroft, I shall soon arrange myself for steady work. You have no idea how difficult it is to write while thus on the wing. However, I inclose something for your perusal, which, if you don't want to print, at least keep the copy for me.

We leave here day after to-morrow morning, and go *via* Paris to London. I shall have but five days in London, but shall see as many old and make as many new friends as possible. As it is in August I fear that dear old Barry and the Thackerays may be absent. I want to see Swinburne again, and Morley and Morris.

I have taken passage in the Germania, which leaves Southampton on the 21st, and expect to be in New York by September 1st. Since Longfellow left England I hear no more about his movements. He was said to be in Heidelberg, but I could not find him there the other day. He is very popular here, and the German authors, also, would like to do him honor. Lucky poet! but he deserves it all.

The Germania reached New York September 2d, and the travelers immediately returned to Cedarcroft, where Bayard Taylor prepared for the press the volume of "By-Ways of Europe," the only substantial product of his year abroad. It appeared at once, too soon, indeed to include the latest of his papers, "The Suabian Alb," which had not yet been published in the "Atlantic." He brought back only one book to show for his year's labor, besides the large collection of sketches and paintings, but he had not gone for work. He had gone for a holiday, and the enforced rest which his illness in Florence gave him made him eager now to plunge into the work which had been rising before him in his mind.

CHAPTER XXI.

A YEAR AT CEDARCROFT.

1868–1869.

> But since I am sated with visions,
> Sated with all the siren Past and its rhythmical phantoms,
> Here will I seek my songs in the quiet field of my boyhood,
> Here, where the peaceful tent of home is pitched for a season.
> *Proem* (to "Home Pastorals").

THE preface to the volume of "By-Ways of Europe" is in the form of a "Familiar Letter to the Reader," from which we have already several times quoted when treating of Bayard Taylor's successive travels. It is, in effect, a poet's apology for having been a traveler, and a leave-taking of this form of literature: "In laying down the mantle of a traveler," the writer says, "which has been thrown upon my shoulders rather than voluntarily assumed, I do not wish to be understood as renouncing all the chances of the future. I cannot foresee what compulsory influences, what inevitable events, may come to shape the course of my life; the work of the day is all with which a man need concern himself. One thing, only, is certain; I shall never, from the mere desire of travel, go forth to the distant parts of the earth. Some minds are so constituted that their freest and cheerfulest activity will not accompany the body from place to place, but is dependent on the air of home, on certain familiar surroundings, and an equable habit of life. Each writer has his own peculiar laws of production, which the reader cannot always deduce from his works. It amuses me, who have set my household gods upon the soil which my ancestors have tilled for near two hundred years, to hear my love of home questioned by men who have changed theirs a dozen times."

The reader will have noticed already how increasingly difficult Bayard Taylor found it to carry on any sustained work while away from home, and how impatient he was to get back to his library at Cedarcroft. His year abroad had stimulated his growing desire for a life free from interruption and given to literature. He had dreamed for years of an ideal career. He would be under his own roof in the midst of his acres, rejoicing in the generous country life, unplagued by cares of money, devoting his fresh hours to the writing of great poems, giving expression to the fancies and schemes which thronged his active mind, resting by congenial work upon his plantations, enjoying the pleasures of hospitality, and broadening thus into a rich, catholic life. He built no castle of indolence in his dreams. Necessity compelled him to be busy with his pen, but he needed no goad in literature; and if all care for the provision of his family and those who leaned on him were to be removed, there was no fear that he would drop into an amiable enjoyment of literature and art. The springs of mental energy were so vigorous, and his delight in production so keen, that affluence would not have dulled his activity, and stringency of fortune could only divert it into undesired ways.

As soon as he had fairly seated himself at Cedarcroft he betook himself to his work, and for a year enjoyed as near an approach to the ideal career which he had imagined as was ever possible to him. He refused all invitations to lecture, and was only occasionally absent from his home. The great work which engaged his mind was the translation of "Faust." The studies which he had made abroad and the books which he had collected were now put to use, and the deeper he plunged into the work the more thoroughly interested did he become, and the more confident of final success. He worked by himself, but there were one or two who shared the knowledge of his labor and with whom he took counsel. Chief of these was the Rev. Dr. W. H. Furness, of Philadelphia, who gave him the benefit of special criticism.

Besides the "Faust" there was abundant work upon articles and poems. Since he was not to lecture, Bayard Taylor needed to supplement his income by constant literary activity, and it was impossible for him to withdraw himself wholly to work which was delightful but unremunerative. Applications from various quarters pressed upon him, and he was, besides, so fertile in thought that for his own comfort he must needs rid himself of the conceptions which crowded upon him. His first business was to complete his series of "By-Ways" for the "Atlantic," since he had been unable to work up the latest material gathered in the hurried days which followed in Germany and London.

TO JAMES T. FIELDS.

KENNETT SQUARE, *September* 7, 1868.

. . . To-day I begin work, and you shall have my Corsican article by the end of the week. Moreover, a story just as soon as possible. . . . While in London and Leipzig I sounded certain publishers about my translation of "Faust," and think I shall have no difficulty in arranging a simultaneous publication in the three countries. Longfellow's success will be some wind in my sails ; but the main thing remains to do my work, and do it as it should be done. How is Whittier, the dear, good friend ?

I am overwhelmed with applications to lecture, but have decided not to go forth this winter. We are very happy here, and my best policy seems to be to use the fresh working mood on matters more important than the repetition of an essay, which is about what my lecturing amounts to.

KENNETT SQUARE, PA., September 13, 1868.

I send you " The Land of Paoli," which I greatly desire should get into the November " Atlantic." I think it will make about fourteen pages, but not too much for the subject. The other two (if you want both) will follow speedily, and then I shall write a story. I am ready enough to give you short stories, but sadly lack good material. Whither can I turn for the latter ?

I return the " Sunshine of the Gods." While in London I read the first draft of the poem to Swinburne, who, while liking it, thought there ought either to be more rhyme or none at all. Singularly enough, I could not recall the changes I had made ; but I find, on reading the poem carefully, that Swinburne's criticism does not apply to the amended copy. It is the result of a mood, — of a flash of the sunshine of the gods, — and ought not to be touched in colder blood. You were right in your warning. I will only suggest this : would stanza VIII. be improved by adding these lines to the end : —

And think'st to tame the fortune,
And force its week-day service, —
To clip the wings of the bright one ? —
Alas ! to tame is to kill !

Ponder this carefully, you and A. W., and if you think it good add the lines ; if not, not.

I am glad that you withheld " Orso's Vendetta." It was written during my convalescence, and I now see physical weakness in it. I shall recast the story, which is too good to lose.

As to the " Lincoln " for children,[1] I am much inclined to do it. Having decided not to lecture this season, I shall have more time. Only, when must you positively have it ? And, besides, I should like a page or two of proof of Stoddard's or Stedman's

---

[1] Mr. Fields had asked him to write a poem upon Abraham Lincoln to accompany some pictures in color, in a series to which Mr. Stoddard and Mr. Stedman were also contributing.

poems, to see just about what plane of intelligence is addressed. Perhaps the matter will keep till I come to Boston ; but if not, pray oblige me so far.

How much I enjoy reading up the " North American Review ! " There is no better periodical in the language.

TO T. B. ALDRICH.

CEDARCROFT, KENNETT SQUARE, PA., *September* 13, 1868.

I went away from home with the hope of writing to you and hearing from you from time to time, but what with my " Atlantic " papers, and my severe sickness of last winter, and a number of other things that turned up on the way, the golden leisure in which correspondence flourishes never came. Moreover, I always heard of you through Fields, and perhaps seemed nearer for that reason. Now this quiet Sunday morning, at home again, I feel inclined to tell you that you have never been out of my memory or my heart, and to reach you my hand (writing) in a fresh greeting. I think I never before was so glad to get back from a journey ; and the prospect of getting to work again in the old track, but with renewed courage, is very pleasant. I have at least three or four years' work on hand, have resolved to cut short my lecturing, and shall live altogether more rationally (for an author) than hitherto. The illness was a mental as well as a physical crisis, which meant either death or a new birth. Happily, it proved to be the latter.

The golden wedding of Bayard Taylor's father and mother was celebrated at Cedarcroft October 15th, and the house for a week was the centre of merry-making which was not conducive to continuous work.

TO MRS. JAMES T. FIELDS.

KENNETT SQUARE, PA., *October* 19, 1868.

. . . We had a delightful commemoration. There were at least a hundred and fifty members of the family present, besides neighbors and friends. I wrote a little masque of characters, which was successfully performed, a song which was sung, and Boker and Stoddard (both of whom were here) read poems. From two in the afternoon until midnight the house was crowded, and I hardly know which were happiest, the golden couple or the friends who came to congratulate them. It is the third golden wedding in a direct line in the family, — my father's father and grandfather having had theirs ; but to have mine I must live to be eighty-two. . . . We have had our house full of the family for a week, but are to-day finally left to ourselves, and I take up my interrupted work. I want to finish the most pressing claims by election day, so that I may find time to run over to Boston soon afterwards and see you all again.

The little masque of characters was a quaint and simple device which the poet used to give expression to the unusualness of the occasion. When the company was gathered, he welcomed them with a few words and then said: "You must expect no more from me than a hearty welcome to each and all, with my thanks, and the thanks of my parents, wife, brothers, and sisters, that you have come together to keep fresh the ties of family and of old friendship. On such days as these, however, we have other help. The invisible Spirits that keep familiar watch over men — the Virtues which both lead and follow, and bless them — the Spirits of the Lands through which the family is scattered — become visible to mortal eyes and give report of the fifty years that have gone by. I have heard a whisper — no matter how or whence — that these Spirits will come to us to-day, and I know that they will keep their word. So I summon them from the sky and the air and the earth! Come, Fairy of Domestic Life, thou who watchest over hearths and homes and family ties! Come, Virtues that accompany us, exacting hard service at first, but blessing us in the end! Come, Spirits of Lands and of Countries, that divide families only to bind them more firmly, — that seem to separate us yet teach that God is equally everywhere, and will bring us all to his peace at last! Come! appear!"

Thereupon the Fairy of Domestic Life appears and acts as the leader of the masque. She greets the couple with tender lines, and then goes forward with two attendant fairies, a boy bearing a crown of golden myrtle and a ring for the bride, a girl with a ring and wreath for the bridegroom. Then, obedient to the Fairy, Truth comes forward with a wreath of amaranth which she lays at the feet of the couple, for, as she says, —

> In the lapse of fifty years
> No single act or word appears
> That is not honest, clear, and true.
> None ever was misled by you :
> Your path was open to the light ;
> Your skirts are clear, your souls are white ;
> Your honor in the land shall be
> A sign and evidence to me.
> I give the garland that endures :
> My crown of amaranth is yours.

Next follows Charity with a wreath of cedar : —

> I will not praise in studied words ;
> The tree that feeds the winter birds
> Must give the wreath that tells of me ;
> And green as is that kindly tree
> In loving hearts your memory be !

Temperance bears a goblet of water and drinks to those

> Whose lives have shown
> The strength that comes from me alone.

America, with a wreath of laurel in her hand, sings of the sacrifice which the father and mother have made ; Africa, with a wreath of ferns and tropical flowers, gives thanks for the steadfast sympathy which her oppressed race has received from these two who have from early days borne contumely for their sake.

Then Switzerland brings a wreath of life-everlasting representing the edelweiss of the Alps, in token of the son whom a daughter of the house had brought from Switzerland, and Germany with a wreath of oak leaves signifies likewise the daughter whom a son had brought. Then all the characters, who had retired a few paces, now form a circle and unite in singing a song written by Bayard Taylor. Mr. Stoddard and Mr. Boker followed with poems. The song and poems were afterwards published in "Lippincott's Magazine," and Mr. Lippincott generously printed them with the "Masque" in a little volume, for the pleasure of those concerned. The three poets added photographs and gave the volume as a surprise at Christmas to Bayard Taylor's mother.

Mr. Donald G. Mitchell was at this time editor of a new weekly journal, "Hearth and Home," which aimed at stimulating a healthy interest in country life. It was for this journal that Bayard Taylor wrote some papers descriptive of his experiments at Cedarcroft, an extract from which has already been given.[1]

TO DONALD G. MITCHELL.

CEDARCROFT, KENNETT SQUARE, PA., *November* 16, 1868.

I found your letter at the Astor House in passing through New York on my way home from Boston. There was no time or I should have called upon you and had a little talk concerning the enterprise which I had already seen noticed, and hailed with delight.

I have withdrawn from the lecturing field this winter, because my engagements to write are sufficient to occupy all my time, and thus enable me to live quietly and much more comfortably at home. I should hesitate about accepting any more work just now, were not your proposal so agreeable, and so easy to perform, — for you want a simple, clear narrative of facts which are all ready to hand. When will the journal commence? and

---

[1] *Ante*, pp. 361-364.

when do you need the articles? I could send you a photograph of the house and make out a ground plan myself, if you think it would interest your readers. With regard to the gardening experiments, I can only tell my story up to the present moment. I have other things on hand, but not sufficiently developed to write about. What would your publishers pay for an article equal to, say eight pages of the "Atlantic Monthly"?

No man can do better work for this country and people than to create such a taste for country life as will elevate and refine the character of our country society. I have read your articles in the "Atlantic Almanac" with great pleasure, and hope that your success in the new enterprise will be equal to your knowledge of the subject, and your ability to illustrate it.

I write hurriedly this morning, but I want you to believe, at least, that I am earnestly interested in your plan.

TO E. C. STEDMAN.

CEDARCROFT, *December* 30, 1868.

. . . The season has been propitious thus far; my seat at the library table looks directly through a glass door into the greenhouse, and the western window of the oriel gives me wonderful sunsets. The cedars around and about us are never so green as now, and the distant hills are no bluer in summer. With my writing, — now that I have worked off a colossal dead horse for Fields, Osgood & Co., — it goes cheerfully, and every evening I take a little of "Faust" as a self-reward for the morning industry. Goethe says (in "Tasso") : —

"Es bildet ein Talent sich in der Stille;"

"Talent develops and forms itself in seclusion," — which I hope may be half true in my case.

TO JAMES T. FIELDS.

CEDARCROFT, *January* 1, 1869.

This poem[1] (just written) is properly a pendant to "The Sunshine of the Gods." That celebrated the poet, and this the unknown receiver of the song.

I hope the thing will be clear to your mind on reading; it is to mine, and I could not write it in any other form. If you like it, pray postpone the "Run Wild," and let this come first. If my reader of the "Sunshine" should remember it, he will be pre-

[1] "Notus Ignoto."

pared to understand and accept this ; at least, so it seems to me.

Perhaps you can tell whether *Notus* may be used in a personal sense. If so, the title is correct — " The Known to the Unknown." I think I should risk it, in any case, but would like to have the opinion of a good Latinist. If you see Lowell pray ask him for me.

I write this on the evening of New Year's Day, the sleeted trees rattling and crashing with a terrible sound. Many happy New-Years to both of you !

CEDARCROFT, KENNETT SQUARE, PA., *January* 14, 1869.

. . . As to the poem,[1] the difficulty seems to be that you have entirely misfelt it. It is one of those purely imaginative dithyrambics which have a law of their own, and in which the rhythmical march is the main thing. Like similar things of Shelley, it may be read here and there with a wrong accent, and I suspect this is just what you have done. Of all your criticisms I only feel that what you say of the last two lines of the first stanza is partly true. Those lines are rather grave and heavy for the airy, spiritual movement of the poem. The other lines, which you call " especially bad," are not only good, but some of them *especially* good, and I don't know that I can change one of them. As for the "inadequate termination," this is just one of those poems which can have no purposed beginning or end. It is much better than the " Sunshine of the Gods," and it ought properly to follow that poem. I am always glad to get criticism, no matter how adverse, and I always accept it when it carries with it that mark of sympathetic understanding which shows that my poem has been truly felt. But all the criticism in the world will not make me change a line which I feel to be the true expression of my thought. " Notus Ignoto " is not the sort of poem to keep by one's self and file at, like most poems. It is like one of those effects in painting which must be done with a sweep of the brush, and not touched afterwards. But to one who does not feel it instantly and wholly, the poem is mere sounding brass. It is one of the very darlings of my brain, and is, to me, as good as anything that ever was, or ever can be, of its kind. I don't think I shall ever touch a word of it, — and there will some day

[1] The one referred to in the previous letter. Mr. Fields had returned it with objections.

be somebody to know what it is. As you like its predecessor, I felt tolerably sure that it would have touched you in the right place, and I have not often been so taken aback as by your remarks upon it.

But enough of this. I merely want to show, or try to show, how we differ. I should not write anything about it, only I know that you are sincere, and that you honestly think the poem a poor one.

My wife joins me in love to yours.

The first draft of the translation of the First Part of "Faust" was completed with the year 1868, and the new year was begun immediately by an attack on the Second Part. He knew well that he should be obliged to overcome a general prejudice if he would persuade people to read the Second Part; but he had long held the belief that the First Part by itself was only a fragment, and needed the Second to bring out its full meaning. The great work drew him, and the incontestable difficulties only stimulated him.

TO REV. W. H. FURNESS.

CEDARCROFT, *January* 14, 1869.

. . . I think a translator should have a nearly equal knowledge of both languages, in order to get that spirit above and beyond the words which simple literalness will never give. The best condition is that in which one knows both languages so well that he does not need to break his head in the hunt for words, but keeps his best strength for that part of thought which subtly expresses itself in metre and harmony. This is my chief effort ; the sense of the original has, so far, given me little trouble, — but, how to put the same sense best into the same form ? However, I guess you see what I am trying to do by this time, and therefore prefer specimens to theories or views. I am much more delighted with the Second Part — now that I take it line by line — than I expected to be ; and it makes a much better appearance in English. Bernays and Anster should have been knocked on the head before prejudicing English readers against the poem by their stupid translations. No wonder people think it so dull !

I have just obtained a third translation of the Second Part — Macdonald's — so now, I believe I know all that have been made ! and they are equally bad. If you are familiar with it, I shall greatly enjoy your suggestions after a while.

I do not intend to commence the revision of the translation until I have put

" Das Ewigweibliche
Zieht uns hinan "

into English. The first draft of the work requires warmth ; the revision, coolness. I only inclose your MS. because I am uncertain whether you have another copy. If you have, or after you have used this, pray return it when you have leisure, as I wish to use it when the proper time comes.

Tell Mrs. Wistar that I would like to oblige her, — that I have all confidence in her discretion, — but I am afraid of accidents, and must beg her to have a little patience with me. It would be, as the Germans say, *hoechst fatal* to me, if even a stanza or couplet of the work should stray from me before I am ready to give the whole. Perhaps I am unnecessarily nervous ; but two years ago I said something about my commenced translation to a friend, and within three months there was an article in a New York paper misstating my design, criticising it in advance, and predicting failure. Since then the statement of my being engaged upon the work has been so frequently made, that it is no longer a secret, and I am so far advanced that I am quite ready to show and consult about passages, where I feel safe, as I do with yourself. What I have sent to you is the first and only specimen that has gone out of my own hands. But need I make further explanation to an author — nay, two authors ? I am very glad that you like my German proem. It is rather a rash undertaking, and I must either succeed *well* or not try.

TO JAMES T. FIELDS.

CEDARCROFT, *Sunday evening, January* 17, 1869.

I had no idea that Bryant's "Iliad" was so nearly finished. It will be a success, and I am very glad you are going to bring it out.

Now, if I can do equally well by "Faust," it will be something remarkable that the three greatest poems outside of the English language should appear so near together in American translations. I am working like a beaver on the first act of the Second

Part, the First Part being finished. To morrow I begin work on my novel, so it is pretty sure to be finished by June.

The novel was "Joseph and his Friend," which Bayard Taylor had agreed to write for serial publication in the "Atlantic Monthly." It was not completed so early as he had hoped, but occupied him at different times during this year and part of the next.

TO JAMES T. FIELDS.

CEDARCROFT, KENNETT SQUARE, PA., *January* 22, 1869.

. . . I also have since sent my poem [1] to two poets, asking their views about the lines and expression to which you object. Their judgment almost exactly coincides with mine.

The first two lines mentioned are pronounced rather too heavy ; all the others are declared good. I know perfectly well that I shall not change the line commencing "His nostrils," etc., nor those ending with "starvest" and "harvest." The latter is an unusual, perfect, and delightful rhyme. *My* critics consider the poem better than "The Sunshine of the Gods," as I do. So we are equally balanced, as far as authority is concerned. . . .

One thing, however, I claim, and I think you will find it reasonable. Each poet has his own individual mode of expressing his conceptions, and now and then inevitably makes use of words, lines, and rhymes which others would wish to see changed. Who does this more than Browning? Who in America, more than Lowell? Even the patient and fine-minded Longfellow sometimes commits flagrant offenses against my sense (and no doubt yours) of beauty. It is so, and must be so, with all poets. Now, a poet is very wrong not to correct a fault made evident to his poetic sense, but equally wrong to change a word, if its faulty character is not so made evident. That is my creed, and I must stand or fall by it.

But I beg of you, my dear Fields, don't let my paternal zeal prevent you from giving your views always and freely. If I seem to be stirred up at first, on being stroked the wrong way, you may be sure it is only a temporary electrical snapping, and I shall soon be purring again.

My wife joins me in best love to yours. When, oh, *when* shall I get Browning's second volume ? [1] I pine for it.

[1] "Notus Ignoto."
[2] *The Ring and the Book.*

JAMES T. FIELDS TO BAYARD TAYLOR.

BOSTON, *February* 3, 1869.

Thank you very much for your kind note of the 22d of January. If my hand were not lame, and I could manipulate the pen with such perfection of chirography as you have always done, I would gladly always shake my own fist over the paper at you. But nowadays I can just make out to sign my name, only, and this must be my excuse for all amanuensory letters you get from me. I never quarrel with a poet's individuality, and offer any strictures on a piece of verse with great editorial modesty, but if the poem I returned is really better than " The Sunshine of the Gods," I will eat a complete set of your works, and have dear old George Putnam thrown in, for sauce. However, some day I hope to be out of this business and quietly laid away in some uneditorial corner.

BAYARD TAYLOR TO MRS. JAMES T. FIELDS.

CEDARCROFT, KENNETT SQUARE, PA., *February* 7, 1869.

. . . I want to give you a water-color sketch in place of that dreadful Arcadian temple, which I did n't know was so bad until I saw it again. I think I had better make it the same size, in order to feel more sure that you will take the other one out of the frame ; so, if you will let me have the dimensions, I will have the picture ready by May and give it to you when you both come here with Whittier. Then, you may give the Arcadian temple to your amiable cook with my compliments, only she must not look at it while compounding sauces or salad-dressings. If she don't want it, let it be hung up the chimney and well smoked for three months, when it may pass for a Byzantine landscape of the ninth century. Even then, I doubt whether it would be safe to have it on hand in a cholera season.

We have the loveliest weather here ; sometimes, but not often, the thermometer gets down to eighteen degrees ; the willow and lilac buds are swelling, and it is delightful to lounge about in the open air. This a little reconciles me to the loss of Emerson's readings, and the other good things which you lucky folks enjoy.

Don't forget the picture-measure !
To make a new one is a pleasure,
And I shall do it in April leisure !

TO PAUL H. HAYNE.

CEDARCROFT, KENNETT SQUARE, PA., *March* 6, 1869.

. . . For your kind appreciation of my poems I am sincerely grateful. I place little value upon what is called "popularity," since it is generally based on the more obvious qualities of poetry. To estimate the soul and spirit requires a higher culture than the mass of one's readers possesses. Now, for instance, you are the second man who has ever spoken of my "Desert Hymn to the Sun," — yet I felt when I wrote it, and still feel, that it expressed what I intended. I almost think that the real excellence of a poem is in inverse ratio to its popularity.

I shall be delighted to send you my "Picture of St. John." As it happens, I have not a copy in my house at present, and must first send to Boston ; but you may look for it in a fortnight, at the latest. I shall also send you the previously collected edition of my poems, published in 1864, which will replace some things you have lost. If *I* had been with Sherman's army, I would have tried hard to save your library and Simms' also. I am so near the (former) border that while I was in Russia during the war, my parents, just before the battle of Gettysburg, buried all my manuscripts. If my place had been sixty miles farther westward, my books would have gone too. But I trust we shall all outlive the scars of these late terrible years.

TO MRS. MARIE BLOEDE.

CEDARCROFT, KENNETT SQUARE, PA., *March* 20, 1869.

I am most heartily obliged to you for the passage from Grimm. In my Introduction to "Faust" I intend to say something of the kinship of the two languages ; for I find that Goethe's method of using German approaches some features of the English language. This passage of Grimm is just what I want, and I shall quote it in my Introduction to the translation. I intend to try to prove that no great poem can be *transferred* with less loss than the German of "Faust" into the English language, — and to make this a part of my justification for rigidly preserving the original metres. Thanks, again !

Since I saw you I have succeeded in untangling the semi-Gordian knots of the "Classische Walpurgisnacht," and it now seems tolerably clear to me. It is necessary to separate the extraneous matter from that which strictly belongs to Goethe's original plan. Singularly enough, the German commentators have not done this fully. My task will be to simplify the explanation of "Faust," and exhibit it as a clear and comprehensible (though not always consistent) whole. In doing so, I must clear away the rubbish cast upon the poem by —— and that class of expounders. But it is a delightful, refreshing, satisfying labor, which attracts me more and more. I confess that the result of my experiment with you — in reading passages from my first revised translation — has given me great encouragement. The number of my friends who know both English and German equally well is small, and when they approve, I feel safe. I feel that this is a most important work : indeed, an English "Faust" seems to me the next thing to writing a great original epic. I am determined that English readers shall have a chance of knowing Goethe's greatness, which they never can through the translations heretofore published.

Did you see a ballad of mine — "Napoleon at Gotha " — in " Putnam " for March ?

Mrs. Bloede, in replying to this letter, offered a criticism of the poem, " Napoleon at Gotha," in which she said, " I am of opinion that it runs on too broad and comfortable a track, though otherwise it may be faultless. You will understand what I mean. The intensity of feeling loses always in proportion as the thread is spun out smoothly to its full length. A more condensed, concise form, even if more rugged, would render it more effective." To which the poet replied : —

TO MRS. MARIE BLOEDE.

CEDARCROFT, KENNETT SQUARE, PA., *April* 29, 1869.

I am always glad to get your criticisms, for they are both honest and good-natured. What you say of the poem may be true : I can only answer that I told the story in my way, which is rather the contemplative than the sensational. I don't say it is the best, but I do say that an author should study his own qualities and adopt that character of expression which best befits them. This I have done, or rather, tried to do ; and therefore, whether the poem be good or bad, I could not have written it so well in a condensed and rugged form. As it is, it is received by some classes of minds ; for I had an enthusiastic letter about it from a well-known poet the other day. On the whole, I feel that *repose* is the secret of Art : if I carry it too far I do wrong, but the tendency of the popular taste just now is for "fine writing." This, I am sure, is false, is temporary ; and the next twenty years will overturn some present brilliant literary reputations. In trying to keep clear of the fashion of the day, I may err on the opposite side ; this is very easy, but also easy to be corrected.

TO E. C. STEDMAN.

CEDARCROFT, *May* 5, 1869.

. . . I am working on the Fifth Act of the Second Part of "Faust," and have just received a great package of German, French, and English criticism and translation, a glance into which gave me new courage, for I see that I have solved various things which are still mysteries to the aforesaid critics. Blaze and Marmier, I find, appreciate Goethe, but they can't translate. The material is increasing and growing richer, and my bother will be what to omit. I intend to add the Paralipomena, and supposed I should be the first : but Blaze got the idea before me, I find. I shall have to dip deeply into the mysteries of the early Greek mythology, and read up certain geological theories, — indeed, there is no end to the lateral studies which "Faust" requires.

Our woods are green, lilacs and laburnums coming into blossom. My prospect for fruit is astounding, and I hope this year to get some tolerable returns for much patience, care, and expense. I hoe and sweat two or three hours every day, work regularly and faithfully at my desk, and seem to be growing into a fresh productiveness. The other day I wrote a *good* poem of two hundred and forty lines, — "Shekh Ahnaf's Letter from Bagdad," — and the sprouts of new poems are coming up as thick as the white-weeds in my strawberry-patch. Moreover, I have written a speech which it will take me an hour and a half to deliver (where, I won't yet say), and am revolving in my brain the Ode for the Gettysburg Dedication. This is true life, and I am most happy in being able to lead it.

On the 15th of May, Bayard Taylor completed the first draft of his translation of "Faust." He immediately turned to the composition of the ode which he had engaged to write for the dedication of the national monument at Gettysburg on the 1st of July. Profoundly moved as he was by all that Gettysburg meant to him, with its personal as well as national associations, he yet dreaded a task which was so foreign from his habits of mind. While working upon the translation of "Faust," he had stopped now and then, to free himself of a poem which came unbidden but welcome. To write poetry when he was giving shape to images which visited him was always an exquisite delight. He would spare no labor in perfecting the form, although indeed the form was almost born with the image, and his part was but to set down that which passed like the flight of a heavenly bird through his mind; but to elaborate, with toilsome art, a conception sought for to fit a certain need, — that was unnatural to him and rarely gave him satisfaction. There was a freedom in the normal action of his imagination which was fretted by the limitations of an occasion.

The Gettysburg ode was followed a few days afterward by the address given at Guilford, Conn., on the occasion of unveiling the statue erected to the memory of Fitz-Greene Halleck.[1] In the midst of these occupations, Bayard Taylor was solicited to accept the post of non-resident professor of German literature at Cornell University. The duties of the place were confined to the delivery of a course of lectures, and he accepted the office with pleasure, since it would enable him to speak of matters which lay in the direct line of his studies. The work on "Faust" had been so absorbing that he had laid aside his novel for a

---

[1] Republished in *Essays and Notes.*

time, since he wished to give each in its turn his full thought.

While these larger and graver works gave a continuity to his thought and life, he was busy in the intervals with literary labor which would have been sufficient occupation to most men. Shortly after his return from Europe he had engaged to prepare for "Putnam's Magazine" the monthly chronicle of foreign literature and art, and this labor he continued to perform until the magazine was discontinued. He was constantly contributing to the "Tribune" also special criticisms of books, which were of course anonymous. "Pray don't let it be known," he writes to Mr. Reid, "who reviews these poets, or some of them will be after me like hornets;" but there was an absence of any personal feeling in such work, so far as he could suppress a thoroughly affectionate nature. He valued the universal in criticism too highly to allow himself the cheap luxury of praising his friends at the expense of honest inquiry into the excellence of their work.

His country life brought as usual a stream of visitors to the house, and gave him also the opportunity of enjoying certain other felicities and trials pertaining to the country gentleman. He bought more land and was continually devising improvements upon his estate. There was an immense satisfaction in pruning his own trees, but he was too deep in the toils of a great place to withhold his hand from changes which draw a chain of other changes after them. Then he found himself, like other landed proprietors, called upon to protect his place. A neighbor proposed to the township to cut a road through it, and the poet-proprietor, who valued his place for what it was to himself, had to fight hard to keep his wild woods from falling before the axe of the road-maker. The neighborhood had always criticised Bayard Taylor, and he had quite refused to order his life and conduct by the canons which were accepted about him. Nor would he quietly go his own way and pay no attention to the criticism. It offended his sense of justice and of catholicity. He found a satisfaction in going before his neighbors in one of their customary conventions, and declaring distinctly just what he understood by reform, and what was its relation to art, for art was one of the great laws of his life.

It was impossible that the constant friction should not weary him. He wished to lead a poetic life, free and wholesome. He was driven by the demands which his estate made upon him. He had a hearty, unaffected welcome for his friends, and they could not stay too long; but others, who had no claim upon his friendship, made one on his hospitality. He was vexed and teased by the petty gossip which assailed him, and by the direct assaults upon his freedom. This constant stream of ignominious troubles was wearing away his patience, and gradually lessening the enthusiasm with which he had turned to Cedarcroft as containing the satisfaction of his earthly desires.

Nevertheless, this return to his native place and his familiar life there summer and winter bore other fruit. It is only those who have been away from the country who are able to see it as it is, and Bayard Taylor, coming back to Kennett Square, after going the rounds of the world, was keenly observant of the characteristics of the people and nature about him. He had already reproduced some of the impressions in his three novels, especially in "The Story of Kennett," but he was to give a higher expression through a higher form of art. The volume containing "The Poet's Journal" had included, among the other poems, the ballad of "The Quaker Widow." The form and subject both pleased him then, and in the spring of this year he added two others, " The Old Pennsylvania Farmer" and " The Holly Tree." He was conscious that he had opened a new vein, and now, later in the season, he wrote the poem to which he gave the name of " An August Pastoral," and so published it in the " Atlantic," but afterward gave it a place in the series of " Home Pastorals." Into this poem he poured the sunshine of his Pennsylvania home, and suffered the motes of a half-playful, half-serious reverie to float in the beams. Nowhere else can one find so well the confession of this poet, written at a time when fortune and fame seemed to be parting company, fame awaiting him in the near distance, and fickle fortune turning her back upon him. It was, moreover, a time when he looked almost wistfully at nature, loving her with a backward glance, since the great drama of human life, as embodied in " Faust," had so engrossed his thought that it was to be in vain for him thereafter to content himself with anything less than the cosmic in nature and humanity.

The choice of form in these pastorals and ballads led him to study closely the structure of the hexameter, and to take great interest in similar productions. His friend, Mr. Stedman, had lately been essaying this verse, and to him naturally he turned with his thoughts. His " Faust " work also continued to enter into his correspondence.

TO E. C. STEDMAN.

CEDARCROFT, KENNETT SQUARE, PA., *August* 14, 1869.

. . . I am over busy, having all sorts of work going on exter-nally on the farm, and trying with all my might to finish a new novel by October. We have had an immense rush of visitors (and not always the right kind) this summer, and my regular habits have been broken up.

I saw Lowell's review of the "Prince," — friendly and candid I think it. What he says of hexameters is exactly true. The Germans *have* discovered the best modern hexameter. I can rap-idly give you an idea of it : —

Four feet dactylic, with an occasional trochee to vary the music.

The fifth *inevitably* a dactyl.

The sixth generally a trochee, but now and then a spondee, in-troduced when necessary to rest the ear.

No spondaic feet in the middle of the line.

This is the usual form, and it is very agreeable : —

$$-\cup\,|\,-\cup\cup\,|\,-\cup\cup\,|\,-\cup\,|\,-\cup\cup\,|\,-\cup.$$

Try a dozen lines, and I think you will be able to get the effect.

In spite of other work, and my manifold distractions, I have written several good short poems this summer. The Lord grant that your bondage in that awful human wilderness of the Gold Room — or whatever it is — has not been in vain !

TO R. H. CHITTENDEN.

KENNETT SQUARE, PA., *August* 12, 1869.

I cannot allow Dr. Bloede to return to Brooklyn without tak-ing to you my thanks for the work you forwarded to me through him. I already possessed it, but it was not therefore any the less welcome. Your translation of "Reichlin-Meldegg's Com-mentary" has the advantage of brevity and clearness, and is of special service to those who can only know "Faust" through translations.

My own translation of both parts is completed, but I shall require nearly a year more for the notes and the final revision. I wish to give the sum of all German criticism and comment, — briefly, of course, — and especially to make the Second Part clear, in spite of the assertions of Hayward and Lewes. I am glad that you are evidently so interested in the Second Part.

If I am right in inferring from your translation of the "Chorus Mysticus" that you have already translated the whole book, I shall look forward to reading it with the greatest interest. If you will allow a little criticism in a line or two, I will venture to give it. *Das Unzulängliche* is not precisely "the unattainable : " the exact meaning is "the insufficient," or "the inadequate." For *Gleichniss,* also, I prefer the word "parable." The whole stanza is a contrast between the life of earth and the future life ; and the meaning of the first four lines is, "all that is transitory on earth is a symbol or parable of what *exists* in the higher sphere ; what is insufficient there (on earth) for the needs of the soul, *here* is an actual event (*Ereigniss*)." My own first rough translation (which is still to be carefully and rigidly tested) of these lines runs thus : —

> " All that is perishable
> Is as parable sent:
> Earth's insufficiency
> Here grows to Event."

It is impossible to retain the measure and all the rhymes : this, however, is the only instance in the whole work where I have not done so.

However, I only meant to thank you for your kindness, not to start questions of interpretation. When I go to New York next winter, for a month or two, I shall be glad to talk over the Second Part with you.

R. H. CHITTENDEN TO BAYARD TAYLOR.

BROOKLYN, *August* 18, 1869.

. . . "Faust" has been my hobby ever since I began to understand it, and no one among your readers will welcome your forthcoming rendering of the Second Part more cordially than I. I am sure it will do more to secure you a permanent place among the poet-thinkers of our times than all you have published.

This I may say in advance, for my friend Bloede says he has heard you read it, and I perceive from your letter that you have found the Goethean standpoint. And besides, you have what Goethe said was an indispensable prerequisite to comprehension of "Faust," *i. e.,* "lived and looked about you."

With respect to the "Mystic Chorus," you have the authority of Meyer (Meyer, "Studien," Altona, 1847, p. 191) to support your rendering of *unzulängliche*, "the insufficient." Still, I am disposed to believe that Faust's triumph at the close was the realization of his longing after the unattainable, which marks his first appearance. I prefer "symbol" to "parable." Was not Goethe something of a Swedenborgian? That is, did not he regard the finite as the symbol of the infinite, the material and transitory as the type or counterpart of the spiritual reality?

In my opinion, Goethe in the Mystic Chorus not only meant all you so well express in your letter, but much more.

Dr. Bloede tells me you translate "Das Ewigweibliche" "woman's-soul." I have spent many hours over those two last lines, with very unsatisfactory results, as you have seen.

It is clear that the poet, by the Eternal Womanhood means Divine Love, — of which the pure and true woman is the most perfect human expression, — love that, coöperating in Faust's better nature, overcame Mephisto, and draweth his rescued spirit upward and onward forever toward God. Please pardon me, for I believe I am afflicted with Goethemania. . . .

Your Dedication Ode at Gettysburg is the best poem I have read in a long time.

BAYARD TAYLOR TO R. H. CHITTENDEN.

KENNETT SQUARE, PA., *August* 21, 1869.

I don't think I stated that although my translation is complete it must still receive one final and thorough revision. I have used the word "parable" because it seems to me to present Goethe's meaning more clearly to the English mind ; but I may still change it, and many other of the more important lines. Dr. Bloede did not correctly give you my translation of the "Ewigweibliche." My lines are : —

> "The Woman-Soul leadeth us
> Upward and on,"

which is a very different thing from "Woman's Soul." I am aware that some of the critics consider the word as typical of the Divine Love, — but I only look upon that as a secondary meaning, and find a connection between it and the line : —

> " Wenn er dich ahnet folgt er nach."

Goethe was ethico-philosophical, never theological. He meant (I think) *primarily* to say that the Woman-element attracts and elevates the Man-element, here and hereafter ; that love is an eternal, purifying, and redeeming force. This reading harmonizes with the introduction of Gretchen, and the line I have quoted. Of course it will also bear the other interpretation, in addition, and won't break under the strain. For my part, I find the best explanation of "Faust" not in the critics, but in Goethe's other works, in Eckermann, and in the correspondence with Schiller, Zelter, and others. I have made it my first business to study Goethe's manner of thought and his habits of composition. The best brief commentary on "Faust" is that recently published by Dr. Kreysig. But I have not time to discuss these points, and only meant to indicate my view of the lines you mention. I need hardly say that all this is confidential : I do not wish to have a single word of my work made public until after the last revision, and I have not yet consulted with Lowell and other German scholars in regard to a few points. I have laid my translation aside to rest, and shall not go over it again until after the notes are finished, — next spring, probably. I here copy the Opening Chorus of the Second Part.

.   .   .   .

You will see that my object — not only here but throughout — is to reproduce measure and rhyme, and also the rhythmical *tone* or *stimmung* of the original. My only charge against Mr. Brooks is that he neglects the latter quality, which is something apart from the mere scansion. "Faust" in this respect is superb. Whether I can do it or not, others must judge. . . . In the greater part of the "Helena" the translation is strictly literal, but every foot and cæsural pause of the choruses is retained.

I am cheered by your encouraging words, and am also very glad to get your commendation of my Gettysburg ode.

TO E. C. STEDMAN.

CEDARCROFT, *Friday, August* 20, 1869.

. . . Lowell's notice was in the "N. A. Review." What he says of your "Theocritus" is cheering. I gave you only *one* line as a specimen ; of course the order of dactyls and trochees can always be varied in the first four feet, and an occasional spondee break the closing trochaic feet. The German hexameters — at least those of Goethe and Gregorovius — are *never* monotonous. The October "Atlantic" will have a "Cedarcroft Pastoral" in hexameters, which I specially want you to read. We are overrun by visitors, or I would write more.

The open life which Bayard Taylor led at Cedarcroft made it easy for the general public of magazines and newspapers to share in the hospitality which he gave so generously. He was asked at this time by a friend who had been his guest to allow her to give a description of his home and surroundings in a new magazine. His reply to her request is an illustration of his own reserve when writing of others: —

TO MISS LAURA C. REDDEN.

CEDARCROFT, KENNETT SQUARE, PA., *September* 15, 1869.

In regard to ——, I know what he wants, and it is a want which ought not to be gratified. I have always been opposed to the reporting of an author's conversation, or personal habits, at least during his life. I have never done it myself, and I know no author who would not be annoyed by it. It is the most difficult thing in the world to make a fair report of free, unreserved talk. A single sentence, taken from its context, and repeated without the tone and mood and manner, may convey a totally false impression. For this reason I earnestly hope that you will repeat no " opinions " of mine, and give no more minute details or incidents of my household life. I have no objection to your describing my own habits of study and composition, if you should wish to do so, and if you remember any of our conversations on that point. Whatever concerns me as an author may be detached from my private life as a man. Thus, you may repeat any of my views in regard to the poet's vocation and duties, or in regard to my own continuous development, etc. my ideas of what poetry is, and how severe an art, etc., etc. I think you will understand me without further explanation. If you choose, I will myself write to ——, and tell him the same thing.

The Stoddards left last Saturday, and I have now recommenced work in the quiet house. My novel will now advance more rapidly. The new pond is beginning to fill up, and we rejoice over this additional beauty of the place. We have a superb vintage, and to-morrow the gardeners will make a barrel of wine.

Alas for his fine hopes! The demon of neces-

sity still pursued him, and late in the fall he was
forced to drop his home life and work and set out on
another lecturing tour, which he devoutly hoped would
be the last which he would be compelled to make. It
kept him engaged until the close of the year, and besides the familiar worries, brought new ones in the
shape of pestilent slanders and accusations, which made
him indignant and outraged, even though he was determined to pay no attention to them. He had now
been so long a familiar personality in the country that
a plentiful crop of stories about him had come to maturity in the journals.

TO REV. H. N. POWERS.

CEDARCROFT, *December* 8, 1869.
Thanks for your note, which has just arrived. Whoever wrote
the article to which you allude took the trouble to send a copy
(marked, of course) to my wife. She threw it into the fire, and
can't even remember the name of the paper. Now, I should like
to know the latter, because the people who do such things are
often the very ones who call upon you for a favor a few years
later. Moreover, I saw in a Pittsburgh paper the other day the
announcement that "B. T. and the Rev. Dr. H. are *flaying each
other* in Chicago." (!) I can only guess that this must refer to
the same thing. If so, here is one result of it : the Y. M. C. A.
(it should properly be P. — for " Pharisaic " — instead of C.) of
———— ————, has broken my engagement to lecture before it, on
account of "the immoral tendency" of my lectures ! I fully
share in your disgust towards the miserable herd of persons in
this country, to whom anything but commonplace is an intellectual offense ; but I have resolved never to notice anything but
an actual assault on my personal character. These persons may
have a temporary influence with the crowd, but they can neither
make nor unmake an author's reputation. I am content to *try*
to do some genuine literary work, satisfied with the encouragement of the few who can appreciate it, and, unfortunately, there
are only a few among us who value the highest aims.
Whether my lecture was sound or not, these very attacks

prove the necessity of something of the kind being said. "*In omnibus caritas*," says St. Augustine, but this is just what we don't have in America.

My wife and mother heartily join in reciprocating your Christmas wishes, and in returning a "Happy New Year" to you and yours.

Toledo, Ohio, *December* 11, 1869.

I received your very kind note after the lecture last night in Detroit, and this is my first chance of replying. It is three or four years since that lie about Humboldt has been everywhere contradicted, and any man who uses it now must be either very ignorant or very malicious. It was invented by Park Benjamin, who confessed the fact shortly before his death, when it was immediately published. I had no agency in the matter. All that I have ever said you will find in my "Familiar Letter to the Reader," in my "By-Ways of Europe," published last spring.

Do not, pray, take any special trouble to answer such a stale slander. These attacks are simply a part of that absence of fairness and refined tolerance which at present characterizes American society. I have long since given up the expectation of any general recognition of the best things I do ; the few honestly and broadly developed minds, here and there, will always judge me kindly. The degree of petty spite which every conscientious thinker must encounter is sometimes rather saddening, but it is hardly worth one's indignation.

Believe me, I appreciate most gratefully the generous spirit in which you write. If there is really anything forcible in the article you have seen, I would be glad if you could forward me a copy to Kennett Square. An intelligent hostility is not always a disadvantage. But if it is merely a coarse, flippant assault, of course I don't care to see it.

CHAPTER XXII.

This plant, it may be, grew from vigorous seed,
Within the field of study set by song.
Sonnet.

AT the beginning of 1870 Bayard Taylor removed with his family to New York for a couple of months. He devoted himself to continuous work upon his novel, the publication of which had been begun in the "Atlantic Monthly," although he had not been able, in spite of his intentions, to finish the writing. He continued also his monthly notes for "Putnam's Magazine," wrote reviews for the "Tribune," notably one on Bryant's translation of the "Iliad," and answered the demand whenever a poem called for expression. He made short lecture trips, but his experience in this grew more and more discouraging. He had not the exuberant vitality with which he was once wont to encounter the physical discomforts of a lecturing life, but he still had the indomitable will, and the contempt for sickness, which led him to attack his work as if he were in the best of health. A wretched catarrhal trouble afflicted him, and before he went back to Cedarcroft he was overtaken by a cough which proved to be whooping-cough. In the intervals of his lecturing he was with his family, and enjoying as before the social life which gathered about him whenever he was in the city. His hospitable ways and his hearty interest in all that concerned literature and art continually brought others to him, and made him a welcome guest at studios and dinner-tables. He was able, also, while working upon " Faust," which had the first place in his mind, if not the greater part of his attention, to avail himself of the friendly counsel of Mr. Chittenden, Dr. Bloede, Mr. and Mrs. Conant, and Mr. Macdonough. Since so many of his friends were within call, he wrote few letters during his stay in New York.

On the 9th of March he returned with his family to Cedarcroft, and began at once to prepare the six lectures on German literature which he had agreed to give at Cornell in April. In a month he had completed them and was again at work on his novel. He spent the latter half of April in Ithaca, delivering his lectures, and giving what hours he could snatch to writing upon his novel.

TO T. B. ALDRICH.

CEDARCROFT, KENNETT SQUARE, PA., *April* 5, 1870.

M. reminds me that I have not yet explained to you why I did not call to see you and L. in New York ; but the same reason applies partly to my not writing sooner. The simple fact is I had the *whoooping-cough,* and in the most violent form ; and I did not dare to go anywhere within a quarter of a mile of babies.

We had arranged to leave on the Monday after lunching with Launt Thompson, but remained a day longer on account of my having so wrenched one of the pectoral muscles, in one of my convulsions, that I was not able to travel.

M. would have gone to see L. but for the fear of carrying some of my atmosphere in her dress, for the ways of whooping-cough are past finding out.

The journey home aggravated my case so much that I have not ventured out of the house until within a week, and every storm still irritates me.

I have been obliged to postpone my lectures at the Cornell

University until next month. But they have been written and I am now free from literary work. You will find another pastoral in the May number, and I have, besides, several poems in MS. I shall finish "Joseph" this month, and will have nothing on hand but "Faust" and will undertake nothing more until that is complete. I work hard, but am happier in working than ever before, and you know I always liked it.

TO JERVIS M^CENTEE.

CEDARCROFT, KENNETT SQUARE, PA., *April* 12, 1870.

You must not measure my satisfaction at receiving your letter with the time I have taken to answer it — but yes, you may, for both are *much!* The fact is this : I have had *six* lectures on German literature to prepare for Cornell University, and the time was so short (I begin to lecture next week) that I, perforce, postponed everything else until the work was done. Yesterday I finished it, and to-day I turn to you, not with the sense of performing a neglected duty, but rather with the delight which we always have in holidays of the mind. The lectures were somewhat of a task, because my whooping-cough became much worse after leaving New York and robbed me of ten days' work. The next thing on hand is to finish the novel of "Joseph and his Friend," which I hope to accomplish by May 1st, and then there will be nothing left for me but — "Faust!" I have sketches for other things, but I like to look at a blank canvas (as I 'll bet you do) and lay out in fancy what I shall put on it. I find that my severest and most serious labor does me most good, so I look forward to a time when the best things may be accomplished with tolerable ease. There is not such a great difference between the mental processes of the painter and the author — chiefly that which springs from the vehicles whereby they work. We have, at last, exquisite weather. I have a bed of hyacinths in blossom on the terrace, and the pear and peach buds are just bursting out. Our grass is quite green, and the new pond at the bottom of the lawn shines like steel. The place never seemed so lovely to me as this spring. Everything is coming on finely. We have had lettuce and radishes for a month past, and to-day have our first "cukes." Rhubarb will be fit for pies in a day or two, and tomatoes are six inches high. We have plucked almost two dozen oranges from our trees, besides lemons which make me think of Sorrento. I have just had a present (from Kansas) of an enormous buffalo head, cured, stuffed, and mounted on a shield, as fierce as life itself. It is to go opposite Stedman's Adirondack stag, in our dining-room.

My stay at Ithaca will be two weeks, and after I return we shall probably leave immediately for California, not to be back again until the middle of July. Then, I hope to rest awhile : we want to see you two here in the fruit season. There is a great promise of everything this year. The gardener and I are going in for making money, at last, and we have good prospects of success. Literature is down, just as much as Art. No books sell now except such wishy-washy things as —— and ——. We are just now feeling the inevitable demoralization of the war. I don't look for much improvement before two, three, — possibly five years. We must first get down to gold, and then over the depression in values which has already commenced, and into the new prosperity that is surely coming, before there can be much change. I get next to nothing from my books now, and it is so with all but the sensational authors. Even Hawthorne's works no longer sell. So the artists are not alone in their misery. Don't you know that what we produce is a luxury, and is always given up sooner than India shawls, jewelry, suppers, and fast horses ? America is still in the prosaic vulgar stage, and we all are born fifty years too soon for our comfort. Our wealth is generally in mean or ignorant hands, and therefore can't go where it should. But, bless me ! this is not a leader I am writing ! Hold up, Pegasus ! why should I think of anything but this glorious spring sunshine ? I won't, except to remember the few friends who make life worth living, whether books sell or not.

The unremunerative work on " Faust," together with the cost of running the estate at Cedarcroft, had so drained his supply of money that he needed to replenish it by some special effort. The returns from publishers were insignificant, the last lecture season had been more of a loss than a gain, and he planned as a means of relief a trip to California. He hoped to repeat something of the experience which he had enjoyed when lecturing there eleven years before. Then, in the first flush of Californian prosperity, he had made a successful tour, though at the time it was less remunerative than he had hoped. Now, he received invitations which gave him confidence that he could win so good a return as to enable him to make an end of lecturing altogether. At first he designed taking his wife and daughter with him, but the rumors of Indian difficulties determined him to go alone. He went, expecting to be absent for two months, but returned in a month, utterly discouraged. He not only did not make a fortune, but actually came back poorer than he started.

TO JAMES T. FIELDS.

CEDARCROFT, KENNETT SQUARE, PA., *May* 6, 1870.

I have just received your note, with check, and thank you heartily. Now it is really too bad, if you meant to visit us this spring, — I mean too bad that we are going away, — for we have been expecting your visit so long and vainly that we had almost come to regard it as one of the unattainable pleasures. The facts are simply these : I have been completely overhauling my pecuniary interests this spring, and reorganizing on a more convenient basis. A certain number of shekels is necessary to make the new truck run without friction, and an invitation of the Mercantile Library Society of San Francisco, with the additional prospect of giving twenty-five more lectures in the smaller towns, offers me the means of doing all I wish by July 1st, and then having the field clear for "Faust." My wife will go with me, and we start next Wednesday. And if you will come in July, or August, or September, or October, — while we have leaves in the forest and fruit in the orchard, it will be another promise of the summer. When I think that seven weeks' work, and the final and complete winding-up of my lecture-business will give me ease and leisure, how can I resist?

CEDARCROFT, *June* 25, 1870.

I reached home four days ago, after a trip of seven days from San Francisco. A note from Howells to my wife relieves me of doubt about the MS. He has all but the last two or three chapters, which I shall write at once and forward.

My parents are going to Switzerland for a year, and will sail on the 12th of July. I should like to run on to Boston for a day or two, then, and possibly may do so. We are so unsettled by the preparations, and various other family matters, that we should prefer to have you come to us in September, when the weather is most perfect, the fruit most plentiful, and when (this season) we shall have quiet and leisure for you and ourselves. Pray so arrange your summer plan as to include this excursion.

I am provoked that my trip to California (a most useless journey, as it has proved) interfered with your plan of coming this spring. I expected to earn a certain sum by my lectures there (the representations made to me being very flattering), and then to be able to rearrange my time and labor comfortably, since I shall lecture no more. But I have been hideously deceived ; the population in California is the deadest I ever saw. Nobody, now, seems to read a book, or go to a lecture, except a small class in San Francisco.

The consequence is, I lost instead of earning money, and come back, ready to undertake some sort of drudgery, for lecture I will not.

The end of Dickens haunts me like a warning ; there were twenty years more of life in him, had he not worn out his vitality. It was not the writings, but the readings, which killed him. I should rather have never heard him read, if we could have had the man twenty years longer.

Cordial greetings to A. W., and salute all friends from me.

Bayard Taylor estimated that his lecturing since the beginning of the year had cost him five hundred dollars. The explanation of his failure, where before he had repeatedly made a success, is to be found not in any change in his matter or manner, but simply in the change which had come over the country. When he entered upon lecturing, the nation was in a state of political ferment which had a strong influence upon intellectual life everywhere. The political habits of the people had made public assemblies a common incident. The religious habits had made the pulpit to be a power. A third force had arisen out of these two in the lecture system. The platform had become the vantage-ground from which apostles, who were either excluded from the pulpit, or wished for a freer condition of address, stirred the people with their reformatory doctrines in every department of morals and social philosophy. No apparatus was needed beyond a gathering place, which the town-hall or meeting-house supplied, a lecturer, and his audience. There was little range of entertainment either in towns, or in cities, and for several years the Lecture was the most available form of entertainment and instruction.

Now, all was changed. The war had intervened, with its rough overturning of old social ranks. Money and leisure were in the power of people who had little intellectual training, and small taste for such plain entertainment as a lecture would afford. The sensational element in literature, the drama and all forms of art, had for a while almost undisputed sway. The growth and prosperity of the newspaper press had given, besides, a means of becoming familiar with the world which was open to the inhabitant of the most distant village. All these causes tended to depress the old-fashioned lyceum. Lecture courses were made palatable by the introduction of musical and dramatic entertainments, and even a well-earned reputation stood the lecturer in poor stead for the power of saying something exceptionally "smart," startling, or witty. The trip to California was a rude awakening to Bayard Taylor, but he saw the drift of public taste, and he could only accept the situation and wait for a return to healthier conditions.

After his return to Cedarcroft he was busy with preparations for the departure of his father and mother, who were going to Switzerland to spend a year with a married daughter. When they had left New York, Bayard Taylor and his wife made an excursion to Boston and neighborhood, and then returned to Cedarcroft, where he devoted himself assiduously to work on "Faust." His work consisted in completing a thorough revision for the press, and in the preparation of the voluminous notes which he designed to accompany the work. Part I. was to be published before the end of the year, and Part II. early in the year following.

It was the summer of the Franco-German war, and Bayard Taylor with his intimate knowledge of modern Europe took the strongest possible interest in affairs. His work on "Faust" was not ill-timed, when Goethe's country was disclosing so dramatically its almost unrecognized power. In the midst of his work, he was called upon by the "Tribune" to furnish an elaborate article upon Louis Napoleon's career, to be used in the event of the emperor's abdication, and though remote from important sources of information, he gave himself to the task with his customary energy, and in half a week had written enough to cover a page of the "Tribune. When the news came of the surrender of MacMahon's army, Bayard Taylor was so stirred that he wrote at once a German "Jubellied eines Amerikaners," which was taken up with enthusiasm by the Germans in America, set to music several times, and translated into English by some one ignorant of its origin. He furnished for the "Tribune," also, a metrical translation of the "Wacht am Rhein."

Meanwhile with all these interruptions he completed "Joseph and his Friend," wrote the remainder of his "Pastorals," and kept assiduously at work throughout the autumn upon his "Faust" and Notes.

As soon as proofs began to come, his labor was not lessened, but it took on a hopeful character.

TO JAMES T. FIELDS.

KENNETT SQUARE, PA., *August* 18, 1870.

I am still waiting for the first proofs as the signal to send on a big batch of MS. But nothing comes. The delay in the printing-office must terminate soon, or the publication will have to be postponed. I am sure of doing my part, and will meet the printer's requirements.

I have laid aside the " Faust " for a few days in order to write the last two chapters of "Joseph." I have also written part of a "November Pastoral," meant as the concluding number of the Trilogy, which I want to finish while the material is fresh and urgent for expression. Do you feel inclined to publish a third (and final) installment ? Having occasion to write to Howells about "Joseph" this morning, I mentioned the "Pastoral" to him. I know you both liked the other two, as *individuals*, but I have no means of knowing whether they attracted sufficient notice from the reading public to make a third profitable to the magazine. Please let me know your candid view of the matter. The poem will probably be finished (having now begun, I cannot stop) before your answer reaches me.

TO WHITELAW REID.

KENNETT SQUARE, PA., *Thursday morning, August* 18, 1870.

Your letter of yesterday has just arrived, but not yet the " Paris in 1851." I suppose the latter is Ténot's book. The article in the " North American " was not of much service ; I found three in " Westminster " for '59, '60, and '61, which were better. In an article of five or six columns I could not give much prominence to any particular event, and describe motives and results also. I have therefore attempted a comprehensive sketch of the whole life. Pray read it if you have time, then send me the proofs, and at the same time any suggestions of change which you may wish to have made ; for instance, of more prominence to certain portions, and less to others. I will then do what further may be necessary, and in the mean time you will have the article as it now is in case of sudden need. This is better for you than if I had retained it here. I have done my best for the time allowed me.

I can, of course, review the new book at once, within a day after it comes. But it will not do to suspend the MS. of "Faust" any longer, as the printers have commenced work on it. By the 10th of September I shall be at liberty again. It is not merely the time, you understand, but also the entire rupture of trains of thought, not all of which can be easily taken up again. I want to finish the other reviews this week, and have a clear field for "Faust" at last.

TO JAMES T. FIELDS.

KENNETT SQUARE, PA., *September* 1, 1870.

A thousand thanks for your promptness in sending me the check. I inclose the receipt you desire. The Preface and German Proem herewith sent are not yet for the printer. I want your opinion about my references to Brooks, Hayward, and Lewes. You know the former, and can judge whether the gentle criticism would disturb. I meant to be friendly and appreciative, while sincere.

Then I should be very glad if both Longfellow and Lowell will take the trouble to run over the MS. and note down any exceptions they may take to what is said, or any hints of anything which might fittingly be added. Here, as you know, there is no one with whom I can consult, and it is not always good to be alone.

It is eleven days since I received and returned the first proof, and I have sent about seventy pages of text and twenty-five of notes, and have about as much on hand ready to send. I have written to Welch, Bigelow & Co. two or three times, asking them to let me know at what rate they would want the copy furnished, etc., but have received no word of reply. I cannot account for the delay, and want you to understand that I am in no way responsible for it. I have worked in the sweat of my brow for a month past, by day and night, to fulfill my promise ; and now, if any delay has been contemplated, I should like to know at once.

CEDARCROFT, KENNETT SQUARE, PA., *September* 8, 1870.

The silhouettes [1] came last night. I agree with you that it would be an advantage to have the explanatory passages from my

---

[1] Roberts Brothers were about to publish Konewka's silhouettes illustrative of *Faust*, and an arrangement had been made by which the text was taken from the forthcoming translation.

translation. They will be the most ordinary specimens, of course, — as the artist takes actions, not thoughts, and his selection is not especially good, — but that will probably make no difference with the public.

I have also heard from Welch, Bigelow & Co. I return the proofs by the next mail in every case, — sometimes in two hours' time, and they have MS. far ahead ; so no delay can be fairly attributed to me.

It was just upon that point where I wished counsel. You and Longfellow are probably right. I *must,* however, take sides against a prose translation, and Hayward will be implied, whether he is mentioned or not. It seemed to me, therefore, fairer to come out squarely with his name. I was doubtful about the reference to Brooks, and in this case a doubt ought to be equal to a decision. Nevertheless, I should be obliged if you will send the MS. to Lowell before returning it to me. I should like to have Longfellow's and his opinion of the Proem.

My "Jubellied" in Tuesday's "Tribune" is copied into all the German - American papers, and is another bit of grist in Faust's mill.

The "Notes" turn out satisfactorily. I *know* they are more complete than have yet been given, for I have many things which have escaped even the German commentators.

KENNETT SQUARE, PA., *September* 22, 1870.

I have finished the text of "Faust" and the greater part of the notes, and do not send all the MS. now, because the printing is so far behind the copy in Welch, Bigelow & Co.'s hands. They promised me fifty pages per week, but I only received thirty pages ten days ago, and since then only four pages of the Notes. I always return the proofs by the next mail.

I wrote to you in August that we were ready for you whenever you could come this way. Now don't simply say that you wish you could be with us, but pack your trunk and take your railroad tickets ! The weather is simply heavenly here, and there is not yet a touch of autumn on the woods. Do take a holiday next week and come on. We only need notice enough in advance to enable us to meet you at the station, which is one mile from Cedarcroft. My wife joins me most heartily for the eleventh (or twenty-seventh) time in repeating the persuasion. If you could only persuade Whittier to come along !

How good Dr. Hedge's article is ! His translation of Goethe's "Coptic Song" is perfect ; if he had undertaken "Faust," my work would have been unnecessary.

Please send me the MS. of Preface as soon as possible, for I intend rewriting it ; or, best of all, bring it with you.

TO T. B. ALDRICH.

CEDARCROFT, KENNETT SQUARE, PA., *October* 5, 1870.

I have just expressed to you a small box containing six figs from my trees, and two pawpaws, which grow wild in our Pennsylvania woods. As the figs only ripen a few at a time, and will not keep well on account of their *lush* nature, I can only dispatch a few, but I hope they will recall an old flavor to your palate. My trees are still young, and I shall not have more than a peck this year ; but the quality is good. There will be three pomegranates in a fortnight more.

I have been working day and night on "Faust" since I saw you, and now that the work is just about finished, I shall feel thoroughly worn out, exhausted, used up, collapsed, effete, intellectually impotent. I only hope there will be some little recognition of my labors in the end.

The coming of autumn and of cooler weather brought little relief to Bayard Taylor. He had toiled incessantly through the hot weather. He had been compelled to give his energy and time to a literary work which could not, even in the future, be very remunerative, withdrawing himself thus from labor which would at least have made the wheels run easily. He had been shut out from congenial society, and had suffered from wearisome interruptions incident to his country life. The near approach, also, to the end of his great task made him hunger for association with people who cared for what most interested him, and he was conscious of growing power which he longed to expend on great work, — work of a kind which could be done only if he were free from the unending perplexities of his situation. He burst forth in a letter to his mother with expressions of dissatisfaction which are not those of a querulous man, but of one who turns with rage upon his broken ideals.

TO HIS MOTHER.

CEDARCROFT, *October* 6, 1870.

. . . I am very tired of working so hard to keep up a place which gives me no return. My last trip to Europe (which I believe saved my life) cost me, as you know, five thousand dollars to keep the place going during my absence. This, and the purchase of McFarland's land, without being able to sell mine, have so burdened me that all the many losses of this year come very hard upon me, and my health suffers from the worry and the extra work I must do. We three can easily economize, but I must either let the place run down, or pay and feed six men besides. Ever since the house was built there have been but two years (1865 and 1866) when I was tolerably free from care. If I had known, in 1859, how prices were to change, and labor to be dear and unreliable, and the neighborhood to go backwards instead of forwards, I never should have built at all. What was comparatively easy then is very difficult now. My pleasure in the place as a home is spoiled by all this drain upon me, and hard as it will be I must leave for my own sake, unless there is a turn of good luck very soon. . . . It is wrong to live in this way and waste the prime of life, or sacrifice it to a sentiment, for I am doing the latter. However, I shall wait until next spring, and if there is no improvement by that time I shall do what I ought to have done four years ago. Few men of my age have gone through so much or done harder work ; and it is time that this continual wear and tear must come to an end.

TO J. B. PHILLIPS.

CEDARCROFT, KENNETT SQUARE, PA., *October* 26, 1870

I have been so busy finishing the last copy for " Faust " that I have delayed answering your last. Now everything has gone to the printer, — text, notes, title-page, preface, and appendices,— and I am free from the mental strain of three months past. The Notes are a very important feature, for they are unlike anything that has yet been done in former translations. I have given the essence of fifty volumes of criticism, besides many things of my own.

I am delighted with the way in which my "Spirits' Chant" impresses you. If that is so successful, the rest is sure ! It was a tremendous job, I assure you ; I wrote it three times, with intervals of a year or two between, coming a little nearer each time. I don't say it can't be done better, but I do defy any human being to retain the exact rhythm and order of rhyme, and at the same time come nearer the meaning of the original. I took Roget's "Thesaurus" for nearly every word, and ran through all the synonyms for it in the language. I wish I could send you the "Archangels' Chorus," but I have only one copy of the proof of that. The "Easter Choruses," I think, are fully as well done. I have kept the five dactylic rhymes in the last, which no translator ever attempted before. Yet, after all, the translation was not more laborious than the preparation of the Notes, as you will understand when you come to see the latter. . . .

CEDARCROFT, *October* 31, 1870.

I can at last send you another specimen, Margaret's prayer to the Virgin, "Ach, neige," etc. This is another very difficult passage, on account of the passionate intensity of appeal in the original. Don't let it go out of your hands until the book appears.

I should like to send you my proem, "An Goethe," but have dispatched my only copy to Germany. Now the work is all done, I breathe freely again. I am satisfied that little, if anything, has been neglected, and nothing slighted. The labor has been an immense advantage in the way of drill ; it has forced my mind into new directions, and will surely give a different character to my future work. I have many plans on hand, and several years would not suffice for their fulfillment. Do you ever see the "Atlantic" ? I have a novel in it this year — decidedly my best — which is now nearly finished. Also there have been three Pastorals,— May, August, and November, — descriptive of life here, which may interest you, if you can stand hexameter. I am hard at work all the time, but my brain seems to fill on one side as fast as I empty it on the other. However, literary labor is my true place, my all-absorbing interest, my happiness ! I am only just now beginning to do genuine work : the past has been but an apprenticeship, my *Lehrjahre* ; and now comes (so God will) the *Meisterschaft*. But if not, no difference ! My life is at least filled and brightened. . . .

TO JAMES T. FIELDS.

KENNETT SQUARE, PA., *November* 3, 1870.

. . . I have changed the Preface in such a way as, I think, will obviate your and Longfellow's objection. Lowell wrote to me, agreeing with my plan of mentioning Brooks and Hayward by name, and suggesting one or two changes, by which the doubtful passages might be made agreeable. I think all is right now. Brooks will very much prefer my reference to him to being wholly omitted; and as for Hayward it does not seem manly to attack prose translations (his being the only one) and not indicate whose views are opposed. I have, however, changed many expressions, and balanced my objections by recognitions. I feel sure they will stand, and that is the main thing.

You can probably estimate by this time the exact period when the volume can appear. If so, pray let me know. What are the aspects of the business by this time? In September they seemed favorable.

We have a wonderful fall here. Cloudless skies; no frost yet; some old oaks still green; my figs ripening day by day; and only wood-fires necessary on the open hearth, mornings and evenings. Tomatoes, egg-plants, and lettuce still flourishing in the gardens. Can you match that about Boston?

TO HIS FATHER AND MOTHER.

CEDARCROFT, *November* 8, 1870.

As I have written to A., I ought to have been less abrupt in my letter [of October 6th]; but the matter has been in my mind for a long time, and it "came to a head," like a slow boil, all at once. You know how things have changed since the house was built. Nobody then dreamed of the war and its consequences. If I had had the least idea of what was coming, I should never have built. But it is just as well: we have lived through the difficult period. Cedarcroft has been a central point for the family. We are all settled in one way or another, the old farm is sold, and you are at least free from trouble for the rest of your lives. I cannot feel now that any further duty requires me to stay here, while my interest calls upon me to leave. You cannot understand all the associations which I need as an author; but for the last two or three years I have seen very clearly that I am losing more than I gain by living here instead of in New York. . . . I thought that possibly my circumstances would enable me to spend half the year in New York, and the other half here. But there is no hope of that. I can only go to New York for two or three months by doing extra work enough to pay for the stay there. In order to live without over-work, I must decide either to live here altogether, or there alto-gether. I like country life, except in the winter ; I like the place, for I have made it what it is, and I have some few good friends in the neighborhood ; but I cannot give up my main ob-ject in life for the sake of a sentiment, however strong. It is not the place where I ought to be now. You both know how very difficult it is to get the right persons in the house or out of it ; how almost impossible it is to arrange things so that they will go on as well while I am away as when I am here. An-other man might perhaps succeed ; I can't. . . . I have explained to A. what a difference it will make in my income ; but the chief difference will be in my peace of mind and freedom from an-noyance. I have plans of more important works than any I have yet written ; I am just now in the prime of my powers ; I need (more than ever before) to have the aid of libraries and the most intelligent society, and I cannot afford to give up all for the sake of a place, no matter how I am attached to it. It has taken me a long while to come to this decision, and it is very hard to make ; but there is no use in shutting one's eyes to what is best and right. If I had done so formerly I should never have accomplished anything. I am at last tired, and tired to death, of this extra work to make both ends meet. I need com-plete rest, and I must and will have it, not merely the rest from work, but also the refreshment of intercourse with minds which can assist and benefit me.

TO JAMES T. FIELDS.

KENNETT SQUARE, PA., *November* 21, 1870.

I should have written sooner, but I have been working hard on the text of Part Second, in order to get well in advance of the printers. My labors on the First Part were so severe and steady that I narrowly escaped a fever, and some rest was absolutely necessary. Now, thank Heaven, I feel as fresh as ever, and the previous discipline will make the remaining work lighter.

Your note was a great encouragement, for I had almost made up my mind for a partial failure. There are so few persons

capable of judging. What research and exactness and literary
self-control is involved in such an undertaking !

The public, moreover, are very uncertain just now, and this is
one of those cases where they wait for some one to take the lead
and tell them whether, and what, to admire. I am in the pre-
dicament of a general who must change front in the face of an
enemy. Nine tenths of those who read made up their minds in
regard to my capacity ten years ago, and they will thus measure
my performance now. In other words, I have given up my old
audience and have not yet obtained a new one.

I have been expecting, all along, that "Faust" would bridge
over this gap, and you give me fresh hope that it may. Nevertheless, we have fallen upon (temporary) evil days. There is
certainly less sound intelligence and less taste in the country
than there was ten years ago. The war seems to have also
shaken up and disturbed the moral and intellectual elements,
and they have not yet had time to settle into their new forms.
I think we have reached, perhaps passed, the worst period, although burlesque and sensational trash seem as current as ever.

If my "Faust" is what I mean it to be, it will have a permanent place in translated literature. No one else is likely, very
soon, to undertake an equal labor. An immediate success will be
much more important to me than that of any work I have yet
published. You may therefore guess with what interest I await
its appearance. I am tolerably good at waiting, but there are
times when one likes to make a rapid advance. Besides, I think
the aspects are good just now. The German ascendency in
Europe, Marie Seebach's acting here, and various similar influences, may all be so many indirect helps. I beg you, therefore, to take all usual measures to set the work fairly afloat,
and catch up every little side-wind that may be turned towards
its sails.

TO HIS MOTHER.

CEDARCROFT, *November* 25, 1870.

. . . I have no expectation of selling the place under a year,
and perhaps longer. But I mean, just as soon as possible, to
arrange my property so that I shall have the income of all, and
be free to carry out my more important plans as an author. I
want to get rid of all the little needs of life, which I must look
after here. I shall be satisfied to buy bread, vegetables, fowls,
eggs, butter, water, gas, to hire my horses just when I need

them, and to be where we can step out and get our dinners if a servant leaves us suddenly. I am tired of having to do with blacksmiths, millers, threshers, harvest hands, hydraulic rams, and all the endless minor interests of life in the country, and I don't take half the same interest in crops and fruit raising since there is so rarely any success. In short, my attempt to combine farming and literature is a dead failure, and I have been carrying it on now for several years since I felt it to be so, out of stubborn unwillingness to admit that I was mistaken. Now since I have made up my mind what to do I am immensely relieved, and am only sorry that I happened to send *the crisis* to you in a letter. I am sure that if you look at the matter from my point of view as an author (and I must be that as long as I live) you will agree with me. I value associations as much as you do, and am almost the only one of my generation who has proved it.[1] I have done my best to make my permanent home here, but I have failed.

TO J. B. PHILLIPS.

KENNETT, *November* 28, 1870.

I have been too busy with the Second Part of "Faust" to acknowledge the receipt of your two translations. In Goethe's ballad you selected one of the most difficult specimens, where entire success is next to impossible. The original of the other I never saw, but it seems to me well translated, except here and there an unnecessarily imperfect rhyme. I notice in both what I see in all your previous translations, a true feeling for the rhythm and tone of the original, with a disinclination to take trouble enough in elaborating all the details of form. In other words, your design is ahead of either your industry or your technical skill (whichever it may be), and you must try to bring the latter up to a level with the former. I say "industry" purposely, because indolence, in just such features, is a universal characteristic of the American mind, and some of our brightest thinkers are not free from it. Some years ago I had it also, and I think this Faust-work has done more than any one thing to help me overcome it. Really, we must have a passion for symmetry, harmony, balance of thought and expression! Very likely you think I lay too much stress on what may seem minor

---

[1] He is speaking of the circle of their connections and acquaintance in Chester County.

things, but a sculptor who is satisfied if the head is good and leaves the fingers and toes half modeled is a poor artist. If you were unable to avoid these little imperfections, I should say nothing, but you are abundantly able, therefore I will admit no excuse.

By the bye, the original MS. of the "Wacht" has just been published in Germany, and the title is "Die Rheinwacht," which fully justifies my "Rhine Guard." We say "watch" in English for a sentinel, or a small body detailed for watching ; but a whole people massed along a frontier line can only be called a *guard*. . . .

The First Part of "Faust," including the critical notes, was published by Fields, Osgood & Co., in a volume uniform with the quarto editions of Longfellow's "Dante" and Bryant's "Iliad," on Wednesday, December 14, 1870. In honor of the publication Mr. and Mrs. Fields had invited the author and his wife to dinner on that day to meet a company of authors. Mrs. Taylor was unable to leave Cedarcroft, but Bayard Taylor took a holiday and enjoyed the occasion as only he could who had been working by himself on a truly monumental task, and now came out into the sunshine of hearty recognition from his peers and elders. A statue of Goethe stood in a bed of flowers in the centre of the table, and the guests present were Mr. Longfellow, Mr. Lowell, Dr. Holmes, Mr. Howells, Mr. Aldrich, and Mr. J. R. Osgood. Mr. Emerson and Mr. Whittier sent letters of regret, but their letters were partial compensation for their absence.

R. W. EMERSON TO JAMES T. FIELDS.

Concord, *Monday, December* 12, 1870.

I cannot come on Wednesday, more's the pity for me, for I wish to see Mr. Taylor and congratulate him on a day of such mark, retro- and pro-spective. I owe him also special kindnesses, repeated oft, — was his guest in Pennsylvania, have received good books, and a good drawing which I keep and prize, and have read with great content his travels in Mediterranean Islands, and lately wondered whether Clough had risen again and was pouring rich English hexameters until I pleased myself with discovering the singer without external hint of any kind, only by the wide travel. He has certainly acquired great mastery of his harp, and I am interested in the new ambition which you told me of, though I am no lover of " Faust," and like everything of Goethe's better.

Thanks for the kind remembrances of your note. But I have been reading of Thackeray with delight.[1] Nothing can be better than this admirable description which shows me, for one thing, that I never saw the man, though I met him twice, and that he was far better worth seeing than I had guessed.

J. G. WHITTIER TO JAMES T. FIELDS.

AMESBURY, 12th 12 mo., 1870.

I very much fear that I shall not be able to be with thee on Wednesday evening. Still, as it is barely possible, I shall not give up entirely the hope of it. Such opportunities are quite too rare to be lost ; life, at the best, is *so* short and uncertain. I take up the lamentation of Falstaff : "There are but few of us good fellows left, and one of them is not fat but lean, and grows old." It would be pleasant to sit down with thy special guest, my dear friend Taylor, and with others whose poetical shoe-strings I hold myself unworthy to untie : the wisest of philosophers and most genial of men from Concord ; the architect of the only noteworthy "Cathedral" in the new world ; and his neighbor, the far-traveled explorer of Purgatory and Hell, and the scarcely less dreary Paradise of the great Italian dreamer. I would like to join with them in congratulation of our Pennsylvania Friend, who introduces to English-speaking people the great masterpiece of Teutonic literature. It seems to me that he is precisely the man of all others to do it. In the first place, though he labors under the misfortune of not having been born in sight of Boston meeting-house, he inherits from his ancestry the Quaker gift of spiritual appreciation and recognition, the belief not only in his own revelations, but in those of others. In the second place, he is a poet himself. Thirdly, he has studied

---

[1] The reference is to a paper in the *Atlantic* by Mr. Fields on Thackeray, the first of the series, "Our Whispering Gallery."

man and nature in all lands and in all their phases, and fourthly, he has brought himself into the closest possible association with the culture and sentiment, the intellect and the heart of the Germany of Goethe, by bringing under his roof-tree at Cedarcroft an estimable countrywoman of Charlotte and Margaret, Natalie and Dorothea. The best translation of Tasso is that of the Quaker Wiffin, and now we have the best of Goethe from the Quaker-born Taylor. With something of pride, therefore, I stretch out my congratulatory hand, and thank him. God bless him, or to use the words made sacred by the memory of one dear to us all, "God bless us, every one !"

Monday. — P. S. Have got thy note. Will come if I can, but it is quite doubtful.

The recognition which Bayard Taylor received went straight to his heart, for he loved his work, he loved poetry and all high art with a passion which made recognition not a delicate perfume to be enjoyed in indolent gratification, but a stimulus and encouragement to higher endeavor. The work upon the Faust literature had already borne its fruit in a new conception, the plan of a comprehensive, interpretative life of Goethe and Schiller. The plan had occurred to him earlier, but had been ripening during his labor. The first impulse, therefore, was now to order his life so as to enable him to execute it. To look forward to a great achievement, — that gave him a bound of life, which never could come from any rest in a thing done. It was with peculiar pleasure, therefore, that he received from Mr. Longfellow on the occasion of his visit, a hint to the same effect. After his return to Cedarcroft, he wrote to the elder poet : —

TO H. W. LONGFELLOW.

KENNETT SQUARE, *December* 19, 1870.

When you have read the volume can you perhaps take fifteen minutes to tell me wherein I have fallen short of my design ? I

have been living so near to the work without the advantage of
other eyes and minds, that your judgment will have an especial
value to me just at present, while I am busy with the Second
Part. Do not fear that you can be too frank. You have recognized my literary endeavors so generously for years past, that I
acknowledge your fullest right to correct me.

It really gives me a new faith in myself to know that you hit
upon the very plan which has been haunting my brain for a year
or two. It is a grand undertaking, and I have been visited by
doubts of my capacity to perform it, but a little more time, I
hope, will give me full courage as well as better skill. My wife
was delighted when I told her of the coincidence, and I also take
it as an auspicious omen.

H. W. LONGFELLOW TO BAYARD TAYLOR.

CAMBRIDGE, *December* 23, 1870.

I was reading the "Prelude" when your letter came. It is an
admirable bit of translation, and if the rest is like it, you are
safe. I foresee that if any criticisms are to be made, they will
be only verbal, and not on the general execution of the work.

I read very slowly and deliberately, because I hate a glut of
anything, and wish to ponder and enjoy. The after-taste that
poetry leaves in the mind is what we really judge it by. Anything that strikes me as dubious I will mark and mention to you
when you come again. I am glad you enjoyed the dinner at
Fields'. I did extremely. It was a joyful occasion, and I still
regret that your wife was not there.

BAYARD TAYLOR TO HIS MOTHER.

CEDARCROFT, *December* 26, 1870.

. . . M. wrote to you about my glorious visit to Boston, and
dinner with the authors. "Faust" is everywhere pronounced a
great success, and will give me a permanent place in our literature. Now all this is just my business in life, and when I am
not working I ought to have rest, diversion, and profitable society ; not worry, loneliness, and a neighborhood which can avail
me nothing. I see, more clearly than ever, that I must change
my surroundings. If I keep my vigor I have twenty years of
steady growth and improving work before me, and cannot afford
to lose any further chances. A singular circumstance is that
Longfellow came to me in Boston, and suggested that I should

do the very thing which for a year past I have determined to do, the literary plan which will take me to Germany for two years. He said it was *the thing* which I should undertake, not guessing that I had already hit upon it. I have never been more cheered and encouraged.

Simultaneously with the publication of the First Part of "Faust," the novel of "Joseph and his Friend" was completed serially in the "Atlantic," and published as a book by G. P. Putnam.

CHAPTER XXIII.

A BUSY MAN'S REST.

1871.

But the thing most near to the freedom I covet
    Is the freedom I wrest
From a time that would bar me from climbing above it,
    To seek the East in the West.
I have dreamed of the forms of a nobler existence
    Than you give me here,
And the beauty that lies afar in the dateless distance
    I would conquer, and bring more near.
                           In the Lists.

THE Notes to "Faust" had cost the writer no small part of the labor which he expended upon the entire work, and finding the preparation of those for the Second Part more than he could accomplish in the country, Bayard Taylor went with his family to New York before the end of January, and remained there till April. He worked under the stimulus of frequent and hearty congratulation at the success of the volume already published, but he knew that he had much to do in overcoming the general prejudice which existed against the Second Part, and he regarded that portion as a severer test of his powers as a translator and interpreter. He bent all his energies toward a satisfactory completion of his task, and knew no relief until the work was finally published.

TO E. C. STEDMAN.

CEDARCROFT, *January* 17, 1871.

Your letter came to me as a beautiful birthday gift, and made an inner sunshine under the cloudy sky. I was especially glad to find that my letter was an encouragement to you. It was not half what I meant to say ; when I read it over, it seemed cold and imperfect ; and I could not have guessed that you would so instantly feel how much more lay behind the words than they strictly expressed.

Your hearty and generous commendation of "Faust" is one of the most welcome which has come to me. I am thoroughly satisfied with the book's reception. The first reviews struck the keynote of judgment, and thus far I have neither seen nor heard of a discordant sound. The private letters of congratulation are unexpectedly numerous. Longfellow, Dr. Furness, Mrs. Wistar, Chittenden (a Faust scholar), A. D. White, Rev. Dr. Powers of Chicago, and various others have written to me. Osgood announces that he is entirely satisfied with the result, and will do his best to make the work a publishing success. So, in the words of Daniel Webster, " I have great reason to be proud."

The difference you notice between MS. and print is partly owing to the severe final revision, in which I tested every word once more and sternly struck out whatever seemed to have the least reflection of *me*, though it might have been more agreeable to eye and ear. I can see nothing, now, that is not Goethe. You are right as to Brooks ; he fails in rhythmical quality and dignity of tone, but he is very conscientious, and deserves a great deal more credit than he receives. The Second Part you read was Birch's, about the worst specimen of translation ever inflicted on the world. I feel sure you will enjoy my Second Part, and also (I hope) my explanatory Notes, which are really important. If I have not made all the enigmas tolerably clear, I have miserably failed.

In the Notes to the First Part, I rejected four times as much as I gave. My object was to furnish all that is necessary, and no more, and to present that in such a form that the unscholarly reader may read it. So in the Second Part, renunciation must also be one of my virtues. Here, however, there is a great deal more of my own independent criticism. The material is wonderfully rich and varied, and the field, being newer and esteemed far more rugged, has a special attraction for me.

But enough of this : I have barely time to write these few lines, with twenty-five volumes open around me on chairs, and proof to be read before the next mail goes. We go to New York in two or three days, — probably on Friday, — and shall descend at the Irving, Broadway and Twelfth, where I hope to see you on Saturday or Sunday.

TO MISS LAURA C. REDDEN.

CEDARCROFT, KENNETT SQUARE, PA., *January* 18, 1871.

You are really magnanimous to overlook my long delay in replying to your last summer's letter, and to punish me by kindness and congratulation. It is not a rose-leaf (although that would have satisfied me, Sybarite), but a warm, hearty clasp of the hand which you give ; and I return it as heartily. As for the cup running over, when did ever an author's cup of success actually run over ? When was it ever so full that it could hold no more ? Not in my experience : but this time, I admit, it is well-filled, and the beverage is both agreeable and tonic. I should be very unreasonable if I were not gratefully satisfied with this last and best success ; I should be very foolish if I allowed it to weaken my resolution to achieve still better success. But there is long, severe, and conscientious labor in the volume, so I accept something as having been fairly earned, and my feeling of jubilation is not exalted enough to interfere with my untangling of the Gordian problems of the Second Part, from which I have a headache at this present writing. In three weeks, D. V., the MS. of that, also, will be completed ; and I foresee that the long foregone freedom will make me seem quite lost and restless, — as a man suddenly thrust out of penitentiary, after seven years of solitary labor ! My only remedy will be to begin something else ! . . .

TO HIS MOTHER.

NEW YORK, *February* 5, 1871.

. . . My translation of "Faust" is a great literary triumph. The reviews have been splendid, and all one way, — nothing but unbounded praise. Last night, at the Century Club, everybody congratulated me. Reid told me that he had never known an instance of such complete success. The book is considered a more successful (because more difficult) work than either Longfellow's "Dante" or Bryant's "Homer." Everything that I have heretofore done all together has not given me so much reputation as this one undertaking. People say that no one need ever translate "Faust" again, because no one can surpass my translation. The Second Part is more than half in type. I have about ten days more to work on the Notes, and then my long labor will be at an end. I shall not make a great deal of money on this first edition, because it is so large and expensive, but I ought to have a fair, permanent income from the popular edition, when it is published.

I will tell you my plan confidentially. It is to write a biography of Goethe and Schiller, such as has not yet been written. Goethe occupies the same place in German as Shakespeare in English literature, and his works are more and more studied in this country. My studies for "Faust" will enable me to undertake the biography; but to do something better than any one else, I must go to Germany for at least two years, become acquainted with all the places where the poet lived, collect materials and qualify myself in every way for the work, as I could not do at home. What I shall do will not be labor but simply occupation; the collection of material will be, really, a recreation for me. When A. wrote that I had done enough, and could afford to rest on my laurels, she did not reflect that further and better work is for me only another name for *life*. I have had enough of mere temporary popularity, and am tired of it; but I have now begun to do the things that shall be permanent in literature, and have not only the strength to undertake and carry them out, but they have also become necessary to me, a source of happiness as well as a means of success. I think you can understand what I mean. When you notice that I am constantly changing, you should also remember that change is the sign of growth, and that if I was now just the man I was ten years ago, I could never hope to accomplish anything more. For my part, my prayer is that I shall *never* stop, but go on changing, and therefore growing, while I live. You must not apply to me the same standard as to the others with whom I grew up. I have a different nature, different duties, and therefore a wholly different life. No one can decide for me, because no one knows what I am able to do and must do.

. . . There is a satisfaction in planning, and the more you do of it, the better you will be prepared to do whatever shall be best when the time comes. All I want is that you shall make such an arrangement as will give you most comfort and least trouble. I am very glad that you are in Europe now, because I know the rest will do you good, in spite of yourself. I heard a physician say, last night, that brain-work, alone, hardly ever breaks down anybody ; but violent emotions, worry, distress of mind or heart, everything that affects the feelings — bring on apoplexy, paralysis, softening of the brain, and all the other miseries which come upon so many persons. He is perfectly right. What we all need is, not to live without work, but to be free from worry.

TO J. B. PHILLIPS.

44 CLINTON PLACE, NEW YORK, *February* 8, 1871.

I have really not been able to write sooner. I am busy day and night with Part II., which is not nearly all in type, and the Notes not yet finished. I am so pulled down, physically, by this work, that I must stave off everything which must not necessarily be done. Ten days more, D. V., will free me from the long captivity.

For once, all petty spites are silenced, and I hear a universal chorus of congratulation. The reviews are all one way, and the private expressions even stronger. English and German critics say the same thing, and the substance of all is that no other translation approaches mine in reproducing the meaning, spirit, tone, and music of the original, — also that the lyrical passages cannot be better done. In short, that I have given *the* English "Faust," which will henceforth be the only one.

Those who know the original best are the loudest in congratulation. I get many letters from strangers, — the other day two from the West, begging pardon for doubting my ability in advance, and confessing to an unjust prejudice. . . . I cannot go into details of your translation of the "Gods of Greece," for no distraction can be allowed until my Notes are finished. When you tell me that you wrote it at one sitting, however, I am surprised. With all my years of practice in translating, I should not undertake to do it in less than three days. Remember what Mahomet says . . . "Haste is of the Devil." Believe me, that is not the way to do good work. The poem is very difficult, for the reason that the lines must be so closely translated in order to produce the same effect. What would you say to my hunting up twenty or thirty synonyms for every chief word in a quatrain, and then spending two or three hours in making them fit in the best possible form? Then, a year later, in many cases, all the work was done over again, in order to get a better combination. Nobody ever succeeded in rapid translation, — not even the highest talent. . . .

44 CLINTON PLACE, NEW YORK, *March* 8, 1871.

I have not been able to write sooner, for the conclusion of the Second Part not only occupied all my time, but so exhausted my strength, that now, ten days after finishing the work, I am only just beginning to recover my ordinary vitality. When you see the volume, you will guess how much laborious research was necessary. The printing is now going on, and it will be published about the 25th. It will not be generally popular ; it is too high for that ; but I think it will excite some curiosity. As a piece of literary work it is superior to the First Part, and some portions — the " Helena " especially — are more successfully translated. I feel quite calm about its reception, for the first volume has succeeded altogether beyond my expectations. The first wholly invidious notice appears to-day in the ——, written by a Rev. Somebody (I forget his name), — a splendid specimen of the orthodox-snobbish style. . . .

I get grudging recognition from other quarters, but I do not mind it. Indeed, this is natural : for I have done a great deal of imperfect work hitherto, and there is a reluctance in many writers for the press to admit that I am really capable of better things. With such men as Longfellow, Lowell, Emerson, and Whittier I stand on another footing, and so can easily bide my time. The true poets are not only tolerant but generous ; they see the aim and the aspiration. But the intermediate class is made up of narrow, prejudiced, semi-developed minds, who suspect all success until it has been sealed by those above them. Even they will in time do me justice. We are living through a very curious, unsettled stage of literature. I may be mistaken, but I think I can already separate the transient from the permanent elements. I am fighting my way from an old place to a new, and this is much more difficult than it was to win the former.

What you say of " Joseph " delights me, for you have recognized exactly what I attempted to do, — that is, to throw some indirect light on the great questions which underlie civilized life, and the existence of which is only dimly felt, not intelligently perceived, by most Americans. I allowed the plot to be directed by these *cryptic* forces ; hence, a reader who does not feel them will hardly be interested in the external movement of the story. The book is not what it might be, if I could have given more time and study to it ; but I would rather miss a high mark than hit a low one in the bull's eye. I will tell you, now, that *I* consider it my best novel, with all its deficiencies. So do a few others ; but the blessed half-educated public sees nothing in the book but dullness.

44 CLINTON PLACE, NEW YORK, *March* 23, 1871.

I have just received your letter, and as I may not have much leisure again for a fortnight, I scratch off a few lines now. We go to Boston to-morrow. My Second Part will be published on Saturday, when I am to dine with all the authors at their club. Sunday we spend in Cambridge with Lowell and Longfellow, and at the end of next week shall be in Cedarcroft again for the rest of the year. I greatly enjoy these visits to Boston ; there I am at home, and feel that I am known and helped.

I thought the ——'s review would amuse you. Don't be deceived by the fellow seeming to know English. What he says of *impermeate* is infernal nonsense. I suppose he would say that *immingle* means not to mingle. He does n't know that *im* is the Latin *inter* in this case, and perfectly correct. So much for the prevalent *charlatanerie* in criticism ! Now if you want a fine specimen of the dignified idiotic, read the ——'s notice this week. Observe the careful misrepresentation of my Preface, and the curious contradictions of the closing paragraph. I do not know a better example of a man trying to *seem* to say something, while he *means* to say nothing. How literary history repeats itself ! This is, for us, a repetition of the time when Nicolai boasted that "he would soon finish Goethe," and when Count Stolberg called Schiller " vulgar and atheistic." One's lasting hope and comfort must be, that whatever is merely smart and flippant only serves the taste of the day, and may to-morrow be supplanted by something else equally smart and flippant. If I found the least trace of honest, sincere purpose in these fellows, I should take their sneers more seriously. But they are a tribe of half-cultured *blasirte*, whose motto is, " Say nothing good of the living ! " If I live long enough, I shall finally be annoyed by their shallow, patronizing praise, from which I pray Heaven I may be spared !

TO WHITELAW REID.

March 29, 1871.

I am just from Boston, where we had a jolly time. Dined with the Saturday Club, lunched with Howells, dined with Long·

fellow, *tead* with Whipple, and launched the Second Part of "Faust," "a haughty volume," as Emerson said to me. Wife and I came back happy. I go to Cedarcroft to-morrow, but shall be back for Saturday evening at the Century, and Sunday evening at Stoddard's, hoping to see you at both places.

The Second Part of "Faust" was published March 25, 1871, by James R. Osgood & Co., who had succeeded Fields, Osgood & Co. since the publication of the First Part in the December previous. "Faust" was issued in the style which had already expressed the dignity of Mr. Longfellow's "Dante," Mr. Bryant's "Homer," Mr. Norton's "Vita Nuova," and was afterward to be used for Mr. Cranch's "Virgil," a notable series of works indicative of American poetical scholarship. Once before only had the First Part of "Faust" been translated by an American, the Rev. Charles T. Brooks, and this honored scholar and poet was one of the first to congratulate Bayard Taylor upon the final completion of his task : —

CHARLES T. BROOKS TO BAYARD TAYLOR.

NEWPORT, *April* 3, 1871.

I take the earliest opportunity to thank you for the very acceptable gift of your *magnum opus,* — your *exactum monumentum,* — the translation of the Second Part of "Faust." The mere labor of reproducing rhyme and rhythm must have been enormous. I know something thereof by experience, having tried my hand at the introductory scene at the time I finished the First Part.

I have only been able yet to glance at your execution of the beginning and end, from which I feel confident that you have had great success in this laborious undertaking.

I shall be very glad to be convinced (if you are right) of the high claim you set up for this Part as an intellectual creation. I confess I have been accustomed to think that only the two extreme piers or abutments were finished, and then all sorts of magnificent material was thrown in to fill up the chasm. But I speak modestly about this, because, after all, I am very weak in the Faustian literature, my work upon Part First having been a simple labor of poetic love.

I incline to think that you have hit it at last in regard to that old puzzle " Zeig' mir die Frucht," etc., although I confess I have some lingering difficulties, the chief one being that upon the assumption of Faust's saying the thing in such a slighting tone, as if he would take all the poor Devil has to give, it is hard to *motive* Mephistopheles's answer : —

> " Ein solcher Auftrag *schreckt* mich nicht."

That word *schreckt* was what drove me to the supposition of a peculiar wild challenge on Faust's part in the " Eh' man sie bricht."

The English edition of the translation of the entire work was published by Strahan in July, the German edition of Part First by Brockhaus, of Leipzig, at the end of the year. The Second Part did not follow in Germany until 1876. "In concluding this labor of years," Bayard Taylor wrote, when dismissing the Second Part from his hand, "I venture to express the hope that, however I may have fallen short of reproducing the original in another, though a kindred language, I may, at least, have assisted in naturalizing the masterpiece of German literature among us, and to that extent have explained the supreme place which has been accorded to Goethe among the poets of the world. Where I have differed from the German critics and commentators, I would present the plea that the laws of construction are similar, whether one builds a cottage or a palace ; and the least of authors, to whom metrical expression is a necessity, may have some natural instinct of the conceptions of the highest."

The colloquial knowledge of German which the translator possessed was of avail, since it enabled him to think in the language ; but the modest and reserved expression in the last sentence of the above passage discloses the real power which enabled him to cope with the profoundest difficulty in translating " Faust." He was a poet. It may be said, indeed, that his poetic power lay at the foundation of all his linguistic attainments. He apprehended foreign speech and foreign life in all its forms through that poetic faculty which is of the nature of intuition. Not that labor was wanting, but labor served to bind and complete what had been caught at and appropriated by the appreciative and penetrative power of a poetic mind. Moreover, in the growth of his own nature, Bayard Taylor had come to think and create in sympathy with Goethe. No doubt the study which was given to " Faust " had much to do with the subsequent development of Bayard Taylor's genius, but it did not lay the foundation of that development; it came when from other causes his mind was ripe for Goethe's thought. When, therefore, he was absorbed in the work of translation, he was very far removed from a mechanical task, however delicate. On the contrary he was in a creative mood, constructing part by part a great poem which lay alongside of " Faust," singularly harmonious with the original, as all critics granted, because the harmony consisted in the very subtle likeness of the movement of his mind with that of Goethe's.

It was not the least of the endowments which qualified him for his task that he had a remarkable memory. Occasional hints of this have already been given, and the testimony of his friends, who never ceased to wonder at the exhibitions given by his memory, is very striking. " He could quote by the hour," says Mr. Boyesen, "English, German, Italian, and even Swedish poetry, and apparently have inexhaustible treasures still in reserve. I remember on one occasion we were debating the merits of the various translations of Tegnér's 'Frithiof's Saga,' and I was maintaining that after Longfellow's exquisite rendering of 'The Temptation,' and a few other separate poems, no poetaster who chose to translate the whole work had any right to try his unskilled hand on these, but ought simply to incorporate Mr. Longfellow's renderings ; of course, with proper acknowledgment of their source. 'And still,' I added, 'there is in single passages of the original a flavor so subtle that even so sensitive an artist as Longfellow fails to catch it. It is so fleeting that it utterly refuses to be translated into another tongue,' and I began to quote,—

Straxt är gamle kungen vaken. 'Mycket var den sömn mig värd,
Ljufligt sofver man i skuggan, skyddad af den tappres svärd.

Here my memory failed me, and Mr. Taylor promptly continued, —

Dock, hvar är ditt svärd, o främling ? blixten's broder, hvar är
    han ?
Hvem har skilt Er, I som aldrig skulle skiljas från hvarann ? '

and so on for five or six verses.

" I have frequently heard Mr. Taylor complain that his memory was an inconvenience to him. He would read by chance some absurd or absolutely colorless verse, and it would continue to haunt him for days. One single reading sometimes sufficed to fix a poem indelibly in his mind. The First Part of 'Faust' I verily believe he could repeat from beginning to end ; at all events, I never happened to allude to any passage which he could not recite at a moment's notice. Even the Second Part, with its evasive and impalpable meanings, he had partly committed to memory ; or rather it had, without any effort of his own, committed itself to his memory." [1]

[1] *Lippincott's Magazine*, August, 1879.

This power was of great value to him in his work of translation, since it released his mind from the necessity of a fatiguing hunt after particulars, and enabled him to hold steadily before his imagination the large thought of the verse, to make comparisons with instantaneous readiness, and to move freely and unembarrassed through his material.

Before returning to Cedarcroft, Bayard Taylor had arranged with Messrs. Scribner, Armstrong & Co. to edit for them a series of volumes, entitled a "Library of Travel." He began at once the preparation of the first, on Arabia, and was busy with this, with contributions to the "Atlantic" and the "Tribune," and with the preparation of a second course of lectures on German literature for Cornell, until the end of May, when with his wife he went to Ithaca to deliver his lectures. This work, necessary as a means of livelihood, necessary also as an outlet for his untiring mental activity, was yet in a measure a relief after the strain laid upon him by his Faust work, and while engaged upon it he was in a more or less reflective mood, taking note both of his own intellectual experience and of the movement in literature about him.

TO JERVIS McENTEE.

CEDARCROFT, *Saturday, April* 29, 1871.

I have an ache, or a neuralgia, or some other "cussed" thing in the back of my head, which prevents me from working at my compilation of "Travels in Arabia" for Scribner & Co., a piece of labor which I have undertaken for money, and for money alone. Let that be a comfort to you, — if it is any comfort to know that others are in the same boat with you, and unable to *skull*. But I am capable of answering your welcome letter, for it is no harder to think to a friend than to talk to him ; and yours, albeit grave, not to say desponding, suggests many things.

It is true, we have fallen on evil times. I think it will be ten years before either literature or art will be as popular and profitable as they were ten years ago. With all the splendid patriotism which the war called forth, we cannot escape its consequences. The people have become materialized, their culture is temporarily disturbed because not well grounded, the very best of the younger generation are lost, the rage for mere diversion and intellectual excitement taints the public taste, — and so nothing is left to us artists but to possess our souls in patience until the better time comes. My chief comfort is the belief that we are now just about passing the climax of discouragement, and any change will be for the better. I think it prudent, however, to revise and recast my plan of life, to cut loose from all extra expenditures, adopt some simpler and more convenient form of living, and secure myself (if I can) against the necessity of writing for bread. While the necessity lasts, I must submit ; but I am somewhat weary, after so many years of hard work, and crave the power of saving my strength and enthusiasm for the literary plans which are really a part of my life. I am glad that you have come to the same conclusion, so far as a secluded life is concerned. That might answer in England, or in some parts of Germany, but seclusion in our country means nothing but moral and intellectual stagnation. The creative natures are few and far apart, except in New York and Boston, and they need all the development, all the comfort, all the encouragement which comes of association. There is not even an appreciative class in the country, and the lack of this will pull down an artist whenever he tries to rise. I am also like you in regard to making new friends : I am growing fastidious, because I find fewer persons who combine character and communicative intelligence than formerly. I am not satisfied with the half - refined, over - demonstrative, "gushing" class, who seemed so agreeable when I was younger. At the same time I welcome every revelation of the deeper and truer nature of genuine men. When you speak of "weakness" in betraying feeling, you mean, or should have said, *strength*. Our stiff, hard, damnable Anglo-Saxon habit of heart is a *weakness*, and the worst kind. A man really among us shows courage in expressing what he feels, and one who does not respect him the more for it is not worthy to be his friend. I believe in a frank, hearty, trustful communication of one nature to another, even in reciprocal revelations of real weakness, as the very crown and blessing of friendship. I never think of any of my few dear friends (of whom you are always one, old fellow!) without a sense of longing, a warm desire for the real, bodily presence. We make fewer friends, it is true, as we grow older, but the few become more to us year by year. I don't find that I shut my nature against any new approach; but I have not the same easy faith in strangers, and require a longer experience, except in those rare cases where you feel instantly the harmony of another nature, and are sure of each other the first moment. Now, in regard to my work, I have almost succeeded in being satisfied with the appreciation of the few; at the same time, as Longfellow said to me the other day, the recognition of what one has done, or tried to do, is like a good draught to a fire. You don't lack the appreciation of the best; your reputation has grown, not fallen off, and I think the present apparent neglect is a sign of it. For my part, I know that I am doing better things now than ever before; I know also that my market value is not half what it was five years ago; yet I devoutly believe that I shall outlive many of the apparently brilliant successes which are now blazing around us. Nothing endures but genuine work: of that you may be sure.

Now, my dear McEntee, I propose that we shall hold together in patience, bind each other's wounds, support each other's stumbling faith, and keep on doing our best. The joy and the reward is in the work itself after all. I wish you were here this quiet Saturday evening. The woods are all in leaf; tulips and lilacs in blossom, all the country green as ever May was, and every glimpse out of the window is an ecstacy. But this is not enough; I'd give it all, to be nearer my real life. This has come to be only a magnificent exile.

TO PAUL H. HAYNE.

KENNETT SQUARE, PA., *May* 11, 1871.

I owe you, in the first place, "ever so many" (as the English girls say) apologies for my long delay in answering your letter. When it came I was just on the point of starting for Boston; then I had to transfer my little household from New York to this place; then I waited to get a copy of Part II., so as to send both at once; then I was ill for a few days, and got behindhand with a piece of literary work (of the "hack" order, for money which I needed), — in short, this is enough, although I could easily make a longer catalogue. The fact is, my labors in "Faust" almost broke me down completely, yet I could take very little rest afterwards, and to-day, after returning from a business trip to New York, is my first sensation of release from the long strain upon mind and body.

I have now to prepare a course of lectures on Mediæval German Literature for Cornell University, and then I shall be free, at least from hard work, for the rest of the year. I think I deserve a little rest, although the law of my life seems to be labor for the sake of growth. No matter what I write, I am dissatisfied with it in three months after it is published, and look forward to some new work. But I would not have it otherwise. I am only happy when I feel that I am gaining, no matter how little, upon my past.

Shortly after his return from Cornell, Bayard Taylor took an excursion to the eastern shore of Maryland, the results of which appeared in a paper in "Harper's Monthly," "Down the Eastern Shore." Later in the summer he accompanied a party of friends, invited by Mr. Jay Cooke, to the Red River of the North, and published in the "Tribune" letters descriptive of the excursion.

TO MISS LAURA C. REDDEN.

CEDARCROFT, *Friday, June 23, 1871.*

. . . I am delighted that my first volume gave you so much pleasure. As it was wholly and purely a labor of love, I like to see it heartily accepted by other minds. The Archangelic Chorus was the first thing I translated. I decided that if I could succeed in that I could succeed in all, if not, not. To me it is one of the most wonderful things in literature ; and you truly feel its grand, planetary, cosmic harmony. But not quite so fully as in the original ! This work, as I think I must have said to you before, is a bridge between my dead literary Past and my (as I pray) living literary Future. It is therefore a great joy to me to see that it bids fair to stand firm. My chief delight is the enthusiastic words which begin to come to me from Germany. The First Part will be republished in Leipzig this month, and I have had an intimation (this is strictly *entre nous*) that Bismarck will be glad to receive a copy from me. . . .

The reception of "Faust" in Germany was very warm, and special recognition was given to the Notes which accompanied the work. The volumes sent by Bayard Taylor passed through the hands, in some cases, of Mr. George Bancroft, who was then Minister of the United States at Berlin. Mr. Bancroft wrote on his own account: "Your letter reached me on Tuesday last; the books on Friday. I go to bed usually as near ten as I can that I may rise at five; your volumes kept me up till nearly two in the morning of Saturday; the like of which has not happened to me in five years. . . . The Second Part of 'Faust' I studied seriously a year or two ago, using the commentary of Carrière. Your translation and notes would have saved me a world of trouble. You impart clearness to what is obscure, and give a thread of continuity to what might seem fantastic and unorganized. Here is seen the energy of Goethe's political feelings; his contempt for the follies and crimes of misgovernment of German princes was the sincere expression of the thoughts which he carried along with him all his life; only their vices were so deeply seated that he to the last appears to me to have despaired of German union." Madame von Holtzendorff, of Gotha, summed up the excellency of the work, and the reason of its excellence, when she wrote: "You not merely have reproduced faithfully word and form, — which I in no way esteem lightly, — but you have so entered into the spirit of the wonderful poem and our language, and made yourself one with it, that your translation is the perfect equal of the original. And this is what seems

to me worthy of the highest gratitude. We Germans
have reason to be proud that a man like you has as-
similated to himself our nature, our mode of thinking
and feeling, to such a degree as to understand us perfectly."

TO JERVIS M^CENTEE.

KENNETT SQUARE, PA., *August* 24, 1871.

I am the sinner this time, but if you have seen the "Tribune,"
you will know that I have been away in Manitoba, in the Hud-
son Bay Territory, on a five weeks' trip, with twenty editors and
correspondents. I had previously made a flying excursion down
the eastern shore of Maryland, out of which I made an article
for "Harper's Monthly;" since then I have written a paper on
Humboldt for "Harper's Weekly," and a "pome" for the
"Atlantic" (that is, if it is accepted!), so you may imagine
how busy I have been. I thought of you during our trip, and
wished you had been with us. . . . The company was a jolly
one, from beginning to end, or I could never have traveled
those five thousand miles, including four hundred of staging,
ten days camping out, and no end of salt pork, muddy water,
dam — *condemnable* coffee, mosquitoes, black dust, gad-flies, and
bugs !

I came home very brown, but much stronger, except my
stomach, which was so fatigued that it is only now recovering a
healthy tone. My father and mother arrived from Europe while
I was away. I find them very well and jolly, and full of stories
of Rome, Florence, Lausanne, and Gotha. By the bye, I see
that Yewell is coming, or has come, home. Let me know where
he is, or will be; I want to write to him as soon as he arrives.

Through M.'s meeting with G. on the boat, I know that you
must now be somewhere among the Catskills, also that you have
sold another picture or two, which latter news is music to my
ears. I wish I could sell one thousand dollars' worth of "Faust,"
but alas ! I shall probably not get a cent from the large and luxurious edition. I have copies of the London and Leipzig editions, both of which are very handsome. Yesterday came a
most friendly letter from Bancroft, who writes to me that he has
sent a copy to Bismarck. Bancroft says that he sat up nearly
all night to read it. I can see, by various slight indications, how

much the work has done for me in a literary sense, and am therefore satisfied. If we could do with less money (why can't we?)
it would be a blessing; but I must be happy in having a much
lighter burden now than I had last year. I try to think that too
much good luck is not healthy, and I'm better off with a very
moderate portion, but now and then the flesh rebels against the
spirit. I am, naturally, a most luxurious devil; I dream of velvet, gold, and ivory, well knowing that reps and stone-ware are
just as good. After all, any simple thing, *good*, is always a luxury, as a glass of Milwaukee lager when you are thirsty; an
old-fashioned, high-backed splint chair; a bath in a mill-pond;
a corn-husk mattress, under a roof, when it rains; two good
cigars, with a friend attached to the other one !

I have ten days of hard hack-work, and then a tolerably easy
Fall before me. I have made an arrangement to give only sixteen lectures for two thousand dollars about the end of October,
and hope to reach New York and settle for the winter by the 1st
of December. We are still uncertain about the future. It does
not seem to be a good time to sell real estate, and I can't afford
to force a sale and make a sacrifice. Rather will I rent the
property next spring. We must do one thing or the other, in
order to go to Europe. But something may turn up any day.
If I can only keep my physical vigor, which I have partly recovered since last spring, I shall unravel and smooth out the
threads of our fate. Well, this must suffice for to-day. Do
write to me soon, and my next shall be a great deal more prompt.
Tell me all the news of everybody, for I've not been in New
York since the riot, when I saw the blackguards clubbed with
the greatest delight.

TO WHITELAW REID.

KENNETT SQUARE, PA., *September* 18, 1871.

For the last week or two I have been trying an experiment
which I have long had in view, in regard to those imitations. I
have written two or three chapters, something like the " Noctes
Ambrosianæ " in form, as the proceedings of a club of wild
young *littérateurs* in the back room of a New York lager-beer
cellar, taken down in short-hand by a concealed reporter. There
is conversation, much free-and-easy criticism of dead and living
authors, discussion of all sorts of current literary topics, and
occasional fun and banter, — all as a proper setting for the imi-

tations. The thing takes hold of my fancy, and constantly suggests new features. I have already a list of forty authors, and about a dozen copies, to be included, and the matter, therefore, will be a tolerable volume.

Now you wanted the imitations as they were, — which won't answer. If I carry out my present scheme they take a different character, and become less appropriate to the columns of a daily paper. They are not only specially adapted to a literary magazine, but would be more likely, when so published, to be a literary " success." Not that it would make a great deal of difference either way ; but if there should be fun enough in the work to make a volume of it temporarily popular, I think the chances would be better if it first appeared in the " Atlantic " say, rather than the " Tribune." Now, what do you think ? . . . Pray you, look at the matter in all these lights, and give me the benefit of your judgment. Don't consider the " Tribune's " interest only, but mine also. I 'm not at all sure that Howells would publish the chapters. I would if I were in his place, and pay a round sum for them. My wife says the plan so far is very successful. I have written new imitations, and improved the old ones, and, moreover, mean to crowd a good deal of serious matter, under the guise of fun, into the conversations. They would run for six months, which would enable the volume to be published in May for summer reading.

I shall say nothing until I hear from you. If you seriously think it will be better for the articles, and the later publication, to have them in the " Tribune," I 'll — well, I 'll do my best to think so, too. It does not seem so to me now.

Please deliberate soon, and write. I thought to have heard from you before, but I suppose the breaking of the Ring claims all your energies.

The imitations referred to in this letter finally took the form of the " Diversions of the Echo Club," published serially in the " Atlantic Monthly," and afterward in a book. The reader will recall the frolic of Bayard Taylor's earlier life in New York, when with Mr. Stoddard, Mr. Aldrich, Mr. O'Brien, and occasionally with others, the young poets entertained themselves with parodies upon each other, upon classic authors, and upon the popular favorites of England and America. Since then, the clever verses had sometimes leaked out or had been printed by others of the number. Bayard Taylor now conceived the notion of giving a certain body to the fun. He was half vexed, half entertained at the sudden rise in America of the dialect school of poetry. It suggested trains of thought which could be followed in a playful yet sincere manner, and he fancied that he could make his parodies not only bits of fun, but sly criticisms as well. Throwing aside all the previous parodies except a few of his own, he turned to and wrote thirty or forty skits in rapid succession, — an extraordinarily varied lot, and after some changes made upon consultation with friends published the jest in the "Atlantic." It was intended to keep the authorship a secret, but his name was pretty authoritatively mentioned before the series had entirely appeared. As might be expected his good-natured raillery cost him if not friendships, yet some moments of friendship.

TO WHITELAW REID.

KENNETT SQUARE, PA., *October* 14, 1871.

. . . Not hearing from you I wrote to Howells the other day about the imitations. I am working them into a literary dialogue, serious at bottom, though with an external rollicking tone. But the matter is hardly light enough for a daily paper, and I think the result will be that Howells and Osgood will make a "feature" of it for the "Atlantic," and pay me about twice what the "Tribune" would, say about —— for four monthly articles. I am rejecting many of the old, and writing new ones. If the plan succeeds it will make a volume which will have a good chance of popularity. I think when you see the framework you will agree with me that this is the best thing to do with the material. . . .

Just returned from the West to-day. My first thought is : Has there yet been a dividend, and how much ? I need to know just as soon as possible in order to begin arrangements for going to New York for the winter. Please say simply *yes* or *no* by return mail, and greatly oblige me.

I had, on the whole, a good time in the West. My lecture on " Schiller " was really popular, to my own surprise. Your " Cincinnati Gazette " treated me handsomely, or, at least, a Mr. Maxwell did, whom I met. Everybody West, and in the cars, was rejoicing over the redemption of New York. . . . There are lots of things I 'd like to mention, but no time to-night. I want to go on, with wife and child, in a fortnight. . . .

It was during this fall that Mr. Longfellow published his " Divine Tragedy." Bayard Taylor took a very strong interest in the work, especially in view of the comprehensive plan of " Christus " which the author had disclosed to him. Mr. Ripley introduced the work in a long summary and analysis in the " Tribune." That was his function as literary editor. But Bayard Taylor was dissatisfied with the result, the more that he was in possession of Mr. Longfellow's scheme, which enabled him to present the subject from a new point of view. Accordingly he obtained permission from the poet to use his knowledge, and from Mr. Reid to embody it in a special contribution to the " Tribune."

H. W. LONGFELLOW TO BAYARD TAYLOR.

CAMBRIDGE, *November* 3, 1871.

I have to-day received your letter of Sunday, and hasten to thank you for your generous judgment of my new book. It is, I assure you, extremely gratifying to me, and makes me feel that I have not wholly failed in treating a rather difficult subject.

By to-day's post I send you the Interludes and Finale, connecting and completing the whole work, presuming that Osgood told you something of my plan, and that this new book is only the first part of a work, of which the " Golden Legend " and the " New England Tragedies " are the second and third ; and which, when the three parts are published together, is to be entitled " Christus." This is a very old design of mine, formed before the " Legend " was written.

The " Introitus " belongs to the book as a whole, and its proper pendant or correlative is not the Epilogue of this first part, but the Finale, which I send you to-day. This will explain the seeming want of proportion and balance which you have noted.

BAYARD TAYLOR TO WHITELAW REID.

CEDARCROFT, *Monday night, November* 27, 1871.

Yours of Friday is just received. With it came one from Osgood, from which I quote : —

" Mr. R.'s review is good, but the publishers and author would have been vastly more gratified if you could have had the opportunity of saying in print what you said to Longfellow in your admirable letter."

This indicates just my own view in regard to R.'s article. It is thoroughly kind, sympathetic, and graceful ; but it is not a review of the " Divine Tragedy." Its general tone is admirable, but there is not one salient point in it, — nothing that tells you how Longfellow has treated the subject ; no comparison of his attempt with others ; no statements of the difficulties to be overcome ; no setting forth of the special excellences of the work, the points wherein his design is less successful ; nor, indeed, what design he had in view. The article expresses a mild, indolent, sympathetic mood, not a clear, well-defined judgment. I don't know that I can come any nearer to a full expression of my opinion. You will no doubt understand just what I mean.

I have had a very pleasant letter from Longfellow, with further proofs of poetical interludes connecting the " Divine Tragedy " with — something else ; but I have no authority to print anything.

Remember that I write the above because you ask it, and I don't want this repeated to any one. R. has unusual ability, and his reviews of theological and scientific works are masterpieces of clear statement ; in judgment he is timid. When he comes to *Belles Lettres* he seems more timid than usual, and his criticisms swerve a little to one side or the other of a non-committal line. Thus he never fully satisfies and never fully offends, but is safe more frequently than most writers could be. I like him heartily personally, and I respect his scholarship and literary ability ; still I don't think he exercises the power which a critic should in correcting the literary aberrations of this confused and bewildering generation in which we live, — neither keenly pricking faults nor sturdily applauding special forms of virtue.

H. W. LONGFELLOW TO BAYARD TAYLOR.

CAMBRIDGE, *December* 12, 1871.

I have just got your letter, and hasten to say that I see no possible objection to what you propose. On the contrary, I see great furtherance in it. I am delighted that you take such friendly interest in my work. Osgood, in his advertisement to-day, announces the book as "the first part of a poem, of which the 'Golden Legend' and the 'New England Tragedies' form the second and third parts." The publication of a few links of the connecting chain can do no harm, and may do good in helping to give an intelligible idea of the whole.

Bayard Taylor, meanwhile, had removed with his family to New York for the winter.

TO WHITELAW REID.

12 UNIVERSITY PLACE, *Wednesday*, 3 *p. m.*, *December* 13, 1871.

Longfellow is evidently very much pleased with the proposition, and gives me full liberty to use the new material. I begin at once, and shall finish the article to-morrow. Do you want to publish it immediately ? If so, I can take or send it down to-morrow (Thursday) afternoon. I go to Boston on Friday. The article will make, I guess, two and a half columns, as I give quotations from the unpublished Interludes. I think it will be a good thing for the "Tribune." If you have anything further to say, send a note to-morrow morning. I should have gone down this afternoon, but the weather is bad and I'd rather write.

Thursday morning.

I write (since you will get this to-night) to suggest that there might well be an editorial reference to the review, — not hinting, of course, about our priority of notice, but as an interesting event in our literary history. Since Milton's " Paradise Regained" and Klopstock's "Messiah" the theme has not been handled by any competent poet ; so Longfellow's work is both a daring venture and (probably) a success all the higher for the failure of others.

Perhaps you have already done something of the kind, but if not, give it thirty seconds of consideration.

TO GEORGE H. BOKER.

12 UNIVERSITY PLACE, NEW YORK, *December* 27, 1871.

Surely you over-praise my poetic farewell ;[1] but I shall not protest. I think the idea of it was graceful and appropriate, and I don't need to tell you how deeply and frankly it was felt ; yet I think it might have been better in a simply artistic sense. However, I managed to say what I desired, so far as substance was concerned, — to give the public my farewell (and that of all the younger tribe) to you, as a poet, yet to keep the strongest and tenderest expression for you alone. How glad I am that I succeeded ! For I wrote the stanzas, as I know you feel, with something in my throat and my eyes ; and it was not easy to read them with a steady voice. I knew that the audience would chiefly note the playful stanzas, and I hoped that you would recognize what they were intended to hide.

[1] On the occasion of Mr. Boker's departure for Constantinople as Minister of the United States.

CHAPTER XXIV.

THE MASQUE OF THE GODS.

1872.

> But out of life arises song,
>   Clear, vital, strong, —
> The speech men pray for when they pine,
>   The speech divine.
>
>   *My Prologue.*

> Now, if the tree I planted for mine must shadow another's,
> If the uncounted tender memories, sown with the seasons,
> Filling the webs of ivy, the grove, the terrace of roses,
> Clothing the lawn with unwithering green, the orchard with blossoms,
> Singing a finer song to the exquisite motion of waters,
> Breathing profounder calm from the dark Dodonian oak-trees,
> Now must be lost, till, haply, the hearts of others renew them, —
> Yet we have had and enjoyed, we have and enjoy them forever.
>
>   *L'Envoi* (to " Home Pastorals ").

THE winter life in New York, besides its social attraction, was constantly opening to Bayard Taylor
opportunities for literary work.   His wide experience
of travel, his training in different forms of composition, and his readiness which was partly a gift, partly
the result of newspaper activity, made him exceptionally well qualified to undertake schemes proposed by
publishers.   " The time goes very fast," he wrote to
his mother in the first days of 1872 ; " but we are all
well and in good spirits.   I can work very well here.
In fact, if we were living here, I should have no
trouble in earning four or five thousand dollars a year
more than now."   The contrast to life at Cedarcroft
was so strong on this side that he was more than ever

determined to break away from the entanglements of that place. He saw clearly that if he were once rid of it, he could maintain himself with ease and have freedom and strength for the work which concerned him most. So he put his estate into the hands of an agent, with instructions to sell if possible; if not, to lease it, and for himself determined to carry out the plan which he had proposed of making a long stay in Germany for the purpose of gathering material for his projected scheme of a double biography of Goethe and Schiller.

"Faust" had opened other paths for his mind. The influence of a great work of art, dealing with profound themes, is never so great as when the student has himself wrought in its lines. The creative work which Bayard Taylor had expended upon the translation had deepened the growing tendency of his mind to occupy itself with the large movements of thought. The eloquence which had been so marked a characteristic of his poetry from the beginning was the sign of a nature which could pour its feeling into strong moulds. It was only the due expression of his growth, therefore, when immediately after his return from a terrible experience in Western travel, in the depth of winter, he sat down and in four days wrote, almost at white heat, his poem, "The Masque of the Gods." Into it he discharged the philosophy and faith which had been, since his sickness at Florence, underlying his thought and forming themselves into substance and shape.

TO J. R. OSGOOD.

12 UNIVERSITY PLACE, NEW YORK, *February* 20, 1872.

Shall you come on this week? I meant to wait, but I have a little project which I must tell you at once. I have written a poem of between six hundred and seven hundred lines, called " The Masque of the Gods." It is in dramatic form. Except my wife, no one has seen it or will see it before publication, but I must bring it out at once, in a little volume, like Lowell's " Cathedral." What do you say to this ? I am determined to publish without regard to popularity or profit. A small sale would pay the expenses, but I should think you might depend on fifteen hundred, — possibly more. I want to get it out by the 20th of March.

If you come soon, come and see me and *it ;* if not, please write at once. Meantime, tell no one of the matter.

12 UNIVERSITY PLACE, NEW YORK, *February* 23, 1872.

. . . Here is the MS. of my " Masque." I think you will agree with me that it ought to be published alone, and there is no reason for delaying publication. As little or no poetry is announced for this spring, it may get a little more attention than under other circumstances. It may be assailed, but that will [do] no harm.

As for copyright, I should prefer that you would charge me with the cost of the plates (which would then be mine), and pay me fifteen per cent. on the sales. I say " charge," because the cost of plates, at least, will be returned in a few days, and I need not, in this case, send the money or have a separate bill made out. Your arrangement of the matter will save trouble to both of us.

I leave all the details of publication — time, manner of announcement, etc. — to your judgment. I should think, however, that the 15th of March would be a favorable time — or earlier, if possible.

I shall be curious to know in what way the MS. strikes your mind.

12 UNIVERSITY PLACE, *February* 29, 1872.

Heart and eyes are delighted. The proofs are simply exquisite, and the " Masque " reads even better than the MS., which I was afraid it would n't. I 'll keep the sheets one day, to be perfectly sure that no word or letter is wrong. Then I 'll return them, and the printing may commence.

My own impression is, that the speediest publication will be best. But I leave all to your wiser judgment. Announce and launch as you think best : only, if you send advance sheets, it were prudent to send to several papers at once. My connection with the " Tribune " renders it impolitic to favor that paper specially in this case.

In writing about the " Masque," Mr. Osgood had also called the author's attention to a passage in the " Diversions of the Echo Club," then appearing in the " Atlantic," which reads: " By the bye, I wish some one would undertake to write our literary history, beginning, say about 1800," and had suggested that here was a subject for him.

TO J. R. OSGOOD.

12 UNIVERSITY PLACE, NEW YORK, *March* 4, 1872.

Yours of yesterday is just at hand. It gives me that rare pleasure which comes to an author when his performance is not only recognized, but his plans anticipated.

I shall be most heartily rejoiced if you can do anything with my " Masque " in England. You can guess better than I where and how to propose the matter, and I leave it entirely in your hands. It seems to me that the " Masque " expresses what thousands of the best people already feel, and what (as you say) all must finally come to. I wrote it in such a heat and exaltation of spirit as I never felt before in my life, and the same feeling urges me to give it to the world immediately, and bide the consequences. There are a great many in England who will understand and, I sincerely trust, welcome it. Your opinion is the first I have received (except my wife's), and it gives me great cheer.

I mean to telegraph to you at once, to catch Wednesday's mail to England.

As to the " History of American Literature," *rem acu tetigisti!* I have been seriously thinking of it, from time to time, as something to be done in the future, when I shall have money enough to have leisure enough. It ought not to be dry and encyclopædic, — not merely dates and names, — but a live work, full of blood and breath. I am not able, and really not prepared, to undertake it now : but the plan will keep. In the mean time, if it should be undertaken by some competent hand, I shall be satisfied. We can talk over the matter more in detail when you come on.

Perhaps the "Fortnightly" or some other magazine might take the "Masque," and pay for it. Of course I should prefer to get something, but the main thing is to have it appear in England. Do this, and I shall be ever grateful.

TO T. B. ALDRICH.

NEW YORK, *March* 5, 1872.

. . . Not a soul here has read the "Masque" except my wife. Your letter (and Osgood's yesterday) gives me the first note of approval, and warms the inmost cockles of my heart. I 'll tell you what I chiefly meant. The gradual development of man's conception of God : first, a colossal reflection of human powers and passions, mixed with the dread inspired by the unknown forces of nature ; then, the idea of Law (Elohim), of Order and Beauty and Achievement (love and Apollo), and of the principles of Good and Evil (Persian), and of the Divine Love (Christ).

But over all is the ONE supreme Spirit, yet unnamed, and whom men only now begin to conceive of, — the God of whom all previous gods gave only faint and various reflections, — to whom Christ is still nearest, but who was also felt, more or less dimly, in all creeds. The poem is not *un*christian at all, but, in its relation to the conventional orthodox idea, *over*christian. I don't doubt that you have interpreted it correctly.

Thanks, dear old fellow, for your generous interest in what I do. I know your constancy and honesty, and fully depend on both, now and always, in matters like the present. I can't guess in advance what fate the poem will have, but it possessed me with the force of seven demons while I was writing it, and it must be published, and must be welcomed and abused.

The writing of a new poem so different in its plane from his previous poetry led Bayard Taylor to review what he had written and published hitherto, with a view to a possible selection, rearrangement, and reissue ; a plan, however, which was not carried out this year. He had also collected, at Mr. Putnam's request, a number of his short stories, and a volume was published at this time under the title, "Beauty and the

Beast, and Tales of Home." He had gone back with his family to Cedarcroft, and having decided, in any event, to go to Germany in the summer, found abundance to do in making arrangements for the management of his place, and in putting his affairs and house in order. He had left his friend, Mr. McEntee, in New York, just recovering from a dangerous illness.

TO JERVIS McENTEE.

KENNETT SQUARE, PA., *March* 21, 1872.

I have given you the benefit of a week's increase of strength before writing, for I am sure you must be stronger and heartier by this time. I hope this unprecedented, incessant cold is kept out of your rooms. Here the northwest wind has been blowing a hurricane for two days. This morning the mercury was down to 10°, the country is as dead wintry as it can be, and spring seems months off. Don't think of going to Rondout until the season turns, — if it ever does !

All of us, as you know by this time, have been very anxious about you ; but I am glad to say that *I* never lost my faith in your recovery, for the same reason that I believed in my own when lying so low in Italy. I have faith in your powers, and know that they have not yet borne their ripest fruit ; it is therefore necessary for you to live. I shall be much surprised if you do not have my own experience in another form, — modified, of course, by the difference of the art. Let me tell you what I think it will be. First, you will imagine yourself entirely restored some five or six months before you are actually so. You will feel the impulse and the need to paint, and what you paint will seem remarkably good at the time ; but you may discover, afterwards, that there is a languor and a lack of vigor in it. By next fall, however, you will find that your mind has become singularly free and active ; some sort of intangible inclosure which limited its action will be broken down. You will easily grasp conceptions which you have been accustomed heretofore to hold with a strong effort, and new ones will come to you without seeking for them. That will be the beginning of a new life much more satisfactory than the old. I am convinced that a serious illness, at your age, to a man who uses the finer qualities of his brain is always an intellectual as well as a physical crisis. The change is not immediately felt, for one's tastes and desires always recover first, and the power follows a long way behind. If this should be all fancy on my part, let it go for such; only, wait six or eight months before you decide.

I have been busy collecting the scattered poems of the last ten years, examining and arranging them with a view to bringing out a volume in the fall. There are enough to make two hundred pages, even after omitting some that are poor. My "Masque of the Gods" will either make or break me, but I am not the least bit nervous about it.

. . . Now, I did n't mean when I began this letter to introduce any but agreeable themes, but I am so accustomed to giving my mind a loose rein in writing to you that she (or *he* or *it*) bolted off on one side before I knew it. The fact is, the weather is so severe that we hardly stir out of doors. We hope from day to day, but in vain, for milder suns, and I am conscious of a slow resentment against the season.

M. packs up a little every day; L. says her Latin lessons to me and reads her "Family Shakespeare;" my mother mends and darns, and my father studies the "Tribune" as if it were a commentary on the Bible. So we wait in our isolation, regretting the better life we left behind in New York. You see there is nothing to write about. I am lazy, and my conscience does not reproach me for it. If you knew how very indolent I am by nature you would have more faith in the something-or-other which makes me work. I am not credited with much of a moral sense, yet I think my industry, under the circumstances, is almost a moral quality, for it has been very difficult to acquire. I inherit laziness from every generation of my father's line, and there is hardly a day of my life when I am not obliged to take myself by the collar and say, "Sit down to work, you idle devil!"

Don't think of answering this. Perhaps G. will write just one line to say how you are. I 'll write again soon.

TO PAUL H. HAYNE.

KENNETT SQUARE, PA., *March* 25, 1872.

Your welcome volume only reached me a fortnight ago when I was on the eve of leaving New York, where we have been during the winter. I take the first chance now of acknowledging the receipt, and thanking you for kindly remembering me in this way.

I think this much the best volume you have published. The poems show a finer finish, a greater symmetry, both of form and idea, than your earlier ones. I am very glad to see this, because it confirms my impression that you recognize the true nature of the poetic art, which, indeed, is that of all art—proportion. Some of our authors, who are quite popular,—in the sense of sale, at least,—seem to have no comprehension of this truth. I saw and valued the same quality in poor Timrod. It was evident in your former volumes, but they show less patient elaboration than this last. I speak freely on this point, because it is only within the last four or five years that I have been able to perceive my own shortcomings in poetry, and have set myself seriously to work to remedy them.

I have seen two or three very favorable reviews of your poems already, and am sure that all honest critics must pronounce the same judgment.

If you see the "Atlantic," you may find some amusement in some papers of mine published anonymously,—the "Diversions of the Echo Club." They were written rather as a pastime, but I have tried to give a few earnest hints in regard to certain aspects of our popular literature just at this time.

I have also a new poem in the press,—"The Masque of the Gods,"—a copy of which I shall be able to send you in a fortnight. It is something "new and strange," and may make a "sea-change" with me, so far as the critics are concerned. I anticipate as much blame as praise, and am most comfortably indifferent; but the opinions of poets, and poets only, have a true value.

TO MRS. JERVIS M\u1d9cENTEE.

KENNETT SQUARE, PA., *March 25, 1872.*

Your letter, though so welcome, was a sore disappointment to us. I hold firmly to my original faith, and Jervis must have additional patience; but we shall have spring yet, and then summer. The fact of his feeling so much better already is a good sign. I should be more anxious if such secondary attacks were not very common in pneumonia. If he is careful of his lungs for three or four months he will then be beyond the tendency to any chronic weakness in them. He may *play* with his colors as much as he pleases, but must not really *work* before next fall; also, don't let him take much exercise for a long while after he

wants to and seems strong as ever. Six months after I was up
and about in Italy I tried to do a little up-hill walking among
the Alps. At the end of an hour I gasped for breath, and came
near having some sort of convulsions. M. was quite fresh when
I felt half dead. It is humiliating to us big animals, but it can't
be helped. Really, the season is almost unendurable. On Saturday I felt the *grippe* of a fierce influenza in head and bones. I
took eight grains of quinine and a hot Scotch whiskey punch on
going to bed, and knocked the ugly thing on the head, so that it
has shown no signs since. (But don't tell your homœopathic doctors about the quinine !) . . . We had our first *cuke* to-day at dinner, and a few slices made me feel as fresh as Nebuchadnezzar.
(Do you know, the idea of going out to grass was always pleasant to me !) My mother has just returned home, having bought a
small cook-stove at auction for seven dollars, and is supremely
happy; so we manage to extract some sort of comfort out of this
dark, gusty day, with a strong south wind and congested sky. In
fact, the firmament needs a good rainy sweat, and then it will feel
better. Nature has her troubles and disorders as well as the rest
of us ; but I hope Jervis does n't catch or reflect any of her condition to-day. There will be rain to-night, I hope, to soften the
deep, persistent frost. Don't you know that slow moaning and
crying of the wind, as if something ached ? I hear it all the
time as I write. When it sounds that way I can't work. I long
for friends ; I think of the blue Mediterranean ; I want to be an
angel, and with the angels stand, — or anything else to keep me
from sympathizing with all out-of-doors, and being as miserable
as it seems to be. So I write immediately, though I have really
so little to say. All I could say to you two would be only the
most commonplace didactics, — which I won't say, there ! You
know that our thoughts and closest sympathies are with you, not
only while this trial lasts, but always ; and there 's some stubborn
old **Anglo**-Saxon element in me which keeps me from being· demonstrative of my feelings, even when I wish to be so. (Jervis
knows exactly what I mean.) However, I guess a few friends
know that the thing is there, and that 's enough. Now, if I have
kept myself from listening to all that outside whimpering of Nature, and diverted the minds of you two for a few minutes by
this reckless chatter, it is about all I set out to do.

KENNETT SQUARE, PA., *March* 25, 1872.

I send to-day, per Adams's Express, the collection of my
poems since 1862, omitting all that seemed to me imperfect, or
without some distinct poetical character. You will see that I
have taken the "Pastorals" to give title and character to the
volume : with the addition of the "Proem" and "Envoi," they
really make one poem. The "Ballads," and many of the other
poems will be new to you, and I think you will find that this volume contains a very different kind of poetry from that in "The
Poet's Journal," the collection published in 1862. Indeed, the
difference is so marked, and (as it seems to me) so unusual, that
I desire more than ever to have this volume published separately. If the material were added to the blue-and-gold simply
to make a completed edition of all my poetry, the change would
receive little notice. I think T. B. A. would take the same view
of the material.

I am satisfied that it would be best not to reprint the "Echo
Club" now. I cannot help giving some slight offense here and
there, and this would be aggravated, in the opinion of the *of-
fendees* (not *effendis!*), if the articles were reproduced in a volume. Besides, they have an ephemeral character. . . . Don't
forget to send me about twenty-five copies of the "Masque" as
soon as bound. I hope you 'll have it at the Trade Sale, and
also publish punctually on the 6th. Please let me know what
Trübner writes : you ought to hear from him in a week. The
last numbers of "Frazer's" and the "Westminster" satisfy me
that a large class of readers in England is ready for such a
poem, and I am very anxious to hear that it will be published.

TO MR. AND MRS. JERVIS McENTEE.

KENNETT SQUARE, PA., *March* 28, 1872.

The last letter was so consoling to us that I have waited
another day to see if we shall retain this heavenly weather.
It is so warm and sweet that I 'm sure you must feel it through
the walls of the Studio Building. There have now been two
days of it, with a third (from the omens) secured in advance.
We already see changes in maples and willows and grass, and
this morning I found the first scented white violet out, under a
protecting box-border.

. . . I forgot to answer your question about the house. No, it is not rented, and I am beginning to fear it will not be. I have no luck in money matters ; I never hit the fortunate season in any such dealings. What I possess is the result of hard, incessant work. Many another would have been luxuriously rich by this time from the use of my personal earnings. The agent in Philadelphia says there ought to be no difficulty in finding a summer occupant ; but we ought to hear of it now. However, I'll not give up the hope for another fortnight. People are hardly thinking of summer yet.

I have only two bits of news. We have just consumed an immense fresh cauliflower, sent from San Francisco by a friend. Secondly (*entre nous*) I have written a Node for the Shakespeare statue celebration, April 23d, to be used in case nothing better can be procured. I'm hardly satisfied with my work, and have only done it with the above proviso. Lowell would be the proper man.

. . . We drove to the village this afternoon, through fearful mud, and the laziness of spring is now in all my bones. I have an idea that a storm is brewing about a thousand miles off ; the depression which precedes it is upon me. Or is it a remnant of the squelched influenza ? Perhaps you know that peculiar feeling, which I once saw accurately described in an old newspaper, " The nerves fall into the pizarintum, the chest becomes morberous, the diaphragm is catichose, and the head goes *tizarizen ! tizarizen !* " I hear the locomotive whistle ; it is twenty minutes past nine. This is quite late for us : we are generally in bed by this time ; but we get up when we see the broad yellow splash of sunrise on the wall. I have been sorting letters all day, and find lots signed " J. McE." Some day, when I write my " Yesterdays with Artists," I shall publish them. It gives one a singular feeling to rake up the past so completely ; I can see very plainly that I must have been more shallow and sensitive and conceited ten years ago than I had any idea of at the time. There is evidence in the correspondence (not with Jervis) that I let myself be annoyed with all sorts of trifles, which I should laugh at now. The other day I looked into a volume of my travels, published in 1859. Ye Gods ! what a flippant style ! I assure you some things made me wince, with a feeling almost like physical pain.

M. has just come down-stairs to see whether I am going to

stay up abnormally late, or, perhaps, fearing that a burglar may break in upon me, sitting here alone in the library. The wood-fire on the hearth has gone out, and I must even close, with her love and mine. . . .

KENNETT SQUARE, PA., *March* 30, 1872.

I suggested to Osgood, in sending him the material of a new volume of poems, that perhaps you might be able to look over them, and give both him and me the advantage of your impressions. The main point is this : Osgood proposed to bring out a new collected edition of poems in the fall, adding these, which are the waifs of ten years (since "The Poet's Journal" in 1862). This plan he seemed to like better than that of bringing the latter out in a separate volume of about two hundred pages. But the collected edition to be complete must include "St. John" and the "Masque," which would make two volumes instead of one ; and I don't believe that I have popularity enough as a poet to carry that much weight.

Moreover, in collecting and arranging these last poems (from which several have been omitted, owing to lack of distinct character), it seems to me that they mark a "new departure" for me. "Canopus," which I have placed last, is the only one belonging to my old régime of sensuosity : all the others have a graver and stronger character. They exhale quite a different atmosphere. Whether or not better than my former things, they are *other*. Therefore, *I* should prefer to try what impression they may make, what success they may have, unconnected with my other poems. The distinctive character would hardly be noticed, if they were attached to the latter. This is a point concerning which I'd like to have your frankest opinion. You know I'm not nearly so sensitive now as I was ten years ago.

. . . We have at last some hope of spring. I found a fragrant white violet in blossom yesterday. M. is busy with a sempstress, and L. is working at Ovid ("Philemon and Baucis"). We have not yet rented the house, but are, nevertheless, preparing to sail in June. I am languid and lazy, partly from the warm air and partly the reaction from my late poetical *spell*.

KENNETT SQUARE, PA., *April* 5, 1872.

Your letter is a genuine cheer and comfort. I am very glad to find that I *can* look at my work with some degree of objective criticism. What you recommend is precisely my own wish and plan. I am afraid to anticipate much success for the "Masque," there is so little dependence on the whims of the American public. But the conception of the work is both new and important, and I am sure that its construction is tolerably up to the mark ; so it ought to have some recognition. I hope Osgood will give it a fair chance in the matter of announcement and publication. If it falls flat of course the poems could not be published now, or very soon ; but if the auspices are good, I think the opportunity should be used. In any case I am resolved that they shall appear (whenever they do) separately. The "Pastorals" are sufficient to give a special character to the collection.

TO JERVIS M^CENTEE.

KENNETT SQUARE, PA., *April* 7, 1872.

This misty, rainy Sunday evening I must write at least a few lines to say how glad we are to hear that you have at last got into your broad-bottomed chair in the studio. The news came yesterday in ——'s letter to L. after we had begun to feel quite uneasy on account of less favorable reports in a note from S. But I know that you could n't get down into the studio without strength enough to get better still ; and, moreover, the fearfully trying season must be over now. Winter, and trouble, and pain, and discouragement, and all other misfortunes, can't endure forever ; the most unpropitious fate gets tired of following men ; in short, there 's no lane but has a turning. I have half a selfish interest in trying to encourage you, because I always encourage myself in doing so. One who is naturally impatient (and I should n't wonder if both of us were !) needs to go over his lesson as regularly as the Lord's Prayer ; in fact, to make a sort of philosophical litany for himself, which one part of his nature must read and the other respond to. As thus : —

> From all sensation and clap-trap :
> *Preserve me, my soul.*
> From doing hasty work for money :
> *Preserve me, my soul.*
> From satisfaction with ephemeral notoriety, etc., etc.

Last night Osgood sent me three letters from London, about

my "Masque." One publisher says it is "too good" (!) for the public ; another fears that it "will not be acceptable ;" but Trübner, who seems very much impressed by it, says he will do his best to get it printed. Judging by these signs, a few people are going to like the poem greatly, and many will denounce it. I rather expect much abuse and misrepresentation in this country, but we shall soon see ; it will be published on Wednesday. The fate of another (new) volume of poems depends on it, so that a failure in England may be a double one for me. But I feel quite easy about the matter, willing to bide my time ; yes, really willing now, and simply because I feel, at last, that I have some qualities which are my own, not simulated or borrowed.

But enough of this egotism. We are in a misty state in-doors as well as out. The house is not rented yet, and no certain prospect of it. The old order of life here is dissolving into a blur of color, and we don't yet see the new picture. I am sure it will come after a while, — if not so bright as we hope, still I shall be satisfied while I have wife, child, health, and courage as now. If I only had more power of disposing of the little *businesses* of life ! Holmes, in his last paper, has a capital plea for poets, claiming that they are as much entitled as artists to shirk encounters with the material aspects of life. So they are ; and I 'd rather work hard for months, than have to do with a real estate agent, contracts for rent, catalogues of furniture, repairs, and all the rest of the miserable bother ! If I ever get this place off my hands I shall be afraid to own any more real estate, unless it 's something so small, simple, and conveniently situated, that it will be always marketable.

The country is dismally brown and dreary ; we are about sick for a little green on the meadows and willows. As in "Christabel," "The spring comes *slowly* up this way." Would this were a gayer epistle ; but it 's already as much as you ought to read at once. So, good-by, with love from all of us to both of you !

KENNETT SQUARE, PA., *April* 19, 1872.

I 've only time to write a line, since my "Masque" goes to you by this morning's mail. I shall be very much interested in learning what impression it makes on you and G.

Singularly enough, all our uncertainties were solved within three days. I sold a tract of sixteen acres, cut off by a road, and of no immediate use, which I had been vainly offering for sale for three years past ; I received the best April dividend from the "Tribune" we have had since '68 ; and I rented the house for three years. Now I have only to sell the carriage and horses, and then everything will be arranged.

The Lord be praised ! We can now prepare to start, with funds enough for nearly a year, all business in order, provision made for some necessary payments during our absence, and no further necessity for that headlong work and anxiety which nearly killed me the last time. Well, I have had so much and such various bad luck for three years past that I take this as a rightful balance on the credit side of the books. Nearly all the secret of life is in being able to wait, after all.

Let me know how you are feeling up in your belated spring. We have at last hyacinths and early wood-flowers.

Fortune's smile proved to be an April one, but it was pleasant to be in the sunshine if only a few days. The congratulations of his friends also began to reach him when the "Masque" was published. Again Mr. Longfellow was one of the first to give him a poet's greeting, and Mr. Whittier hastened with his congratulations.

H. W. LONGFELLOW TO BAYARD TAYLOR.

CAMBRIDGE, *April* 19, 1872.

I congratulate you on your new poem. It is a lofty theme, and you have treated it in a lofty manner, and in a style solemn and impressive. You may safely write under it, *Fecit, fecit*, the double mark of Titian.

To the common and careless reader it may at first be something of a puzzle ; but no one can read it through without seeing your noble aim and meaning. I am delighted to see you taking so high a flight, and heartily say God speed !

BAYARD TAYLOR TO JOHN G. WHITTIER.

KENNETT SQUARE, PA., *April* 24, 1872.

Your kind note of congratulation was a most unexpected delight to me. My little poem has a very ambitious air, I know, and it is a flight where, if the wings are not strong enough, one falls *all the way down*. It is a great encouragement to me that you see signs of a "sure hand" in it.

I do hope you will not find the spirit of the poem irreverent. I know that I wrote it with a feeling of the deepest reverence for the awful, wonderful Deity, whom, it seems to me, the race is only now beginning to recognize. In regard to details, of course, there will be differences of views and feelings. But I never could feel that the older Hebrew Elohim was the same conception of God as the Jehovah of the Psalms ; and I never could feel either that the æsthetic part of the Greek faith could possibly conflict with Christianity. I mention these two points because I expect to see them picked out for attack. . . .

Longfellow has also written me a delightful letter about the " Masque." I am very grateful for this immediate and generous recognition from both of you, and shall try hard to deserve it by doing better work henceforth. You have already armed me with new patience, and inspired me with new hope. In this isolation such greetings have a double value.

I may be in Boston for a day, towards the end of May. If so, I hope we shall meet ; but in any case, I want you to believe that my old affection cannot change by time or absence.

TO JERVIS McENTEE.

KENNETT SQUARE, PA., *May* 1, 1872.

I got your letter and G.'s (most welcome they were !), and noticed the invitation ;[1] but inasmuch as I had already written to you that we were to sail June 13th, and was over head and ears in the worry of settling all sorts of minor business, I did not think it necessary to write immediately ; since it would be simply impossible to be at Tufts College on the 20th of June.

We have since changed our date of sailing to June 6th, in order to go with our good old Captain Schwensen. And now, to be perfectly frank with you, although I meant the date of sailing to be sufficient reason for declining the invitation, I will say that I am firmly resolved never again to write, or to attempt to write, a poem for an occasion. I have resisted at least a hundred applications in the last fifteen years. This spring, I yielded : let me tell you the result. —— came to see me twice, just before leaving New York, about writing an Ode for the dedication of Ward's Shakespeare Statue in the Central Park, and would take no denial. Lowell had declined ; Literature must be represented by somebody, and their only hope was in me. I finally promised

[1] To deliver a poem at Tufts College Commencement.

to consider the matter, and after reaching home, here, did write an ode, of over one hundred lines, which I sent to ——. After waiting ten days for an answer, I wrote to him again : waited a second ten days, — in vain : then wrote a brief note, demanding to have the MS. sent back to me. Then it came, with the most insufferably snobbish letter from —— which you ever read. "Some things" in the Ode were "felicitous ;" I "might have done better in another metre ;" still, when I had "worked over" certain parts, and they had "received their final form," he "did not doubt but that it would be worthy of me." Did you ever hear of such damnable impertinence ?

Won't you, or G., simply reply for me to Tufts, giving the time as sufficient reason for declining? My brains are worn down to the stump : I pray only for rest and recreation, and, really, I would n't write a poem, now, at the request of the Archangel Gabriel.

. . . I 'm greatly cheered about the "Masque." Longfellow and Whittier have sent me the most delightful letters of congratulation, and the newspaper notices have been pure glorifications, so far. It pleased me specially that the poem suggested landscapes to you and a symphony to G. Here I must close ; do write again soon. We 'll be in New York in a fortnight from to-day.

IRVING HOUSE, NEW YORK, *May* 22, 1872.

We 've been here just a week, and I write a line to say that I most earnestly hope you 'll be able to come down before we sail, June 6th. I don't believe we can possibly run up to Rondout : I 've a horse to sell (a most disgusting and demoralizing business for me), and no purchaser yet, also must finish certain jobs for the publishers. After our sudden turn of good luck, the Fates are after us again : we have no end of little worries and wearinesses. I 'm hard at work, running my legs off every day, and will only be serenely happy when the steamer is twenty-five feet from the Hoboken pier, heading down the bay. You 'll see my *rejected* Ode in to-morrow's "Tribune ;" there is an *added* scorpion-sting in it, which I think you 'll discover. M. joins me in love to G. and hopes, with me, that you may both have an errand here.

TO T. B. ALDRICH.

IRVING HOUSE, NEW YORK, *May* 29, 1872.

Thanks for your kind and welcome letter. I have at last sold my horse, and the small poems, and have, by good luck, a sufficiency of means for this summer, after which "the Lord will provide."

What you say of the "Masque" is quite true. I thought of an anonymous at first, but did not believe the secret would be kept, and, anticipating attack, believed it would be more frank and courageous to give my name at once. If this public won't accept my better work, I must wait until a new one grows up. I thought ——'s notice timid and rather awkward ; it gave me the impression that he did not really like the poem, yet, out of personal regard for me, did not want to say so.

. . . I am, however, wholly satisfied with what the best men say. The letters of Longfellow, Whittier, and Holmes, your judgment, and Osgood's faith in the work are all I could ask, and I say to myself, "Patience ! the better time will come." . . . One thing I swear to you. I will go on trying to do intrinsically good things, and will not yield a hair's breadth for the sake of conciliating an ignorant public. If there is any virtue in faith, I 'll try to deserve that, if nothing more.

CHAPTER XXV.

LARS.

1872-1873.

I hold anew the earliest gift and dearest,—
The happy Song that cares not for its fame !
Ad Amicos.

BAYARD TAYLOR and his family sailed for Hamburg June 6, 1872. Before that date Mr. Greeley had been nominated for the presidency by the Liberal wing of the Republican party, and later by the Democrats. Bayard Taylor was greatly moved by the incident. His long intimacy with Mr. Greeley had made him a staunch friend, and he admired in him the qualities which marked him as an American of strong convictions. But he dreaded the impending political canvass with its inevitable personal character, and its very doubtful effect upon the fortunes of the " Tribune," in which was invested all his property which yielded any income. It was upon the dividends that he relied to meet the expenses of his life abroad; upon these and upon such incidental work as he might do.

He had not, however, carried with him a great deal of work, nor laid his plans for thus occupying himself while absent from America. He needed to prepare the remaining numbers for the series of volumes of travel which he had undertaken for Messrs. Scribner, Armstrong & Co., and he had engaged to write for Messrs. Appleton a school history of Germany; this

volume he was to have stereotyed and provided with
illustrations in Leipzig, sending the plates home to
America, where they would be printed. He could expect no return from this work for a year yet, but he
looked to it as likely to yield him a regular and considerable income.

He was thus reasonably free from care. He had
let his Cedarcroft estate for three years; he had provided for the payment of such liabilities as he had left
in America; he was in receipt of a fair income from
his investment, and could add to it with little labor;
he had even the hope, not long after going abroad, of
selling his estate, and thus unburdening himself of his
heaviest load. His freedom he meant to devote to
such rest as he was willing to take, and to the accumulation of material for his Goethe and Schiller biography. He found himself exceptionally well placed for
this. His translation of " Faust " had at once made
him a marked man in Germany. Already well and
favorably known, this work had given him special
claims for consideration. He entered on his life,
therefore, with light heart.

TO HIS MOTHER.

HAMBURG, *June* 20, 1872.

We reached here yesterday after a delightful voyage of twelve
days and a half to the mouth of the Elbe. . . . We started with
the loveliest weather, finding the ocean so smooth that everybody
went to the dinner-table. Next day was the same. . . . We had
three or four rainy days, which were unpleasant, but no gale, not
even half a gale, no rough sea, and no cold winds. On Sunday,
the tenth day, we saw the Scilly Islands about one P. M. The day
before and the morning had been rather foggy and overcast, but
after passing the islands the sky cleared and the sea was like a
lake. We reached Plymouth at ten P. M., and after an hour and
a half left for Cherbourg. Early Monday morning we were sail-

ing along the beautiful coast of Normandy, and at seven were at
Cherbourg. The Channel was smooth as glass, the sky without a
cloud, and by dusk we passed Dover. On Tuesday morning we
found the North Sea just as quiet, the weather just as lovely,
ran along the coast all day, and reached Cuxhaven about midnight. Yesterday morning we took a small steamer and came
up the Elbe, reaching Hamburg at 9.30. H. and I. were waiting for us on the pier. . . . The voyage was by far the most
agreeable we ever made. I already feel myself much fresher and
stronger. We are going to loaf for a few days, and I shall not
write again until after we reach Gotha.

TO JERVIS M^cENTEE.

GOTHA, GERMANY, *July* 3, 1872.

Here we are, at last ! I can scarcely believe that nearly a
month has gone by since you and Launt left us on the steamer's
deck at Hoboken. The intervening time has been so pleasant
that one day has only repeated the impression left by the previous one. We went out on the smoothest of oceans that day, and
carried calm weather with us. I was not the least sea-sick, for
the first time in my life, and M. only for half a day. The passengers were agreeable, the fare and attendance remarkably
good, and so the time went by so rapidly that the Scilly Islands
seemed only a short distance from the light-ship off Sandy
Hook. We touched at Plymouth on the evening of the tenth
day, found the Channel a sheet of glass, Normandy and Cherbourg flooded with sunshine, the Strait of Dover in a most benevolent and Christian mood, and the dreaded North Sea an imitation of the Mediterranean. At Hamburg my brother and sister-
in-law were waiting for us on the quay. We landed at their
door, and sat down to their table with much the same feeling as
if we had gone from New York to dine in Brooklyn.

Two more weeks have gone since then, and now I am quietly
settled here in my father-in-law's house, with my books, papers,
and amateur sketching-traps in his old library at the foot of the
astronomical tower. I breathe an atmosphere of old vellum
binding, queer instruments, dust, and astrological mysteries, very
much like Faust in the opening scene. Under me is a garden
of gooseberries, then the trees of the park, a bit of the old ducal
castle, and a good, broad stretch of sky. Here I mean to write,
dabble in colors, smoke, and " invite my soul " to whatever sort of

banquet she may prefer. I tell you, old fellow, it does one great good to get away, now and then, from the grooves in which one's life must run. Distance has the effect of time, in a measure. You walk farther away from your canvas in this great studio of the world, and see the truer relations of the work in hand. I have a smouldering instinct that I must give this summer to physical interests mainly ; therefore, we still hold to the plan of a watering-place. But we shall not go until some time in August, and thus hope to hear from you before we leave. My brother-in-law from Russia is here with his family, — wife and five children, — and the stately old house is full of noises. I am "uncled" from morning till night. But there is one sad figure in the merry family circle. M.'s uncle [Mr. August Bufleb], who traveled with me in Egypt twenty years ago, and through whose friendship I was first brought here to find the best of my life's fortunes, has been so lamed and maimed, bodily and mentally, by paralysis, that he is almost lost to us. I could get used to his helplessness, his half-incoherent words (the tongue being also lamed) ; but the indifference to everything in which he once took an interest, the death or sleep of all his finer qualities of mind and heart, makes a very painful impression.

For my part, my brain has been enjoying the brief season of rest. Yesterday, in a book-store, I saw, in a German literary periodical, a notice of my "Masque," which the critic declared to be "one of the most remarkable and original poems which has been written in America." I had not been expecting any notice of the work here for a long while to come ; and, of course, am all the better pleased. Sometimes my heart sinks a little when I think how many years have passed before coming to my mature work, and how few years of growth remain ; but, after all, one can only do his best with what he has, and no more. The joy in doing, thank Heaven ! remains as keen as ever.

M. joins me in best love to G. and you, and Vauxes and all our friends. Both of us feel more clearly than ever before how much we have left behind, — how much that we cannot expect to find anywhere else in the world. Our ties, now, have the light and sparkle and strength and smoothness of ripe old wine, and this is the best gift the years bring. Do let me hear from you soon, and tell me all your plans and interests and labors.

TO A. R. MACDONOUGH.

GOTHA, GERMANY, *July* 16, 1872.

I write to you to-day, not because you care to hear about a smooth voyage and all manner of family junketings after arrival, — not because this is Germany and that is America where you are, — but because I honestly and earnestly mean that our companionship, in the highest and best sense of the word, shall not only endure, but become closer and more beneficent. Since the distance of the ocean has shoved last winter away, as if far back into the past, I have thought much of you; and my predominant feeling was one of wonder, that we should have met for so many years without either having acquired any genuine knowledge of the other. But perhaps I should only speak of myself. I was, for a long time, over self-conscious, and guarded my aspirations as jealously as if they had been vices; hence, I now see, I must have missed many chances of discovering kindred qualities in other men. I always recognized the extent and variety of your knowledge: how was it that I did not see or suspect, until within a year or two, the strength and delicacy of your æsthetic instincts? Just what I most value, most need, in a friend, — the nameless, indescribable freemasonry of the spirit (I won't use the colder word " intellect ") wherethrough there is the freest giving and taking, diverging in particulars only to unite more warmly in essentials, — just this I must have missed, God knows how! But now that I have found it, I have the rare comfort of again opening all my doors, — or, rather, of giving you a pass-key by which you can enter at will. This, I need hardly say, leaves you your old freedom to test and criticise. I shall always feel free, so long as I recognize in a friend the reverence for an equal standard of art, though it be not the same as my own.

I have done nothing since leaving home, except to read a few books which I shall need to consult for Goethe's biography. But last week I went with my wife on a three days' trip to Ilmenau, Rudolstadt, and the region thereabouts, — classic localities! At Ilmenau a curious thing happened. The *Oberkellner* said: " The hotel is full; I must put you in Goethe's room." It was the room where Goethe celebrated his last (eighty-second) birthday, in 1831; and there I discovered a new fact in his biography. It is interesting, rather than important; and proves, among other things, that Lewes took more from Viehoff's " Life

of Goethe " than he acknowledges. The next day we stopped at
Volkstedt, and saw the room where Schiller lived in 1788, then
crossed the Saale and walked to Rudolstadt by the path he followed when he visited the Lengefelds. We saw also the *Grenz-
hammer*, a forge where he studied the *staffage* for his ballad of
" Fridolin." Unfortunately, the lodge on the Kickelhahn, where
Goethe wrote " Ueber allen Gipfeln " with a pencil on the wall,
was burned down about eighteen months ago. I have just discovered an unpublished (and unpublishable !) youthful poem of
Schiller, and mean to get hold of Goethe's " Tagebuch," which
was surreptitiously printed in Berlin in (I think) 1867. It is
said to be no worse than Boccaccio or Faublas. I mean to
put the two men back into their original flesh and blood before I
begin to write about them.

There is not much stirring in literature now in Germany.
Freytag is at work, about two miles from here, on a new romance. I have not yet visited him. The latest sensation seems
to have been E. von Hartmann's " Philosophie des Unbewussten,"
a big octavo of eight hundred pages, which has reached a fourth
edition in a little over a year. . . .

TO JERVIS MᶜENTEE.

LAUSANNE, SWITZERLAND, *September* 13, 1872.

Your most welcome letter reached me at the baths of Bormio,
about three weeks ago. I was not in a favorable mood for writing at the time, — probably on account of a certain physical languor, from bathing and drinking disagreeable water, — and so
have waited until reaching here. We have had, on the whole, a
very agreeable summer trip ; from Gotha to Switzerland, leaving
railroads at Chur, whence we posted over the mountains to the
Engadin, then by the Bernina Pass to the valley of the Adda, and
so to Bormio, at the very foot of the famous Stelvio Pass into the
Tyrol. There is only one large hotel, standing alone in the midst
of a wild and desolate landscape, four thousand four hundred
feet above the sea. The springs have a temperature of about
ninety-five degrees, but I could not discover that there is any
specially bracing or healing quality about them. The guests
were mostly Italians of the aristocratic class and English, — on
the whole, a pleasant company ; the Americans have not yet discovered the place. We stayed three weeks, more benefited, I
think, by the delightful air, exercise, and freedom from work,

than by the bathing. Among other excursions we went up the Stelvio, nine thousand feet, and always covered with snow. Leaving Bormio we went down the valley of the Adda to the Lake of Como, crossed to Lugano, and then to Lago Maggiore, and over the Simplon to this place, a trip of six days, during which we scarcely had a cloud in the sky. Every day was a fresh delight. All the main lines of travel this year are swamped under the crowds of Americans and English. I never saw such multitudes ; but I manage, by displaying the airs of an old, case-hardened traveler, to avoid over-charges. I always commence by offering the landlords and waiters their choice of French, Italian, or German, which is usually sufficient. If they say any-thing about places or routes, I answer : " I know all that, I have seen everything a dozen times." It makes a difference in the bill, I assure you. Except in Germany, expenses are no greater than they were four years ago.

Your letter had a special interest for me. How well I under-stand the mood you describe ! I had it through the summer of 1868, and still have it at intervals. In fact, I was too hasty in writing to you from Gotha that my own delight in work had come back to me. It was a delusion. For two months past I have done nothing, and your letter found me in that sort of de-pression which sees no good in anything done, and no chance of anything better to come. I think, when the mind has been a lit-tle overtaxed, a kind of morbid activity may be produced, which one easily mistakes for returning vigor. In Gotha I began writ-ing a long poem, the plan of which I had been brooding over for at least five years ; but I did n't finish more than a hundred lines before the heat died out of me, and left me with a cold, flabby sensation. I determined that I would not worry about it, and the travel and rest at Bormio have been a complete restorative. The desire for activity which is now slowly growing upon me is the genuine, healthy thing. I am sure your experience will be similar. I fully expect that this will find you at work, cheerful and hopeful. Why, if one's art is not a permanent possession, it is the vilest cheat ever invented by the Devil ! There is a heal-ing influence in the very telling of such experiences. Probably no true author or artist is ever entirely free from them ; the only confident and happy souls are the —— and —— and —— !

How glad I am to be away from home this summer ! I can even smell the stench and feel the venom of the campaign at this distance, and there are few features of it which do not create disgust. My only consolation is the hope that after such a stirring up there may be such a universal nausea that all parties will have relieved their stomachs and returned to plain and decent fare. Thank Heaven there are only two months more of it !

I made about a dozen water-color sketches at Bormio, and was glad to find Goethe's test hold true, that if one improves while resting, finding himself doing better on recommencing work than on leaving off, it is a sure indication that the ability is inherent, native, not the result of mere technical skill. We constantly thought and talked of you and Gifford, and I don't know how many pictures we selected for you in glens and valleys which you may never see. After all there is no more charming life than that of an artist who is not obliged to depend wholly on his art for his living. Think what cant and abuse you escape, in the form of "moral and religious tendencies," etc. No one can say that a landscape is not moral, or that it in any way conflicts with "Christian doctrine." Pharisee and sinner come to you alike, and you are free to Catholic and Rationalistic walls. The temperance people buy your grape-vines, and the strong-minded women your ivy clinging to the oak. There is no sting in your nettles, and no blight falls from your upas tree. You cannot "corrupt youth," or "bring an indignant blush to the cheek of outraged virtue." Happy, thrice happy painter ! Let this immunity balance a thousand dissatisfactions with your fate. Well, I am cultivating a thick hide, so that our fortunes may be more similar. Now, good-by ! Write to me at Gotha, where we shall be again in a fortnight.

On his return to Gotha Bayard Taylor settled himself to work. He was busy with one of the Scribner volumes, and he took up again the poem which he had begun early in the summer, and had laid aside from lack of energy to go on with it. He never could work at poetry in a languid or even in a deliberate fashion. He was unwilling to write unless he was so possessed by his subject that the difficulty was in stopping, not in beginning work.

TO E. C. STEDMAN.

GOTHA, GERMANY, *October* 6, 1872.

I 've not written many letters this summer, or you would have
had one before. The fact is, I was more listless and lazy than
ever before in my life, and it has done me good in every way. I
thought I should write a few things, merely to keep my hand in :
but no ! my brain *bucked,* and refused to budge a step until it
pleased. I yielded, knowing full well that the old pace would
come back again soon enough — as it has. The watering, exter-
nally and internally, the air of the high Alps, the glimpse of Italy
on the lakes, the determined banishment of all uneasy subjects
from my thoughts, have been followed by a complete restoration
of health and fine spirits. I hope your Old Colony sojourn has
done as much for you. I have read your letters with real relish ;
the last was especially good. Now what will you be at ? What
new form of the old business ? What variety of literary activity ?

I am slowly gathering material for Goethe's life. It is very
rich, and very attractive. In July I took a carriage, and with
M. and L. went to Ilmenau and Rudolstadt, studying Goethe and
Schiller localities. It was a charming trip. At Ilmenau the
landlord put us into Goethe's room, where he spent his last birthday, and there, by a singular coincidence, I came upon a very
interesting fact for his biography. In Frankfurt I got upon the
track of many curious particulars. Oh, if I had but all my time
to myself, how I should plunge into the work ! but I must first
buy my time by these wearisome compilations for Scribner. Although I am now sticking to the latter, with an aroused conscience, after my summer idleness, I cannot help writing a little
every evening on a poem which has been haunting me for at least
six years. It is an idyllic story, in blank verse, wholly mine own
conception. I have written about two hundred lines, and don't
see how I can finish under two thousand. When I am farther
on, I 'll tell you more about it, — now, I dare not. But I don't
write so much to tell you of myself, as to evoke news of yourself
from you. I was greatly disappointed to miss your good-by before sailing ; but I trust the Lord has still many How-are-yous
in store for you and me. . . . I am in a slight state of uncertainty just now, about some home matters, and am not "laid
out" (to translate a German expression) for one of my long-
winded, effusive epistles. But keep your faith in my old affec-

tion, nevertheless. I have not been silent from neglect or indifference, only heartily tired of pen and paper, and with a most languid intellect. You don't know what delight there is in a letter from an old friend, when one is so far away from all home-friends, or you would have heaped coals on my head before this. Be sure and give me, also, all the news and gossip.

TO J. R. OSGOOD.

GOTHA, *October* 28, 1872.

Since I wrote to you, three or four weeks ago, I have so worked myself into the new poem that I can't stop. The first and second books are finished, and the third (and last) grows daily. It has been maturing in my head for so many years that all the incidents are complete in advance. I write slowly, revise carefully, and shall have little to change when the last line is written. It will make about 2,100 lines, or one hundred and thirty pages like the "Masque." Have you courage to publish it, say early in March? As a narrative poem, with a touching and quite original story, the scene of which is partly in Norway and partly in Delaware, it ought to attract ten readers for one of the "Masque." I send you an episode from Book I.

. . . Long before I hear from you, the poem will be finished, and ready to send. The title is "Lars." Book I. is laid in Norway, Book II. on the Delaware, and Book III. in Norway again. Strange as it may seem, the story is not only highly moral, but religious ! ! ! Yet there is no purposed moralizing : all is action, talk, and description, as in the passage I send. If your decision gives me hope, I shall try to arrange with Strahan, and herein a word from you would help. I can have the MS. copied here, and a few days priority of publication in London will secure him.

I meant, at first, to have told you more of the story ; but I guess it's hardly necessary. The specimen must answer ; and besides, such things easily get out. Pray do not mention the matter yet, or show the MS. to any besides Howells, Aldrich, Fields, and Longfellow. If Whittier should drop in when you get this, he may read all, over your shoulder, also.

Give my hearty love to all the above, and let me hear from you in regard to this, as soon as you have consulted the stars.

TO T. B. ALDRICH.

GOTHA, *October* 28, 1872.

. . . Osgood will show you what I am about, and I hope the plan will strike you agreeably. If he should decide on publishing, may I rely on your exact eye and good heart, old boy, to read the proof of 2,100 lines of blank verse? Of these, 1,500 are written, and the remaining part is so sketched out that I can very nearly guess its proportion. I have no audience or adviser here but M., who is all the keener because a loving critic. She encourages me greatly, but — woe is me ! — I no longer build on anything I write being specially popular. This poem of "Lars" has been floating and growing in my brain for at least six years. I did not mean to undertake it this fall, but it *would* out, and I am glad ; because another idea, which it covered or overlaid, now stands clear before my mind.

A week ago the Grand Duke of Saxe-Weimar invited me to visit him at the Wartburg ; this on account of "Faust." We dined in the Hall of the Minstrels, where Tannhäuser sang, — actually the same old Byzantine hall, — and sat on mediæval chairs. All their five Roilighnesses (as Yellowplush says) were very amiable, and the two Princesses were charming. This invitation is a good thing for my plans ; for the Grand Duke invited me to Weimar, and all the Goethean records and archives will now be open to me. At present I am only collecting materials, which will be a work of some months.

Here we are living very quietly. I work half the day compiling for Scribners, and thus earn the right to use the other half for myself. Moreover, I paint in oil, and of such is *not* the Kingdom of Heaven ! How I should like to have an autumn evening at Cambridge with you, and Longfellow, and Howells !

Tell Longfellow from me that the Weimar Princesses have read all his works, and the Hoffräulein, Baroness ——, a very charming person, begged me to say that her enthusiasm for him is so great that it led her to cut his name out of a traveler's register at Bruges. This was at the beginning of dinner, and all the ceremonious Highnesses showed so much interest in Longfellow that I forgot ceremony and felt quite at home all the evening. So that I owe to him !

GOTHA, GERMANY, *October* 28, 1872.

Your letter and the MSS. have been forwarded to me from New York.

It is very difficult to give an absolute opinion in regard to poems, and yet be just to the writer. Many other things must be considered, — age, circumstances of life, temperament, mental and moral force independent of the poetic faculty, etc., etc. If you are young, for instance, you have the power of finally producing much better verse ; if no longer young, you can only hope to produce that which manifests poetic taste and feeling. You have a decided rhythmical sense, yet with many roughnesses and some awkward lines. —— is the most complete and agreeable of the poems. In —— and ——, there are good stanzas, but the execution is uneven, sometimes careless. A man who means to write poetry must know how *to work.* One might as well hope to become a painter without studying the laws of drawing and color, and all the technicalities of the art, as to become a successful poet without devoting an equal study to rhythm, language, and the forms of thought. This is all I can say, and I am aware that it will not be satisfactory to you. But what can I do ? In poetry, each man must work out his own salvation. If I simply censured, I should be unjust ; if I simply praised, I should do more harm than good.

Begging you to believe, at least, that what I have said is meant to be in the most friendly spirit, I remain very truly yours.

TO JERVIS M^cENTEE.

GOTHA, GERMANY, *November* 18, 1872.

Your letter came four or five days ago, and I take my first leisure to answer it. I take it for granted that this will find you in your Tenth Street rooms, which are so clear in my memory (even to the little flat alabaster dish for cigars), that a letter is more like a personal meeting to me than when you were in Rondout. You somehow manage to bring your own bodily self before me when you write : I see your eyes and beard, and the changing expression of your face, as I read, and the sound of your voice accompanies the written words. Thus your letters are most welcome, no matter what you write, and I don't care how many jeremiads you send me ; only, my dear old fellow,

don't look to me for strength and comfort at a time when I myself can only keep cheerful and hopeful by sheer force of will.
I have a great mind to cultivate *phlegm* and indifference ; I believe I should get along just as well as with my present sensitive
nerves and confoundedly wakeful imagination. If anybody in
this world has, during the past three months, buffeted and tram-
pled on himself, and shut his mind up in a dark closet like a
naughty child, whenever it began to dread and misgive, that man
is myself. I get no end of bad news : the man who took my
house threatens to break his contract ; the gardener has given
me six months' notice of the termination of *his;* an arrangement I made for my parents has been spoiled by the neglect or
bad memory of the friend who offered to see it carried out ; the
money I have been expecting from four different quarters does
not come, — not a stiver, — and my whole worldly wealth at this
moment consists of fifteen groschen ! Mixed with all this bad
luck there is one possibility of a great good fortune soon ; but
I dare not hope. I am in a state of suspense ; ten years ago I
should have lost appetite, sleep, and capacity for work. Now I
say to myself : "Keep cool, you old sinner ! " and *I am cool.*
There !

I have one positive happiness. I have just finished a poem
which has been haunting and tormenting me for at least six
years. It is an idyllic story, in blank verse, quite unlike anything I have done, making three books, and about 2,100 lines.
I don't think you would take it for mine if you should see it
printed without a name. This poem has helped me amazingly
over all the weeks of discouragement and uncertainty : so my
counsel to you is — *Paint!* Schiller was right : "Occupation
that never wearies ; that slowly creates and nought destroys " is
one of the secrets by which we can control our natures and make
our lives smoother. I have also compiled a volume for Scribners this fall, and have purposely laid out some more mechanical work for myself, in order to carry me over the remaining
period of suspense, — about a month yet. Pray let me keep
silence about this matter until the suspense is over, and then you
shall know all. But I assure you (and M. will testify to it) that
I am composed, cheerful, and not uneasy more than fifteen minutes in each week.

I read a review of ——, with extracts, in the "Tribune."
Great Jove ! how can the man so coolly display his marvelous

ignorance of the whole Grecian world ? To make unconscious Calvinists of the Rhodian sculptors ! I am not surprised that he should have 8,000 (or 80,000) readers ; he puts a broad phylactery on his books and the sect takes them on the strength of it. You and I will never see the end of glorified crudity in the United States ; but we shall see the growth of an independent, cultivated class, the guardians of the temple where we worship.

TO A. R. MACDONOUGH.

GOTHA, GERMANY, *November 24,* 1872.

I was beginning to wonder whether I should ever hear from you, when your letter arrived. Gout, after the Canadian forests (which means salt pork, biscuits, and an occasional trout !), is something incomprehensible. Yours cannot be the genuine article, and for your sake I will hope your doctor is mistaken. How can I think of you, on monthly evenings at the Century, without a glass of punch in your hand ?

I quite share your disgust in regard to this year's political campaign, and I suppose I am as glad as you can possibly be that the thing has come to an end. I feel sorry for Greeley on personal grounds, but have no fear of what Cushing calls a " cataclysm," because he is not elected. I must confess, also, that the " Tribune " of November 8th — the last I have received — is much more agreeable reading than any number since June has been. I now hope for, and try to believe in, the disintegration of both parties, and the formation of new (and let us hope, decent) ones, by 1876.

What you suggest about writing a life of Schiller indicates to me that I could not have told you, in detail, my plan of Goethe's biography. I mean to include the biography of Schiller within it, for the very reason that the two lives run together during so many important years. Let me try to make it clear by a diagram : —

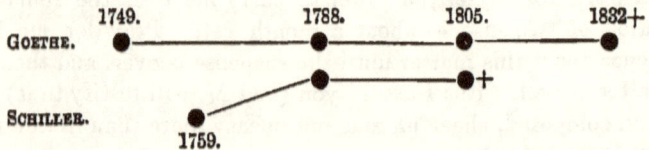

The action of the two minds upon each other, the radical differences in their methods of development, yet the similarity of their directions, give opportunities for a series of contrasts, whereby each explains the other. In many respects they are complementary. There is no work of the kind, even in Germany ; no attempt has been made anywhere, so far as I know, to write a double biography of this kind. There are difficulties in the way, I admit ; but if I can succeed in keeping each biography from interfering with the interest of the other, up to the point where they join, the rest will be easy. I am collecting material for both at the same time, and also studying the composition of society in Weimar and Jena during the classic period. It is now possible to draw another and a much more real portrait of Schiller than you will find in Carlyle's life, and a far completer picture of Goethe than Lewes gives us.

Three weeks ago the Grand-Duke of Saxe-Weimar (Carl August's grandson) invited me to dinner, for Goethe's sake. We dined in the *Sängersaal,* in the Wartburg, between the old Byzantine pillars, against which certainly must have leaned Wolfram von Eschenbach and Walther von der Vogelweide. The Grand-Duke is a special admirer of Hawthorne, and is quite well acquainted, *überhaupt,* with American literature. The most important result of this visit to me was a pressing invitation to visit the *Herrschaften* again in Weimar, and a promise from the Grand-Duke that I should have all necessary facilities in making my Goethe researches. This makes my way clear in advance.

But I can't undertake any real work upon the biography before next summer. There is still one more pot-boiling task to be finished — a matter of six months — before my time will be my own. The delay does no harm ; I collect *Briefwechsel* of all sorts, read, assimilate, and quietly mature the plan, so that when I finally begin I shall be used to the weight of the material, and not too much oppressed by it.

Moreover, this fall I have cleared my brain of one poetic disturbance. I have written a semi-idyllic, semi-dramatic poem in blank verse — about 2,100 lines. For years the conception has been haunting me, but postponed ; held off, because there was no fitting time or mood. It returned upon my indolence this summer, would take no denial, forced me to begin ; and when one begins, you know, one is securely caught. Well, the thing is done. It is in three Books, is entitled " Lars," begins and ends in Norway, but shifts over the ocean to Delaware in Book II.

The poem is (for me) very simple and unrhetorical. *I* like it for its unlikeness to all my other poetry. Whether it will be specially liked by others I can't tell, nor do I trouble myself with speculations thereupon. When, five or six years ago, I saw clearly that I had achieved no real success as an author, I said to myself : "This first battle is lost, but there is still time to win another." If I live I think I shall win it, but only legitimately, by a slow and steady advance along the whole line. The "Masque," for instance, is not popular, — cannot be, — yet it has given me a little more ground. So my "Lars," which has been a great delight, and leaves a singular feeling of relief behind it, will force another small portion of the resisting public to yield.

While writing it you were often in my mind. I felt the need of your rhythmical instinct, in the way of sympathy and counsel ; but if Osgood, to whom I have written, has not lost faith, the poem will be published in March. I sent him a small specimen brick, and would send you one if I had but time to copy. Just now I have a new and rather curious task on hand. I am writing a lecture *in German* on American Literature, to be delivered here in a fortnight, for the benefit of a *Frauenverein* (Benevolent, not Strong-Minded). I have never tried such an experiment, — have never, in fact, written so much German at one time ; but thus far my wife gives me good encouragement. Were it not for the *atra cura* of small business matters, which visits me again and again in letters from Pennsylvania, I should have no complaint to make against my present fate. It often seems as if we were never allowed to possess a gift without paying for it ; the Gods are hard creditors.

I wish you would take my plan of the double-biography into consideration, and tell me what you think of it. You may be able to see some difficulty which has escaped me, or a way of avoiding one which is directly evident. I find, already, that the plan will oblige me to give a tolerably full account of the whole Weimar circle : but this, if well done, will be an advantage. Were I to make two separate works, the most interesting years (1793 to 1805) must be repeated in each. . . .

Here I must close, for this time. I have hardly given you anything but egotistical gossip, but really I have nothing else to send. Our life here is very quiet and monotonous, and perhaps the days would drag if I did not work so steadily. We shall be here until the beginning of January ; so, pray, write soon, and I shall get your letter before leaving. I think we shall go to Florence or Rome for the rest of the winter, but cannot yet decide until we get further news from home.

My wife heartily returns your greeting. She has just finished a prose translation of my "Masque," for the private benefit of many friends or relatives who read no English.

The references to the circumstances of his life intimate that all was not going well. In truth, things were going very ill. The ease and contentment with which he had begun his life abroad had given way to anxiety and the most helpless perplexity. Almost every resource upon which he relied failed him. No letters came in response to his inquiries. The "Tribune" passed its quarterly dividends twice. The tenant at Cedarcroft made no payment. The prospective purchaser of the estate hesitated and delayed in the most trying manner. Remittances on which he had confidently counted failed to come, owing to mistakes, and upon top of it all came in quick succession news of the disastrous defeat of Mr. Greeley, the death of Mr. Greeley, and the tempestuous condition of the internal affairs of the "Tribune."

Bayard Taylor mourned Mr. Greeley's death sincerely. He had been associated with the great editor ever since he had himself entered the field of journalism, and in the quarter-century intimacy had learned to know him well. With the knowledge had come only increasing respect, and when in 1876 he was called upon to accept, in the name of the people, the monumental bust of Horace Greeley, which an association of printers had placed in Greenwood Cemetery, he mingled his own personal regard with his recognition of Mr. Greeley's public services. " I should like," he said in his address, " to speak of his tenderness and generosity. I should like to explain the awkward devices of his heart to hide itself, knowing that the exhibition of feeling is unconventional, and sensitive lest its earnest impulses should be misconstrued. But the veil which he wore during life must not be lifted by the privilege which follows death; enough of light shines through it to reveal all that the world need know. To me his nature seemed like a fertile tract of the soil of his native New Hampshire. It was cleared and cultivated, and rich harvests clad its southern slopes; yet the rough primitive granite cropped out here and there, and there were dingles which defied the plough, where the sweet wild flowers blossomed in their season, and the wild birds built their nests unharmed. In a word, he was a man who kept his life as God fashioned it for him, neither assuming a grace which was not bestowed, nor disguising a quality which asserted its existence."

The whole period was one of public and private loss to Bayard Taylor. He learned soon after of the death of his dear friend Mr. Kensett, the artist, and of his long-tried associate, Mr. Putnam, the publisher. These private griefs deepened the gloom into which his affairs were cast. He found himself at a distance from the scene of action, unable to protect the interests of his property in the "Tribune," the prey of conflicting purposes, absolutely adrift. It was impossible to work, it was impossible to avoid the terrible depression which overtook him, and which was lifted only when he received at last such intelligence as persuaded him of the substantial integrity of his interest in the "Tribune." Then he threw himself eagerly into the plans of his associates, heartily commended them for carrying out the building scheme, and expressed the most entire faith in the future of the paper under its new auspices. Nevertheless, he was so completely thrown out of his calculations that he was compelled to part with one of his shares in order to gain time for recovering himself. He retained his remaining shares, well content, he said, to wait for the return of prosperity. He waited indeed, for no dividends were paid on the Tribune stock until after his death, and from this time forward there was no release from arduous labor, incessant daily toil to meet the demands of maintenance. The higher work which he was yet to do was done because he must do it, not for gain, but for the satisfaction of his nature, and it was done in contempt of toil and rest. He was not again to know any true mental leisure.

Meanwhile he took a lively interest in the publication of "Lars," waiting with some impatience to see how it would be received.

TO WHITELAW REID.

GOTHA, GERMANY, *December* 2, 1872.

The news of Greeley's death came yesterday. I am too much shocked and stunned to write much about it, further than to send the inclosed, which I beg you to publish at once. I have ventured to speak for all of us, you will see, and hope there is no line which Greeley's other associates will not indorse.

Pray write to me immediately. I must wait long until I get any particulars of the sad — nay, the tragic event ; and the "Tribune" will not give me *all*. Do take half an hour for my sake, and tell me everything. I feel it as a hard blow, — so hard, indeed, that I cannot yet write about it. But the poem wrote itself : it ran hot from my mind, as it stands.

TO J. R. OSGOOD.

GOTHA, GERMANY, *December* 16, 1872.

I almost fancied I should never hear from you again, when your letter came on the 13th. . . . I have just had a letter from

Mr. Isbister, now the head of Strahan & Co. His edition of
"Faust" has very nearly paid expenses, and the sale continues
steadily good. Fifty copies more will clear the whole edition,
and then I shall get at least five shillings on every volume sold.
He promises me good returns for next year. Moreover, he is
anxious to publish "Lars" in London a few days before you do
in Boston, and offers me half profits.

I am more than ever anxious to have "Lars" published early
in March, say the 8th or 10th. Congress will then have adjourned, and after a year of debauch the public stomach, it seems
to me, will be ready for the mild maguesia or seltzers of such a
poem as "Lars." I send in this envelope Books I. and II., and
you will get Book III. by the next mail. When you have the
entire MS. in your hands, light a cigar on the first rainy Sunday
morning that comes, sit down, and read the whole poem. I think
you will then understand why I want to publish in March rather
than wait until next October. In fact, Strahan's offer obliges me
to insist upon the former date. I am neither surprised nor mor-
tified if you have little faith in the popularity of my poetry, but
I must ask you to try once more. If this venture does not have
at least a moderate success, I shall hereafter publish my poems
myself as a private luxury.

The cheap edition of "Faust" can much better be postponed
until next fall. By that time I can get the plates of both volumes from Brockhaus — if you are willing, that is, satisfied with
the type, etc. — and send them to you. It will surely be much
cheaper for me than to have them made in Boston, and I think
the two will make one handsome volume by using a better paper
than Brockhaus'.

I am very sorry to learn that you have lost by the fire.[1] I
knew, from the public accounts, that your quarters were un-
touched, and was ready to congratulate instead of condoling.
The loss of the illustrations must be serious, unless you were in-
sured. Greeley's death is a severe blow to me. I had given up
the hope of his election three months ago, but believed that he
would live many years yet and do the more good because of this
year's experience. I do not think his death will injure the
"Tribune" pecuniarily ; but there must be a partial reorganiza-
tion of the editorial corps, and I am not at all satisfied to be away
at such a time.

[1] The Boston fire of November 9, 1872.

I have two MS. copies of " Lars," one for Strahan & Co. My proposition is that they should publish on March 1st, and you on March 8th. I had suggested this to them, before receiving your letter. I can arrange to send you the sum necessary for payment of the plates — about one hundred and fifty dollars, I should guess, — by the end of February, and you need not begin with more than two thousand copies. The story will surely justify that number to begin with. You may take your own way of having attention called to it, by advertising, extracts in advance, etc. . . .

TO E. C. STEDMAN.

GOTHA, *December* 22, 1872.

Your letter was almost like the sight and sound of yourself to me. In these short, dark, Northern days, and the many uncertainties which follow me here, I miss the old circle of friends more than ever. I am pursued by disappointments of all sorts, and for the last fortnight have given up all work through sheer inability to fix my mind steadily upon any subject. Greeley's death, as you may guess, is a hard blow to me, and I am only just now beginning to accept it as a part of the inevitable. However, since yesterday, when the sun stood over Capricorn, I have passed the climax of discouragement. This " darksome hollow " of the year is always my worst season.

Well, the poem is finished, and one copy of the MS. is half-seas over, on the way to Osgood. It makes just 2,135 lines of blank verse. The title is " Lars," — only that, and nothing more. The story is wholly mine own invention, and seemeth unto me entirely original. I think the poem will interest you in one sense : it is very simple, unrhetorical, and the characters are all objectively drawn. The Norwegian scenes ought to interest many readers ; but I do not dare to anticipate any special popularity for the poem.

I have, however, one piece of good news. Strahan & Co. (London) write to me that the sale of " Faust " has very nearly paid the expenses of the edition ; it continues good and steady, and they will have some profits for me next year. Wherefore, they offer to print " Lars " a few days in advance of Osgood, and thus secure an English copyright. I have made another MS. copy for them, and shall send it in a few days. This will be the first publication of any poem of mine in England, and may the Gods favor the venture !

I have already two offers from London for the biography of

Goethe, but shall make no arrangements until the work is well under way. The mass of material to be scraped together is immense, but new and inspiring vistas are already opening through it. I am in no hurry, for I can only manage the great mass by slow assimilation. . . . I am constantly finding new sources of private and personal aid. So, as far as this plan is concerned, there is various and increasing encouragement. I only fear that other worries may force me away from it, for a time.

Yesterday a file of " Tribunes " came, with your poem, " Before the Burial," which must have been written at precisely the same time as I wrote. We have three expressions in common, I notice. Your poem is calm and artistic, mine personal and almost passionate. I think yours one of the best things you ever wrote : it is at once touching and noble in feeling.

I quite understand your restless desire to write, without having any definite theme. I have several times passed through the same phase, but I find that it always results in the finding of a theme. Of late years my chief trouble has been the accumulation of poetic subjects in my mind. " Lars," for example, has haunted me for a long while, and persistently stood between me and a much more important conception, for the expression of which I am hardly yet ripe enough. Now that the first is completed, the latter stands out clear and unobstructed, and I have a fresh delight in contemplating it.

. . . Our plans are all in suspense. We shall leave here in about three weeks, put L. in a school in Baden-Baden, and then go to Lausanne, where we shall stay with my sister until certain business matters are settled one way or another. Beyond that point I plan nothing. Scribners have announced to me the stoppage of the " Library of Travel," so I have now only a school history of Germany to prepare for Appletons, and then I shall be free for my own especial task. I have given up all idea of resting or merely loafing here in Europe. Both necessity and conscience force me to work. . . .

TO JOHN G. WHITTIER.

GOTHA, GERMANY, *December* 30, 1872.

The " Pennsylvania Pilgrim " came to me as a Christmas gift, all the more welcome because so unexpected. I have just finished reading it, and can now return intelligent thanks for your thoughtful kindness in sending the volume so far. Yet one

reading cannot exhaust the fullness of meaning and of feeling in
the chief poem. I was not more attracted by the story of Pas-
torius (of whom I knew almost nothing) than by the warm,
bright background of tolerance and mellow humanity, upon
which his figure is drawn. The latter is like the ground of dead
gold which the early Italian painters gave to the forms of their
saints, only more luminous.

But, mixed with my delight in the poem from first to last,
there is a feeling of surprise which I can only explain by telling
you what *I* have been doing. Three months ago I was moved to
begin a narrative poem, the conception of which had been haunting my mind for five or six years. Once begun, I could not
leave the subject; I dropped all other work, and by the beginning of November had finished an idyllic narrative poem of more
than 2,100 lines, in blank verse. The title is "Lars," and the
scene is laid partly in Norway and partly on the banks of the
Delaware.

I have brought Quaker peace and Berserker rage into conflict, and given the triumph to the former. The one bit of fact
out of which the poem grew is the circumstance that there is —
or at least was — a small community of Friends at Arendal in
Norway. The story is wholly of my own invention. Now, in
describing a "silent meeting" I have expressed the same
thought which I find in the "Pilgrim," —

> "The gathered stillness multiplied
> And made intense by sympathy."

And the conclusion of my poem is exactly the same thought,
in other words, as the conclusion of yours. I will quote from
my MS. : —

> "Though the name of Lars
> Be never heard, the healing of the world
> Is in its nameless saints. Each separate star
> Seems nothing, but a myriad scattered stars
> Break up the Night, and make it beautiful."

It is pleasant to me to know that we have both been busy with
the same, or kindred thoughts. When I sent the MS. of my
poem to Osgood three weeks ago, I also sent a dedicatory poem,
which is more than ever justified by this coincidence. I requested
Osgood to let you see the MS. or the proofs if there should be
opportunity. But if any charge of plagiarism is made, it will
fall upon me! The absence of music, color, and external graces
makes the Quaker a difficult subject for poetry, unless the lat-

ter touches only his spiritual side, which I have endeavored to do. I depend on my Norwegian characters for whatever external picturesqueness seemed to be necessary. I feel sure that there are some things in the poem which you will like, and I hope there may be nothing in it to make the dedication unwelcome. I am not ashamed to say that I cried over many passages while writing.

The collection of materials for my biography of Goethe goes rapidly on, but the work itself must be done slowly. I shall take my time to it, and meanwhile be able, I hope, to work out other poetic ideas which are waiting for their turn. After many wanderings of mind and fancy, I seem to have found my true field : at least I am happy in my work, as never before.

Three weeks ago I gave a lecture here, in German, on American Literature, in aid of a charitable society of women. It was my first experiment of the kind, but proved to be successful. Among other quotations I read an excellent translation of your "Song of the Slaves in the Desert," which made a deep impression upon the audience. I have several times, since then, been called upon to read it in private circles.

We shall go to Switzerland, perhaps to Italy, for two or three months, and then come back here again to my labors. If you should be able to read my " Lars " within a month after getting this, I should be glad to hear what impression it makes upon the one who was most in my mind as I wrote. The memory of Elizabeth, also, came back to me very clearly and tenderly.

TO JERVIS MᶜENTEE.

GOTHA, GERMANY, *December* 30, 1872.

Your letter came as a Christmas gift, and G.'s followed the next day. Well, — your moral heaven is brighter, and so is mine : that 's the best news. I allow for depression in others much more readily than in myself, I suppose because it conflicts more violently with my born nature, the latter being joyous, hopeful, almost epicurean in some things. But, good Heaven ! if I had written to you on the 18th of December instead of the 18th of November ! At the latter date I was still making a tolerable fight against disturbing circumstances. I held out until the 10th of December ; then, as the enemy pressed harder and no relief corps showed itself, I ignominiously hoisted the white flag, saw all my breastworks of pride and philosophy carried,

gave up my sword, and was sent to the rear. Such a self-sur-
render is all the more abject when it follows a long resistance.
With me it expressed itself in painful nervous restlessness, an
inability to work, a morbid dislike to society, and an utter lack
of faith in the future. For ten days I was honestly wretched ;
then the mood, having exhausted itself, passed away, and better
news came immediately. All my depression was unnecessary ;
as it was, I think it was the shock of Greeley's death which gave
the finishing stroke. I am still in a state of considerable doubt
and uncertainty, but endure it now cheerfully, and have all my
usual hopefulness again.

I had a strong personal affection for Greeley : I partly grew
up with him and the " Tribune ; " he was always kind and helpful, and to be trusted in any emergency, so that his death comes
nearer to me than would that of many a relative. Besides, it
came upon me so suddenly. One day the telegraph simply reported that he was ill ; but I knew his good constitution and felt
no anxiety. The next day — he was dead ! This sudden ending, after all the vile and cruel abuse poured upon him through
the campaign, was really tragic. I wonder how such men as
Douglass, Gerrit Smith, etc., feel now. For my part, I am
done with political parties from this time on. I see no more
personal honesty or fairness in the leading Republican politicians than in the Democrats. The war is over, and its results
secured ; now I am free to support a good man wherever I find
him, and to hate the character of our party strife on one side as
well as on the other.

. . . Did I tell you that I was to give a lecture here, in German, on American Literature ? It came off on the 12th, and
was a great pecuniary success for the Ladies' Charitable Society.
I read several poems, both English and German, — among others, Poe's " Raven " in German, — and greatly astonished the
people by what they considered a very artistic declamation, but
which in America would be the ordinary lecture tone. The fact
is, we are, in simple, common-sense views of Art and Literature,
ahead of any people in Europe. I see now, more clearly than
ever, that if you and I (for instance) are true to our high calling
in New York, we shall receive in the end a heartier appreciation
there than we could ever get abroad. Where a people are in
their pupilage there is always more earnestness, more force of aspiration, than when they think themselves fully developed, and

— as now in Europe — have become a little *blasé*. Let us only hold on : if we live long enough, a day will come to reward our faith !

I wish you had told me a little about Page's "Shakespeare : " I am curious to know something of it. Also, what do you think of Le Clear's me ? How are all the good fellows at the Century ? It gives me a slight pang to think of that old smoky corner. You can't possibly miss us more than we do you. When we get back, I think we shall be less willing to leave than ever before. But I must get the material and make the studies for my biography of Goethe while here, and also give L. the advantage of a good school. We keep our health, fortunately ; I am physically much stronger than a year ago, and one or two troubles I had have nearly disappeared. I find that with every additional year my anxiety about the future becomes less, — and this is a gain to balance many minor losses. Your letter really cheered both of us, and some cheer (although the worst was over) was needed. I feel entirely free to give you, always, an honest picture of my mental and moral condition, and you must not withhold your depressions in return, for they belong to your life. This is the great relief and blessing of our correspondence, and any feeling of restraint, on either side, would take away from its value.

TO HIS MOTHER.

GOTHA, GERMANY, *January* 3, 1873.

. . . I have entirely gotten over my discouragement, and am at work again. We have enough to pay everything, including the advance on L.'s schooling, and to live in Lausanne until the middle of February.

By April next I think everything will be decided, — the sale of Cedarcroft, your pension, my connection with the "Tribune," my new volume, and other minor matters. So let us have patience for three months more. Even if every other prospect proves to be unfortunate, the sale of one share will enable me to wait for better times. . . . I have begun work on my School History, which, if it prove successful, will yield me more than all my Tribune shares. I hope to finish it by July. The one necessity now is money and freedom from anxiety, which the sale of a share will give me. Since I have decided to do this, I feel perfectly easy in mind.

The MS. of " Lars " reached America safely, and was read by Mr. Osgood and Mr. Aldrich, who both advised the substitution of some other name for the title of the book. They doubted if the public would take kindly to a poem so briefly, and, to most, unintelligibly named. It was curious, when the announcement of the book was made, to see what blunders that part of the public made which is engaged in instructing the rest of the public. One critic pointed out the error in the Latinity of the name. It should be " Lares," he said. Another explained that Bayard Taylor was indebted to Macaulay for the idea of the poem, which was taken from the story of " Lars Porsenna." His friends also suggested to Bayard Taylor the expediency of putting the poem out anonymously.

TO J. R. OSGOOD AND T. B. ALDRICH.

LAUSANNE, SWITZERLAND, *Sunday, January* 26, 1873.

The two letters of the 10th, anent " Lars," reached me last night. I should be quite willing to try the experiment of an anonymous publication, but, unfortunately, it is too late. I have written about the poem to several friends in New York and Pennsylvania, have signed the contract with Strahan & Co., and sent the proofs, and I don't think Strahan & Co. (who now seem very glad to get the poem) would be willing to drop my name, to which the " Faust " has given some little value in England. The main fact is, the secret could not be kept now; had I thought of it sooner, it would have been quite easy, but the idea of "making a sensation" never entered my mind.

As for the title, I assert that no title can be "fatal" to a good poem; and I think "Lars" rather better than average titles. It is brief, strong, Scandinavian, and therefore picturesque, has never been used, and is the only name which can be applied to the whole poem. " Brita's Lovers " would only apply to Book I., and, moreover, it is a title after Miss Braddon's, or Mrs. Henry Wood's own heart! "Mildred's Lovers!" "Sylvia's Lovers!" No, no! none o' that! "Lars" is a great deal better than

"Enoch Arden." The fact is, fancy titles have been run into the ground : a good work will always make its own title popular. Now, look at the list of titles of the principal idyllic poems in literature : Voss, "Louise ;" Goethe, "Hermann und Dorothea ;" Lamartine, "Jacqueline ;" Tennyson, "Enoch Arden ;" Longfellow, "Evangeline." Except the last, and perhaps "Hermann und Dorothea," "Lars" is as good as, if not better than, these names. Your objection, T., must arise from some sort of personal dislike to the sound of the word. Nevertheless, I have given it thorough consideration : I have tried all other possible titles, but with each one a spirit whispered in my ear, "Lars! Lars !" I feel that "Lars" becomes my complexion best, and "Lars" it must be. If you had given a distinct reason for your dislike, I could better feel its force, but I can imagine no reason against a simple name, except its sound. I'll predict one thing : if the poem is well received at the start, the name will immediately become popular.

I cannot telegraph this decision, for the simple reason that I've not money enough in pocket for the dispatch. I've had to telegraph twice to New York concerning my interest in the "Tribune," and an expense of fourteen dollars (gold) just now would bankrupt me. We have exactly enough to pay for lodging and plain fare for a fortnight, when my remittances are due. So the venture must be made as it stands ; but if you both think there's a chance for decided success, pray give my poem the benefit of all legitimate devices. Strahan's publication and the English notices (if favorable) may be a considerable help. If the same public which read "Enoch Arden" can be made to look at it, I think the story will make its way. It cannot be assailed, except on literary grounds. Its moral and religious character is unexceptionable.

Your verdict, T., brought joy to my heart : it was exactly what I wanted to hear said of the poem. In spite of all previous disappointments, I can't help hoping again. My next poetical plan is something equally as different from all former verse of mine, something entirely new, and, in fact, almost startling, in which the dull public (or even critical) mind will never recognize me. In a year or so, I hope, I shall be able to conspire with you for an anonymous publication.

TO J. R. OSGOOD.

LAUSANNE, SWITZERLAND, *January* 30, 1873.

Eureka! I think I have discovered a way to assuage the anguish which I fear you must have felt, on reading my last letter. I knew that both you and Aldrich would be disgusted with my stubbornness, and yet, for the life of me, I could not change the title. Why did n't I sooner think of a sub-title? I don't know: but to-day, still pondering on the matter, it flashed across my mind as a possible compromise between our views. Thus: "Lars: A Pastoral of Norway." Does not that make the publishing side of your heart thrill? Think of Björnstjerne Björnsen and the Norwegian idyls! — by the bye, I won't say *idyl,* because of Tennyson. "Pastoral" is the word; it is more grassy, clovery, and homelike. I can understand that multitudes would not know whether "Lars" was a name, a chemical substance, or a plant; but the sub-title ought to be explanatory and attractive at the same time. I shall send it to Strahan & Co. at once, and you may announce it on enormous yellow posters.

When I see you you will regale me with broiled oysters for this concession, or cod's tongue, a dish I have only found in Boston. May we then be able to drink to the 150th thousand of "Lars: A Pastoral of Norway."

The weather during Bayard Taylor's stay at Lausanne was exceedingly disagreeable, and brought on a bronchial difficulty which gave him great trouble, but he would not relinquish work. He had placed his daughter in school at Baden-Baden, and in the middle of February he left Lausanne with his wife for Italy.

TO HIS MOTHER.

FLORENCE, ITALY, *February* 27, 1873.

. . . We went direct to Marseilles, and there found sunshine and warmth. Traveling along the Mediterranean shore toward Genoa, through magnificent orange-groves, with roses, violets, and anemones everywhere in blossom, green peas and fresh tomatoes on the table, my cough and hoarseness grew lighter every day, and now I am perfectly well, always hungry, and with a great capacity for sleep. We reached here last Saturday, and came direct to Mrs. Baranowsky [Casa Guidi], where we have very nice quarters. Grahams [1] wanted us to go to them, but we declined on account of my needing at least half of each day for my own work. Dr. Wilson came round immediately to see us, and finds me looking remarkably well. Powers has not been well for some months, and looks a great deal older than when we saw him last. The weather here is very mild (about like the early part of May with us), but there is a good deal of rain yet, and we can only walk out about every other day. Still the sight of green grass and flowers and fruit-trees in bloom is very delightful.

TO JERVIS M^CENTEE.

CASA GUIDI, FLORENCE, *March* 12, 1873.

It is an unconscionable while to make you wait for an answer to yours of January 19th. It reached me in Lausanne, just as I was taken with a severe bronchial cold, accompanied by loss of voice, so I was not able to write with any comfort. We left there before I was quite well, went down the Rhone to Marseilles, then along the shore to Cannes, Nice, and by the Cornice Road to Genoa. It was a heavenly change from the slushy weather of Switzerland : we plunged into summer, sat under palm and orange trees, plucked red anemones by the road-side, basked in perfect sunshine, and were happy. We reached here on the 22d, found rooms in the Casa Guidi, and have been quiet and laborious Florentines ever since. Of course I am perfectly well again, and Dr. Wilson, who pulled me back to life five years ago, says I am an excellent specimen. I brought my work along, and manage to write about the substance of seven or eight printed octavo pages every day. You may judge of my application by the fact that I had not set foot within a gallery until this morning. I am again a drudge, and working solely for money, but my job is interesting and rather attractive than otherwise, so I must be content. It is a great blessing to be here, in the midst of flowers, with the young green thickening over all the trees.

I called on Miss S. as soon as we got settled, and we have both met her since at Gray's [2] reception. She is looking very well, and seems to have a great attachment to Italy. She has

---

[1] J. Lorimer Graham Jr. was at that time American Consul at Florence.

[2] H. P. Gray, the artist, then in Florence.

not yet found a chance of going home, but I believe expects to have one in July, if not sooner. Gray is nicely fixed here : he has painted two very good pictures, one a portrait of Mrs. Graham, and they have brought him fresh orders. . . . I have called on all the old residents and friends here, except Hart and Mead, whom I shall see soon. Powers has not been well ; he looks thin and spiritual, and his eyes are brighter than ever. I fear he will not be long with us. Dix died at Rome yesterday. I spent last evening in company with Emerson and his daughter at Graham's. They have a charming place, spacious and luxurious, but not oppressively so. They received us with open arms, and are the same hospitable, generous creatures as always heretofore. . . . We have seen much of them since arriving, and are very glad to find them unchanged. Florence is more homelike to me than ever ; I find that I have not forgotten a street, hardly a house, but go about as if I had always lived here. I think there must be near one thousand Americans here ; three hundred came to Gray's reception, and they were certainly not more than one third of all. In spite of the capital being moved to Rome I never saw the streets so crowded, and whole blocks of houses are going up. The new drive around San Miniato is one of the finest things in Europe.

We shall go to Rome for ten days, in about a week, then remain here until April 20th, when we return to Germany. . . . I shall very likely go to Vienna, to write for the "Tribune," during May. My history will keep me busy until the end of July, and I can't take a holiday sooner. I want to stay until the summer of next year to complete the studies for Goethe's life. I have been collecting material for some months, but cannot undertake the work seriously until this task is off my hands. Emerson seems to feel a great interest in it ; we had a long talk about it last evening. Since the "Tribune" is safe in Reid's hands, I feel easier about the future. The other matter is still undecided, but I have ceased to worry. The one thing is to keep occupied, and then the blue devils drop their tails and run. I now wish the days were longer : they go too fast for me. What a waste of time there is in "calls"! Really, one is forced to choose between society and serious work. No man can do his conventional duty, and then accomplish anything else, — and the absurdity is, people expect it of me ! I dread being introduced, lest I should receive another "call," which must be answered, or offense is given. This carrying New York and London with one wherever you go is growing to be a curse.

Well, my new poem is out, and I shall wait with great interest to hear your verdict. I have heard none as yet, except from Aldrich, who votes "yea." How I long for the leisure to begin something new which already haunts me! But I must hold it off at arm's length, with a tight grip on its throat. The sheet is coming to an end, and I have hardly said anything. Your letter, with all the particulars about dear old Kensett, was most welcome. *I* shall like your commemorative picture. What you say of the reaction against foreign art is encouraging: I have been waiting for this. Next we must have a reaction against the fashions in literature, and that will come, I know, sooner than the successful quacks anticipate. . . .

TO T. B. ALDRICH.

FLORENCE, *March* 29, 1873.

Last night we returned from an eight days' trip to Rome, and I find a "Lars" in sheets waiting for me. It is much handsomer than Strahan's edition. I ran through it rapidly, and found only one error, — "Rin*k*an" instead of "Ri*u*kan," — which is not a painful one; since the few who are familiar with Norwegian names will see that it is a misprint. Otherwise, it seems to me perfect, and I owe you many a good turn for your kind attention to my sense, spelling, and punctuation. I've already seen two notices, in the Boston "Advertiser" and "Globe," both just the things I hoped would be said. So, thus far, the aspects look well, and I will dare to hope for a meek, modest success.

Emerson was here a fortnight ago, and I saw him twice. He tells me that Lowell is still in Paris. In Rome I saw Story (who has *sculped* a magnificent Jerusalem and Electra), who does not expect Lowell in Italy this season, so I shall probably not meet the latter. Story told me that Browning sent him the "Echo Club" last summer, with a note saying it was the best thing of the kind he had ever seen, and that if he had found the imitations of himself in a volume of his poems he would have believed that he actually wrote them! The American painters in Rome had also read the "Echo Club," and chuckled over it in my presence, not suspecting the author. I really thought the articles had fallen upon the "Atlantic" readers without effect, and here I find an evidence to the contrary.

We are living very quietly here. I have brought my work along, and write five or six hours every day, which accounts for my not writing to you sooner. My " History of Germany," for schools, is going on steadily, and I hope, when finished, that it will kindle a better fire under the household pot than all my good work has done. I must also take six or eight months to complete the collection of material for Goethe's life before returning home. This, however, will be no labor, but an unmitigated delight.

TO HANNAH M. DARLINGTON.

FLORENCE, ITALY, *April* 5, 1873.

. . . You will have seen before this what I wrote last fall. I do not know how it will be received by the public, but the few friends who have read the poem are satisfied with it. The plan has been in my head for five or six years, and as it is probably the last poem I shall write embodying home (that is, Pennsylvania or Quaker) elements, I tried to do my best. The story is entirely my own invention. I must say that if the Quakers are not satisfied with my presentation of them and their peaceful creed, they do not deserve a place in our literature. My experiences, however, have taught me not to hope for much immediate recognition either of this work or of any other I may write. But I am quite content with the appreciation of the few best minds. I would rather exercise a slow and cumulative influence than enjoy (?) any amount of temporary popularity. There is a great satisfaction in working up towards an ideal which at least seems high to one's own eyes. I doubt whether any author can estimate his own success or failure. . . .

The length of our stay in Europe is still uncertain. I cannot complete my History before July or August, and therefore cannot sooner than then begin my studies for Goethe's life. I have collected a good deal of material, but that is not enough. My plan is, to have all I need prepared or collected before going home, and then I shall begin to write. It will be a work of three years' labor at least. As for our return to Cedarcroft, I do not, I must confess, see the way clear. It was a great mistake to suppose that I could attend to the details of business in a country home, and go on with a serious literary work at the same time. The absence of large libraries and such literary counselors as can be found only in a large city is an equal drawback.

So long as I wrote merely superficial descriptive works I did not feel the difficulty ; but now, when I must divide my time between earnest, absorbing study and entire rest and recreation, a change in our manner of life becomes inevitable. If Philadelphia were Boston, and Kennett Concord, I might manage to stay, by reducing my property to a few acres. Few men, I think, are more attached to their early associations than I am, but when a more important duty, when the necessity of my aim in life comes between me and them, what should I do?

" Lars " was published in London March 1st, and in Boston March 8, 1873.

CHAPTER XXVI.

THE PROPHET.

1873–1874.

And still some cheaper service claims
The will that leaps to loftier call ;
Some cloud is cast on splendid aims,
On power achieved some common thrall.
Implora Pace.

MR. REID, in his plans for the rehabilitation of the
"Tribune," was glad to take advantage of Bayard
Taylor's residence in Europe to obtain from him some
special letters upon the Vienna Exhibition, then about
to open. The "Tribune" might make no dividends
to its stockholders, but it was a good paymaster to its
contributors, and Bayard Taylor, compelled now to
live from hand to mouth, dropped his work on the
"History of Germany" and went to Vienna for a
month, for the purpose of describing the enterprise in
general terms and especially of reporting promptly
the scenes at the opening. It was not proposed that
he should describe the Exhibition in detail. That was
left to his associates, Mr. W. J. Stillman and Mr.
E. V. Smalley, who were on the ground with him and
remained after he left.

He threw himself into the task with all the ardor
of a newspaper man who is carrying the colors of his
enterprise. He not only succeeded in distancing the
representatives of other papers and sending a series

of letters which gave full and graphic reports, but he
worked indefatigably for the interests of the paper in
other ways, making it the most conspicuous of the
American journals in the eyes of the Viennese. This
done, he hastened back to Gotha to take up his History, which he was impatient to complete.

TO WHITELAW REID.

VIENNA, *Saturday evening, May* 3, 1873.

I am pretty well used up, physically, by this evening, but shall
be all right again after a good night's rest. Stillman and I have
been working together ever since April 24th, when I arrived, and
have done all we planned to do. Everything relating to the opening was made difficult by the delay and confusion of the Austrian
officials. They kept no promises ; the cards of admission, the
advance copies of the speeches, and other minor privileges, could
only be obtained after repeated personal interviews. The hacks
were all on a strike, and we ran back and forth on our own legs.
The landlord threatened to turn us out by announcing a charge
of twelve dollars per day for my room, instead of four dollars,
and there was no time to hunt other quarters. Finally, I got a
small back chamber for three dollars.

You will see how we divided our work. Stillman had his copy
ready by two o'clock, and got possession of the wire, which we
kept (having made a previous arrangement with the officials) until we finished. I sent half of mine at three, and took the other
half at four, when —— of the —— made his first appearance.
Our first number was 112 and ——'s 129. Then came Forbes,
of the London "News," and after him the rest ; but all had to
wait for us. The New York —— sent a special messenger to
Queenstown to catch to-day's steamer, while by telegraphing we
have caught Thursday's. Smalley got his share finished about
half-past five.

. . . I did my best, at the journalists' banquet, to make capital for the "Tribune," and succeeded. It was a little *too* cool in
Yates to get up and be presented as an American, and speak in
the name of the American press (in fearful German), without
calling upon one of us natives. I did what I never did before, —
privately demanded of the president a chance to speak, — and in
ten minutes stirred up the only real enthusiasm of the evening.

Austrian editors and Prussian, French, and Swedish, crowded around me to shake hands and to thank me for striking the keynote of what journalism should be. I made, accidentally, a new German word,[1] — an entirely correct one, — which has greatly tickled the fancy of the editors here. One of the dailies has since used it for the title of a leading article. Dr. Schlesinger, Rodenberg, Etienne, and others of the leading German journalists, have since personally expressed to me their great satisfaction. I inclose the report of the "Deutsche Zeitung," with a translation of the part relating to my little speech, which you will see is only an echo of the "Tribune's" position. I don't ask you to publish it, — indeed, I am not sure that it would be in good taste to do so ; but I want you to see exactly what I said. I had no idea of making such an impression. I hear of the thing wherever I turn, and I hope it will do us some good.

VIENNA, *Friday morning, May* 16, 1873.

. . . The weather continues frightfully bad, and there are comparatively few arrivals. The great show has been so retarded, and is still so incomplete, that I have found some difficulty in deciding what to write about. I am afraid you will be disappointed in your hope of getting "brilliant" descriptive letters from me, since that quality is a thing which cannot be manufactured ; it must come from the object described. Even the opening was so brief and simple that I doubt whether any correspondent succeeded in making an impressive account of it. I have seen none in the German or English papers which was either so full or so correct as ours.

The Tribune Bureau is now tolerably well regulated. I think —— anticipates a little too much in the way of advertising and circulation, as I wrote to him to-day ; but no very serious expense has been incurred, and we have at least already acquired a prestige in Germany, Austria, and Hungary which leaves all other American papers out of sight. The —— people have been bewildered and worried at finding the "Tribune" ahead of them everywhere. The ——, after a feeble struggle, gave up competition, and all the other papers come under our wings for a little comfort or counsel.

---

[1] The word, a new German compound, was *Weltgemüthlichkeit*, and was received with no end of applause. The German speech was praised in all the papers, and said to be full of the sprightliest *aperçus*.

I shall write three letters more, and then I must go back to my neglected History. My wife has been quite unwell in Gotha, and will not come here for a few days as she hoped. E. V. S. has gone out to Baden (twenty miles from here) temporarily, on account of *his* wife's health. He and W. J. S. will be quite enough to report the future progress of the Exhibition, and they will so divide their duties as not to conflict or overlap.

GOTHA, GERMANY, *May* 24, 1873.

I finished and sent off to you this morning my last letter anent the Vienna Exposition. This makes (including the report of the opening) ten letters and two translations which I have sent from Vienna in all, so now I propose that we square accounts for the present. As there was no agreement in advance, I must leave the remuneration to your estimate of the service rendered, only begging you to remember that *all* my time in Vienna was given to Tribune work, half of which, and perhaps the most important half, is not represented by my correspondence ; and also that inevitable and necessary expenses for the month I have given, including the journey to and fro, are a little over three hundred dollars, gold. Please just lump together all I have done, Italian letters, etc., up to now, and send me a draft for the amount (on Berlin) to this address. I must give myself wholly to the History from this day on until it is all written and stereotyped, so cannot undertake any more service for the "Tribune" before September.

. . . I am tolerably tired, after a month of bad weather, bad fare, and endless running to and fro in Vienna. My wife has been quite unwell also, so we propose to go to a little town in the mountains, only a few miles from here, for three or four weeks. I shall take my work along, and get my mails daily as here. I am very desirous of hearing something about the new building, and again beg you to send me an unmounted photograph of the plan as soon as you have one. When you answer this, pray tell me as much as you have time to say concerning that and other business developments.

TO HIS MOTHER.

GOTHA, *May* 26, 1873.

Yours of the 9th inst. came on Saturday and found me already here. I did not write from Vienna, because I was just as busy

as I could be, doing work for the "Tribune," and had a severe
attack of rheumatism in the right (or write) arm, which made
writing difficult. I cured it with quinine before I left, and am
now all right. The weather was bad there, the cost of living
very high, and the Exhibition unfinished ; consequently I am
very glad to get back again. My only consolation is that I
earned a little money. You will see my letters in the "Tribune,"
so I need write nothing more about my visit there. . . . We shall
go to Friedrichroda in two days to stay a few weeks. It is
quieter there, and I can work better. I shall be very busy until
August, and may not be able to write long letters ; but when the
History is once finished, it will be a great relief. . . .

TO WHITELAW REID.

GOTHA, GERMANY, *July* 23, 1873.

The "Tribune" is admirable, and I no longer wonder at its
success. What Ripley tells me of the profits is most encouraging ; but it is only a foreshadowing of what is yet to come. I
am heartily glad that I have been able to do a very little, and
should like to do more.

Here, I have a proposition to make, and beg you to answer it
solely as you may judge the interests of the paper require, without regard to any personal considerations. I am quite anxious to
see Egypt again, after twenty-two years, next winter. I have a
bronchial difficulty which threatens to become chronic, and a winter in Egypt would make all right. So much has happened there,
such changes are going on in the Orient, that I think a series
of letters would be interesting to the "Tribune" readers — and
possibly valuable for the weekly and semi-weekly, if announced
early in the fall, as H. G. used to do. With my present means I
could go, provided I could earn eight hundred to one thousand
dollars by writing while there, — and as I formerly wrote, not by
measure, which does n't answer well for the kind of correspondence I have in view, but for the service as a whole. As far back
as 1850, I was paid thirty dollars per letter, without any regard
to length, and if I spent three or four months in the Orient, I
should hardly write less than twenty-five letters. I mention this
now, that you may consider in time ; it might help the weekly a
little, if mentioned in the coming programme. But if you decide
against it, I am sure it will be for sufficient reasons. When I
return home next summer, I want to stay for a good many years,
D. V., in New York.

GOTHA, *July* 26, 1873.

. . . I think I never stuck at any work so steadily as this " History of Germany," for it requires the closest attention, and besides I have engaged to finish my part of the work by the 1st of August. Consequently I have let everything lie ; for after working seven hours a day, and then walking one hour, I really felt as if I could not touch a pen. If I keep my health and strength, which so far have supported me wonderfully, only four days more, I shall be done. Wednesday will be the 30th of July, and I shall have one day to spare. After that I don't mean to do more than I please for a month or two. The History has been a big job, but I hope it will yield me something handsome, which it is sure to do, if once properly introduced into the schools. I feel the labor less, I think, than I did a month ago, for as I draw so near the end the pressure diminishes.

His estimate of his powers was exact. The work was finished, so far as the writing was concerned, upon the 30th of July. The stereotyping of the plates had meanwhile been going on at Leipzig, and by the first week of September Mr. Brockhaus wrote that the plates had been shipped to New York, ready for printing. He added in his letter : " In the course of its progress here, I have taken great interest in becoming acquainted with your work, and I feel glad, as a German, that the history of our country has found in you such an excellent interpreter ; for it is certainly not easy for a foreigner to make clear the often very clouded and obscure passages in our history. You have really rendered a great service to Germany by this work, since it will no doubt help toward a better knowledge of our development as a Nation." There was little other satisfaction for Bayard Taylor in the book. The publication was delayed in America, owing to dissatisfaction with the illustrations, and the end was that the author never received the least return for his labor.

TO E. C. STEDMAN.

GOTHA, GERMANY, *August* 9, 1873.

You made your short note so pleasant that I can't scold you for its brevity ; yet I should like to. There might have been so much more of what may seem personal or domestic " nothings " to you, yet have such value at this distance ! As for the Vienna letters, I went there reluctantly, and expected to hear that my reports were stupid and prosy : if you suppose I made any effort to do fine writing, you are mistaken. Nothing in my literary experience ever surprised me more than to hear, from a great many sources, that they were especially good. The other things which I write in exactly the same fashion, under the same moods, on the same literary plan, are not so fortunate. Why is this thus ? Of course I am always glad to do a thing well, — glad, in this case, for the "Tribune's" sake, — but I can't have any feeling of exultation about mere ephemeral work. .

. . . However, "Lars" has been so long published that my interest in him is now about as slight as that of any reader. I have been working for seven months, interrupted only by a month at Vienna, on my "History of Germany," which I hope will be damned alive by everybody and sell tremendously. This work I have done for money : now let us see whether the sordid impulse will not be more fortunate than the purer aspiration ! Since I must earn my living for the present, I pray for pecuniary success, and for none other ; a few months will probably decide.

I must be thankful for health, after all this labor, — and for the last ten weeks I have studied, written, and corrected ten hours a day, Sundays included, — and for the absence of physical and mental depression, which I had two years ago. I shall take the holiday of a few weeks which I have fairly earned, gather Goethe-material in a slow way, and gradually look out for fresh paying work.

. . . We live, in fact, like the early Christians, not taking much thought of the morrow, yet reasonably happy and hopeful. In fact, life is full of useless misery, — if we could but shake it off !

TO W. J. STILLMAN.

GOTHA, *September* 12, 1873.

. . . I can fully understand your longing for America. I am beginning to count the months which must intervene before my own return, and when I get there I shall not leave again soon. There must certainly be good, remunerative work for you there, for the work you can do is sorely needed. I think the people are ripe for a purer artistic instruction than they have yet received. Unfortunately the chances of finding one's place are more or less accidental, and one must generally wait a little for them. If you should not go before I do, and still keep in the same mind, I can easily ascertain what hope there is in New York. I do not know Boston so well, and have not an entire faith in the permanence of its æsthetic culture. Much there depends upon a small circle, the members of which are getting old, and I do not see any signs of a younger generation. In New York it is just the younger ones who are developing in the right way.

I have finished my History, and have been for the last fortnight painting. It is, perhaps, a foolish, but a harmless, passion with me, and I am very happy over every little sign of improvement. Moreover, after a long dry spell there have been a few poetic showers, and they always give me fresh life. So I take all other discouragements easily, and keep in cheerful spirits.

TO E. C. STEDMAN.

WEIMAR, *October* 14, 1873.

. . . I have carefully read all the *German* biographies, and recently Lewes over again, with a most encouraging result. The man and poet, Goethe, is not clearly or fairly drawn in any of them. The material is immense, and I must know it all without using more than ten per cent. of it. But the farther I go the more courage I have to take hold.

I have only been here two days, but have made two most valuable acquaintances, and learned the streets of the little capital by heart. I always liked Weimar, and now it has a veritable fascination for me. I shall stay about six weeks now, and return in the spring. This study of the localities is delightful. Already both Goethe and Schiller come out of the limbo of shadows, and are growing into existences of flesh and blood for mc. Yesterday, passing Goethe's garden-house, in the charming park along the Ilm, I stopped at the gate and found myself wondering whether *he* had planted the bed of marigolds under the window. The table where Thackeray used to take tea with Ottilie von Goethe was covered with fallen leaves ; but there were white curtains at the windows, and a bouquet of asters in a pot. Most of the trees are still green ; the days are very bright and sunny, though night comes much too soon here in lat. 51°.

TO JOHN B. PHILLIPS.

GOTHA, *November* 22, 1873.

. . . You exaggerate what you consider my successes, and hence, very probably, the effect which you imagine them to have upon my nature. From 1854 to 1862, or thereabouts, I had a good deal of popularity of a cheap, ephemeral sort. It began to decline at the time when I began to see the better and truer work in store for me, and I let it go, feeling that I must begin anew and acquire a second reputation, of a very different kind. For the past five years I have been engaged in this struggle, which is not yet over. I dare not pause to rest, for my own sake ; the change in my nature gives me the energy of a new youth, and I know this cannot last many years more. I am giving the best blood of my life to my labors, seeing them gradually recognized by the few and the best, it is true, but they are still unknown to the public, and my new claims are fiercely resisted by a majority of the newspaper writers in the United States. Out of a dozen intimate literary friends in New York and Boston, only three have sent me a word of congratulation about "Lars." . . . And now comes a report from Strahan, the London publisher. "Lars" is the first poem of mine ever published in England, and I hoped for some impartial recognition there. Well, the sale is just one hundred and eight copies ! My translation of "Faust" is at last accepted in England, Germany, and America as much the best. It cost me years of the severest labor, and has not yet returned me five hundred dollars. The "Masque of the Gods" has not paid expenses. The sale of my former volumes of travel has fallen almost to nothing, as is natural, for they were doomed, from the first, to a transient existence. For two years past I have had no income of any sort from property or copyrights, and am living partly upon my capital and partly upon mechanical labor of the mind. Within a year I have written "Lars," compiled a volume on Central Asia for Scribners, done the Vienna Exposition for the "Tribune," written a complete "School History of Germany" (working on it ten hours a day for months), and have just returned from six weeks of Goethe studies and researches in Weimar. I am very weary, indeed, completely fagged out, and to read what you say of my success sounds almost like irony. The fancy that you may think me spoiled by it makes me laugh. It would take a great deal more praise than I get to make me feel that the one resolute aim of these later years is at all generally appreciated. . . .

The hints which Bayard Taylor had dropped to one or two of his most intimate friends of a mysterious work upon which he was engaged point to his drama of "The Prophet." Several years before, when walking with a friend, their conversation fell upon the Mormons, and his friend sketched a drama which he meant to write some day with the Mormon superstition for an historic basis. At that very time Bayard Taylor had projected a drama, which was to make use of the same materials, although the use was to be very different. He was so taken aback by the coincidence of their thought that he was dumb for the rest of the walk, and could not bring himself to speak of his own scheme, but waited until he had gone home, when he wrote of it to his friend. There was no real conflict of purpose between them, but the incident points to a characteristic of Bayard Taylor's habit of construction, whether in poetry or prose. Rapid as his work was, it waited upon a full projection, and sometimes waited long. The conception came ; he suffered it to grow, to become full-formed in his mind before he gave it expression. Then, when it pressed for a concrete form, he saw it from beginning to end, and the very fury of his composition was in his eager haste to overtake the conclusion. There was no hesitation about the work ;

because the conception lay perfect in his mind before he conveyed it at all to paper. He was willing to wait for the full growth of his idea, because the ideal which he always had before him was of perfection in art, and he believed too emphatically in the possibility of this perfection to suffer his work to be begun in uncertainty, with the expectation that somehow it would shape itself. The creative instinct which he had so strongly was an intelligent and conscious one. His works were not happy accidents, but clearly determined forms. The one unmistakable property of all his writings, except the merely narrative and descriptive works, was this clear conception of ultimate form. Thus, although he had conceived the main purpose of " The Prophet" long before, he had waited until he could impose it upon a sure basis of historic fact, and now that he was satisfied with the structure as it was formed in his mind he wrote as one transcribes.

The completion of " The Prophet " left the writer wearied from the strain which the composition had imposed upon him. He began writing it at the end of August, during his short stay in Gotha. The first act was completed in September, and the second act begun. The visit to Weimar did not interrupt the work. Indeed, it rather stimulated his mind to greater activity. The delightful intercourse which he there had with intellectual people, and the association with Goethe which was made more intimate by the distinct purpose of his visit, quickened his mental life and hastened the completion of the drama. On October 18th he wrote to his wife, " I have nothing more to send you, for I shall bring the new scenes with me. I write something, whether much or little, every day, and find it the only way to prevent the Goethe-interests from interrupting

me. I want to go on with the main action while I am
possessed with it." So deeply had he become absorbed
in his task, that social engagements, researches, and
visits to neighboring towns seemed merely outside incidents, which deprived him for the time of actual
writing, but did not retard the growth of the drama in
his mind, so that in the intervals of his busy life he was
always ready to put quickly upon paper the acts and
scenes which had been taking form. On the railway
to Gotha, the second stanza of Livia's song was composed and noted down in pencil. In the middle of
November, after having completed Act IV., he resolved
not to begin Act V. until a week later, when he expected to have a few quiet days at Gotha. But before
getting there, on November 18th, he wrote, "I began
Act V. last evening, — could n't help it. To-day, D. V.,
I shall finish Scene II. There 's no use of waiting,
while I am in the humor to write." The last two
scenes of the drama were written at Leizpig, November 24th and 25th. He was hardly aware, until the
work was done, how heavily it had taxed his nervous
system.

TO J. R. OSGOOD AND T. B. ALDRICH.

GOTHA, GERMANY, *November* 30, 1873.

I unite your names, intending this for both of you, because I
have a secret to confide to both, and most earnestly request that
it shall go no farther.

The plan you, T. B. A., suggested in regard to "Lars" can
now be put into execution, and with a far better chance of success. There were many passages in "Lars" which would have
betrayed my hand : there is scarcely one in the new poem, just
completed, which any one will recognize as mine. A much more
ambitious and important conception, which I have carried in my
head for seven years past, is at last put into words. For nearly
four months I have been secretly at work ; no one here, except
my wife, has any suspicion of what I have done, and of course

no one in America. It is a dramatic poem called "The Prophet : a Tragedy," or "The Prophet's Tragedy," whichever may be considered best. I prefer the former. It is in five acts, and makes 3,400 lines of verse, without counting descriptive passages or stage directions. The following are the Dramatis Personæ : David Starr, the Prophet; Elkanah Starr, his father ; Hannah Starr, his mother ; Rhoda, afterwards his wife ; Nimrod Kraft, afterwards High Priest ; Livia Romney, a woman of the world ; Peter, an orphan, David's serving-man ; Simeon, Mordecai, Hugh, Jonas, members of the Council of Twelve ; Sarah, wife of Jonas ; Colonel Hyde, Sheriff ; Hiram, a member of the church ; a Preacher ; men of David's neighborhood ; members of the Church, women, Colonel Hyde's followers.

The time is between 1840 and 1850.

The scene of Act I. is in a New England State ; of the other four Acts in a Western State.

The substance of the drama may be thus roughly given : Act I. The development of the prophet-nature in an earnest, excitable young man ; love ; miracles. Act II. Emigration to the West ; Zion founded ; new elements introduced ; another woman. Act III. Polygamy : two passions at work. Act IV. Secret rebellion ; desperate measures to establish a hierarchy ; ambition of the High Priest. Act V. Conflict with state authorities ; *denoûement* of a plot in which two wives, Prophet, Priest, and Council of Twelve figure ; death of the Prophet in the Temple.

The history of the Mormons is a background to the poem. Nauvoo is suggested ; but the conception of the Prophet's nature is quite independent. The poem is a two-edged sword, cutting the fossilized Orthodox to the heart no less than the Mormons. It is full of passion and intrigue ; among the scenes are : A camp-meeting ; miracles in a mountain valley ; camps on the prairies ; the Temple of the New Zion ; secret councils of the Twelve ; and at last battle and death. The plot is the result of years of constant thought ; as a piece of literary art the poem will rank vastly higher than "Lars." It has a terse, compact, vigorous character, which is quite unlike the latter ; the action is uninterrupted from beginning to end, and there are many very strong dramatic situations. In short, it is a poem to make or break a reputation.

My suggestion is this : I will send the MS. by mail in the spring. During the summer the work may be heralded by mysterious hints of a new author. (If need be, I will write two or three poems in some striking manner, to be used.) I expect to return home about September 1st, and if it comes out about the middle of that month, suspicion will be averted from me. This seems to me the very best chance for trying the experiment. The poem will certainly attract a great deal of attention, — possibly, of controversy. I assure you in advance of its originality and of its power, as contrasted with my former works. The conception struck me at first as so important that I kept it so many years in order to grow up to it. What I have written to you is the driest skeleton, not even giving you the plot. But I hope the material will enable you to judge. It will make a volume of two hundred pages, printed like Longfellow's "Divine Tragedy." There are thirty-five scenes in all, and nine songs or hymns introduced. The catastrophe is quite startling, solving the complication introduced by the two wives of the Prophet, and in a way which (I think) will satisfy everybody.

There! I need say no more. The work is done, must and will be published, and it is for you to decide whether in this way or another.

I may add that the religious element is a background on which human passions are projected. David is a Hamlet-nature, and the germs of his final fate are in him from the first.

I write this now, that we may have plenty of time. All that was suggested last winter is now possible, and I will go into the plot with all my heart if you agree. Please answer me soon to this address.

TO GEORGE H. YEWELL.

GOTHA, GERMANY, *December* 5, 1873.

I have just finished my Weimar studies for this fall, and brought my wife back from Leipzig. . . . I feel quite sure that it (Egypt) will be the very climate for my wife. I found the winter-climate of Egypt bracing as well as soft; three days out of four there was a north wind, and the *Khamseen* (something like the scirocco) only came about once a month. It was sometimes quite warm between eleven and three o'clock, but the evenings were always perfect, and the nights cool enough for blankets. I am more than ever bent on going, because I feel sure the trip can be made with tolerable cheapness from Naples, *via* Malta, in the Rubattino line. It will hardly cost more at a

hotel in Cairo than in Rome, — say about fifteen francs a day.
If five of us go together, I will undertake to make the journey
from Rome to Thebes and back for six hundred dollars apiece,
counting *everything* : possibly for five hundred dollars.

I am obliged to economize in every way, as we have almost no
income of any kind, and are eating our way into our very moderate capital ; but I estimate that the letters I can write from
Egypt will yield enough to pay more than the difference of expenses between going there and staying in Italy. So you may
bring back two or three old temple interiors which will pay you
in the same way. Don't give up the idea yet ; if you will say
yes, now, I will say so too. We can leave about the middle of
January, and be back about the middle of March, after which we
want to stay a month in Rome before returning to Germany.

This is our dark time of the year, when every letter is sure to
have bad news. Within three or four weeks, my mother has
been sick, my old father fell down a staircase, a niece in America and another in Germany have died, remittances have gone
astray or never been sent, and I don't know how many minor
anxieties have come to us. But I console myself with the idea
that Fate, after taking so much, will owe me something after
a while, — that I shall earn a little good luck by being patient
with the bad. . . . We shall turn our faces southward about
January 1st, and probably make the trip from here to Bologna
— forty hours — without stopping.

. . . We both long for Italy again, and it is a great delight
to think that, D. V., we shall be there in four weeks. Don't
wait as long as I have done with a letter ; you must remember
that, writing all day at my work, a little more writing is sometimes hard, and I rather wait than turn a letter to a friend into
a task.

TO T. B. ALDRICH.

GOTHA, *December 6, 1873.*

I sent a joint letter to you and Osgood two or three days
ago, with a confidential message, which I hope will reach you
safely. I feel rather sure of your concurrence in the proposed
plan. Indeed, the idea is solely yours of last winter, and I
shall owe my success to you if it succeeds. Inasmuch as I
don't get some important letters long since due, I begin to fear
that there may be a leak somewhere in the post, and therefore,

to be quite sure of your getting my message, will briefly repeat the substance of it here.

I've written a dramatic poem in five acts, — "The Prophet : A Tragedy." It is wholly American in scene, character, and plot ; in fact, the story could not happen in any other part of the world. The rise of the Mormons under Joe Smith, the building of the Temple at Nauvoo, and the death of Joe Smith there form a sufficient historical background. My Prophet, however, is a totally different person ; his doom may be distinctly traced to teachings of Orthodox Christianity. Upon the latter he bases polygamy and a despotic hierarchy. The poem is full of dramatic situations, and its religious element is only the ground upon which human passions are drawn. The poem is by far the best thing I have ever written. The blank verse has a vigorous, compact character, quite unlike that of "Lars," and I'm sure few persons will think of me when they read it. If I'd a set of devout disciples, like Emerson or Lowell, I should not feel safe ; but having positively not *one* (that I know of), I think we may play a little comedy without any one looking under the mask. My letter tells more of the poem, and I hope its safe arrival will make this superfluous.

I've just returned from a stay of nearly two months at Weimar. While there I got well acquainted with the grandsons of Goethe, Schiller, Herder, and Wieland, and with many elder persons who knew Goethe intimately. I *lived myself into* (as the German phrase is) the atmosphere of the place, and learned a great deal in a short time.

. . . I'm getting immensely homesick, but next summer, D. V., will see us back again. Pray let me hear from you soon after this reaches you. Direct to care of J. L. Graham, United States Consul, Florence, Italy. We'll go there in four weeks to finish the winter in a softer air. And now good-by !

TO HANNAH M. DARLINGTON.

GOTHA, GERMANY, *December* 29, 1873.

Your letter of the 7th inst. was most welcome and interesting. . . .

I'm glad to hear that "Lars" is finding favor among the Friends. I know that it is not strictly true to all their observances, but that makes not the slightest difference. The more correct it is, in that respect, the less poetic it becomes. The dis-

cipline of the Friends is antagonistic to all poetry. I have used
the only poetic element they possess, — the direction of the Spirit.
The "plan of approach," of which you speak as being so contrary
to their ways, is chosen because it is dramatic and true in a general human sense, no matter how untrue in a technical sense. So,
if the story is "horrible," as you think, can you not feel that the
two extremes are positively necessary ? If "Lars" had not been
so violent a nature, the triumph of the peace-principle would be
greatly lessened, the story would become weak and tame, and the
final impression might be lost altogether. What success I have
achieved lies exactly in overcoming brute passion in its fiercest
form by a moral courage so strong that it prohibits the suspicion
of physical cowardice. The laws of poetic art are never in conflict with those of human nature in its broad, unhindered development ; but every sect, and the Friends as much as any other,
cramps, dwarfs, and distorts such development. The highest nature is that which is bound by no sect, but freely accepts the good
of each and all. You must, therefore, not judge "Lars" from the
standpoint of the rules and regulations of the Friends ; no poem,
in fact, can be submitted to such a standard of judgment. . . .
I am steadily at work all the time. I have really done more during the last fifteen months than ever before in my life in an equal
period of time. Whether my work will find immediate acceptance or not does not concern me. I try to fulfill my own ideal of
excellence so far as possible, and trust to final recognition by the
minds capable of it. . . .

TO JERVIS M^CENTEE.

GOTHA, GERMANY, *January* 8, 1874.

Your welcome letter of December 21st reached me yesterday,
and I reply at once because we are on the eve of starting for Italy.
In fact, we meant to leave to-morrow, but L. has been in bed two
days with a severe bilious attack, and we shall hardly be able to
get away before Monday next.

. . . Our plan now is to get to Italy as soon as possible, but
not to stay there. We shall push on to Egypt by the 1st of February, and remain there until the end of March ; then return to
Rome for April, then back to Germany in May, when I shall go
again to Weimar for six weeks. My studies completed there, we
shall all be ready and eager to go home.

Now, you may wonder how I should undertake a trip to Egypt

in my state of suspended income. The secret is, I go there to write for the "Tribune," and to make half a dozen magazine articles of more interest than I could prepare in Italy. Thus, although the expense will be greater, I shall be able to earn more than enough to cover the difference. Besides, the perfect climate of Egypt is just what is needed for M. and me. My bronchial irritation is not bad, but very stubborn, and African air will cure it in a few weeks. Moreover, I don't feel certain of again coming to Europe for such a long stay, — at least, I hope not, — and I must refresh my soul, my whole nature, beside the Nile, where I felt the fullness of life twenty-one years ago as never since. If we were only already there !

The short delay which Bayard Taylor anticipated in getting away from Gotha proved to be a month. His daughter's illness was more serious than at first appeared, and the family remained from day to day and week to week, waiting until it was safe to travel. The delay compelled them finally to shorten their stay both in Italy and in Egypt, where they could not go beyond Cairo. The closing weeks of 1873 and the early months of 1874 also were marked by most unpropitious weather, so that the holiday which Bayard Taylor had anticipated was passed under many discomforts. He was so occupied by many cares connected with his daughter's illness that he did little work during the month of forced stay in Gotha, except to write a long article for the "Tribune" on Schliemann's discoveries, one of the earliest and most comprehensive résumés of a work which was then just coming into notice. He wrote also a story for the "Atlantic," "Who was She?" The delay gave him opportunity to write more at length to his friends.

TO E. C. STEDMAN.

GOTHA, GERMANY, *January* 16, 1874.

. . . We meant to have left here on the 7th for Florence and Rome, but on the 5th L. was taken down with bilious fever, and

still lies in bed, although, D. G. ! the crisis is past, and she begins to mend. The winter climate here is unusually trying. I
have a stubborn cough, and M. is beginning to give way, after so
much night-watching. However, to-day I engaged Sister Engel-
berta and Sister Blanca, two fresh and fair Catholic nurses, to
take turns in sitting up, in M.'s place ; and we hope five or six
days more will relieve us from all further care and anxiety. But
it will be the end of the month, or nearly so, before we get away.

So much was crowded into my two months' sojourn in Weimar,
that I hardly know where to begin to tell you about it. I had
not been there many days before I discovered that my translation was generally and favorably known ; so I began to call,
without ceremony, upon the people I wanted to know, and was
received with open arms. During the last three weeks I was invited out to supper every evening, and thus drew deep draughts
of the social atmosphere. I made no secret of my plan, and
every one seemed desirous to be of some service. With Baron
Gleichen, Schiller's grandson, I established a hearty friendship.
I am to go with him to his father's castle of Bonnland in the
spring, and examine all the MSS. and relics of Schiller which
the family possesses. Wolfgang von Goethe, who is both eccen-
tric and misanthropic, thawed towards me, and I assure you it
was a great satisfaction to visit him in Goethe's house, and to see
the same luminous large brown eyes beaming on me as he talked.
I was startled at his personal resemblance to the poet. Herder's
grandson invited me to supper before I ever saw him, and Wieland's granddaughter, a sculptress, invited me to give my German
lecture on American Literature in Weimar. One evening, at the
hotel, an interesting looking man of forty, with a brown beard,
took his seat opposite to me, and we fell into conversation. Presently Mr. Hamilton (of the noble Scotch clan, who lives in Weimar) came in, and introduced him to me as Baron von Stein,
grandson of Frau von Stein ! Fräulein Frommann, foster-sister
of one of Goethe's loves (Minna Herzlieb), though a woman of
seventy-five, knows and remembers everything, and she told me
many interesting anecdotes. She was for many years companion
to the present Empress Augusta, and enjoys much consideration;
so when she said to me, " I feel *safe* with you ; I can tell you
all knowing that you will use it only as I could wish," and repeated the same thing to others, I was at once placed in the very
relation to all which I wished to have established. I called on

the famous old painter, Preller, whose illustrations of the Odyssey are finer (because simpler and severer) than anything of Kaulbach's. I remarked that he had a copy of Trippel's glorious bust of Goethe, and said : "I have this bust at home, and opposite to it the Venus of Milo, as the woman form corresponding to this male form." His eyes shone ; he rose up without a word, grasped my arm, and turned me around. There was the Venus of Milo, opposite Goethe ! "I never pass her," said Preller, "without pausing an instant, and saying to myself, 'My God, how beautiful she is !'" Well, after that, Preller and I became fast friends. He was a protégé, a half-pupil of Goethe, whose son died in his arms. Afterwards, when Goethe lay dead, Preller stole into the room and made a wonderful drawing of the head. Now, after forty years, he voluntarily made the first copy of it, with his own hands, as a present for me ! You may guess how I value it.

Schiller's grandson is an excellent artist. His pictures are astonishingly like McEntee's. I spent many hours in his studio. Schoell, one of the best Goethe scholars in Germany (now chief librarian at Weimar), is enthusiastically in favor of my biographical plan. He is utterly dissatisfied with Lewes. He told Lewes many particulars which Lewes distorted in the most ridiculous manner. Several persons told me that Lewes pumped lackeys and old servants while in Weimar, and took no pains to get acquainted with the intelligent intimate friends of Goethe. I can't say how much truth there is in this ; *I* am most happy to find that I have nothing of my own conception of Goethe to *unlearn*, after knowing Weimar. My plan, at last, stands round and complete before my mind, and I only need life and health to give it a permanent form. I wish I had space to tell you more of what I learned, and how immensely I have been encouraged.

My lecture was a great triumph. It was given in the hall of the Arquebusiers, a society dating from the Middle Ages. The whole court came, Grand-Duke and Duchess, Hereditary Grand-Duke and Duchess, the two charming Princesses, and Prince Hermann, with adjutants and ladies of honor. The Grand-Duke came up to me with a mock reproach, and said : "There's one serious fault in the lecture : you have not mentioned yourself ! But come and dine with me to-morrow, and we'll talk more about it." Which I did. The dinner was superb ; two Weimar friends of mine were invited, otherwise only the family. I assure you it gave me a thrill of pride to stand in Weimar, with the grand-children of Carl August, Goethe, Schiller, Herder, and Wieland among my auditors, and vindicate the literary achievement of America. I lashed properly the German idea of the omnipo-tency of money among us ; recited passages from Halleck, Poe, Emerson, Bryant, and Whittier, and said a good word for E. C. S., R. H. S., T. B. A., and W. D. H. The lecture seems to have made considerable impression, as an account of it has since gone the rounds of most of the German papers.

I must return to Weimar for another month in the spring, and finish my studies there. Then Dr. Hirzel of Leipzig, who has the best Goethe library in the world, allows me to make use of certain materials, which will give me in a fortnight what would otherwise require a year's drudgery. I want to come home next summer, ready to begin to write. The whole work, then, can be done in three years more, even allowing occasional interludes of poetry, as they come to me.

I 'm very glad you like my " Two Homes." The idea is not new, of course, but I think the form is. At least it came to me in a dream, and I did not see why it was good until after the poem was written, when I felt that the change from iambic to anapæstic, terminating with an unrhymed line, expresses unrest growing out of rest. . . . The fact is, my dear old friend, there are eternal laws in literary art ; thought (in poetry) is subject to architectural rules, and the painted and tinseled palaces which just now dazzle the eyes of the public are doomed, — for their very material is ruin. Mere grace of phrase, surface brilliancy, simulated fire, cannot endure : we must build of hewn blocks from the everlasting quarries, and then the fools who say, " Oh, there is no color in that ! " will die long before our work shall dream of decay. . . . The success of your volume of poems is an excellent sign, and delights me to the very heart. Your suc-cess means mine, and that of all honest poets. You may depend upon me : I will never flinch ; my will is like adamant to en-dure until the end. I have large designs yet, and more real po-etry in me than has hitherto come out of me. I see my way clear, — recognize both capacities and limitations as never before, and bate no jot of heart or hope. I hope to have something more ready to show you by the time I reach home, but will not prom-ise. . . .

Here's a third sheet : shall I go on ? Yes ; for you can take a cigar and let me chatter in your ear, while you are relieved of the necessity of answering. I could open the flood-gates and let *myself* rush out upon you. I've had no one near me for a long while with whom I could expand, save a superbly beautiful young artist in Weimar, full of genius but impatient. I wrote a German distich under my photograph which I gave him, which I may translate thus : —

> Never forget, O Friend, that for Art, the true, the eternal,
> Genius is sire that begets, Patience the mother that bears !

Well, if I were to write about myself for six hours, it would all come to this : that life is, for me, the developing, asserting, and establishing of my own *Entelecheia*, — the making all that is possible out of such powers as I may have, without violently forcing or distorting them. You have often, no doubt, wondered at and condemned the variety of things I have either willfully attempted or been compelled to do by the necessities of my life. I see the use of all these attempts now, when I am beginning to concentrate instead of scatter. If I am capable of good and lasting work, there is nothing I have hitherto done which will not now help me to achieve it. All's well that ends well. Yes, but the end is not yet come. It's enough that I am not afraid of it.

Bayard Taylor and his family finally left Gotha February 11th, and by easy stages traveled to Rome, where they stayed a week. They left Rome March 1st, and went to Naples, where they took the steamer for Alexandria *via* Messina. On the 13th they landed at Alexandria, whence they proceeded to Cairo, returning to Alexandria April 6th, and reaching Naples April 13th. Three days later they went to Rome, remained there a week only, and then by Florence, Nürnberg, and Munich to Gotha, which they reached May 1st. Bayard Taylor occupied himself with letters from Egypt to the "Tribune," eleven in all, written under the greatest discomfort of cold and storm, and with one or two magazine articles. He was absorbed for the time in Egyptology, and his imagination was kindled anew. In spite of all the disagreeable circumstances of the entire journey, he gained physically.

TO E. C. STEDMAN.

ROME, *February* 24, 1874.

We reached here on Saturday evening, and the next morning I found your package (E. B. B., Landor, Hood, Arnold, etc., the Dartmouth Ode, and Macdonough's article). I read every line of all of them before I went to bed that evening, and it is long since anything has so thoroughly refreshed me.

. . . At Florence I found Lowell in the same hotel, and had three good days with him. This is our third day here, and we leave on Friday for Naples, to embark for Alexandria on Saturday. We shall only take a month for Egypt, and then come back to Rome for April. In May to Germany, in July to England, in August to America, — such is, D. V., our plan. Here, I have only seen the Howitts, the Trollopes, G. P. Marsh, and (without being introduced to him) Joaquin Miller. . . .

I hope the Eumenides are tired, and will now let me alone for a while. I feel quite bright and fresh mentally, — only morally a little fagged, after such a strain upon my patience. But it's time I were at home. I feel that I can do my best work on my native heath, and this visit shows me that (except the material for Goethe's life) I need not give much more time to Europe. I have now harvested as much as was needed for my own special literary work, and shall not attempt anything more here. My remaining material waits at home.

The letters which Bayard Taylor received *en route* contained answers to those which he had written with regard to his scheme for an anonymous publication of "The Prophet," and discouraged him from the plan on the ground that popular taste was so indifferent in the main to a poem in dramatic form, that his poem would require the aid of his name, instead of piquing curiosity as a new venture of an unknown poet.

TO J. R. OSGOOD.

ROME, *February* 24, 1874.

Your letter of January 31st, forwarded from Gotha, has just reached me. After sickness in my family and innumerable delays, I have just got thus far on my way to Egypt, where we shall spend March, and then come back to Rome for April ; so in April I shall have everything once more revised and fairly copied in a different hand. You may expect the whole MS. early in May. In a venture of this kind the form (to my thinking) is not a very material matter ; a narrative poem would almost inevitably have betrayed me to some few. I don't think any one will charge me with this. The simple fact is, the subject was dramatically conceived in the beginning, six or seven years ago, has been dramatically evolved and elaborated in my mind, so that, even before beginning to write, any other form was wholly impossible. *In hoc signo,* then !

I shall write to Aldrich, also, whose generous concurrence in the plan will be a great help to me. Meantime, now that you are willing to try the experiment, I will turn over in my mind what can further be done to make it successful, — say in the way of fragmentary passages, short poems of a striking character, etc. By the time I get back to Rome I hope to have all such accessories decided upon, subject to your and T. B. A.'s good judgment. The more mystery we employ, the better. I'd send you a passage or two from the tragedy now for your private perusal if I had time to copy ; but we have only two days more here, meaning to embark at Naples on Saturday.

I have hoodwinked all intimate friends, by writing only of my Goethe-studies, and if you bring out "The Prophet" at the beginning of the season, I'm sure no one of them will suspect me.

TO T. B. ALDRICH.

ROME, *February* 24, 1874.

Your most welcome letter reached me last Wednesday in Florence. We had arrived the evening before, and on reaching the Hotel du Nord I found that Lowell was staying there. After dinner we smoked a cigar together, talked of Elmwood and you, and made quite a Cambridge atmosphere in the very heart of the old Tuscan city. We breakfasted together for three days, and dined *vis-à-vis* at the *table d'hôte* with Henry James. Lowell meant to join us for the trip to Rome on Saturday, but was so fagged after finishing a long poem on Friday afternoon that he decided to wait until Monday. . . . We are still, as regards health, a shabby, dilapidated family, and look forward to the specifics which shall restore us. We hope to embark at Naples for Alexandria on Saturday, spend a month in Cairo, and come back to Rome for April.

As regards "The Prophet," I think it can't make any serious difference. It could not, as I conceived it, be anything but a dramatic poem. A story would be very apt to betray me, and this will not. The MS. will be copied and forwarded in April, and you can then judge. Meantime (as I have just written to Osgood), I 'll study ways and means of mystery, provocations of curiosity, etc., and forward whatever I can do in that line to you two, subject to your good judgment. I know you will like the work itself, for it is honest and earnest. When you suggested to me the "Seven Mormon Wives" in the street, I had already my plan nearly complete, and it cost me an effort not to tell you so. I make the origin of the Mormon sect and the Joe Smith tragedy the historical background of my poem ; but my plot has the universal human element. It stirs up more than one question which disturbs the undercurrents of the world just now ; for it is pervaded with that sort of logic which lay behind the Greek idea of fate.

TO GEORGE H. YEWELL.

HOTEL DU NIL, CAIRO, *March* 20, 1874.

I must use the coming mail-day to let you know how we are getting on. Now that the winter finally seems to be at an end, I am more socially inclined than since leaving Rome, for we have all been growling like bears on account of the cold. At Naples we fairly froze ; even burning five francs' worth of wood every day did not keep us warm. Excursions were impossible, for the wind pierced to the marrow. Then, after waiting a week to meet my old friend Boker, I was forced to leave the very same day when he probably arrived.

We had a delightful passage to Messina, and the sun there was a very little warmer. Etna was a solid cone of snow, and even the Calabrian mountains were very wintry. The second night was somewhat rough, and the next day we were all a little sea-sick ; but after that the conditions gradually improved, the sea growing smoother and the air warmer. We saw the Morea,

Cerigo, and Crete, and reached Alexandria in cloudless weather in just five days. On the whole it was a good voyage, although the steamer was small and not very comfortable.

We stayed nearly two days at Alexandria, going about among the bazars and to native cafés. The temperature was 72° in the shade, with clear sky and a soft, cool wind, — a heavenly change from Italy. Then the journey by rail hither was a perfect delight, and when we sat in the garden of palms of this hotel in the evening, we felt that we could ask nothing more. But on Tuesday (17th) a furious north wind blew ; on Wednesday it rained the whole day at a temperature of 45°, and yesterday I wrote my letters wearing an overcoat ! Too late for Egypt, everybody said in Rome. Too soon, *I* say ; for we have really suffered from the cold until to-day. The heavens are now serene again, and this afternoon existence is a luxury. We have not been farther than to the Citadel and the Nile : the wind is still too cool for longer excursions. I think we are sure of fine weather from this time on, after such unprecedented cold. The hotel is capital ; so far, we can live cheaper than in Italy, for wine is the only *extra*. My old dragoman of twenty-two years ago, Achmet, is alive, as I firmly believed, in spite of Gifford's report of his death. He was overjoyed to see me again, and looks after us like a father. My cough and irritation of the throat is all gone, and M. is recovering her strength as rapidly as I could expect. We mean to go one hundred and fifty miles up the Nile by rail to the tombs of Beni-Hassan. The pyramids look grander than ever. We have found lots of wonderful interiors for you to paint. Although Cairo has greatly changed, all the new city being European and not picturesque, nearly all the best things are left. To-day we saw the dancing dervishes, and drove to the Nile under such a delicate, pearly sky as you rarely have seen, if ever, — clouds like dim, lilac-tinted opal, above the warm glory of the desert hills. Against this the white citadel-mosque, under it a brown belt of buildings, and nearer clumps of palms rising above dazzlingly green wheat-fields. You can imagine the effect.

My Arabic comes back astonishingly. I am already nearly independent of interpreters. The natives, most of whom have a smattering of English, open their eyes in wonder when I bring out a full sentence of their own tongue, and instantly become friendship itself. I find that I like them better than ever. I am particularly glad that Egypt makes such an effect on my wife. She came with a little reluctance, but she is now fairly possessed with the indescribable fascination of the land. Would that you were here!

CAIRO, *March* 28, 1874.

We 've about decided to sail from Alexandria on the 7th of April, and shall consequently, D. V., reach Rome by the 15th or 16th. I am sorry to return so soon, for I enjoy Egypt as much, if not more, than ever before ; but we really can't afford any more time. The weather, now, is simply perfect, — 75° at noon, in the shade, always a light breeze, clover-scents in the air, all trees in young leaf, wheat coming into head, — not too cold to sit, or too warm to walk. I have not had such an appetite for a long time, and my whole night's sleep, done in one piece, seems about fifteen minutes long. Moreover, Cairo is hardly dearer than Rome, the Mussulmen are as cheerful and friendly as ever, the old picturesqueness lingers everywhere, and each day is thus a new satisfaction.

We have been to the Pyramids and various palaces and gardens on both banks of the Nile, and to-morrow I go to the Fyoom. Next week we shall visit Suez. From what the American Consul says, I should not be afraid to spend the whole summer here.

NAPLES, *Tuesday, April* 14, 1874.

We arrived last night, after a long and disagreeable voyage, although the weather was not bad. We are all dilapidated : my wife is quite exhausted, and this moment comes the sad news of her father's death. I have had a headache for a week, — a thing I never had before in my life, — but am already better to-day. We shall try to get to Rome on Thursday, and I feel tolerably sure we shall, but may have to wait until Friday, on M.'s account. Will you please engage rooms — *primo piano*, if possible, but certainly not higher than *secondo* — at the Stati Uniti, for Thursday evening. I 'll pay for the day, in case we are delayed until Friday. We are very anxious to reach Rome, on account of letters from Germany. Our plans are quite uncertain, and we cannot take apartments, even for one month.

GOTHA, GERMANY, *Sunday, May* 3, 1874.

I can scarcely believe that it is only a week yesterday since we took leave of you. The trip to Florence was somehow very fatiguing to all of us, but it came to an end, as all things do, and Graham, looking better than I have seen him for a long while, with Boker, were waiting for us at the station. We stayed at the Orsini [Palace] until ten A. M. Tuesday, and our stay was wholly delightful. Dr. Wilson made a thorough examination of my physical condition, which he pronounced excellent, and much better than last year. As you may imagine, I have felt better ever since.

I dreaded the further journey, as M. was still very weak, and L. became indisposed in Florence. However, we took a bottle of beef-tea, extract of ginger, brandy, etc., along, and kept on to Verona the same day, arriving at midnight. There we rested until two P. M., Wednesday, and started again, fortunately securing a coupé for three, with seats and foot-shelves, which enabled us to lie down. By midnight we were on the summit of the Brenner, and soon after sunrise reached Munich. There were 5° of cold in Bavaria, the car-windows sheeted with ice, white frost far and wide, and all fruit destroyed. We really suffered from the cold. At Nürnberg, where we arrived before eleven, we thawed out and rested all day. Finally, on Friday, seven hours more of travel brought us to Gotha. M. stood the journey wonderfully well. She is decidedly better and stronger already. We find her mother somewhat resigned to her loss, and physically better than we expected to find her. The season is almost as far advanced as in Rome, and after two raw, stormy days there is this morning a promise of sunshine and milder air.

I find another "Job's post" (as the Germans say) waiting for me : a letter from Appletons coolly informs me that the new illustrations for my "German History," which they decided to have made last October, have not yet been commenced! Six months thrown away, and the publication delayed for a year after my work is finished, and this, after urging me to perform my part as speedily as possible! Such are an author's experiences ; let them console you whenever you think an artist's are hard. Moreover, I am paid nothing in advance, and the investment of the labor of nearly a year is thus allowed to wait.

Never mind : I have got back my old pluck and hopefulness. I shall jump into steady work now, beginning to-morrow morning.

GOTHA, GERMANY, *May* 16, 1874.

My wife's lack of health and strength has delayed me a week longer, but now I trust that you will have everything by the 10th or 15th of June. There is no one here whom I can get as a copyist, so the labor falls on her. The first and second acts, which I now send, bring nearly all the characters upon the stage, and fairly start the plot ; the remaining three acts have much more action and passion. I shall be curious to get your personal impression and T. B. A.'s of the quality of the work.

Except my wife, the only human being who has seen the MS. is Boker. We came together in Italy a month ago. I can trust him wholly, and, needing the critical judgment of at least one friend, I asked him to read it. He seemed to be especially struck by its dramatic character. I 'll not give his views further, except to say that they were satisfactory to me. But he very much doubts the expediency of publishing anonymously. He thinks, as you do, that a dramatic poem without the author's name is not likely to make a sudden or strong impression on the public, — hence, that its success (in a business point of view) would be much more probable if my name were put upon the title-page. Now, inasmuch as the suggestion of anonymity came first from T. B. A., I am quite willing that you and he should decide the question after you have read the whole of the MS. I shall also write to T. B. by this mail.

I 'll send with the final installment two short poems,[1] which may be used as an additional " blind " if you decide to carry out the anonymous. It will be time enough by August or the beginning of September to set your traps, as you will hardly publish before October 1st. It seems to me the trade must improve from this time on, and that next fall will be a favorable season.

Please acknowledge receipt of these two acts in a line or two. My address will be Gotha for eight or ten weeks to come, as we stay here until ready to start for home.

While hastening to complete the work which detained him in Europe, Bayard Taylor received an

---

[1] The poems sent were three, *A Lover's Test, My Prologue,* and *Gabriel.*

urgent request from Mr. Reid to go to Iceland to report for the "Tribune" the celebration of the one
thousandth anniversary of the first settlement of the
island. "To the few who have never known any
other Alma Mater than the New York 'Tribune,'" he
wrote in his first letter describing the trip, "her (or
its) call is like that of the trumpet unto the war-
horse." He was very impatient to be at home again,
and at first it seemed as if he should be compelled to
abandon the excursion on account of the impossibility
of bringing it within the time which he could give,
in justice to American engagements already made.
But Mr. Cyrus Field was going and had chartered a
steamer. This was an opportunity too good to decline, and Bayard Taylor joined other correspondents
in sharing the use and expense of this conveyance.

TO JERVIS M^CENTEE.

GOTHA, *July* 7, 1874.

Yours of June 14th was a welcome surprise and a hearty cheer
to my soul, as all your letters are. I must write once more, so
that there shall be no gaps to be filled up when we meet, but
each will know just about where the other stands. It seems to
me that there is a sort of relationship between our fates, — perhaps because we both have high aims and have patiently endured
unrecognition. Your experience in art during the last six months
is much like mine in literature. In spite of hard times, my copyright accounts show an increase of nearly fifty per cent. in the
sales of my books. Reid writes that my Tribune letters are
more popular than any I have written for many years, and that
the sneerers and cavilers are growing silent one by one, so I can
fairly hope for a better reception for the works to come. Moreover, having at last finished my Goethe-studies, I find that my
original conception of the plan of the biography was the true one,
and the best scholars in Germany have only confirmed, not specially instructed me. Between over-confidence and self-doubt
there is a delicate line to walk, but I feel as if I had found it,
and as if each step were upon secure ground.

. . . I have done many things which have been not understood by my author friends, because they were inevitable preparations for something higher. When I gave up the sensuous vein of poetry, and grew tired to death of merely descriptive prose, I made some blunders, of course, but they were in the right direction. Even —— has blamed what he called the "metaphysical element" (although it is really psychological) in some of my later works, not foreseeing that I should beat my way through it, and use the experience in the "Masque" and "Lars." How often have the ——s said, "Why don't you write so-and-so, which you used to do so well?" — as if I could recall a lost impulse, or silence a later one! No; if we carefully measure our strength we must, as a matter of natural development, steadily become capable of higher and longer flights, until the decay of force sets in. May the latter period be many years off for you and me!

By the time this reaches you I shall probably be in Iceland. (A secret. Say nothing until you see it announced in the "Tribune.") Reid wants me to report the Millennial Celebration; but I have been on the point of giving it up, until Saturday, when Smalley telegraphed to me from London that Cyrus Field had chartered a special steamer and offered me a berth in it. So I must go, — not very enthusiastically, but I cannot deny Reid, who has been such a helpful friend to me since Greeley's death. I hope to be back in England by the middle of August, and home by the 1st of September. M. and L. will wait in Germany meantime.

I have just returned from Weimar and Leipzig, where I have met with great encouragement. I found Baron von Gleichen hard at work, and developing finely. He has a large picture, six by four feet, — hunter and deer in a brown November copse, — which is capital. He gave me his mother's copy of the life of *her* mother, Schiller's wife. The older Goethe at last opened all Goethe's rooms for me, and the Grand-Duke invited me to dinner or tea almost every day. Everybody seemed willing and anxious to be of assistance in my researches, and I came away feeling really richly fitted out for the biography. In Leipzig I went through eighteen folio scrap-books of newspaper articles concerning Goethe, and this saves me some months of time. I have made a list of one hundred and seventy-five works to be consulted, — in short, am ready, when I reach home and have earned enough to keep the pot boiling for six months, to break ground and push bravely forward with the MS. of the work. I've written a few short poems, but don't mean to publish them immediately. Moreover, I've accepted an invitation to preside at a national convention of the Δ K E fraternity, students north and south, at the University of Virginia, in October. After that begins the lecturing campaign for three months.

I feel like a fallow field waiting for plough and drill, — and this in spite of a great deal of desultory work. Of course I'm in capital spirits. Give me the least bit of appreciation, and the embers break into a fresh blaze at once. Let us only live twenty years longer, and we shall all see our best days ! We must have a closer, yet a freer intercourse of all artists ; the time is ripe for it.

TO J. R. OSGOOD.

LONDON, *July* 16, 1874.

Your brief line of June 26th, saying you had all the copy, reached Gotha just before I left there ; but I fear that I may not get the more important facts of impression, decision, etc., from both you and T. B. A. for a month to come. I leave on Sunday for a trip to Iceland in a private steamer, with Cyrus Field, Tom Appleton, Dr. Hayes, Murat Halstead, and one of Gladstone's sons. (Keep this secret for a week or two.) We shall be back in about a month, after which I shall sail with family immediately for home, expecting, D. V., to reach New York during the first September week. I want to read at least plate-proofs before publication, and there will be time. But there can be no further conference about the manner of publication ; hence the failure to receive any advice or judgment from you (inevitable, it seems) before I start for Iceland is a considerable disappointment to me. I can only say, decide upon the course that seems best to you after reading the MS., and go ahead, in God's name ! Take the beginning of the season, if you can, for I suspect that the business success of the volume, if it come at all, will come after a certain class has read it and begun to talk about it.

The decision of his publisher and friend was adverse to the anonymous publication of " The Prophet," and his own desire for it had grown somewhat feebler. The writing of three poems which were to be in disguise of his own style cooled his ardor. He could write parodies with singular ease, but to write genuine poetry which was not in imitation, and into which he did not put his whole soul, was contrary to all his instincts and reason. The game was not worth the candle. Besides, he was exhilarated by signs of a stronger faith in him on the part of the public, and he was in no mood to play a game. He was more eager to move forward in his own chosen way. He was not disappointed, therefore, at the conclusion of his scheme.

He left Aberdeen July 22d, and was back in Edinburgh August 14th. While absent, and after his return to England, he wrote a dozen letters to the "Tribune" and had the pleasure besides of contributing to the festivities at Rejkiavik a poem, "America to Iceland," which was translated into Icelandic. He returned the compliment by translating into English, an Icelandic poem of address to the king of Denmark, written by Mr. Magnusson. On the 20th of August he rejoined his family in Gotha; on the 26th they sailed from Hamburg, and on the 9th of September landed in New York.

TO WHITELAW REID.

LONDON, *August* 18, 1874.

Smalley can testify to the immense relief I experienced on mailing my last letter to you last evening. The work is finished, and it will be well or ill done ; I 've done my best, under the circumstances, and can do no more.

Putnams have written to me about making a volume out of the Egyptian letters, etc., and Halstead insists that they were so popular that a volume entitled "Egypt and Iceland" would have a large sale. What do you think ? I shall write to young Putnam to-day to see you about it, since, if decided upon, the letters ought not to appear in any of the "Tribune's" special sheets. If I can make a few hundred dollars that way this fall, so much the better.

And now, good-by from Europe for the last time ! I 'm only too glad that I can write it.

CHAPTER XXVII.

IN THE HARNESS AGAIN.

1874–1876.

> 'T is not for idle ease we pray,
> But freedom for our task divine.
> *Implora Pace.*

WHEN Bayard Taylor returned to America in the
fall of 1874, he was full of a new hope. Two days
after he landed, "The Prophet" was published. He
went directly with his family to Cedarcroft, and was a
guest in his own house. Immediately letters poured
in upon him with invitations to lecture. It was like
old times. He set about preparing at once for the
press his volume, "Egypt and Iceland," which was
published by G. P. Putnam's Sons in October, and he
wrote a new lecture on "Ancient Egypt." There were
abundant signs of an increase in his popularity. His
letters to the "Tribune" during his absence had been
of a character to add substantially to his reputation,
and the "Tribune" itself had given him an honorable
prominence in its record of literature and news.

He had need of all this encouragement, for he knew
well what labor lay before him, and how distant was
yet the fulfillment of his dream of freedom from care
and leisure for the highest work. He had brought
with him a library of books to aid him in his Goethe
and Schiller biography; he had rich stores of material
in his capacious memory, and he was eager to begin

the work which opened before him so finely. Poetic schemes also were pushing their way forward in his mind. But all must be postponed until he could provide the means of living. He used a little of his new material in a series of papers, "Autumn Days in Weimar," which he now began for the "Atlantic," [1] but his principal resource for the winter was lecturing, which seemed to have revived not only for him but for lecturers at large. He was vigorous and hopeful. He knew his own mind. Life stretched out before him with fair prospects, and through the hard work, the drudgery which awaited him, he saw those mounts of poetry which made all toil but a light affliction for the moment.

TO T. B. ALDRICH.

KENNETT SQUARE, PA., *September* 16, 1874.

Thanks for your unchanged voice of welcome! M., L., and I return as much love as you can possibly send us.

The Iceland trip, by postponing my return home for a whole month, overwhelms me with work. The copy for the book "Egypt and Iceland" is finished to-day, and I have as much more work as I can do for a month, when I begin lecturing. I must go back to my old "stand-by," thankful for the shekels it will assure me. I want to secure a year's expenses in advance, and then go to work on the Goethe. I may pass through Boston about October 5th or 6th on my way to or from my first lecture in New Hampshire, — otherwise I shall hardly get there before next January. I go West the end of October, and return about Christmas, after which we settle in New York *for good*.

It's a good sign to me that you've read the "Prophet" again, and I'm eager to know what impression it makes on you. If you think your warning in regard to the new critics will alarm me, you're mistaken. I'm preciously indifferent to all criticism that is not sound and intelligent. Let the —— multiply. Even this year's harvest has its Colorado bugs. As for poetry, I shall

---

[1] Since republished in *Essays and Notes*, together with a later paper, "Weimar in June."

go on writing it, whether the public reads or not ; yea, I shall write it and publish it, though I should be forced to pay all expenses and give away the volumes ! Smile, pity, condemn, — but believe !

. . . We come back quite penniless, but never jollier. I get invitations to lecture every day, and have only a little gap to bridge over before I earn instead of merely spending.

TO JERVIS M^cENTEE.

KENNETT SQUARE, PA., *September* 17, 1874.

After escaping from a fearful West-India hurricane, which met us off Nova Scotia, we landed on the afternoon of the 9th, and reached here on the 11th. Your most cheerful and inspiriting letter missed me in London, and only overtook me here ; and I should have written on reading but for the mountain of work waiting for me. Since my arrival I have prepared all the copy for a book on " Egypt and Iceland," and begun to read the proofs. Now I must write a lecture, an oration, and an article for the " Atlantic," all by October 4th, at which time I begin to lecture, and expect to keep it up all winter. Having three different works out this fall, the " Egypt," etc., the " Prophet," and my " History of Germany," I can afford to drop the pen for six months and go to earning money, until I have a year's expenses in advance, when I shall sit down to my life of Goethe. I never said a word about the " Prophet " to you because Osgood first meant to publish it anonymously, and only gave up the plan at the last moment, — but it is my most ambitious, certainly my strongest poem. There are so many typographical errors that I 'm waiting to have them corrected before I send you a copy.

M. will hardly go to New York before Christmas, and I suppose you 'll not go much before ; but I have a mighty longing to see your Michelangelic beard again. We 're a family party here at Cedarcroft, — the old folks, my sister A., husband, and two children, sister E. and two children, and we three, and a French governess. M. and I are visitors, practically, having nothing to do with housekeeping, and it 's a great comfort. I was quite used up by the hardships of my Icelandic trip, and have not really been rested since ; but I feel full of fresh energy and hope, and trust that I shall come out all right. Reid has been exceedingly good and kind, and the Iceland letters seem to be popular all over the country. The invitations to lecture come in as they used to do in my old shallow days, and this time I shall not slight the aid they bring.

TO E. C. STEDMAN.

KENNETT SQUARE, *Sunday, September* 20, 1874.

Our position is just this : I mean to keep Cedarcroft (until there is a good chance of selling) as a home for my parents, my sister A. and family, etc. ; but not to lease it again and risk such losses and abuse of property as I had to endure while in Europe. " Our purpose holds " to move to New York as soon as convenient. We need not do so before the end of the year, and I shall have no funds for the migration and new settlement before the middle of November.

Don't rashly suspect me of over-haste in my work. You know my habit of mentally considering and arranging for months in advance of writing. So it is now, and the speech will not be over half an hour long, nor the lecture more than an hour and a quarter. I have already a fair prospect of eighty lecture engagements, which will lift me out of this vale of penury, and seat me on the modest height of " easy circumstances."

None of the signs of recognition which Bayard Taylor received on his return to America touched him so nearly as the spontaneous, unaffected welcome which his old friends and neighbors gave him. They invited him to a picnic on October 12th, at Mt. Cuba, a lovely spot at the end of the Hockessin Valley, a few miles from Kennett Square, and the scene of the American incidents in " Lars." The pretty pavilion was decorated with autumn leaves and flowers and with verses from the poet's works ; words of welcome were spoken and poems read, and Bayard Taylor, responding to the greeting, spoke as one would speak to a familiar friend, freely disclosing his deeper purposes. The measure of such an occasion is in its power to break down conventionalities, and when he rehearsed his career and declared his hopes, he was bearing witness to the genuine kindliness with which those who knew him most familiarly regarded him.

"I am glad," he said, "it is not a mere formal occasion, but such as forms really a close, confidential circle, where things said are said to friends only, and not to the great world, /listening at the window. I will so speak, as a friend to his friends, face to face. The most grateful feature of the occasion is its recognition of what I feel to be my best work. This honor has not come to me too late; it ought not to have come sooner. It is only in the character of my later works that I feel I have earned it. It is thirty years ago since I first left home for Europe, and in three months I shall be fifty. This is the turning-point of my life. While the springs of nature, I feel, are still fresh, and the enthusiasm of youth has not died out, still at this period one can look back and consider impartially his career. Ten years ago I saw that the work I had then done had no permanent value, and did not express what I felt were my full powers as an author. My books of travel had had a popularity that deceived many of my friends, but I knew that they could not hold an enduring position in literature. A traveler's observations and descriptions stand only until some later traveler sees more intelligently, or discovers more, or describes more agreeably. I therefore resolved now to make good my lost time, for my travels had never been a part of the purpose of my life. I had undertaken them only to aid in my education in the arts, poetry, and the higher forms of literary work. Now such a decision to change the character of my efforts was like changing front in battle, a manœuvre, as you know, always full of peril. In the new endeavors, however, I have been fortunately kept in good heart and encouragement. . . . This welcome of to-day here in the scene of my poem, so spontaneous and from my old friends, has a sanctity to me beyond any ordinary meeting, and I would be totally unworthy of it if I permitted myself to receive it in any vain spirit of exultation. I cannot believe I have done enough to deserve it, though in a life largely of aspiration and effort one cannot fairly estimate what the degree of accomplishment is; but for whatever I have earned of your cordial greeting, the praise from me must be due to the goodness of God. I will still work; I feel myself capable of accomplishment equal to anything yet done, if my life be spared; and let me promise to you that from now I will strive still to do a better, truer, and higher work."

It was with real emotion that he began these words, and the remembrance of the whole scene filled him with tenderness whenever he recurred to it. The open air, the sweet landscape, the grasp of the hand, all gave to the occasion a poetic fitness and beauty which served as a happy omen to him in this new day of work and aspiration. A few days after he gave an address before the Delta Kappa Epsilon fraternity at the University of Virginia.

TO WHITELAW REID.

CEDARCROFT, *Monday, October* 12, 1874.

The welcome on Saturday was the crowning glory of my life. It was pure, beautiful, perfect. All old friends and neighbors, hundreds, came from far and near, the pavilion was splendid with flowers and autumn leaves, passages from my poems were framed in ivy, and the German and American flags were intertwined. The speeches, songs, and poems quite overwhelmed me. It seemed that all I once thought best and supposed to be forgotten was revived ; that all the recognition I craved in vain was poured upon me at once. For three hours I had to keep myself, by desperate force of will, from crying like a baby.

You will see some report of the welcome in the Wilmington "Commercial." I asked to have a copy sent to you personally, because during the past two years you have done more than any other friend to bring about this happy reaction. Therefore take your full share of what I say in the poem I inclose. I should like to have it in the "Tribune," because it will thus be read soonest and by all who were there. My own reply was impromptu, broken, and insufficient, but it was impossible, under the circumstances, to do better. It was hard enough to say anything.

TO JAMES T. FIELDS.

CEDARCROFT, KENNETT SQUARE, PA., *October* 17, 1874.

Your MS. in the envelope was the most welcome I have seen for a long while. I don't know how many times, during my absence, I have meant to write to you. Over and over again I have wanted to congratulate you on becoming a new force[1] among us ; to discuss common aims and common interests ; to keep fresh the intercourse of old days ; to thank you for constant encouragement, and ask your pardon for impatience with a literary judgment which, I now see, was generally in the right ; in short, though driven to silence by the pressure of hard and earnest work, I have felt a constant longing to talk with, and confer with, and cheer (if I could) and be cheered by you (a certainty) !

The other day in Boston I meant surely to see you. But after I had talked business with Osgood, and waited for Howells, — who did n't come after all, — it was time to rush away to Providence for my lecture there. I 'm down for a lecture in Boston January 11th, my fiftieth birthday, which I ought to have at home, but the crowd of engagements does n't leave me even that. I 'm afraid you will not be there either, for I hear of your many engagements all over the country. But let us try to meet as soon as we may. No new friends wear like the old, and you are the first, outside of my home, who is still in the world.

It is a spite of fate that you are to lecture in West Chester on the 9th of November, when I shall be in the West, and M. and L. already migrated from Cedarcroft to New York. I had my time given away before I heard of your coming, or I would have kept a gap for your sake, and each with his audience of one

[1] Mr. Fields, after retiring from business, had devoted much time to lecturing.

or the complemental two, would not have missed the multitudinous listener.

I've just returned from the University of Virginia, where the young Southerners have given me a fresh satisfaction by taking to their hearts the words I was impelled to say to them. To-day I go to West Chester, and a score of letters are to be answered before I start ; here must be the end, with most unsaid.

Bayard Taylor began his lecturing tour October 20th, and continued it with occasional intermissions until the middle of April. His family removed to New York early in November, and now transferred to that city their household goods, for it was Bayard Taylor's purpose to make his permanent home there. He left his parents in occupation of Cedarcroft and the place continued to be the family place, but was no longer kept up as an establishment upon the old basis. The lecturing brought with it its accustomed privations and discomforts, but he accepted these as a necessary concomitant, made as little of them as possible, and, in his jealousy at the expenditure of time required by the business, was wont to turn to account not only the days which he was able to spend now and then with his family, but the chance hours which came as he went hither and thither. He took up thus the study of Greek, eager to repair the loss of early years, and also because he had already formed the plan of a new drama which was closely allied in his mind with Greek art, and the spirit of Greek culture. "The Prophet" had brought him some pleasant letters from friends ; it had received some kindly criticism, but it was misinterpreted in many quarters; the historical movement with which it was inwoven misled those who looked no farther than the outside. The author himself felt that it was in some sense a study for higher dramatic work.

TO PAUL H. HAYNE.

MANKATO, MINNESOTA, *November* 29, 1874.

. . . The critics are mistaken in supposing that my design was to represent a phase of Mormon history. The original conception was totally unconnected with any actual events ; the features which suggest the Mormons were added long afterwards. . . . It is the most steady, conscientiously elaborated, and uninterruptedly carried out work of my life. The main lesson of the drama — the (to me) most tragic element in it — has not yet been perceived by any critic. The London " Athenæum " alone has seen that the work may have many interpretations. I am quite aware that it is not of the fashion of our day, and I am hardly disappointed — certainly in no wise annoyed — that what is best in it has been so far ignored. I wrote it for myself, first of all, and without the least reference to its possible acceptation by others. Still, I consider that the " Masque of the Gods " is on a much higher plane. But if I live, I have more and better work to do. " The Prophet " now belongs to my past, and will not trouble my thoughts any more. I have no time to look back on completed work while so much is waiting its final fashion in my mind.

Later in the season the persistent misunderstanding of " The Prophet " drew from him a more public defense of his motive, which he addressed to a German paper, very likely because however he might hope to receive from his own countrymen, in the wide range of critical judgment, an average recognition, he was unwilling that his German friends, dependent on fewer means of information, should be led into a false conception of his poetic work.

NEW YORK, *May* 3, 1875.

TO THE EDITOR OF THE " NEW-YORKER STAATSZEITUNG : " —

Sir, — To-day I have read for the first time your review of my dramatic poem, " The Prophet," which was published some weeks ago in the " Staatszeitung." While I think that an author should never reply to any distinctively literary criticism, it seems to me time to correct a misapprehension of the design of my work which reappears in every review of it. I have thus far forborne to make any such correction, in the fruitless hope that at least one critic might truly interpret my design.

"The Prophet" does not represent the early history of the Mormons, and David Starr is as far as possible from being Joe Smith. The man who most nearly stands for his prototype in real life was the Rev. Edward Irving, the founder of a sect which still exists in Scotland and Germany. Irving taught the continued bestowal of miraculous powers upon devout Christians, as they were given by Paul to the members of the churches he founded. In David Starr's case the unquestioning acceptance of a doctrine which was formerly more generally preached than now — that the Bible is not only divine, but that every word in it was written from the direct dictation of the Holy Spirit — is the power which impels him : this is the fate which makes the tragedy of his life inevitable. The crashing down of a rock in the first act is an incident related of the so-called "Prophet" Mathias. The emigration to the West and the manner of David's death are the only features that coincide with the story of the Mormons. The poem, first conceived upwards of eight years ago, was worked out in my mind without reference to that or any other sect ; I designed only to represent phases of spiritual development and their external results, which are hardly possible in any other country than ours. For the same reason the tragic element in the poem is placed chiefly in its moral and spiritual aspects, rather than in the action. It would simply be an absurdity to attempt its representation upon the stage.

I do not complain of the misconceptions to which I have alluded. They are such as any author must expect to encounter now and then, even from the most honest and impartial critics. With regard to the general charge that the events suggested are too recent, and the language too realistic, these are faults which will disappear in time, if the poem has any vitality ; if it should have none, they become of no consequence. I only ask that the reader may be made acquainted also with the author's intention.

Very respectfully,   BAYARD TAYLOR.

Popularity brings with it burdens as well as pleasures, and Bayard Taylor found himself at this time so far a public character that he was hard driven to it to secure the quiet and seclusion which he needed for his work. His correspondence became large; his time was broken in upon by people who were more concerned to satisfy their curiosity or secure some aid, than to be of service to the man whom they took possession of. All sorts of applications were made to him, and it was not easy for him to deny any one. Worthier claims also began to be made upon his service.

TO HIS MOTHER.

NEW YORK, *February* 7, 1875.

. . . There was a strong effort made by prominent men at Washington (including two members of the Cabinet) to have me appointed Minister to Russia. I did n't know anything about it until all was over, but I could not have accepted the place in any case. I was told last night that the same friends are determined that I shall have an appointment two or three years hence.

A stranger, who had read "Autumn Days in Weimar," was moved to write Bayard Taylor his concurrence in the views there expressed regarding the reading of blank verse. He sent him an article in which he had taken the same position, and drew from Bayard Taylor a letter in reply: —

TO E. LAKIN BROWN.

31 WEST SIXTY-FIRST STREET, NEW YORK, *March* 19, 1875.

Your letter was mislaid during my absence from home, and my reply is thus greatly delayed. I have read with great interest and satisfaction the article you forwarded. You take the true ground, — the only true ground. We have not, in this country (so far as my experience goes), an actor, an elocutionist, or a public speaker, who reads English blank verse correctly. And the method of teaching in our schools is not only false, but barbaric.

I may hereafter have more to say, or to write, upon this subject, for it is by no means unimportant. The absence of a rhythmic ear among us is something astonishing. I think it accounts for much bad taste as well as bad poetry. I have only time to add that I hope you will continue to preach the doctrine whenever you have a chance, and thus oblige all poets, living or dead.

After the close of the lecture season, Bayard Taylor turned to work which was pressing upon him. He prepared his later poems for publication in a volume, as well as revised his " Faust " for a cheaper edition, and wrote a lecture on Richter, to be delivered with his former ones at Cornell. He went to Ithaca May 19th for ten days, and in the middle of June to Boston, to write for the " Tribune " an account of the Bunker Hill Centennial.

TO PAUL H. HAYNE.

31 WEST SIXTY-FIRST STREET, *June* 28, 1875.

You must have all possible charity for me. I have been overwhelmed by a multitude of private business matters, in addition to the necessity of giving a course of lectures at Cornell University, describing the Bunker Hill Centennial for the "Tribune," and spending a week at Cedarcroft, — my place in Pennsylvania. During this same period, I have revised my " Faust " for a cheap popular edition in the fall, and have collected the scattered lyrics of the last thirteen years for a new volume. All this, with a new poem pressing powerfully upon my brain, and absolutely forcing me to give it such fragments of days and nights as I could snatch from necessary duties, will account to you (I trust) for my few and brief letters. Your volume only reached me a fortnight ago, since when I have been absent from the city. So I barely had time to look through it, note what was new and what known to me, and get a general impression of its character. I saw, at least, that your poems do not lose, but gain, by being collected. The same delicately refined stamp is upon all, so each one throws side-gleams upon its neighbors. But I mean to take the volume with me to the Massachusetts sea-coast, whither we go in two days, and where, for the first time in three years, I hope to have a little rest. I don't believe you in the South know what active, working lives we lead here. I am sometimes inclined to complain, — to long for a quiet nook in the shores of Cos, — but then again it is an advantage to have your muscle always in training, and to feel that the coming labor cannot intimidate you. Well, none of us get just the life we wish for !

Bayard Taylor spent the month of July with his family at the sea-shore in Massachusetts, and for once gave himself up to the luxury of idleness. Only when the month was gone did he redeem a promise which he had made, and send to the " Tribune " the first of a series of " Alongshore Letters," which he continued as he went to Manchester to visit Mr. Fields, and then to New Brunswick. He returned to New York toward the end of August, and went to Cedarcroft, where he was busily engaged for three days on his Ode for the presentation by the Goethe Club of a bust of Goethe to be erected in Central Park. He finished it so near the occasion, that when he came to recite it on the day, August 28th, it was with the glow of composition still upon his mind. His vacation brought him again among valued friends.

TO H. W. LONGFELLOW.

BOSTON, *August* 5, 1875.

. . . I am full of renewed hope and courage this evening, after your cordial words. As you can well understand, there are few to whom I could show the poem [" Prince Deukalion "], — few, perhaps, who would be interested in the leading conception. I have written, thus far, as much from instinct as from purpose ; but I trust the former even more than the latter, and you have given me fresh self-confidence, — not, I trust, self-exaltation. But, as I tried to say, I have never yet met you without receiving some clear, strong, generous encouragement, which confirmed me in my best poetical aims. At the best, we all stand much alone, and there is great strength in one feeling the support of another.

It was at this time also that he made the acquaintance of that fine spirit, Sidney Lanier, then struggling, as he was always to struggle, with adversity. A word of praise from Bayard Taylor had brought a grateful letter from Lanier.

BOSTON, *August* 17, 1875.

. . . I write hurriedly, finding much correspondence awaiting
me here, so can only repeat how much joy the evidence of a new,
true poet always gives me, — such a poet as I believe you to be.
I am heartily glad to welcome you to the fellowship of authors,
so far as I may dare to represent it ; but, knowing the others, I
venture to speak in their names also. When we meet, I hope to
be able to show you, more satisfactorily than by these written
words, the genuineness of the interest which each author always
feels in all others ; and perhaps I may be also able to extend
your own acquaintance among those whom you have a right to
know. . . .

TO GEORGE H. YEWELL.

NEW YORK, *August* 31, 1875.

Your letter, which reached me this afternoon, is at once a delight and a reproach. I have not forgotten that you wrote to me
more than a year ago, while I was in Iceland ; and that *I* have
not written to you since. My wife can testify, how often, during
the past year, I have said : "I *must* write to George Yewell!"
— and how often she has asked me, "Have you not written
yet?" The difficulty with all authors is that the act of writing
is, in one sense, a repetition of their particular form of labor.
Suppose you *painted* your correspondence, — would you not often
drop brush and colors, and let the absent friend wait a little
longer? This is all the explanation I can give for my silence :
I have been steadily at work, and have passed through such
periods of fatigue that I could only rest by keeping away wholly
from pen and paper.

I must give you, first, our private history. In ten days it will
be a year since we landed on American soil. I found a great demand for my lectures, — greater, in fact, than ever before in my
experience, — and it seemed like a special good fortune, in my
condition of debt and suspended income. So I accepted all invitations, started on the work in three weeks after landing, and
kept it up until the end of April, — full six months, during which
I lectured one hundred and thirty times, and traveled about
fifteen thousand miles. The winter was the severest known on
this continent since 1741, so you may judge what I "underwent

and overcame." True, I cleared $11,000 in the half-year, paid $4,000 of old debts, and made myself easy for a year to come, — but it was a task which tested my physical power. I was forced to take a summer holiday by the sea, near Newport, after which my wife and I went to New Brunswick (the British Province) to leave L. with an old friend of hers, and then returned to Cedarcroft for a month. I have come back to New York, to deliver an Ode on the 126th birthday of Goethe, — last Saturday, — and am waiting here for L.'s return, to take her with me to Cedarcroft. As a matter of some possible interest, I inclose the Ode. Bryant gave the oration; the bronze bust of the poet is meant for Central Park. I have also a new volume of poems ready for publication; I mean to send you a copy, as it includes the "Implora Pace" which you so thoroughly understood. Besides this main labor, I have done many smaller things: an oration at the University of Virginia, a course of lectures at Cornell, summer letters for the "Tribune," etc., and have revised the translation of "Faust" for a cheap popular edition. The biography of Goethe has not advanced much, of course; but I have written part of a new and important poem (this is all I can say about it!) and made other plans of future work. Now, how do you suppose I could break away from this activity and go back to Europe? The rumor you mention is not only false, but absurd; my place, my work, my duty, are here! I do not expect to leave America for some years; I certainly do not want to do so. I was met, last fall, by an appreciation which I had never expected to get, in this life; there is a broad field waiting for earnest workers, and I mean to do my share. Although so harried and driven by necessary labor, I never was more hopeful and confident. There *is* — I tell you again, dear old friend — a sure reward for all honest work. Take what cheer you can out of my experience, for you have as much right to your reward as I to mine.

. . . We make our home in New York now, as I have given up Cedarcroft to my sister and Swiss brother-in-law and my parents. I shall have to lecture for a part of the coming season, in order to get funds in advance; but I have also a prospect of steady work in New York, with sufficient margin for my own literary plans. On the whole I take my life gratefully and joyously; it might be better, but it could so easily be worse!

I wish, more than ever, that you had gone to Egypt with us, —

especially since you don't go beyond Cairo. I could have lived the first poetic experience over again, in your company.

My faithful dragoman's name is Achmet-es-Saïdi (pronounce like Italian), and you can easily find him. Mention my name, ask him to show you my photograph, and you will be all right with him. If you go to the Hotel du Nil, mention my name to Herr Friedmann, the landlord. Get Achmet to help you to Saracenic interiors. Take a run up the Nile, by rail, as far as Siout, and — if you possibly can — go to Medeenet-el-Fyoom, where you will find unpainted pictures, purely Oriental.

I 'm heartily glad that you will be so well represented at the Centennial. Why should n't you come over to it ? Our country is still worth something, in spite of all you may hear against it ; and I can't reconcile myself to seeing so many good artists expatriating themselves. But it 's at least pleasant to find that you are comfortable and secure of the near future.

... By the way, the article in "Frazer's Magazine" was not mine, some scamp, so far as I can learn, took my name ! I 'm relieved to hear that the article is good, for I have never read it. My friends here say, "It is just your style !" — and I shrink from acquaintance with a style which might not impress me favorably ! Would you like to see a man whom your friends pronounced to be your second self ? I think not. You would certainly dislike the man. Tell my friends, for Heaven's sake, that I never wrote, " A Professor Extraordinary " ! !

Here I sit late at night, with a window opening on Central Park, and you are looking on the dusky Apennines, — it 's incredible ! If you could bring the material features of your life over here, without benumbing our fresh atmosphere of deed and aspiration, how gladly would I accept it ! But we can't have the two things together, so I forego the delight of the eye, the opiate of the nerves, the indolent delight in beauty, and take my burden as the Lord gave it.

Give our love to Mrs. Gould, if she still lives when this arrives. Tell her, from me, she must not attribute too much weight to anything I may have said against Rome, when I felt too strongly the seduction of the grand old city, — that I shall never find fault with a free Rome, such as may spring partly from the seed she has sown. I am only jealous of that mighty Past which in Rome wiles so many of us to forget that we are of *this* age and must do its work. But *she* has never forgotten.

I have written deep into the night, yet have said little. Do write again before you leave for Egypt, and I will answer at once. My wife is not here, but I know how rejoiced she will be to hear from you again, and I send her love with mine.

TO SIDNEY LANIER.

Thursday afternoon, September 2, 1875.

. . . I can't tell you how rejoiced I am to find in you the genuine poetic nature, temperament, and *morale*. These are the necessary conditions of success (not in the lower popular meaning of the word), — of the possibility of slowly approaching one's ideal, for we never can, or ought to, reach it. All I can say is, "Be of good cheer!" . . .

The form of the Ode agreed so well with the character of Bayard Taylor's genius, and found now, especially, so close an alliance with his poetic designs, that his friends were quick to recognize the singular value of his work in this direction. His comrades were the first to note this, and sent him the cheer which fortified him in his purpose.

TO E. C. STEDMAN.

CEDARCROFT, *September* 9, 1875.

Yours of the 4th, after wandering from Mattapoisett to Boston, reached me yesterday. You forgot that we left the former place more than a month ago. I was in New York all last week, but was told at the Century that you would not arrive until Saturday, so did not call at Lafayette Place. However, we shall be back again in ten or twelve days.

Your impressions of the Ode give me great and lasting comfort. You can easily guess the difficulties of the themes. I could not bring myself to attempt the work until five or six days before the anniversary, and then went at it with such desperate resolution that I wrote it, as it now is, in two days. I recited, or rather yelled, it, to a restless, noisy audience of twelve thousand persons, and left with dark misgivings of failure.

Even now it falls short of my desire and intention; but I am profoundly glad that something thereof has made itself manifest in the strophes, and is accepted by you and other nearest-standing friends and poets. I hope to do better things in the future, and your generous words are to me as a strong additional plank thrust under that hope. I am too old to be injured by warm, hearty recognition, and yet as full of fresh aspiration as ever in my youth. But we'll talk of these things when we meet. There are many years of good work, I trust, awaiting both of us.

I have had many echoes from the Ode already, but not one with as clear and certain a tone as yours.

"Home Pastorals, Ballads, and Lyrics" was published by J. R. Osgood & Co. in October. In the same season appeared also a new and revised edition of "Faust" in a style uniform with "Home Pastorals," and thus more within the reach of the general public than it could be in the large octavo form. Bayard Taylor at this time had established himself in New York in quarters which he retained until he finally left America. The book received at once a cordial welcome from those whose welcome was most grateful. Dr. Holmes wrote, "A thousand thanks for the new volume which I received yesterday. How often does it happen to you to have read a gift book through before you write to thank the giver? It does not happen to me very often, but this time I have read every word, and enjoyed myself very much in doing it. . . . I have not decided which of the poems I like best, but I tell you some of the passages which most struck me; the mullein passage :[1]— 'Yet, were it not,' to the end of the page.

Better it were to sleep with the owl, to house with the hornet.
Truth as it shines in the sky, not truth as it smokes in their
 lantern.

These two lines ought to 'stick,' as C. S. had it.

[1] Yet, were it not for the poets, say, is the asphodel fairer ?
Were not the mullein as dear, had Theocritus sung it, or Bion ?
Yea, but they did not ; and we, whose fancy's tenderest tendrils
Shoot unsupported, and wither, for want of a Past we can cling to,

" I like the whole of the ' Old Pennsylvania Farmer,' but one line of it went to my heart, —

I 'd rather use my legs and hands than plague my brain with thought ;

and the next poem, 'Napoleon at Gotha,' gave me a sensation. 'Penn Calvin' I had read before, and was very glad to read it again. It is full of meaning. Perhaps nothing in the volume is better than the way in which you revive Shakespeare's characters as they show themselves in Broadway and Central Park. I must mention one more passage. It is the last part of Section III. of the Goethe Ode, beginning as far back as ' What courtier,' etc.[2]

" I have read no poetry, or almost none, of late until your book, and I have to thank you not only for your kindness in sending me the volume, but for the great pleasure I have had in reading it."

HENRY W. LONGFELLOW TO BAYARD TAYLOR.

CAMBRIDGE, *November* 12, 1875.

There should be twelve of them instead of three, — these beautiful " Home Pastorals " ! That is what I am saying to myself just after reading them this bright, poetic morning.

We, so starved in the Present, so weary of singing the Future, —
What is 't to us, if, haply, a score of centuries later,
Milk-weed inspires Patagonian tourists, and mulleins are classic ?

[2] What courtier, stuffed with smooth, accepted lore
  Of Song's patrician line,
But shrugged his velvet shoulders all the more
  And heard, with bland indulgent face,
   As who bestows a grace,
The homely phrase that Shakespeare made divine?
  So, now, the dainty souls that crave
Light stepping-stones across a shallow wave,
Shrink from the deeps of Goethe's soundless song!
  So, now, the weak, imperfect fire
  That knows but half of passion and desire
  Betrays itself, to do the Master wrong; —
  Turns, dazzled by his white uncolored glow,
And deems his sevenfold heat the wintry flash of snow!

From time to time, as the season and the spirit move you, I hope and believe you will fill up this admirable framework, and give every month its own : —

December, with its Christmas, and reminiscences of Palestine ;

January, with its snows, changing your hills into spurs of the Himalayas ;

February, with its seclusion and books, a fruitful theme.

And so on, till you have run through the whole round of the months. The three already written are so good, and the verse so sonorous and musical, that I long for more. The rest of the volume I have not yet finished. I read slowly. I was much pleased with Mr. Lanier.

BAYARD TAYLOR TO H. W. LONGFELLOW.

142 EAST EIGHTEENTH STREET,
NEW YORK, *November* 14, 1875.

Again your voice of cheer ! And how welcome it is after the stupidities of several so-called reviews which I have just been reading ! Two of them assert that my " Pastorals " resemble " Locksley Hall," and a third says they suggest Tupper !! Really, unless one poet helps another in this country, where shall we get encouragement ?

Last night at the Century Club, a man whose poetic instinct is marvelous for one not a poet said to me, " You should go on and write more of the ' Pastorals,' filling out the design already indicated, by other pictures of life and nature." Here was your thought again, and, to be frank, my own secret hope, waiting to be justified by the verdict of a friend. I only ask for two or three to give some recognition of the character and aim of my poetic work. I shall go on, as leisure and inspiration allow, but I probably should not do so if no one had spoken the right words.

You can imagine the interest with which I have read your " Pandora." The choruses are as fine as anything you have ever done, and I read them three times before laying down the book. Their rhythmical character is another point of resemblance to my drama, and I anticipate the charge of imitation from the same refined and intelligent reviewers when I come to publish. However, I shall not let that trouble me since you know the truth.

I am very glad you like Lanier. He seems to me a genuine poetic nature. I should not otherwise have taken the liberty of giving him a letter to you, knowing how much of your time is claimed by strangers.

TO J. B. PHILLIPS.

NEW YORK, *November* 26, 1875.

I 'm glad you 're occupying yourself again with poetry ; there 's no intellectual delight equal to it. . . . I have been exceedingly busy of late, M. having been quite ill, and much accumulated work on my hands. I have to do a great amount of needless correspondence, absurd applications, answers to questions, and the Lord knows what all. Then I am personally assailed to make speeches, write occasional poems, etc., all which I refuse, but the visits and the explanations take time.

There were some requests, however, which he could not lightly refuse. The United States Centennial Commission was in full blast, arranging for the great exhibition and celebration at Philadelphia the coming summer. General Hawley, the President of the Commission, gave Bayard Taylor the choice of writing the Hymn or the Cantata, or both, for the opening day of the festival, and when he chose the Hymn, begged him to name some one to write the Cantata. Mr. Lanier's musical education and his great enthusiasm for poetry in its large forms at once marked him in Bayard Taylor's mind as the right person, and he advised General Hawley to apply to him.

TO SIDNEY LANIER.

NEW YORK, *December* 28, 1875.

I write in a hurry, — but have something to say. General Hawley, President of the United States Centennial Commission, has invited me to write a hymn for the grand opening ceremonies. There is to be also an original cantata, the text of which was to be asked of Stedman ; but he is gone to Panama, and neither Theodore Thomas nor Dudley Buck (the composer) will wait his return. General Hawley asked me to name a poet not of New England, so I suggested a Southern poet for the cantata. I feel quite sure you will be the choice.

I write in all haste to say, you must accept, if it is offered. The cantata should not be more than from forty to fifty lines long, of unity of conception, yet capable of being divided easily into three parts, — an opening chorus, a bass solo, and a finale, either general or alternating chorus. The measure ought to be irregular, yet sufficiently rhythmical. My additional suggestion is, — and I think you 'll pardon it, — to make the lines simple and strong, keep down the play of fancy (except where it may give room for a fine musical phrase), and aim at expressing the general feeling of the nation rather than individual ideas, though the latter might be much finer.

I have just had a visit from Theodore Thomas and Mr. Buck, and we talked the whole matter over. Thomas remembers you well, and Mr. Buck says it would be specially agreeable to him to compose for the words of a Southern poet. I have taken the liberty of speaking for you, both to them and to General Hawley, and you must not fail me. . . .

Now, my dear Lanier, I am sure you can do this worthily. It 's a great occasion, — not especially for poetry as an art, but for poetry to assert herself as a power. I must close, being very busy. This is to prepare you a little, and set your thoughts as soon as possible in the direction of the task. . . .

SIDNEY LANIER TO BAYARD TAYLOR.

BALTIMORE, *December* 29, 1875.

If it were a cantata upon your goodness, I 'm willing to wager I could write a stirring one and a grateful withal. Of course I will accept, — when 't is offered. I only write a hasty line now to say how deeply I am touched by the friendly forethought of your letter.

BAYARD TAYLOR TO SIDNEY LANIER.

NEW YORK, *January* 7, 1876.

. . . I am very glad you accept so heartily. . . . "Occasional" poetical work should always be brief, appropriate in idea, and technically good. One dare not be imaginative or particularly original. . . . Don't overvalue my friendly good-will, nor ever let it impose the least sense of obligation upon you. I am very glad when I can give some encouragement to a man in whom I have faith.

Then followed an interesting correspondence between the two poets in which Mr. Lanier's frequent drafts of the cantata were subjected to searching criticism, branching out into discussions of poetic form. Bayard Taylor was compelled, however, to write always on the wing, for he was in the midst of his lecturing until the beginning of March, when he brought his tours to an end. He had for some time been considering the expediency of giving up this nomadic life, and finding his means of support in a less remunerative, but also less irregular way. The wear and tear of constant traveling was enormous. Better the confinement of a desk with all its drudgery and its tyranny of hours. He had already accepted from Messrs. Appleton the task of overseeing the editorial work upon "Picturesque Europe," and he now made an engagement with the "Tribune," by which he was to take a desk in the office and give his principal working hours to work upon the paper. The wide experience of the world which he had enjoyed gave him special qualifications for commenting upon current affairs in Europe; his convictions in literature stood him in good stead when called upon to give quick criticism of new books; his facility in reporting impressions enabled him to give independent descriptions of interesting occasions in the city.

It was no light thing for Bayard Taylor to return thus to the bondage of journalism. However lightly the yoke might be laid upon his shoulders, it could not help galling him. But he accepted the situation and made himself master of it. He had work yet to do. He had his life of Goethe and Schiller to write;

" Prince Deukalion," partly written, was in his desk; poems came, he had no thought of a day when they would not come. All these things, which made his life a joy, must wait upon that inexorable demand which was laid upon him to earn his living, and having once decided upon this course, he did not shrink from what it involved. He made the cause of the " Tribune " his cause, and wrote editorials, criticisms, reports, as if there were nothing else so well worth doing.

CHAPTER XXVIII

Ah, hark ! the solemn undertone,
On every wind of human story blown.
The National Ode.

THE hymn which Bayard Taylor had written was
to be sung at the opening of the Philadelphia Exhibition, but the great day of the feast was to be the
Fourth of July, when the centennial of the Declara-
tion of Independence was to be celebrated. The celebration centred about an oration to be given by Hon.
William M. Evarts and an ode. The Centennial
Commission had applied in turn to Mr. Longfellow,
Mr. Lowell, Dr. Holmes. Each had declined. Early
in March General Hawley wrote to Bayard Taylor:
"I have written to Mr. Bryant. I presume he will
decline. You were so kind and patriotic as to say
that in that case you would undertake the work. . . .
Time is passing. If I telegraph you to-morrow morning that Mr. Bryant declines, I shall at the same time
write you a formal invitation to take the place."

The next day the dispatch came advising Bayard
Taylor that Mr. Bryant had declined. He sent his
own acceptance and withdrew his hymn. He did not
covet the place. Neither was he moved by any shallow pride to refuse because he was not first asked.
He was overburdened with routine work; he lacked

the spring of vitality which had once been his, but he
was unwilling that so important an office should go
begging. He had an honest pride which would not
suffer his country to be weakly represented. Mr.
Lanier had written a long analysis and criticism of
his hymn. In replying to it, he told him of his new
task.

TO SIDNEY LANIER.

NEW YORK, *March* 17, 1876.

. . . I don't entirely agree with you in regard to a rigid *architectural* structure for the hymn : a strict appropriation of three
stanzas to the three manifestations of the Deity, with a union of
all at the beginning and end, would give a too-conscious air of
design. Here, again, is an instance where you cannot apply the
laws of Music to Poetry. The hymn is to be sung by many, not
divided into parts, and its fitness depends on the whole expression much more than upon a finished artistic form.

However, my part has been changed within two days, and the
hymn will not be sung at all. I have been asked to write the
Ode for the grand national celebration of the Fourth of July,
and have accepted. Bryant, Longfellow, and Lowell declined,
and Whittier and Holmes urged my appointment. I dare not
decline ; yet I feel the weight of the task, and shall both work
and pray ardently for success. Of course I have withdrawn the
hymn, as it would be manifestly improper for me to do both.
Some one else will be appointed immediately. Please don't mention this matter for four or five days yet, by which time it will
be officially announced. I shall miss your poetic companionship,
for which the oration will not compensate me ; but you will readily see that I cannot do otherwise.

NEW YORK, *March* 23, 1876.

. . . The announcement of my Ode was made yesterday, and
I inclose you what Bryant says about it. I 'll add (in confidence,
as yet) that Whittier will probably write the hymn in my stead.
I had a letter from him this morning, and he does n't *decline*, at
least. I am just now a good deal busier than usual, for my
Tribune work takes more time at first, I having been out of
harness so long. Then there have been a great many delayed

(almost *protested*) social debts to be paid, which are more or less fatiguing, however pleasant. Pray be charitable to my enforced brevity this morning.

142 East Eighteenth Street,
New York, *March* 26, 1876.

After all, I can't reply at length, even to-night, to your penultimate letter. You are quite right in your application of your scheme of song to many of my poems : I am well aware of the deficiencies of my early work. Nor do I disagree with you at all in regard to the necessity of strictly-proportioned form ; only there is no single *schema* for all *themas,* and my nature bids me elaborate and round a poetical conception in my brain before I write, letting it find its own manner and form. Poetic ideas have a willful being of their own, and there are cases where they are best expressed through an apparent disregard of form. Of course I don't refer here to my hymn, or to anything of my own.

While keenly feeling, and trying more and more to apprehend the beauty of perfect form in verse, some instinct in me shrinks from too rigidly defining it. Is this comprehensible to you ?

The response to the announcement of my new appointment has been far more cordial than I dared to hope for. Bryant's generous notice struck the keynote which a great many papers have echoed. But all the greater is the cloud of responsibility hanging over me. I feel as if my nerves and muscles were slowly setting for a desperate deed, as in one chosen to lead a forlorn hope. But I can only give what is in me, and if my possible best (under the depressing circumstances) is counted failure, I hope some little courage of nature will not be denied me.

I have seen no single notice of your part in the opening solemnities that was not friendly. Since it is almost certain that Whittier will write the hymn, the appropriateness of the two selections is admitted by everybody. You can now easily make yourself (as you are) the representative of the South in American song.

I am now doing, and shall probably continue to do, regular daily work on the "Tribune." It's a little hard at first, after twenty years' holiday from such labor, but I'm slowly working into it. I must give up much of my lecturing, or I shall *never* get on with my life of Goethe ; and six hours a day given to potboiling leaves me at least three for my own dear, unpaying work.

Bryant probably declined on account of his age, — eighty-two;

Longfellow from his neuralgia in the head ; Lowell urged illness as his excuse . . . Whittier and Holmes both urged my appointment, and so — here I am! Some day, I hope, the circumstances will be known, and I shall get at least a little credit for patriotic willingness to step in and fill up the breach at the eleventh hour. . . .

TO PAUL H. HAYNE.

142 EAST EIGHTEENTH STREET,
NEW YORK, *April* 3, 1876.

Pardon me for having delayed answering your letter for five days since it came. But I have been absolutely overwhelmed with business of all kinds, and such an unusual number of letters demanding immediate answers, that I have been almost distracted. I must even reply hurriedly now, for it is late at night, and I am, to use a German phrase, "dog-tired."

Your letter to the "Star" is exceedingly kind and generous, and I thank you most heartily for it. By a singular coincidence, Bryant said almost the same thing, but briefly, in noticing my appointment as Centennial Poet ; and the opinion has been echoed in many papers all over the country. I only accepted the ode after Bryant, Longfellow, Lowell, and Whittier declined ; but this fact has not saved me from some ill-natured comments, and will not save my work from abuse and attack. However, the announcement has been received far more favorably than I dared to hope, and I shall both labor and pray to be successful.

. . . My head is full of floating ideas for the ode, and I have been so constantly interrupted of late that the quiet wherein such ideas take coherent and harmonious form seems to be totally denied to me. The conception, as a whole, will probably fall upon me suddenly, and then I must lay everything else aside until it is embodied in verse.

Before the ode had been written, Bayard Taylor was required to go to Philadelphia to describe for the "Tribune" the exercises attending the opening of the exhibition. He went thence to Cedarcroft, to secure the freedom from interruption which he needed for his great task. There he threw himself into the composition, and in a couple of days returned to New York with the first rapid draft of the ode.

TO JOHN B. PHILLIPS.

TO JOHN B. PHILLIPS.

NEW YORK, *May* 18, 1876.

I have delayed writing until I could send you my volume. . . .
Besides, I have had to go to Philadelphia to write unusually
much for the " Tribune," to work on my ode, to answer an immense rush of letters and applications, — in short, I have been
hunted like a wild stag.

. . . I meant to have written to you during the winter, but
when my own beloved poetical work must stand aside, my
friends may well bear with me. You can have no idea of the
thousand really unnecessary claims which the unthinking public
makes upon an author. Since March 8th I have been doing
daily editorial work on the " Tribune " in order to live, for I
cannot stand so much lecturing. It is something of a pull upon
me, but the best thing I can do under present circumstances.

Marvelous to say, my ode is finished. Bryant has read it over
with me, and both Stedman and Stoddard indorse it, but somehow I don't feel very confident. The task is one to wreck brain
and heart, and I foresee a great deal of spiteful abuse. I have
always gone straight forward in my own way, catering to nobody's prejudices, and such a policy is always resented in this
country. It does n't worry me now ; if I live ten years longer, I
shall see the end of it.

I have been working for the last fifteen months at intervals on
another poem, which will be the work of my life. It is a little
more than half written, but must now wait. I can hardly hope
to see the end for another year. Meanwhile, I can feel that I
am slowly gaining ground, and am therefore content. This is an
egotistical scrawl, but I am writing late at night after a hard
day's work, and can't stop to consider. It will at least show
you that I am ever your friend.

TO JAMES T. FIELDS.

NEW YORK, *May* 19, 1876.

. . . I am immensely glad that my ode made a good impression on you ; but somehow I can't feel much confidence about it.
I put forth my best powers and did what is now possible to me;
nothing, however, equals my conception of what it should be, and
I dare not look for any loud or general echo.

I shall make very few alterations : further criticism begins to be confusing, and little change is possible without change of form, which I shall not make.

As for Pan*theon*,[1] I am tolerably satisfied that the word is right as it stands. The accent is Greek, πάνθεον, the last syllable from θεός, not θέος. Webster gives both, putting Panthéon first, — but damn Webster, so long as general custom is based on the true Greek accent. Even Byron's line can be read, if you put the accent strongly on the *on*, as the Greeks did.

As for " feather-cinctured," I suppose I must change it, although, personally, I don't care at all that Gray has used the compound adjective already. There is none other so good ; and I 'd as soon be a thief of a good word as maker of a poor one. I shall be abused, anyhow, so what boots one little crime the more ? If I can find something that will *decently* serve, I 'll make the change ; if not —

I 'll omit Strophe, etc., though it 's like throwing a sop to Cerberus.

NEW YORK, *May* 20, 1876.

I have tired my brain to no purpose about the epithet. These are the lines : —

> No more a Chieftainess, with wampum-zone
> And feather-cinctured brow.

Now, I can't say either " feather-girdled " or " feather-belted," after using *zone*. There only remains " feather-banded," which sounds flat and *millinerish*. Gray says " feather-cinctured *chiefs*," referring to a feather petticoat, hanging from the waist ; and in the same line he steals "dusky loves" from Pope ! Why should n't I take what, after all, is probably not Gray's own ? Is it worth while to be tender towards such an intolerant old thief as he ? As for what may be said of me, I don't regard it at all.

I swear to you, I never thought of Gray till you mentioned the fact. The adjective came of itself, and therefore insists on staying. There is no poet living, or who ever has lived, who does not occasionally take a marked word from another. Even Goethe took Schiller's *Donnergang*, and got all the credit of it, until I first pointed out where it came from. Tennyson is full of such use, and so is anybody you can name.

Give me an equally good epithet, and I 'll burn incense under

---

[1] In the line,

> Invade thy rising Pantheon of the Past.

your photograph ! But I shall not spoil my invocation to our native goddess unless I can get something equally good. There ! *Dixi!*

Those who shared in the festivities of the centennial Fourth of July are not likely soon to forget it. They are not likely to forget the blazing sun which rose with fierce determination, and beat down upon the mass of people with an unstinted fury all day long. Certain invited guests — the governors of the States — met at nine o'clock at the Continental Hotel, which was swarming with curious lookers-on. Bayard Taylor's mind was so absorbed in the task before him that he was oblivious of the people whom he met, and did not even return the greetings of his friends. With his wife and daughter, he marched in the procession which formed at the hotel, and proceeded to the square, where an immense platform had been built, running the length of Independence Hall. It had seats for four or five thousand people, who were partially sheltered from the violence of the sun by awnings stretched above them. In front of the platform was a dense, surging mass of people, who were at the sun's mercy for five hours. A few enterprising ones had climbed the shady trees and were ensconced in the branches, whence they peeped out upon the multitude below, but all were full of enthusiasm. They greeted with cheers the guests as they took their places. The last to come was the Emperor of Brazil, who came without ceremony, and with the alertness which he always showed at what was going on about him.

The overture from the band at the other end of the square could scarcely be heard from the platform, so restless was the great crowd. At last Bayard Taylor's part came. He stood upon the speaker's stand, without manuscript or notes of any kind, and in his full, strong voice began, —

Sun of the stately Day.

There was something in his presence, erect, impressive, filled with a solemn sense of the moment, something in his voice, clear, penetrating, sonorous, and charged with profound emotion, which stilled the noise and tumult of those before him, hushed even the lively creatures in the branches, and made the vast audience listen. He had mastered the situation in a moment, and filled with his theme, he poured out his ode with a majesty of expression which held the people to the close. It was a real victory for Poetry. When the last word was uttered, a great shout rose from the enthusiastic people. Shortly before the close of the exercises, Bayard Taylor and his party watched their opportunity to escape. General Sheridan was just leaving, and the crowd opened to allow him to pass. They followed close behind. People were packed like a wall on both sides, some on the shoulders of others, and as they caught sight of him, they called out eagerly, "That's Bayard Taylor! That's the poet! Hurrah for our poet!" and hands were thrust out to seize his in the general excitement and enthusiasm. Whatever criticism might be given in cooler moments to his ode, Bayard Taylor had the rare pleasure of knowing that his lofty strains had fallen upon the delighted ears of the common people. Nor was this the only tribute, for as soon as the ode had been published in the journals, letters from friends and strangers rained down upon him. "It is in full accordance with the great occasion," Mr. Whittier wrote, "and will link thy name honorably with it forever. I felt thee could do justice to the theme, and I am sure all will agree with me that thee has done so. I wish I could have heard thy recitation of it." Bayard Taylor's own sensation when it was all over was one of thankfulness that he could have passed through such an experience, and then of extreme exhaustion, for he had wrought to a high pitch his already overtaxed brain.

TO REV. H. N. POWERS.

142 EAST EIGHTEENTH STREET,
NEW YORK, *July* 6, 1876.

A thousand thanks for your unstinted congratulation! It came yesterday, with a dozen warmly appreciative newspaper notices, and three disparaging sneers. So the balance is firmly on the fortunate side. What gratified me most deeply, because so utterly unexpected, was the way in which the great universal crowd below the platform received my stanzas. I never before saw *the people* silenced, moved, and kindled into flame by poetry. As we passed out through the immense masses there was such cheering and offering of hard hands as never before came to me. In fact, the whole experience was taken out of the old Athenian days. I am indescribably grateful to have had it once in my life.

I was wholly absorbed in the lines as I repeated them, and made myself heard by ten thousand persons without spoiling rhythm or expression. But the reaction came yesterday, and I am scarcely over it yet. My wife joins me in love to C., and thanks for your generous sympathy. The latter is just as necessary in good as in ill fortune, but is not so often given!

TO GEORGE H. BOKER.

142 EAST EIGHTEENTH STREET,
NEW YORK, *July* 8, 1876.

It was a great disappointment not to see you on the Fourth. M. especially regrets it, since now she will not be able to see you at all. I regret it all the more on account of the unfortunate cause.

I felt such a reaction afterwards, and the evening was so oppressive, that I gave up going to Drexel's, as I was obliged to leave by early train next morning. But I was already overwhelmed by the immediate effect of the ode, — a thing upon which I have never reckoned. I made myself heard by ten thousand people without spoiling expression or rhythm, and the mass below the platform was breathless until it burst out into flame. I never before saw the common people silenced, then inspired, by poetry. As we went out through the mass, hundreds of hard hands were stretched to me, and there was a continual succession of "Three cheers for the Poet!" It was simply amazing, and I can yet hardly comprehend the effect. Well, such an experience is worth living for, to say nothing of the hearty and generous voices of friends. Thank you, dear old fellow, for your magnanimous words ; for, according to the small ideas of newspaper critics, we ought to be envious rivals ! What you say of the general verdict at Drexel's is most grateful to me, — and so is Peacock's notice, which I had not seen. We have to win our way slowly by single steps, but this last is a little higher than usual. I can already see that it has modified the tone of certain journals towards me.

In the midst of congratulation and praise came the notes also of envy, depreciation, and slander. Stories flew about that the poet was the unwilling choice of the Commission, and it was in answer to one of these evil reports that the President of the Commission wrote the following note : —

J. R. HAWLEY TO BAYARD TAYLOR.

PHILADELPHIA, *July* 14, 1876.

. . . You have been misinformed as to alleged opposition to selecting you as the poet of the celebration. Mr. Longfellow was first chosen last autumn, but his refusal was hardly at all a surprise to us. Some of us were quite ready to come early to you, but the general sense of the committee demanded that we should first ask those several gentlemen of an earlier age, — Mr. Lowell, Dr. Holmes, and Mr. Whittier. You kindly consented to write the hymn for the opening. Nobody so well as I knows how absolutely unselfish, how free from vanity, how patriotic you were in all this matter. You labored to induce others to take honors that you had every right to aspire to. You wrote a most admirable hymn for the opening, and offered your services for any duty that we might impose upon you. When I was happily left to offer you the poem of the Fourth, I wrote the Executive

Committee and received a prompt response from every one approving the proposition. Your kindness was understood by them, and most gratefully appreciated. I never heard an unkind or hostile word about you in the Commission. Since the Fourth some one expressed great pleasure over your success because of an alleged hostility or unfriendly criticisms in Philadelphia, — some old affair, I suppose, for I got a very indistinct idea about it.

We are all more than satisfied, — profoundly gratified. How old Homer recited his verses, or how effective the elocutionary skill of the troubadours may have been, I have no satisfactory evidence, but I am sure no poet in this country ever delivered his poem so well. You are quite right in thinking that the great crowd followed and appreciated you. I never saw a mass of the common people like that in front of you so clearly comprehending a poem. Their applause was given instantly and with unfailing judgment.

I 'm sorry you could not come to Drexel's that evening. You would have received a shower of well-deserved praise.

Personally as well as officially I am very grateful to you, and very proud of your triumph.

There was no vacation after this labor. Leaving his family at Cedarcroft, Bayard Taylor took up his work with scarcely an interruption, now and then visiting his family as his errands took him to Philadelphia. During this season J. R. Osgood & Co. published "The Echo Club and other Literary Diversions," for he had included in the original series of sketches his witty travesty-criticism of Browning's "Inn Album" and "The Battle of the Bards," both of which had been published in the "Tribune." It was almost a piece of irony that he should be represented now by a book which might easily seem the jest of an idler; it was worse than irony to him that so clever and skillful a bit of work should have fallen upon an apathetic public.

TO PAUL H. HAYNE.

142 EAST EIGHTEENTH STREET,
NEW YORK, *August* 1, 1876.

If you were not a poet, and therefore able to appreciate all the
evils and troubles and embarrassments and shortcomings of poets,
I should fear to write to you. As it is, I don't know whether I
can make clear to you all that has weighed upon me this summer,
— all the labor, anxiety, disappointment, loss of time, neglect of
correspondence, postponement of cherished literary plans, etc.
But it *is* so. I have not been so pinched pecuniarily, driven by
necessity, thwarted in all reasonable expectations, for twenty years
past. I have sent wife and daughter into the country, but cannot go myself. During a month of such heat as you never had
in the South I have been doing daily work, and a dozen times
when I have taken up the pen to write to you, I have laid it down
again from sheer weariness.

I have been unsuccessful with your poem, as I feared. I am
very sorry to announce this, but I am hardly surprised at the result since learning that this summer is the blackest period ever
known since we began to have literature. The publishers say
that they never knew the like ; absolutely *no books* are sold, and
the papers and magazines are living, as much as possible, on already accepted material. Osgood, after telling me this, or the
substance of it, has just brought out my "Echo Club," and I feel
sure I shall not get ten dollars from the sale ! What is to become
of us ?

People say "better times are coming." I hope so, but I have
little present faith. I don't believe any one can judge fairly until after the excitement of the political campaign is over. Meanwhile, I drudge and sigh and wait.

I have seen Lanier recently. He will stay North for the present. He is a charming fellow, of undoubted genius, and I think
will make his mark. In him the elements are still a little confused, but he will soon work into clearness the power he has
already.

In the same season G. P. Putnam's Sons published
" Boys of Other Countries," a series of sketches orig-
inally contributed to " Our Young Folks " and " St.
Nicholas," Osgood & Co. published the National Ode

in heliotype fac-simile reproduction of his singularly clear handwriting, and Brockhaus, in Leipzig, brought out the German edition of the Second Part of "Faust." Bayard Taylor's work continued through the summer and autumn to be mainly upon the "Tribune," where the editorial force was just then small and overworked; he also wrote reviews for "The International Review," and contributed occasional letters to the Cincinnati "Commercial." At the end of August his family rejoined him in New York. As the lecture season returned he continued to have many invitations, but he was compelled to select such places only as he could visit near at hand without detriment to his work on a daily paper. He gave his lectures on German Literature before the Peabody Institute in Baltimore, traveling back and forth for this purpose, and always carrying with him books for review, upon which he worked while traveling.

The wear and tear of such a life was incessant, yet the public could not be aware of it. He did not slight his work on the "Tribune," but used as much care as if his name was signed to every editorial or criticism which he wrote. He even wrote two or three poems, notably the "Assyrian Song" and "Peach Blossom." Nothing could ever prevent him from writing poetry, when it asked for expression. Through all his laborious days and nights he maintained a brave, cheerful face, which did not betray the weariness which he suffered. The most noticeable sign of the gradual undermining of his remarkable vitality was his silence and absent-mindedness. From being always on the alert, and quick to respond, he seemed now to be preoccupied and absorbed. It was the effort of a strong nature to conceal its wounds and to concentrate itself upon the necessary performance of its functions. Many troubles also came upon his family circle at this time. He used to say half-seriously, half-humorously, that the fall was his regular season for bad news, and that he could not expect anything cheering until the winter solstice was over, and the sun began to return. He found compensation, indeed, in his work. It was a pleasure to call attention to the worthy work of others. It was pleasant to find that his words in such a case had been of service and solace.

SIDNEY LANIER TO BAYARD TAYLOR.

PHILADELPHIA, PA., *November* 24, 1876.

A peculiar affection of the side has almost incapacitated me for any use of the pen, temporarily ; but I must send you a little note in order to share with you, — for I would like you to have half of *all* my good things in this world, — the pleasure which your generous notice in the "Tribune" has given me. I recognized it as yours at once, and I therefore did not stint myself in my enjoyment of its appreciative expressions any more than I would mar my smoking of your cigars, or my drinking of your wine, with *arrières pensées*, for I know that the one was as free as the other.

I was particularly pleased with the light way in which you touched upon my faults, and I say this not hastily, but upon a principle to which I 've given a good deal of meditation. The more I think of it the more I am convinced, that every genuine artist may be safely trusted with his own defects. I feel perfectly sure that there are stages of growth, particularly with artists of very great sensibility who live remote from the business-life of men, in which one's habitual faults are already apt to be unhealthily exaggerated from within, and the additional forcing of such a tendency from without, through perpetual reminders of shortcomings, becomes positively hurtful by proud-fleshing the artistic conscience and making it unnaturally timid and irritable. In looking around at the publications of the younger American poets, I am struck with the circumstance that none of them even attempt anything great. The morbid fear of doing something wrong or unpolished appears to have influenced their choice of subjects. Hence the endless multiplication of those little feeble magazine-lyrics which we all know, consisting of one minute idea each, which is put in the last line of the fourth verse, the other three verses and three lines being mere sawdust and surplusage.

It seems to me to be a fact bearing directly upon all this, that if we inquire who are the poets that must be read with the greatest allowances, we find them to be precisely the greatest poets. What enormous artistic crimes do we have continually to pardon in Homer, Dante, Shakespeare! How often is the first utterly dull and long-winded, the second absurdly credulous and superstitious, the third overdone and fantastical! But we have long ago settled all this, we have forgiven them their sins, we have ceased to place emphasis upon the matters in which they displease us, and when we recall their works, our minds instinctively confine remembrance to their beauties only. And applying this principle to the great exemplars of the other arts besides poetry, I think we find no exception to the rule that as to the great artist we always have to take him *cum onere.*

I have to send you my thanks very often. I hope they don't become monstrous to you. Your praise has really given me a great deal of genuine and fruitful pleasure. The truth is, that as for censure, I am overloaded with my own ; but as for commendation, I am mainly in a state of famine, so that while I cannot, for very surfeit, profitably digest the former, I have such a stomach for the latter as would astonish gods and men.

BAYARD TAYLOR TO T. B. ALDRICH.

NEW YORK, *December* 9, 1876.

Your L. has just left us, and I told her I would not delay writing another moment. When she called with B. last Sunday I said I would write that day, and sincerely meant to do so, but one interruption came after another with my imperative Tribune work still to do. . . . You see what a restless life is mine just now. But you have been present in my mind for weeks past, and every day I have meant to write to you. . . .

Only have a little patience with me in these dismal times. I am trying to do my Tribune work, and at the same time to give lectures enough to secure me two or three months at the Sulphur Springs of Virginia next summer. I have positively no income except from my personal labor ; all my literary plans must be postponed, though it cuts me to the heart. But I don't mean to be depressed, or lose one jot of courage or faith. It will all come right in time. I have some things yet to say, and will say them. Nevertheless, I have not been compelled to work so steadily and strenuously for twenty-five years, and at my age it tells upon me physically. There have been many days when, after getting through with my necessary duties, the answering of the most formal note seemed too great a burden. I have come home from the office tired out, and meaning to rest, when some sudden demand followed to write an editorial late at night. If I had not a great capacity for sleep, I should have utterly broken down long ago. It is a situation from which I cannot escape ; I need not go into any explanatory details, but for two years to come I shall be taxed to the limit of my powers. After that, D. V., I may still be able to do my best literary work ; at any rate, I shall have earned the right to do it.

CHAPTER XXIX.

PRINCE DEUKALION.

1877.

And prophet thought, whose lightning pinions go
Beyond the shores of Time !

The Poet's Ambition.

But in thy scheme lie burning
Keen sparks of yearning, —
The hope that dies not,
The voice that lies not,
The dream, more bright at each returning !

Prince Deukalion.

THE year 1877 began as the last year had closed, with hard work on the "Tribune," varied by exhausting journeys to lecture. There was no rest gained by this change of labor, for besides the privations incident to winter traveling, work always accumulated for him at the office, and needed to be cleared away on his return. Added to this was the demand made upon him for unremunerative, but no less exacting work. He gave freely, and when he did not give, the withholding brought discomfort and irritation to him. He was not given to hoarding time and strength, and he pressed on diligently, for he had two new reasons for labor: his house at Cedarcroft stood in need of extensive repairs, which must be made now to save more considerable expenditure later, and he was warned that he must be absolutely idle in the summer if he wished to save himself. His earthly tabernacle was beginning to show serious rents.

TO T. B. ALDRICH.

142 EAST EIGHTEENTH STREET,
NEW YORK, *January* 27, 1877.

I need n't say how welcome your letter was to me. I did n't answer it immediately, because I have been literally ground to the dust with work and worry. You cannot guess, in your Ponkapog seclusion, how much of an author's time is wasted in attending to requests of friends (especially women) for help in this or that good work, which can't quite be refused. It is getting to be the great bane of my life. In addition, my reputation among the Germans brings upon me no end of solicitations. The invitations to dine with clubs and societies, to make addresses, to do this or that, although I almost invariably refuse or decline, fritter away many precious hours, and exhaust a certain kind of nervous force. Committees call and must be received ; they beg and insist ; I can't turn them out, and though I escape in the end the fresh edge is taken off my capacity to work. The fact is, — and it is melancholy to contemplate, — I seem to be much more popular than my books. If the latter sold I should have more means and time, and one thing would balance the other. But to have the annoyance only, and not the gain, drives me frequently to the verge of desperation. . . .

I hope your book did well, in spite of the dismal season. We are sure to have much better times by the end of this year, no matter who is President. I must do extra work now, because —— prescribes the Sulphur Springs of Virginia for next summer. I 've written two good poems lately, but the main thing, my lyrical drama, lies idle.

In the latter part of the winter Bayard Taylor was urged to give his lectures on German Literature in New York and Brooklyn to audiences chiefly of ladies. The task was an agreeable one and spared him the necessity of traveling, but it was not wholly a relief, for he went carefully over the manuscript of each lecture before repeating it, and often became so interested again in the theme that he forgot everything else in following new lines of thought ; he recast parts, made notes for extemporaneous passages, and added poetical translations for illustration. It was not in him to slight his work. Mr. Lanier at this time wrote a poem, " Under the Cedarcroft Chestnut," published in " Scribner's Monthly," in January, 1878. " I wanted to say all manner of fair things about you, but I was so intensely afraid," Mr. Lanier wrote, " of appearing to *plaster* you that I finally squeezed them all into one line.

" ' In soul and stature larger than thy kind.' "

TO SIDNEY LANIER.

NEW YORK, *March* 12, 1877.

Drudgery, drudgery, drudgery ! What else can I say ? Does not that explain all ? Two courses of twelve lectures on German Literature, here and in Brooklyn, daily work on the "Tribune," magazine articles (one dismally delayed), interruptions of all sorts, and just as much conscience as you may imagine pressing upon me to write to you and other friends ! The fact is, I am so weary, fagged, with sore spots under the collar-bone, and all sorts of indescribable symptoms which betoken lessened vitality, that I must piteously beg you to grant me much allowance.

. . . I must say frankly ("which I should not ") that the " Chestnut-Tree " is very fine. . . . Why not change the title to " The Chestnut-Tree at (or of) Cedarcroft " ? It seems a little less personal. The line you mention *is* fine, apart from mine own interest in it ; too good as applied to me. Somehow I feel as if such things might be said after a man is dead, — hardly while he is living. But that you feel impelled to say it now gives me a feeling of dissolving warmth about the heart. You must not think, my dear friend, that simply because I recognize your genius and character, and the purity of the aims of both, that I confer any obligation on you ! From you, and all like you, few as they are, I draw my own encouragement for that work of mine which I think may possibly live. . . .

I have a great many more things to say, but you 'll pardon me. I am deadly tired, and hardly know how I 've kept up the past year without breaking down utterly. But I must at least tell you how glad I am always to hear from you, — how I pray for your restoration to enough of health to do the work God meant you to do.

Three or four days after this confession of physical weakness, Bayard Taylor achieved a feat which was as much greater than the mechanical exploits of· journalism as the spirit of man is superior to a machine. He received one evening the two thick volumes of Victor Hugo's "La Légende des Siècles," and the next evening delivered to the printer copy for a review which fills eighteen pages of his posthumous volume of "Essays and Literary Notes," and contains five considerable poems, which are translations in the metre of the original. "The translations," writes Mr. Stedman, "are what make the feat so surprising. All are interesting, and the last two, 'Solomon' and 'Moschus,' read like the best and most characteristic of your original poems. 'Moschus' is exquisite. No one would ever imagine it to be a translation."

He did not lack for work, and his fame for versatility seems to have penetrated the region of mental dullness which is illustrated by the following letter:

—, *March* 24, 1877.

BAYARD TAYLOR : —

Dear Sir, — Hearing that you are a poet of some note as well as a good Oration writer I come to ask you this question and I would like very much to have an answer in one or two days as no doubt you can write a very good Oration if so Let me know your price and if you can not write an Oration please let me know of any one that can please do not do as others do but answer my letter as soon as you can and also state your price of writing one for me, in every case in writing directions give no of Box or Street. Yours Very Truly

—— ——,

——,

——.

P. O. Box 98.

P. S. give price and also subject which you would write on.

P. S. Please give me the directions of E. C. Stedman and W. H. Stoddard and much oblige   Yours Truly.

He did not " do as others do," but replied most cheerfully to his anxious correspondent, and gave the addresses asked for with great alacrity : —

NEW YORK, *March* 27, 1877.

SIR, — I have received your letter asking me the price of an oration to be written by me for your use. I regret to say that I am quite out of orations ready-made. The recent political excitement obliged me to prepare a large number for the politicians on both sides ; and I have now taken a contract to write seventy-five sermons for a new sect which will soon come into existence. As it is generally known that I furnish speeches, orations, scientific lectures, sermons, and humorous entertainments, I have more applications than I can fill, and have been obliged to raise my price from $27.25 to $43.60, according to subject and style.

Mr. E. C. Stedman, however, has quite a number of scientific and exoteric orations, some of which have been once used in Texas and Oregon, but are still new in the Atlantic States. His address is 80 Broadway.

Mr. R. H. Stoddard (at 329 East Fifteenth Street) has several orations devoted to moral and spiritual reform. They are serious, but very touching, and I think one of them might suit you quite as well as anything I could write.

I may remark, however, that the price of ready-made orations has increased within a year or two, owing to the greater number of new reputations which we have been called upon to construct.

Yours truly,   BAYARD TAYLOR.

There was a limit, however, to the work which he could do. He had written his letters to the Cincinnati " Commercial " as occasion might prompt, but he decided that he must give up this part of his work, voluntary as it was, and he wrote a long letter to Mr. Halstead, the editor of the paper, in which he was led to free his mind regarding the general circumstances under which he, like other men of letters, was working.

142 East Eighteenth Street,
New York, *April* 16, 1877.

At last I have a free, unbespoken evening, and am not too tired to write ; so I can unburden my conscience of the perilous stuff that has been weighing upon it for the last two months. This will be such a great relief that I shall use it almost as a luxury ; and as I look at the empty rocking-chair beside my table, which you may remember having so comfortably filled when you first made the proposition, the substance of what I said to you then comes back to my mind. Do you remember it ? Probably not ; so, rather than take too much for granted, let me recall it. When you proposed that I should send you letters to the "Commercial," weekly if possible, but with an irregular continuity in any case, I was well disposed to comply ; but I am enough of a journalist to understand the necessity of selecting only such material as may have a general interest, and treating it in a free, lively manner. I was a little doubtful, in the first place, of being able to do this as it ought to be done ; I was almost certain that I could not keep it up for any length of time. Hence I stipulated —that, of course, you remember — that I should be at liberty to discontinue the correspondence whenever it should become too serious a task.

Well, the time has come, and even a little sooner than I anticipated. After finishing my lecturing engagements outside of the city, I supposed that I might at least send you irregular reports of what is going on here. But the experiment of giving my series of twelve lectures on German Literature here and in Brooklyn proved successful. (Whether successful or not, the nervous wear and tear would have been the same.) Now, imagine me giving four lectures a week, doing my daily work on the "Tribune," attending to my correspondence, household and other private matters, to say nothing of vainly striving to snatch an hour now and then for my own cherished and long-delayed literary labor, and judge for yourself what chance there is of my doing good, honest, conscientious work for you and your readers. I see my best friends seldom, except when they are kind enough to come to me ; I deny myself a great deal of social recreation, which I both heartily enjoy and think necessary to a rational life ; I mortally offend numbers of unknown individuals by not answering their unnecessary letters of inquiry : yet I still lack the needful rest of body and brain. The outgo must be contracted somewhere ; if I take off that for which I am just now least fitted, and cease to chat with your subscribers, will you not pardon me ?

But, seriously, now, my dear friend, have you any idea of the life of a man who has attained a certain amount of name (by which I don't mean fame) in literature ? Have you ever considered how many solid claims are made in return for certain very intangible advantages ? I should like to enlighten you a little on this point, for within the last year I have seen the comfortable statement repeated in various newspapers that a man has only to do good literary work in order to be appreciated — and rewarded. Nothing could be more untrue in this country at this time. The public supposes that the mere knowledge of a man's name is the token of his success. If notoriety were success, this would be true ; but it is sometimes the reverse. However, notoriety brings with it the same penalties as genuine fame ; and a large proportion of the very persons who most worry an author imagine that they are cheering him with compliment ! When they do not do this, they boldly assert their claims upon his time and patience. For instance, nothing is more common than for me to receive a package of MSS., accompanied by a letter, beginning in this way : " I ask of you the same assistance which others gave to you when you were young. Will you read my manuscripts, and return them to me with your critical judgment ? " etc. The simple fact is, I never had such assistance when young. I never sent an article to an author who was not also the editor of a periodical ; I never asked another's influence to procure admission into a magazine ; and, with all the sympathy which I still keep for the hope and uncertainty of beginners, I have never yet found that my frank criticism was of any avail, except to make me enemies when the ardent young poet subsides into the reporter or paragraph-writer.

But I meant to go a little more into particulars. This letter is already fearfully long, but I am to-night "i' the vein," and you must e'en have patience to read it. Applications for autographs — when they send *one* card and an addressed envelope — are easily answered, and I can't refuse the boys and girls.

Then follow questioning letters about all sorts of things, for which the writers need only consult a cyclopædia. The other day I had one from Ohio, insisting that I should decide a bet whether the Khedive's private income is greater than the Sultan's! Next come, less frequently, invitations to deliver orations or poems before colleges, college societies, associations of all sorts, public meetings or charities, but each requiring a careful and respectful statement of the reasons for declining. In this class I count personal visits from committees or individuals, pressing similar requests, and rarely to be satisfied under less than half an hour's argument. I could increase the list materially, but this will be enough to show you how much mental and vital force may be dulled and wearied, and all for nobody's profit. Sometimes, for weeks together, I thus lose an hour or two every day.

If you could in some way help to make people understand that no author who is not independently rich can possibly respond to the claims made upon him, and that wealth is never attained in this country, or perhaps any other, by the highest, purest, and most permanent form of literary labor, you will do a real service to our guild. Emerson is now seventy-four years old, and his last volume is the only one which has approached a remunerative sale. Bryant is in his eighty-third year, and he could not buy a modest house with all he ever received in his life from his poems. Washington Irving was nearly seventy years old before the sale of his works at home met the expenses of his simple life at Sunnyside. I have had no reason to complain of the remuneration formerly derived from those works which I know to possess slight literary value. But the translation of "Faust," to which I gave all my best and freshest leisure during a period of six or seven years, has only yielded me about as much as a fortnight's lecturing. I have spent two or three years in collecting the material and making the preparatory studies for a new biography of Goethe, and I have been waiting two years longer for the fitting leisure to begin the work. In order to undertake it I must own my time in advance. No matter how successful it might be considered, it could not possibly bring me more than a tithe of the amount which drudgery for the markets of literature would return, in the same time. But the matter of money does n't enter into my plan. I only look forward and yearn for the chance.

Don't misunderstand me, therefore ; this is not complaint, but explanation. It's absurd to complain about what is inevitable. Almost every American author I know has more or less of the same trouble ; but some have a better fortune to balance it. One, whom we know, loses much time through women who have far more time at their command, but who try to pile upon his shoulders a good part of the burden of their own charitable interests. It is so easy to help, — and get the credit of it, — in this way ! However, we try to be as courteous and considerate as in us lies. I think there is only one thing that upsets my chronic patience : it is when some one comes with a particularly onerous and unnecessary claim, and begins thus : "Oh, you are before the public, you know, so I feel that I have the right to call upon you, and I am sure you will see that your duty," etc. I declare to you I am sometimes so weary with my routine of daily work, so dull for lack of the social recreation which I must forego, so disappointed in not attaining the leisure for my own independent and desired labor, that when a demand of this sort comes it requires a colossal effort to repress all signs of irritation.

Here's now the seventh page, and I *must* stop. But I could write a magazine article on the subject. I foresee that I shall finally be obliged to return to Cedarcroft, to write the biography. If all this interruption and consequent wear and tear won't let me alone, I must get out of its way. When I happen to speak of it, people innocently say, "Why don't you keep a secretary ?" Great heavens ! I'd rather take a secretary's salary and buy up two or three months of my own time. Well, the true secret of life lies in making the most of one's circumstances ; but I can't quite understand why the fact of one's name being tolerably well known should impose upon him so many hindrances. If one could really help ! — but an experience of several hundred young aspirants for literary fame has been very discouraging to me.

I have writen rather ramblingly, having too much to say to be strictly simple and logical. But you will get the drift of my letter, I am sure, and will recognize the necessity I am under of simplifying my work. Some critics have charged me with attempting too much, — trying too many fields. Trying ? — when it was a matter of sheer necessity ! I should only be too happy if I were in a condition to give up everything but the one path of literary labor which I know was designed for me, — if any ever was. *Dixi.*

TO T. B. ALDRICH.

NEW YORK, *May* 7, 1877.

. . . I have had no release from hard work yet. My lectures, although very successful, were a drain upon my strength, as I had to do the usual amount of Tribune work at the same time ; and since then, the art criticism has been added to my burden. Did you see my article on Tennyson in the "International Review ? " In addition to that I have written a paper on Bismarck ; but now the limit of possible work has been reached, and I am forced to give up all magazine-writing for a time. I am longing for the 1st of July, for then we shall go to the White Sulphur Springs of Virginia for a month or two, finishing up with a short season at Cedarcroft.

TO SIDNEY LANIER.

142 EAST EIGHTEENTH STREET,
NEW YORK, *May* 9, 1877.

. . . I have been forced to write six long art-criticisms on the Exhibition, and you 've no idea how exhausting such work is. In fact, it is only within two days that I begin to feel a little lifting of the strain upon me, and wake up o' mornings with the sense of being moderately refreshed by sleep. All this work has been inevitable, owing to necessity of meeting some unusual expenses this spring. But I have laid up enough for two months of summer idleness, for which I pant as the hart for the water-brooks, and so can only be thankful. . . .

At the end of May Bayard Taylor went to Ithaca to delivered his lectures before the University, and a month later went to Providence to read a poem, " Soldiers of Peace," before the Grand Army of the Potomac, a task which he had refused the year before and now took up with extreme reluctance. A few days afterward he went with his family for his much-needed rest at the White Sulphur Springs, where he had taken a cottage. He was asked to give a poem at a celebration of the hundredth anniversary of the massacre at Paoli, September 20th, but declined in the following letter : —

TO T. BAYARD WOOD.

142 EAST EIGHTEENTH STREET,
NEW YORK, *June* 29, 1877.

Your letter has just reached me here, as we have not yet gone to Cedarcroft for the summer. There could be no greater inducement to me to perform the duty you request than the circumstance that it is a Chester County commemoration. Hence I regret the more that I am compelled to decline. I am overworked, and leave on Monday for the White Sulphur Springs (Va.), where I mean to live for a while without using my pen. The poem I have just delivered in Providence, R. I., was written in consequence of a promise made last year, and the experience satisfies me that I must undertake no more tasks of the kind for some time to come. There is nothing more difficult in literature than to write a good poem for a special occasion, and the very anticipation of it would rob me of all peace of mind from now until the 20th of September. Both last year and this, I have been severely taxed, and feel that I cannot and ought not to undertake a new labor.

Accept my sincere thanks for the compliment contained in your invitation.

At the White Sulphur Springs he was joined by his friends Mr. McEntee and wife, and gave himself up as well as he could to complete relaxation, resuming the recreation of painting, and luxuriating in the lovely nature and climate of the resort. Rumors had now begun to fly about that the new administration had it in mind to appoint him to a foreign mission; Russia was named most prominently, and in one of the papers the alternative of Belgium was given. This prospect had no charms for him, and he took an early opportunity to intimate to the government that he should not accept that appointment. He did, however, catch at the possibility of going to Berlin. He would not make application for the office, but he saw in such a position an opportunity to write his life of

Goethe and Schiller, and he began eagerly to build upon this chance.

TO T. B. ALDRICH.

WHITE SULPHUR SPRINGS, GREENBRIER CO., W. VA.,
July 5, 1877.

. . . I have a holiday of two months, during which I shall only put pen to paper in order to write to a few old friends. Mc-Entee will join me here next week, and we are going a-sketching. Talk of your Ponkapog air ! We are here two thousand feet above the sea, yet with mountains two thousand feet higher all around us ; turf as in England, groves of glorious ancient oaks, and an atmosphere like that of heaven. We have a cottage to ourselves, two dark retainers, an ex-Governor on one side and a coming President promised for the other, the most courteous and refined society, and such an amount of kindness since leaving Washington as I have found nowhere else in the United States ! Take away your Saratogas and your Long Branches !

TO SIDNEY LANIER.

WHITE SULPHUR SPRINGS, W. VA., *July* 11, 1877.

. . . As for the mission, I think " Belgium " must be a mistake for " Berlin." It would be singular to offer the choice of a *first* or *fourth* rate place ! In any case, the German mission is the only one I am able to take ; and if it is not offered, I'll even stay at home. But the matter ought to be decided soon : it disquiets me a little, in spite of my best will not to think of the matter.

This is the most complete nest of repose I have yet found in America. The air, the quiet, the society, are just what I need ; I drink the water and bathe, and am feeling like a new man. But, oh ! how supremely lazy I am ! It's an effort even to write a letter to a friend. I walk half a mile, sit down under a tree, look at the rich colors of the wooded mountains, and am animally happy. I only write poems in dreams, and here's a line which came to me thus, the other night : —

" The ship sails true, because the seas are wide."

Let me break off here. This indolence (I foresee) will breed fresh activity ; but I don't want to think of that now. . . .

WHITE SULPHUR SPRINGS, W. VA., *July* 13, 1877.

I am satisfied that I have found the right place. The air here, the sulphur-water, the baths, and the general quiet are precisely what I needed. I am gaining in every way, day after day ; and the influences seem equally good for my wife and daughter. The Southern society here shows the most courteous and amiable temper towards us : the two Governors, —— and ——, are men of culture and refinement, and there are very pleasant people from farther South. I sit under a tree and make sketches with McEntee in the forenoon, and then loaf until evening, when some one generally calls to give us a drive through these charming mountain valleys.

I am a little unsettled (even with the best will to keep perfectly cool) by all the newspaper talk about the Russian and Belgian missions. The government has given no hint to me, yet I suppose there must be some basis for the report. Now, as I told you, I do not want, and cannot accept, either the Russian or the Belgian place ; but I should consider it as a special good fortune to have the mission to Germany. It is of the same rank as the Russian, hence would involve no higher ambition, and I am entirely sure of my qualifications for the place. Knowing Germany so well, I could live in Berlin on the salary (which I could not do in St. Petersburg), and there would be leisure enough in the course of three or four years to finish my Goethe work. The position would at once open to me many archives not easily accessible otherwise. I think the fact that I can make a speech in German, and the chance I should have of furthering communication in the fields of science and scholarship between the two countries, would enable me to be of real service to the government.

I only ask you, in case you hear anything said by those in authority in regard to the matter, to present this view. I am very doubtful whether I could get the place, — certainly I shall not ask for it, — but there may be just a possibility.

WHITE SULPHUR, W. VA., *July* 28 (*Saturday*), 1877.

. . . We leave for Cedarcroft on Wednesday, August 1st. The weather is now intolerably hot, and daily hot sulphur-baths are somewhat debilitating. But at least I am having my system thoroughly washed out, and shall begin a tonic course on leaving here. I meant to write a letter or two, and still may ; but you have hardly room for such now. Perhaps it may do a week hence.

No word from Washington, and I don't expect any while the trouble lasts. But Halstead has written to me that he *knows* that Hayes, Evarts, and Schurz are favorable to me ; that he himself would write immediately to Hayes ; and that Judge Force of Cincinnati (whom I don't know) had written a very strong letter. This letter of Halstead's was in answer to my inquiry whether he, or any one whom he knew, had suggested my name in the first place. He says emphatically no : it was voluntary on the part of the government, — which is all the more satisfactory to me. But I don't allow myself to think of the matter as more than a possibility : I am able to possess my soul in peace, and attend chiefly to my body.

TO JERVIS McENTEE.

· CEDARCROFT, KENNETT SQUARE, PA., *August* 4, 1877.

Yesterday we received your very welcome and interesting letter. Now that the suffering from heat is passing from your memory, I hope that you have the same abiding pleasures of memory as we have. But I must first tell you of our remaining days at the White Sulphur. . . .

Stevensons took our cottage, and began to move in before we got out. Altogether, we went off feeling satisfied. It was a lovely, cool evening ; we all slept well, and woke up at Alexandria. At Washington we had a capital breakfast, went on to Baltimore, took a carriage and drove all over Druid Hill Park, dined, and went home the same afternoon, the weather and temperature being simply perfect. I was glad to come away from the White Sulphur, yet I feel that I should like to go there again. Here we have glorious weather thus far ; I never knew finer, and never saw the country looking so richly and mellowly green. L. had her quiet birthday celebration yesterday. I still mean to get a *cuke* and cabbage-cutter and send on to your mother. I find that my appetite is undiminished : it seems that the effect of the sulphur is now coming for the first time.

Nothing has yet turned up about the mission. I had a letter of good import from Murat Halstead after you left, but I cannot do anything except quietly wait. A secretary has been appointed, the place having been vacant for two or three months, so I suppose the appointment of a minister is next in order. But I am trying to give up all thoughts of the matter. The more time elapses, the less the government seems desirous of having my services, and what seemed such a fortunate chance will doubtless vanish in smoke, — or like smoke. I may be able to say, " What a luck I missed ! " and that will be the end.

CEDARCROFT, *August* 7, 1877.

Go ahead with your bill o' fare,[1] but omit *names !* It ought to run thus : —

SOUP.

Violincelli.

FISH.

Striped Bassoon, baked ; Cast o' Net Sauce.

ENTRÉES.

Trombones of Beef.   Haut-boiled Mutton.
Stewed Chickerings, Steinway Sauce.
Fiddlet of Veal.   Kettle Drum Sticks.

VEGETABLES.

Green Cornet.   Tubas, mashed.   Cymblins.
Violin String Beans.

DESSERT.

Flagi au lait.   Cabinet Organ Pudding.   Mandoline Tarts.
Dulcimers.

WINES.

Sackbut.   French Horns.

They are off for the mail.   Good-by !

Bayard Taylor returned with his family to Cedarcroft, but shortly after went for the sea air to Newport and Mattapoisett, taking a run also to Cohasset for a day.

1 Mr. McEntee had asked permission to give to a local paper a copy of a *jeu d' esprit* which had entertained the party at the White Sulphur.

Shepherdess,

(*Singing in the valley.*)

Uncover the embers!
With pine-cone and myrtle
My breath shall enkindle
    The sacred Fire!
Arise through the stillness
My shepherd's blue signal,
And bear to his mountain
    The valley's desire!
The olive-tree bendeth;
The grapes gather purple;
The garden in sunshine
    Is ripe to the core;
Then smile as thou sleepest,
His fruit and my blossom;
There's peace in the chamber
    And song at the door!

TO SIDNEY LANIER.

142 EAST EIGHTEENTH STREET,
NEW YORK, *September* 6, 1877.

I found your letter waiting for me on Monday, when my holiday closed, and we found ourselves back again in our old quarters. I don't think the White Sulphur helped me much, after all, but the sea air and water did, and I feel more like my old self now.

I was (for me) exceedingly nervous and restless while at Cedarcroft, and also much occupied with *little* matters and family changes, which made our stay there anything but refreshing. Moreover, I was foolishly expecting, from day to day, that decision of the government which has not yet been made, and will probably be delayed another month. I am so accustomed to look forward to some fixed point, and work towards it, that I hardly know how to manage an uncertainty which includes two such radically different fates. . . . Since I am at work again I can more easily banish the subject from my mind. . . . Strange that you should mention my poem, just when I take it up again ! I have written one new scene since Monday. . . .

The poem referred to was " Prince Deukalion." The long period during which he had laid aside the poem was one of drudgery, of exhaustion, and of rest, but his silence had not been directly owing to these causes. He had reached a point in his poem where he hesitated before the problem of the requisite form to embody a critical thought. He could not satisfy himself, and waited patiently for the cloud to lift. Suddenly, early in September, when on an excursion in Boston Harbor, the vision of Deukalion occurred to him; he saw his way clear, and upon his return to New York he threw himself with his customary ardor into the work of completing the poem, which he now wrote rapidly.

During his visit to New England he had also arranged to translate Schiller's " Don Carlos " for Mr.

Lawrence Barrett, the tragedian. In October he was busy with the delivery, twice a week, of his twelve lectures on German Literature, at the Lowell Institute in Boston, — a course which was exceedingly popular.

TO JAMES T. FIELDS.

142 EAST EIGHTEENTH STREET,
NEW YORK, October 8, 1877.

Pardon, pardon, pardon ! You knew beforehand that I enjoy everything you write, and that I must be glad to get your lovely little volume (" Boskage," not *Underbrush*).

Now, it so happened that, after having stuck fast for eighteen months in the very middle of my lyrical drama, — finding a *pons asinorum* I could not cross, — I at last kited a string over the chasm, then a rope, then a tough wire-cable, the which, having become entangled in some distant thicket of the imagination, sufficed to bear the weight of my conception. The crossing, giddy but fortunate, was made in a basket. There was firm ground beyond, over which I ran, breathless, until, on the top of a misty hill, I caught hold of the End ! This happened only yesterday, and now the crowd of delayed duties rushes back upon my conscience.

First of all, my hearty thanks ; the volume is charming, both in bodily form and intellectual substance. I knew the most of it already, whence it was all the more welcome.

I think I shall return hither by night-train until after November 1st, when I shall spend the intermediate days in Boston. I want to show Longfellow Acts III. and IV. ; he has only seen I. and II. You twain have only heard Act I., at Manchester, two years ago ; would you like to hear the rest, *privatissime?* But we 'll talk of this anon.

TO SIDNEY LANIER.

142 EAST EIGHTEENTH STREET,
NEW YORK, October 13, 1877.

. . . Scribners are going to publish your poem on the chestnut-trees and have it illustrated by me ! When I was last at Cedarcroft I made the necessary sketch of the trees for them.

Now, I have a piece of news for you. My " Deukalion " is finished ! The conception overcame me like a summer cloud, during all my holiday time; but the difficulty wherein I stuck fast more than a year ago would not be solved. But, little by little, I worked out the only possible solution — for me. I finished the third act, my great stumbling-block ; then, as the fourth and last act was already clear in my mind, and I still felt fresh for the task, I went on. Now all is complete and fairly copied into that volume which you will remember. But I shall hardly publish before another year. It is an immense relief, as the delight of writing was counterbalanced by the huge difficulties of the subject. Well, there's more of my life and thought and aspiration in this poem than in all else I have written, and if it has no vitality nothing of mine can have.

For a week past I have been giving all my spare time to a translation and adaptation to our stage of Schiller's " Don Carlos " for Lawrence Barrett. It's a new sort of work for me, very interesting, and just what I need in order to let myself down easily from the heights of " Deukalion."

You don't tell me what you are doing — or going to do — in Baltimore. It's too bad that the government is so slow and muddled in the matter of making appointments. I, also, have been kept hanging in suspense for over three months, and now find that my chances are rapidly sliding down to nothing. I've given up all expectation of the place which would help me on in my literary plans, and I won't have any other.

I begin my course of twelve lectures in Boston on Wednesday next. Work, work, work ! but I thank the Lord that my poem is finished.

TO GEORGE H. BOKER.

142 EAST EIGHTEENTH STREET,
NEW YORK, *December* 29, 1877.

I write, trusting this will catch you before you leave St. Petersburg. I must throw myself upon your mercy for not having answered your last letter before you wrote again, but I was really waiting for some solution of my own case, and there seemed to be a chance that I might be able to learn a few things of interest to you, as well as to myself, by waiting a little. I was mistaken ; but at least I know how to explain why you, as well as myself, have been so treated.

Meanwhile I am working, I think, harder than ever before in my life. I am staggering on the brink of mental and physical exhaustion. My lyrical drama — the work of three years, although it only contains three thousand lines — is finished. I have translated, with many changes, the greater part of Schiller's "Don Carlos" for Barrett, the actor; have given my twelve lectures on German Literature before the Lowell Institute in Boston; written for the "North American Review," and I don't know how much else, beside my regular daily work for the "Tribune." I can't stand this strain longer, and so am going to Cedarcroft next spring, to live simply and cheaply, and begin my biography of Goethe. I have read the whole of my new poem to Longfellow, who says it is far ahead of anything I have ever done, and that it is one of the grandest conceptions in literature. I feel, indeed, that I am making progress all the time. I know that my name, in our literature, counts more than it ever did before, and am content to go on working, and get out whatever is in me.

. . . I am glad you are coming back. An American who has any interest whatever in his country makes a fatal mistake when he gives up his residence here and stays in Europe, where he never can be wholly at home. I have tested the two continents pretty thoroughly, and am satisfied that one is always happiest where he is best known, where he knows most, and where his interests are kept alive and active.

I won't add any gossip, for there is nothing of importance beyond what you see in the papers, and you'll soon be here to learn it personally. Then we'll have a good long talk, either at 1720 Walnut Street or at Cedarcroft, and the history of all these six years shall be made clear. One thing I am sure of, dear old fellow! — we shall take up the thread of our divided lives, and weave them together in loving interest, as we have always done.

TO GORDON GRANT.

142 EAST EIGHTEENTH STREET,
NEW YORK, *December* 30, 1877.

. . . A week ago I went into the Fifth Avenue Hotel, and found a nest of politicians, Governor Jewell, McCormick, etc. They pounced upon me, saying I must make an effort, gain influence, etc., for there was no one asking for the place. They also told me that Fred. Seward was exceedingly desirous of my appointment; that Schurz had declared he could not, in any case, go to *Germany*, and added all sorts of persuasions. I answered that I was now satisfied that the nominations were made *by whim;* that the government was perfectly well acquainted with my fitness (or unfitness) for the place ; that the published rumors already proved the favor of the entire American press ; and that I would not, personally, do anything but wait for the decision of the government. I then made a call of respect upon Hayes, who was in the hotel ; he was extremely cordial, and seemed to expect that I should say something, but I did not. So the matter stands. . . .

I have never before in my life done so much work in four months as during the last four. In fact, I have done far too much, and have brought myself to the verge of some physical disaster. Nothing but plenty of sleep and heavenly weather have pulled me safely through the crisis. We have a purely Roman winter, thus far ; until to-day, the greenest turf, dandelions in blossom, cloudless skies, and an air to breathe which creates a new life every day. This morning the temperature fell to 21° for the first time, — but what a day ! And how the perfect days succeed each other ! I have fire in my library only about twice a week. New York Bay is as smooth and deep blue as your Mediterranean at Leghorn. . . . Of course, all this work tells (or will tell) *for* me, but it also tells *upon* me. But the best rest, as I hinted to President Hayes the other day, comes not from indolence, but *entire change of occupation.* I don't know whether he understood the hint ; probably not.

I have left some of your questions unanswered, and can send you, at best, but a hasty, unsatisfactory letter in reply to your many interesting messages. You must have patience with me. I do the best I can now, and will do better when I get back some of my old vigor.

It had been Bayard Taylor's purpose to keep "Prince Deukalion" by him for possible further revision, but when the drama was completed it became, like other of his works, a thing of the past, to be put aside, dismissed, and made to give way in his thought to other designs. He rarely lingered over the accomplished task; its completion only left him free for the new purposes which had already risen in his mind. He was hastened, beside, in his intention to publish by the discovery, after his poem was written, of two poems, an English and a German, which so nearly approached it in design as to convince him that he was in a wide current of thought, and that unless he published now he was in danger of finding his work received as if it were a follower instead of an *avant-courier*. " Prince Deukalion " was, beyond all this, so distinctly a confession of the author's faith that in this earnest hour of his life he felt a strong man's desire to declare emphatically how he stood in relation to the great question of being. Something in a letter from Mr. Hayne drew from Bayard Taylor a response in which he spoke with less reserve than he was wont.

"As to what seems to be your most important question," he writes, " I will be frank, with the understanding that this is confidential. A man's faith is a sacred part of his nature, with which the public has no concern, and I resist all open attempts to make me reveal mine. I *do* most entirely believe in the immortality of the soul. And perhaps I cannot better sum up my arguments than by intrusting you with some lines from an unpublished poem, which I have just finished after three years of study and severe consecration. Urania (Science) asks, —

> Yet why, to flatter life, wilt thou repeat
> The unproven solace ? [1]

The answer is : —

> Proven by its need ! —
> By fates so large no fortune can fulfill ;
> By wrong no earthly justice can atone ;
> By promises of love that keep love pure ;
> And all rich instincts powerless of aim,
> Save chance, and time, and aspiration wed

[1] The immortality of the soul.

To freer forces, follow !   By the trust
Of the chilled Good that at life's very end
Puts forth a root, and feels its blossom sure !
Yea, by thy law ! [1] — since every being holds
Its final purpose in the primal cell,
And here the radiant destiny o'erflows
Its visible bounds, enlarges what it took
From sources past discovery, and predicts
No end, or, if an end, the end of all !

Do not let these lines go out of your hands! The very
wisdom and wonder of the universe and its laws prove
conclusively to me that the intuitions of power and
knowledge in ourselves, which we cannot fulfill here,
assure us of continued being. If those laws are good,
— as we see they are, — then what is ordered for us is
also good. We need not too painfully go into conjunc-
tures of details. *True* harmony between natures in
this life certainly predicts continuance in the next;
but how or in what manner it shall be continued is
beyond us, and I have not felt the least fear. I feel
none now. I can conceive the Infinite much more
easily than I can the Finite; I *know* (but I cannot
demonstrate) that my being cannot be annihilated.
This feeling is in accordance with all that science
teaches me ; if I depended on theology alone I should
have little comfort. If the Divine Law manifest in
matter be good, we shall live on, — we *must ;* if there
is no future for me, a Devil, and not a God, governs
the universe. *Dixi !* "

[1] The law of Science.

CHAPTER XXX.

MINISTER TO GERMANY.

1878.

Slow-paced is Fate:
All crowns come late.
Prince Deukalion.

THE action of the government regarding the mission to Germany was still deferred. The delay was annoying, for it was impossible to work or plan freely with such a decision still impending. But so far as Bayard Taylor's purpose of literary work was concerned, there was no uncertainty. He had determined to enter earnestly upon his life of Goethe and Schiller. It pressed upon him. He had cleared away the dramatic poem which stood between him and this task, and when once he entered upon a great design he was driven by his mental necessity to carry it to completion, whatever the obstacles.

Yet he was almost in despair of securing the requisite leisure for this great work. The pressure of daily labor upon him was very great, and if he continued in America, engaged upon editorial work, he foresaw the extreme difficulty of organizing time for his task. Moreover, the longer he delayed the more insecure did the wealth of material which he had accumulated appear to him. For this material was stored principally in his capacious memory; and confident as he ordinarily was of his power to hold firmly what he intrusted to it, he began now to doubt if this treasury might not be rendered less impregnable by the countless cares and anxieties which were undermining it.

Hermann Grimm's "Goethe" had recently appeared, and was so near in its scheme to his own design as to make him more eager than ever to achieve his purpose. If he went to Germany he would unquestionably have special advantages for doing the work. If he did not go he meant to cut himself off from all other life, bury himself in Cedarcroft, and not emerge until the book was done.

He completed his translation and adaptation of "Don Carlos," and wrote an ode on the death of Victor Emmanuel, which was published in the "Tribune" under the title of "The Obsequies in Rome," and is included thus in the collection of his poems made since his death. In this ode he gave expression to that ardent love of Italy which had been one of his early passions, never to grow weak, and renewed both by his own life in Italy and by the historic movements of that nation, which drew forth his eager interest. It was in the same spirit that he took part in the memorial meeting held by the Italians in New York, and gave a short address in the Italian language, upon the spur of the moment.

TO SIDNEY LANIER.

142 EAST EIGHTEENTH STREET,
NEW YORK, *January* 20, 1878.

. . . I have finished (but not yet revised) Schiller's "Don Carlos" since I saw you, and have done a good deal of magazine work. My only poem is the Ode on Victor Emmanuel, which you may have seen. . . . For the last few days I have been writing as little as possible, in order to rest, having been troubled with a sense of great oppression on the chest. The fact is, I must take more rest than I have been doing.

Speaking of this, the prospect of a good rest abroad is still held out to me ; but after such long uncertainty I dare not count upon it in the least.   I learn that the President favors my appointment, and —— says nothing against it : still they don't make it, and the post has been vacant nearly six months.   I think a decision of some kind will be made in a few weeks. During the fall, when I gave up all expectation of going, I was happy, and I would withdraw my name now rather than be so unsettled but for the great chance of the Goethe work.

. . . Friends come in now and then and keep us cheerful.   I can feel that I am steadily gaining in various ways, and am hopeful of the future.   Keep up your spirits also, but I think you have the blessing of a good natural stock of them.

At last, late in the evening of February 15th, a dispatch was brought to Bayard Taylor from the Tribune office, where it had just been received from Washington, announcing that the President had sent in his name to the Senate as Minister to Germany.   The news was in the morning papers the next day, and immediately there began a series of dispatches, letters, visits, receptions, and dinners which knew no cessation until Bayard Taylor sailed, April 11th.   If ever a nomination was ratified by the people, it was this. The newspaper press, quick to act as spokesman of the popular mind, was nearly unanimous in its emphatic praise of the appointment.   Strong political antipathy, displayed still in a few instances, was generally laid aside in recognition of the fitness of the nomination. Something, no doubt, was due to the *esprit de corps* which made the newspapers proud to be thus represented by one of their own number, but the varied forms of expression of pleasure all centred in a hearty indorsement of the President's action, and a strong sense of satisfaction that the administration had done what the country demanded in appointing to a first-class mission a man who had won the place by his eminent adaptation to it. The German press, also, at once welcomed in anticipation the new minister, for he was no stranger to them.

All this demonstration made a profound impression upon Bayard Taylor. It was an evidence of good-will toward him which came when he was worn in health and spirits, ready to despair of accomplishing the work which he had in mind and almost ready to think his life a failure. It acted upon his impaired nature as a powerful stimulus, and enabled him to undergo a strain which otherwise he could not have borne. There was much cheap witticism in the papers upon the dinners which Bayard Taylor ate as preparation for his work as Minister Plenipotentiary ; but Bayard Taylor himself was profoundly sensitive to popular recognition. When any one told him he loved him, or loved his poetry, his heart responded instantly ; and when various nationalities through their clubs, his associates through their public receptions and dinners, and hosts of friends in more private ways, testified to their hearty pleasure in his appointment, it was not in him to withhold response to any, great or small. He was amazed at the fullness and spontaneity of expression, but he was solemnized by it also. It swept him off his feet at first ; then it gave him a profound sense of the debt which he owed, — a debt to be paid only by the most complete service.

TO SAMUEL BANCROFT, JR.

142 EAST EIGHTEENTH STREET,
NEW YORK, *Sunday, February* 17, 1878.

Croasdale sent me my first telegraphic congratulation yesterday, though many others followed it. I am amazed, yet moved and made solemnly happy, by the outburst (I can't call it anything else) of good-will which the appointment has produced. The press, without exception, so far — everybody here, Democrats as well as Republicans — seems to be delighted. Even strangers stopped me in the street yesterday to shake hands. At the Century last night they at once proposed a dinner to me ; but so many responded that they now think of having two! Bryant himself wrote that delightful notice in yesterday's "Post."

Both Bryant and Reid say that the confirmation is sure, and I can't help thinking so, too. . . . I hope the action will come soon, because I want to arrange with the government about my time of leaving. One month is always allowed, but if I can get six weeks (till April 1st) it will save me much condensed labor.

Luckily, "Don Carlos" is finished, and there is now nothing between me and Goethe! The appointment came after all as a great surprise. I had it by telegraph at ten P. M., on Friday, and it rather spoiled M.'s sleep and mine. But how glad I am that I have kept quiet all this time !

TO GEORGE H. YEWELL.

142 East Eighteenth Street,
New York, *February* 17, 1878.

Impose upon me any penance you please, and I will endure it ! You have simply heaped coals of fire, if not melted brimstone, on my head by your second letter, after my long neglect in answering your first. I have no excuse to offer. I ought to have *made* time for you ; and yet, when I look back, I find myself somehow pitying myself for all the load of labor heaped upon me, and finally performed. The fact is that during the past three years I have done fully as much as in any previous six or eight years of my life. I have had no single day, no hour, I could rightfully call my own ; and some of my severest duties were just those which gave me honor, but nothing else. My former income is wholly suspended in these disastrous times ; practically I am penniless, and must earn every dollar I spend. With L.'s education, a heavy life insurance (but now only one more payment to make !), help for my parents, indirect claims of all kinds, and the necessity of entertaining many friends, you may easily guess what my life has been. My poetry during this time has been stolen from night and sleep. I have been several times on the point of giving up from sheer physical inability. When your second letter came I was under one of these pressures, and was forced to ask Loop to try and explain the matter to you, since I could not possibly have written then.

Yesterday morning daylight came, and I am relieved from all necessity of work (except my own cherished literary labor) for three years to come. After I had given up all expectation of it, the President suddenly appointed me Minister to Germany. The way in which the appointment has been received almost weighs me down with amazement and gratitude. There is one outburst of satisfaction from press and people. Yesterday I swam in congratulations, even strangers stopping me in the street, and the Century Club was like a jubilee. We must now prepare to leave in four or five weeks, and shall be in Berlin early in April. Can't we meet before you return? I write at once, to atone in some measure for my long silence. . . .

TO SIDNEY LANIER.

142 EAST EIGHTEENTH STREET,
NEW YORK, *February* 19, 1878.

There's a rewarding as well as an avenging fate! What a payment for all my years of patient and unrecognized labor! But *you* know just what the appointment is to me. It came as a surprise, after all, and a greater amazement is the wonderful, generous response to it from friends and people. I feel as if buried under a huge warm wave of congratulation. . . .

TO PAUL H. HAYNE.

NEW YORK, *February* 24, 1878.

When I tell you that I have written one hundred and fifty letters since last Sunday, you will understand how tired I am of pen and ink. You have no doubt heard by this time of my appointment to Germany. It has brought upon me such a flood of congratulation as atones for all previous struggles, and precludes me from ever again complaining of Fate. The office will be of incalculable advantage to me in writing my " Biography of Goethe," and thus comes as a wonderful good fortune. We must leave in four or five weeks; that is, should the Senate confirm the appointment. I hear, however, that this is certain, every Southern senator being favorable. At last I see some of my life's best work standing before me !

TO GEORGE H. BOKER.

142 EAST EIGHTEENTH STREET,
NEW YORK, *February* 25, 1878.

It was a delight to me to see your hand on an envelope again.
I could only write very hastily, and cannot write at length now.
There are so many things which one would rather say than
write! and it will take an evening for us to exchange experiences and balance the books of memory and anticipation.

My nomination comes as a great surprise, the reason whereof
and the whole history of the matter I'll tell you when we meet.
But it is not too late for what I want, nor shall I be thwarted in
my main design. I know the force of all you say in regard to
diplomatic duties; but I have had a severe discipline during the
past five or six years, and know thoroughly how to secure my
time, that is, my literary activity. I wanted the place solely for
this end, and I will not lose it, neither will I neglect or slur
over any legitimate duty. . . . It seems almost like too much
good fortune, but I must earn the right to it by steady, conscientious work. A month ago I was on the point of breaking
down, overworked and discouraged; now I am strong and full
of hope. Thanks for your kind words.

TO MR. AND MRS. JAMES T. FIELDS.

February 25, 1878.

M. joins me in hearty thanks for your kind words. You already know what the appointment means to me, and how I shall
use its advantages. The true honor connected with it lies in
the generous, overwhelming reception which follows it. This is
really something to stir up the Eumenides; but I mean to miti-
gate their wrath by doing my best work. How much we shall
lose by going! yet how much also shall we not gain! Come
over while we are away and cheer our exile!

The criticism was made by some that the United
States was sending one of its scholars on a diplomatic
mission in order to enable him to complete a literary
design, and people generally showed a very lively interest in what was, as has already been shown, the im-
pelling motive which led Bayard Taylor to desire the

appointment. His own comment upon the matter, when addressing the Goethe Club at the reception given him, sets it in a clear light.

"The fact," he said, "that for years past I have designed writing a new biography of the great German master is generally known; there was no necessity for keeping it secret; it has been specially mentioned by the press since my appointment, and I need not hesitate to say that the favor of our government will give me important facilities in the prosecution of the work. But the question has also been asked here and there, and very naturally, Is a minister to a foreign court to be appointed for such a purpose? I answer No! The minister's duty to his government and to the interests of his fellow-citizens is always paramount. I shall go to Berlin with the full understanding of the character of the services I am expected to render, and the honest determination to fulfill them to the best of my ability. But, as my friends know, I have the power and the habit of doing a great deal of work; and I think no one will complain if, instead of the recreation which others allow themselves, I should find my own recreation in another form of labor. I hope to secure at least two hours out of each twenty-four for my own work, without detriment to my official duties, and if two hours are not practicable one must suffice. I shall be in the midst of the material I most need, shall be able to make the acquaintance of the men and women who can give me the best assistance, and, without looking forward positively to the completion of the task, I may safely say that this opportunity gives me a cheerful hope of being able to complete it."

At the Century Club a breakfast was given which

brought around Bayard Taylor the men with whom he associated most intimately, on the score of common interests and tastes in literature and art. "The good-fellowship of the Century," wrote Mr. Curtis in one of his Easy-Chair papers, when speaking of this break-fast, "is famous and traditional, and the breakfast to Mr. Taylor assembled some sixty Centurions, with Mr. Bryant at their head, to congratulate Brother Bayard on the honors which had naturally fallen upon an associate. There were, besides Mr. Bryant, three or four of the original members, the patriarchs, the fathers, the founders, of the Century, who had been members of the old Sketch Club, from which it grew, and whose presence gives the Century the true royal flavor, like the lump of ambergris in the Sultan's cup."

TO E. C. STEDMAN.

March 6, 1878, 9 P. M.

I had a talk with Evarts last night. He grants me a month, which enables us to take passage with our good old Captain Schwensen, commodore of the Hamburg line, April 11th. It will be, in every way, more convenient and agreeable to me if the dinner[1] comes late, — say the first week in April, any day except Saturday. W. and S. showed me the letter, which is simply perfect in expression : I could not wish an additional word, or a word changed. But I pray you, dear old friend, *don't* add this burden to those you stagger under. Consider that I have already had enough to make any author satisfied with Fate for a long life ; and more is not needed. Since the honor is decreed (and irrevocably, as it seems), I must gratefully take it ; but I assure you that I bear constantly in mind the fact that it may, or at least should, exalt our art in the eyes of our unæsthetic countrymen, and thus indirectly be a help and an honor to all of our guild.

There is something astounding to me in the response to my nomination. I cannot yet rightly apprehend it ; and I am at the

[1] The public dinner at Delmonico's, in the arrangements for which Mr. Stedman had a conspicuous share.

point of being frightened rather than flattered. I think you will understand this feeling, and perhaps you may also measure, through your own inborn nobility of nature, the character of a gratitude which I cannot express in words. I don't thank you, for that seems commonplace, but you know how gratefully I am ever affectionately your friend.

TO T. B. ALDRICH.

142 EAST EIGHTEENTH STREET,
NEW YORK, *March* 10, 1878.

I returned from Washington this morning, and find your letter. The appointment came, at last, as a surprise, but a most welcome one ; for it enables me to write my life of Goethe. How could you suppose that I would not accept it with that in view ? It comes providentially, also, to save me from breaking down physically ; and I am already beginning to feel like another man.

We sail about April 11th, but must spend ten days at Cedarcroft in the interim, I must go to Washington again, and I have to get through with six dinners and receptions of a large kind, here and in Philadelphia. I am sorry to say that my chances of going to Boston are growing faint. We begin packing up tomorrow, and my duties are almost alarming. In three weeks I have written more than two hundred answers to letters of congratulation, and the visits, from morning till night, interrupt us. The German minister gave me a dinner in Washington last night (with Evarts, Bancroft, Schurz, etc.), and I was forced to rush away at 9.30 for the night express. This is our last Sunday evening, and a crowd is coming. To-morrow evening the Union League of Philadelphia has invited me ; on Saturday the Century Club gives a breakfast, — and so the thing goes on. It is all amazing and overwhelming, and I shall have no sense of rest until I get outside of Sandy Hook. I 'm afraid M. will be laid up, although she holds out bravely thus far. . . .

TO PAUL H. HAYNE.

142 EAST EIGHTEENTH STREET,
NEW YORK, *March* 13, 1878.

. . . As for myself, I am simply overwhelmed by a burst of generous good-will, the force of which I never could have suspected. Every evening until we sail is preëngaged for din-

ners and receptions, mostly by clubs and associations of prominent men, here and in Pennsylvania. It is something so amazing
for an *author* to receive that I am more bewildered and embarrassed than proud of the honors. If you knew how many years
I have steadily worked, devoted to a high ideal, which no one
seemed to recognize, and sneered at by cheap critics as a mere
interloper in literature, you would understand how incredible
this change seems to me. The great comfort is this : I was right
in my instinct. The world does appreciate earnest endeavor, in
the end. I have always had faith, and I have learned to overlook opposition, disparagement, misconception of my best work,
believing that the day of justification would come. But what
now comes to me seems too much. I can only accept it as a balance against me, to be met by still better work in the future.

The cordiality of his neighbors and friends was to
Bayard Taylor one of the most agreeable features
of that general acclamation which greeted him. As
before, when he returned from Europe, he had felt
deeply the spontaneous welcome given him near his
home, so now he was moved by the hasty but abundant demonstration at Kennett Square which came
upon the sudden news that he was to pass through
the village on his way to Cedarcroft. This festivity,
which was every way successful, was unlike anything
ever before seen in Kennett. The town seemed to
have laid aside its traditional Quaker garb, and to
have come out in the dress of the day. Again he received a public dinner at West Chester, where the
county which he had not only glorified, but written of
with candor and faithfulness to nature, showed with unmistakable signs that it was proud of its member, and
knew his sincere attachment to the place of his birth.

The dinner at Delmonico's was more formal than
the other occasions, and was made the opportunity for
a recognition by all the great classes in the community
of the public services of a man who had been conspic-

uous, not by reason of the favors which he had shown political followers, nor of the skill by which he had achieved political position, but by reason of the steadfast devotion to a line of work which had a legitimate crown in the end now attained. The letters of invitation and acceptance were as follows: —

NEW YORK, *March* 19, 1878.

HON. BAYARD TAYLOR, UNITED STATES MINISTER TO GERMANY : —

Dear Sir, — Your fellow-citizens, without distinction of party, have been prompt to acknowledge the eminent fitness of your appointment as the representative of this nation at the court of Berlin. They feel that their government has acted most worthily in thus designating for important service an American whose purity of life and character is in keeping with his reputation as a scholar, writer, and observer of affairs.

In recognition of these facts, and as a mark of our personal affection and esteem, we invite you to accept a public dinner before your departure for that country which has already extended to you a welcome, with which you are connected by the closest ties, and with whose politics and literature you are so familiar. Requesting you to name a day that will suit your convenience, we have the honor to be

Your friends and obedient servants,

WILLIAM CULLEN BRYANT [and others].

REPLY.

GENTLEMEN, — The honor you extend to me is such a rare representation of the highest intellectual and material interests of this great city, coming, as it does, from gentlemen distinguished in every art and profession, that I should shrink from seeming to merit it by acceptance, were it not accompanied by such generous expressions of personal regard. Your kindness leaves me no alternative ; but you will allow me to accept the distinction of a public dinner as a new obligation laid upon me for the future, rather than as having been earned by any service in the past.

I suggest Thursday, the 4th of April, the last convenient day before my departure, and remain, with sentiments of the profoundest gratitude and esteem,

Your friend and servant,　　　　　BAYARD TAYLOR.

Mr. Bryant presided at the dinner, and literature, art, the learned professions, and commerce were represented in the persons of the guests, and by the short addresses which followed the dinner. Besides the abundant flowers and plants which filled the hall, there were upon the tables ingenious decorations in confectionery, representing scenes from "Lars," the "Bedouin Song," "The Old Pennsylvania Farmer," "The Quaker Widow," and "The Song of the Camp." Bayard Taylor's address was as follows : —

"MR. CHAIRMAN AND GENTLEMEN, — You will pardon me for saying that the magnitude of the honor you confer upon me increases, in the same proportion, the test of my capacity to deserve it. I am confronted, before leaving home, by the most difficult of all diplomatic tasks. If I should try to express what I feel on being thus accepted as a member of that illustrious company, which begins with Homer and counts Bryant among its noble masters, I might displease the politicians ; if I dwell too much on the official honor which you all welcome, to-night, I may fail to satisfy my literary brethren. I can only say that the beam is level, because each scale is filled and heaped with all that it can hold. But you are too frank and generous for diplomacy, and I dare not use the dialect of diplomacy in responding. Let me be equally frank, and declare how more than honored, how glad and happy I am, that this God-speed comes not from any party or special class of men, but from the united activity and enterprise and intelligence, the scientific, artistic, and spiritual aspiration, of this great city. I do not go abroad as the representative of a party, but of the government and the entire people of the United States. I shall not ask of any one who comes to me for such assistance or information as I may be able to render more than the simple question, 'Are you an American citizen?' So far as the duties of my position are concerned, I hope to discharge them faithfully and satisfactorily. I am accredited to a court with which our government has never had other than friendly relations, and cannot anticipate any other; and if an important question should arise, requiring the decision of a wiser judgment than mine, I am able to communicate instantly with the head of the Department of State, who, more than any other living statesman, has labored to substitute peaceful arbitration for war, in settling disputes between nations. I may, therefore, without undue estimation of self, look forward calmly and confidently to my coming duties.

"I feel that I may also claim the right, this evening, to magnify mine office. I cannot agree with those of our legislators who seem willing to return to the practices of semi-civilized races, in the earlier ages of the world, and abolish all permanent diplomatic representation abroad. I prefer to recognize the increased, and ever-increasing, importance given to such posts, by the growth and nearer intercourse of all nations. It is a mistake to suppose that a minister is merely a political representative, whose duties cease when he has negotiated a treaty of commerce, or defended the technical rights of his countrymen. Our age requires of him larger services than these. He ought also to be a permanent agent for the interchange of reciprocal and beneficent knowledge, making nations and races better acquainted with each other; an usher, to present the intelligence, the invention, the progressive energy, of each land to the other; always on hand to correct mistaken views, to soften prejudices, and to knit new

bonds of sympathy. Finally, as a guest, privileged
by the government which receives him, because chosen
by that which sends him, he must never forget that
every one of his fellow-citizens is honored or dishonored,
justly or unjustly judged, by the action of him who represents the country!

"If you think my conception of the position a worthy
one, you lighten somewhat the burden of my gratitude
to you; for I shall do my utmost to make that conception a reality. Let me also believe that there is a real
strength conferred by friendship; that there is help
in congratulation, and good omen in good-will! You
have given me a farewell cup, brimming over with un-
mingled cheer and sparkle. The only bitter drop in it
comes from my own regret at parting, for a time, from
so many true and noble-hearted friends."

Just before midnight the company rose from the
tables and passed into the parlors adjoining the hall.
From a balcony, the street below was seen to be
thronged with people. A calcium light made bright-
ness, and just then a torchlight procession came in
sight, headed by a band of music. The band halted
below the balcony, and played a serenade. Then followed a rich chorus of men's voices. It was the German Liederkranz, which had come to say farewell to
the American minister. Bayard Taylor, completely
surprised, and stirred by the occasion, stepped out
upon the balcony to answer the serenade. Without
hesitation, and with no other preparation than the
scene inspired, he gave in German the little speech
which follows in English: —

"My German Fellow-Citizens, — How shall I
thank you for coming to crown so beautifully this, to
me, ever-memorable evening? For Art is the true

crown of Civilization; and your songs breathe upon me like a breeze from the German woods. I hold it as a particular honor that you have taken part in this festival; now all the elements are united which I must represent abroad, so far as I have the power to do it. You have endeavored, as I have, to comprehend the life, the genius, the importance in the world's history, of the two great nations, — I through repeated residence and the studies of years in your first home, you through the circumstance that you have found in mine a second home. I may assume that we have reached the same conviction, namely, that the races are most fortunately developed through mutual knowledge, sympathy, and assimilation of the good which belongs to each. The German Empire and the American Republic have much to gain, and nothing to lose, by continued relations of friendship. Once more my hearty thanks : Long live German Song and German Art!'"

In his account of the Three Hundredth Anniversary of the University of Jena,[1] Bayard Taylor has given a lively picture of the *Commers* which closed the three days' festival. It fell to him now to be the recipient, a few evenings before he sailed, of honors paid in a Commers of the *Deutsche Gesellig - Wissenschaft-liche Verein* of New York, when speech and song were given in the multitudinous and jovial fashion of the ceremony.

It almost seemed as if time and tide waited to give opportunity for more leave-taking. The Holsatia left the pier at Jersey City on the afternoon of April 11th, and a large party accompanied Bayard Taylor and his family down the harbor. A tug bearing the

[1] *At Home and Abroad*, First Series.

German flag puffed along after the steamer, which was most of the time enveloped in fog and rain. When over the bar at sundown, the tug drew up alongside to carry back the friends, who now said their good-bys. But so heavy was the swell that it was impossible for the tug to come close enough to the Holsatia, and to the dismay of some and the entertainment of the rest it steamed away, showing at the same moment a liberal collation which the German consul-general had provided for the returning company. There was nothing to be done but to wait for the morning. The steamer rode at anchor in the outer bay, and when morning came returned through the Narrows to Staten Island, where the tug again made its appearance, and carried off the constrained passengers. Long before they had left the steamer, Bayard Taylor had sought his stateroom, entirely overcome by the strain under which he had been ever since his appointment, — a strain which had tightened as the time for departure drew near. Only when the voyage had fairly begun was he able to secure the needed rest and quiet. Nor could he have this without the aid of sedatives. His brain was abnormally active. As soon as he composed himself for sleep he would begin to prepare speeches in English and German, and there seemed for a time imminent danger of brain fever. His letters, after arrival in England, narrate the new series of social labors upon which he now entered.

TO SAMUEL BANCROFT, JR.

LONDON, *April* 25, 1878.

I was mightily sorry to miss the last sight of you and the rest, but I was really incapable of anything more. The strain had been too great, and the reaction was proportioned to it. I think I was on the verge of brain fever, or something of the sort, for I could not sleep for three days, and only succeeded by taking bromide of potassium. For four days we had wonderfully fine weather, crossed the Banks within ten miles of the southernmost iceberg, and hoped for a fine run across the mid-Atlantic ; but then came four other days with a furious squall of hail and snow every hour, and a high sea. The last two days were lovely again, and we reached Plymouth under a summer sky, with all the downs golden with flowering gorse. Day before yesterday we came on here, and day after to-morrow we go on to Paris. We only stop for business and shopping, avoiding society, but could not help dining out last evening, to meet Max Müller. I resisted an invitation to the opening of Keble College, Oxford, to-day, and also Minister Welsh's plan for a big dinner on Saturday : it would be too much. I am a good deal recruited, but not wholly, and must save my strength for an official appearance at the opening of the Paris Exposition.

Most cordial and delightful letters from Berlin meet us here, and we are assured of a generous welcome there. We shall arrive in a week from to-morrow, glad to have a haven of rest, even if it includes labor.

It was impossible for Bayard Taylor at this time to renew his literary acquaintance in London, but he must needs pay a visit to Carlyle, to whose house he went with Mr. Moncure D. Conway, who had just introduced him to Max Müller. "We found Carlyle," says Mr. Conway, "in the early afternoon alone, and reading. He presently remembered the previous call which the young author had made upon him, and congratulated him that he belonged to a country which preferred to be represented abroad by scholars and thinkers rather than by professional diplomatists. He at once inquired how he was getting on with his life of Goethe, remarking that such a work was needed. Bayard Taylor told him of a number of new documents of importance which the Germans had intrusted to him. The two at once entered upon an interesting consultation concerning the knotty points in Goethe's his-

tory. He referred to Bayard Taylor's translation of
'Faust;' with a good-natured smile, he said, 'Yours
is the twentieth version of that book which their authors have been kind enough to place on my shelves.
You have grappled, I see, with the Second Part. My
belief increasingly has been that when Goethe had got
through with his " Faust " he found himself in possession of a vast quantity of classical and mediæval lore,
demonology, and what not: it was what he somewhere
called his Walpurgis Sack, which he might some day
empty, and it all got emptied, in his artistic way, in
Part II. Such is my present impression.' At last
Carlyle's brougham was announced, and he must take
his customary drive; but he was evidently sorry to
give up this interview. He entered upon an impressive monologue about Goethe, which ended with a repetition of the first verses of the 'Freemason's Song.'
His voice trembled a little when he came to the lines

> 'Stars silent rest o'er us,
> Graves under us silent.'

'No voice from either of those directions,' he said,
with a sigh. Then Bayard Taylor took up the strain,
and in warm, earnest tones repeated the remaining
verses in his perfect German. Carlyle was profoundly
moved. He grasped Taylor's hand and said, 'Shall I
see you again?' The other answered that he must
immediately leave England, but hoped to return before
long. Carlyle passed down to his carriage, but just as
he was about driving off made the driver halt, and
signaled to us to come near. He said to Bayard
Taylor, 'I hope you will do your best at Berlin to
save us from further war in Europe;' and then, after
a moment's silence, 'Let us shake hands once more;

we are not likely to meet again. I wish you all success and happiness.'"[1]

TO WHITELAW REID.

AMERICAN LEGATION, BERLIN, *May* 7, 1878.

I use my first moment of leisure to report progress thus far.
I don't remember whether, in writing to you from London, I
spoke of my most delightful visit to Carlyle, where I also met
Froude. After the old man got into his carriage for his afternoon drive, he called for me, shook hands again, and said, " I 'm
verra glad you 've come to see me ; we may never meet agin, and
I want to say to ye that I desire yer prosperrity." We had hard
work in London to get through with our purchases in three days,
and then went to Paris, Saturday, April 27th, taking Mrs. Smalley along. G. W. S. met us at the station, having already secured the free entrance of all our trunks and our exit in advance
of the crowd through a side door.

We had five days in Paris, and very fatiguing days they were.
I had a fearful time in the official procession, — lost my carriage,
had no umbrella, tramped three miles on foot to the hotel in rain
and mud, and narrowly escaped being killed in crossing the bou-
levard. In the evening, all three of us went to MacMahon's grand
reception at his palace. I forgot to say that through G. W. S.
I made the acquaintance of Louis Blanc (a charming little fellow !), and he took me to spend an evening with Victor Hugo.
To my great surprise, I was delighted with V. H. He was amia-
bility itself, and even hinted at giving me a dinner, if I could
remain long enough. The man is much better than his preposterous *pronunciamentos*. His manners are those of an old-school
gentleman, and his French the purest and most delightful I ever
heard in my life. I stayed to a queer midnight supper with him,
which I have not time to describe now. At the opening I met
him again among the senators ; also Louis Blanc, who was
crushed and unhappy.

At MacMahon's there was what might be called *une exposition sociale et politique.* Think of seeing ex-Queen of Spain Isabella, ex-King of Spain Amadeo, the Duke de Nemours, Prince
of Wales, Crown Prince of Denmark, Gambetta, Alexandre Du-
mas, a Nevada Bonanza lady (?), and what not, all mixed up to-

[1] *A Sketch of Thomas Carlyle.* By M. D. Conway.

gether! The etiquette was curious; there was no usher or other official personage on hand, and I was compelled to introduce myself and family to the Marshal-President. However, he was very amiable, and all went off well. On Thursday evening, Noyes gave a grand dinner-party to Welsh and myself. We begged off from going to the big ministerial reception the same evening, for we were obliged to get up at five the next morning to take the train for Cologne. On entering Germany, everything seemed to have been anticipated. The baggage was instantly passed free, the head railroad official announced that he had reserved a special carriage for us, and all along the road, on Saturday, the officials came to pay their respects at the stations. On reaching here, I was received by the whole diplomatic and consular *personnel.* Mr. Everett wrote on Sunday evening for an interview with Baron Bülow, Minister of Foreign Affairs, and it came off yesterday. To-day, with very unusual promptness, the Emperor received me, and I have just come from the first dinner, given by Bülow, who said, "You must allow me to offer you the first hospitality in Berlin." Three members of the ministry were present; also Curtius and Professor von Sybel. It was a delightful affair. The Emperor, it seems, was quite delighted because I made my little address in German. He was remarkably cordial and communicative. To-day I took full charge of the legation, read up the business on hand, and gave my first official signatures.

In spite of this very sudden assumption of duty, I am gaining strength and spirits day by day; for I am here at last, and can arrange for the needful rest. My wife and daughter left me at Hannover on Saturday, *en route* hither, to visit my mother-in-law, who has been ill; but she is recovering, and they will be here day after to-morrow. If the business of the legation does not materially increase, I am quite sure of three hours every morning for my literary work, and this is all I need. My reception here has been as cordial (though, of course, in a more formal way) as my departure from home, and I have only to keep the ground thus gained in order to make my position easy and agreeable to the end.

I write thus much this evening, because a great round of ceremonial calls begins to-morrow, and I am not sure of much leisure for another week. Of course nothing of this must get into print, but I hope you'll show it to such friends as may be interested in my progress.

Mr. G. W. Smalley, who was with Bayard Taylor until he left Paris, has recorded the impression which he received from the companionship, and relates at some length the incident at MacMahon's reception merely hinted at in the letter just quoted.

"I last saw Mr. Taylor," he writes to the "Tribune" from London, December 22, 1879, "in Paris, whither he came for the opening of the Exhibition on his way to Berlin. He had by no means recovered from the fatigue imposed upon him by the long series of well-meant kindnesses which marked his farewell to America. The letters, the public festivals, the dinners, all the manifestations of private friendship and public admiration which had been lavished on him, had laid a great strain on his already overtaxed system. None the less was he profoundly touched by them, and sensible of the friendliness which prompted them. He spoke of them repeatedly and with emotion as one of the most precious experiences of his life. He spoke of his appointment to Berlin in the tone of a man who was modestly conscious of his worth; who knew that the distinction, brilliant as it was, had been fairly earned, but who was none the less grateful for it. He knew that he was fit for the place, and that the honor bestowed on him was one to which he in turn was able to do honor. He had a just pride in hearing his name associated with the names of Irving, of Motley, of Marsh, of Lowell, — one and all men who had earned their fame in literature before they became diplomatists. He was far too frank and open-natured to care to hide his pleasure. With all his varied and ample experience, with all his knowledge of the world and mastery of social conventionalities, Mr. Taylor retained to the last a certain freshness and candor in expressing his inmost feelings, which belongs only to those souls that have no mean secrets to keep, no false pride or false modesty. He was pleased, and he was not ashamed of being pleased. It is only a man very sure of himself who can venture to take the world into his confidence as he did. Then, as often before, I thought it most honorable to him. It was consistent with great dignity of demeanor, and whoever fancied he could take advantage of it soon found out his mistake. He submitted readily and generously to all sorts of slight impositions. He gave five francs for some service which fifty centimes would have rewarded amply. He would never look too closely into matters where only his own interest was at stake, but where others were concerned, where it was his business to defend interests which had been confided to him, he could be hard, astute, immovable. That was one of his peculiar merits as a minister. In most points no two men could be more unlike than Mr. Taylor and Prince Bismarck, but they had this in common: that they told the truth fearlessly, and found it serve their purpose where the most ingenious mystifications would have failed of their end.

"A single incident, which I hope I may now relate without offense to anybody, will show how thoroughly a man of the world he was in the midst of all his simplicity. On the night of the 1st of May he went to the Marshal's official reception at the Elysée. He found himself on his arrival absolutely alone. No one from the legation in Paris had accompanied him, and no one was at the palace to meet him. The official arrangements were so meagre that not so much as an usher was there to announce him. I don't know what had become of that imposing personage M. Mollard, *introducteur des ambassadeurs.* Mr. Taylor's colleague did not arrive till later. With Marshal Mac-Mahon, the President of the French Republic, Mr. Taylor had no acquaintance. In such circumstances, most men would have gone away, or would have mingled quietly with the crowd. Mr. Taylor made his way to the Marshal, introduced himself by his name and title, paid his due compliment, and asked leave to present his wife and daughter. The Marshal, whatever his political sins, is quick to recognize manly frankness. He greeted Mr. Taylor cordially, carried off the party, and presented them to the Duchess, who in turn received them with marked civility. 'I thought,' said Mr. Taylor, in describing the incident to me, 'that I had no choice. It was known that I was in Paris, and had been asked to this ceremony. If I had gone away without making myself known, my supposed absence would have been set down as a piece of rudeness or carelessness, and I was determined that no such charge should be brought against a minister of the American republic when he was in the capital of a foreign republic.' He made absolutely no observation on the singularity of his position, on his being left to do for himself what somebody else might have done for him. I don't think it occurred to him that any neglect had been shown him. He was concerned with nothing but the discharge of his duty. He did it, let me add, after a day of great fatigue, and when he was quite ill enough to have excused him for going to bed instead of going to the Elysée. He had been on foot all the morning and afternoon at the opening ceremony, missed his carriage, and walked home, arriving in a state of exhaustion."

CHAPTER XXXI.

FINAL DAYS.

1878.

And last, ye Forms, with shrouded face
Hiding the features of your woe,
That on the fresh sod of his burial-place
Your myrtle, oak, and laurel throw, —
Who are ye? . . .

. . . .

"I am Germany,
Drawn sadly nearer now
By songs of his and mine that make one strain,
Though parted by the world-dividing sea!"

Epicedium.

BAYARD TAYLOR entered upon his duties as minister at a time when Europe, and Germany especially, was in an excited condition, and when a foreign minister had need to use his best knowledge of men and affairs. During the summer two attempts were made upon the Emperor's life, and elsewhere the assassin seemed to be striking in the dark at existing powers. The Social Democrats of Germany were making themselves a force in politics. The Berlin Congress for the settlement of the Eastern Question brought together a remarkable body of men, and the United States was at this time significantly represented in Europe in the person of its late President, General Grant, who was traveling with his family.

The American Minister found himself, in his new position, at once among people who knew well his attainments. The court which received him gave him a welcome which was beyond the mere official reception of an ambassador from a friendly power. Mr. H. Sidney Everett, First Secretary of the Legation, had written to Secretary Evarts in March, "I may add here that the appointment of Mr. Bayard Taylor as Minister to Berlin has given the greatest satisfaction in official and diplomatic circles here, and is accepted as proof of the good-will and good judgment of the administration.

TO HIS MOTHER.

AMERICAN LEGATION, BERLIN, *May* 18, 1878.

I write to you again, intending this letter to be read by all. We are very busy just now getting settled and paying the round of formal visits which is required of us. I have already used a hundred and fifty cards, and ordered three hundred more to be printed. The Crown Prince received me last Friday (yesterday week, I mean), with the greatest friendliness. He came up to me with outstretched hand, saying, in English, "Oh, I know you already! My wife was talking about your 'Faust' only a few weeks ago." My hearty reception by the imperial family is known, of course, to the diplomatic corps, and hence all the other ambassadors are very polite and obliging. . . .

M. and L. nearly saw the attempt to assassinate the Emperor. He passed them hardly two minutes before the man fired. I went to the palace at once, and was one of the first to offer my congratulations. Yesterday I received, officially, the Emperor's thanks. Last night there was a magnificent torchlight procession of students.

. We are busy looking out for a residence. We can get a superb one for about fifteen hundred dollars a year (adding the office-rent, which the government pays), with a grand ballroom and no end of bedrooms. I think we shall take it. Furnished apartments can scarcely be had, but furniture is now very cheap, and we think we can save enough from the salary by October 1st to buy all that is necessary. So far as I can judge, the expenses will be just about what I calculated. M. and L. are out this afternoon, leaving cards, with Harris (our mulatto man), gorgeous in his gold-banded stove-pipe hat. No one else has a colored footman except Prince Karl, and Harris adds immensely to our respectability. I find that our experience in St. Petersburg is of great value now. We know what to do, and people are rather surprised to find that we know it. All this tells in such an artificial society as we move in. The business of the legation is less than I supposed ; the two secretaries take all the bother off my hands, and I am in capital spirits about my literary work. The weather is wonderful ; it is full summer ; all windows open, even at night, and cloudless skies, day after day.

A few days after the date of this letter he thought it advisable to consult a physician on account of a continued disturbance of his system, but the advice which he received did not presuppose any serious difficulty.

TO WHITELAW REID.

AMERICAN LEGATION, *June* 9, 1878.

. . . You know what has happened here since I arrived, and can easily guess what an exciting five weeks I have already lived through. My reception has been exceptionally cordial and agreeable, and I am in every way agreeably surprised by my experiences. The Crown Prince met me like an old friend, coming forward with outstretched hand, and saying, "Oh, I know you already;" and yesterday, when I had my first interview with Bismarck, he began with, "I read one of your books through, with my wife, during my late illness." I passed an hour with him alone, in the garden behind his palace, and felt in ten minutes as if I had known him for years. I was astounded at the freedom with which he spoke, but I shall honor his confidence and say nothing for years to come. The duties of the legation are not difficult when one knows the routine, and I find that my former experience in St. Petersburg helps me immensely. Besides, the two secretaries are exactly the men I need, — intelligent, methodical, thorough gentlemen, as the son of Everett and the grandson of Crittenden must be, — and thus willing to accord me every right, and prompt to render every prescribed assistance. We harmonize thoroughly, and there are only about two days in the week when we are obliged to work longer than three hours together.

The main result of all this is that I am slowly and surely recovering my health. I have consulted the best physician in Berlin, whose counsel is, substantially : as little work as possible, eight or nine hours' sleep, one hour's walking every day, light wines with brandy and seltzer, and a stomach tonic which has already restored my normal appetite. Looking back, now, I see how near I was to utter physical ruin, but, thank God, the danger is over. All my functions are coming nearer entire health, day by day, and the office business, since I have mastered its character, is no particular drain upon my strength. In this respect my position here is far better than I anticipated. My books are unpacked, I feel eager for the task, and a fortnight will not go by before I write the opening chapter of my biography of Goethe.

The congress, which meets here next Thursday, will not impose upon me anything more than a few dispatches. I suppose there will be dinners, etc., and I shall see my old friend Gortchakoff again. Bismarck showed me the room where the sessions will be. I advised him to put Beaconsfield at one end of the long table and Gortchakoff at the other. He laughed, and said, " Yes ; I think I shall have to do that." But the thing won't last more than a fortnight, since the main points are all cut and dried beforehand. Of course there is a good deal of excitement arising from the regency of the Crown Prince just at this time, but it seems to me that the worst of the crisis is already over. The Social Democrats (American communists) have overreached themselves, and what has happened here may prevent what otherwise might have happened at home. It is a secret society, and with international correspondence ; hence I think the rabble will be somewhat cautious for the present.

TO MR. AND MRS. R. H. STODDARD.

AMERICAN LEGATION, BERLIN, *June* 10, 1878.

At last, at last, I feel that I can sit down and write to you with somewhat of freedom and freshness of mind. I have really suffered, both before leaving home and since. I had too much to do, bear, consider, receive, accept, reject, etc., etc. (you know what I mean). After sailing I could not sleep for three nights, and must have been on the verge of brain fever, or something of the sort. The voyage was rough; the short stay in London filled with shopping and business, ditto in Paris, and no chance of rest before reaching here. However, I have some rich memories, which will stay, when I forget the worry and fatigue.

. . . I reached here May 4th, and have had my hands full ever since. Besides the business of the legation and the presentations to the high personages, I have already distributed more than four hundred cards in formal necessary calls. Now I am nearly through, — only two princes more. On Saturday I had an hour's talk with Bismarck in the garden behind his palace ; he being accompanied by a huge black dog, and I by a huge brown bitch. I tell you he is a *great* man ! We talked only of books, birds, and trees, but the man's deepest nature opened now and then, and I saw his very self. The attempts on the Emperor's life have produced an effect only a little less profound than the murder of Lincoln. The excitement is all the stronger because it is silent, but now it is subsiding, and to-day (the second Pentecost holiday) the people begin to look cheerful again.

I have been most cordially received, and like Berlin much better than I expected. . . . E——'s family has gone to France for the summer, so we have taken his rooms until October, when we shall arrange our own household. We have hired a carriage — two jet-black horses and coachman in livery — for about one hundred dollars a month, and find that the other expenses will be very nearly what we calculated, and thus the salary will be quite sufficient. . . .

Well, I can't write more than this sheet now. M. and L. send best love to all three of you. They are very busy, packing up to go to the Thüringian Forest for the summer. M.'s mother has been very ill, and we just learn that she will leave Hamburg at once for the mountains, so M. must meet her there. I am under the charge of a good physician here, who says, eight hours' sleep, as little work as possible, an hour's walk every day, and a stomachic medicine. Three weeks of this regimen have almost restored my old self ; I have not felt so well for a year. Do write, and tell me the news. Henceforth I shall have more time, and I never lack the will.

TO SAMUEL BANCROFT, JR.

AMERICAN LEGATION, BERLIN, *June* 18, 1878.

Last Saturday George von Bunsen (son of the scholar Bunsen) gave me a dinner, at which I met Curtius, Mommsen, Lepsius, Helmholz, and Minister Waddington, of France. Think what a company that was ! Last night Lord Odo Russell (English ambassador) had a reception, and I saw Dizzy Beaconsfield, Count

Andrassy, Marquis of Salisbury, and Mehemet Ali Pasha, one of
the Turkish heroes of the late war. To-morrow night Count
Kàroly, Austrian ambassador, has a reception for the congress ;
Friday night the Count St. Vallier, French ambassador ; and on
Saturday Delbrück, ex-minister, and one of the leading men of
Germany, gives me a dinner. My reception here has been so
cordial that people talk about it in society as something unusual.
I thank Heaven that I am at least comparatively well, so that
these social festivals refresh instead of exhausting me. I don't
know how many editors of German magazines and papers have
written to me for contributions, — all of which I refuse, of
course. I have already a dozen presentation copies of volumes
from authors, and have been applied to for photographs to be
engraved, or biographical material ! I cannot candidly say that
I am flattered, or even slightly pleased, by these manifestations,
because I don't know how much is owing simply to my position.
I tell you the whole thing, as if we were sitting face to face in
the Stuyvesant Building, and you must not suppose that the
writing of all this means more than the telling of it to the accompaniment of laughter and cigar smoke. But I think you
may care to know just what I am doing, how I find myself, and
what happens to me in Berlin. The conventionalities of the
office rest on me more lightly than I supposed they would,
and somehow (I wonder at it myself) the diplomatic business
interests and agreeably stimulates me. There is something large,
human or humane, about this business, which comes to me as a
natural interest, and reconciles me to much that is merely mechanical. After all, there is something inspiring in the feeling
that one represents a great nation and speaks with the voice of
that nation.

M. and L. are in the mountains near Gotha, settled for the
summer, and I expect to spend half my Sundays with them : it
is seven hours by rail from here. They are both quite well and
cheerful.

In his official dispatches, Bayard Taylor conveyed
to his government the impressions which had been
made upon him, during the visit of General Grant,
of the attitude which Germany took toward the United
States. The visit gave occasion to some singular ex-

pressions of good-will, and it is scarcely to be doubted that the channel through which they passed was an important part of the expression.

BAYARD TAYLOR TO W. M. EVARTS.

LEGATION OF THE UNITED STATES,
BERLIN, *July* 1, 1878.

. . . It had been announced in various journals that General Grant would proceed directly from Amsterdam to Copenhagen without visiting Berlin, and my first intimation of his coming was through a letter from my colleague, Mr. Birney, United States Minister resident at The Hague, received on the 22d ultimo. I communicated immediately with him and with Mr. A. M. Simon, the United States Vice-Consul at Hanover, and ascertained the day and hour of General and Mrs. Grant's arrival here. It was then impossible — since the stay of the distinguished visitors would be brief — to arrange in advance for such interviews and honors as might be procured for them at a time when both assumed an exceptional importance. The Emperor is unable to receive any one, and I was informed by the proper officials that the Empress, for this reason, would probably feel bound to maintain her privacy in the palace. Prince Frederick Charles is absent on a visit to England, and Count Moltke is residing on his estate in Silesia, at some distance from Berlin. Furthermore, the presence of the European Congress, and the number of prearranged dinners and social assemblages arising therefrom, seemed to limit the amount of attention which at any other time would have been so freely accorded to the ex-President.

On Wednesday, the 26th ultimo, after having arranged for a reception by his Imperial Highness the Crown Prince and by Prince von Bismarck, I traveled as far as Stendal (about sixty-five miles), there met General and Mrs. Grant, and accompanied them to Berlin. The secretaries of this legation, the consular officials, and a number of the American residents were at the station to welcome the distinguished guests ; the hour was too late for any other testimony of respect.

The following afternoon I accompanied General Grant to the palace of the Crown Prince, where he was first received by all the adjutants and court officials of the latter, and conducted to the audience room. The Crown Prince then entered in his uniform of field marshal, greeted General Grant most cordially, and conversed with him for three quarters of an hour. At the close of the interview he invited him and Mrs. Grant, together with myself, to dine at the new palace in Potsdam the next evening.

On returning home I was surprised to find a letter from Count Nesselrode, court marshal of the Empress, informing me that her majesty would receive me on Friday afternoon. From the absence of certain customary formalities on reaching the palace and the quiet manner of my reception, I suspect that it was meant to be private quite as much as official. The Empress took occasion to express to me the Emperor's interest in General Grant's history, his desire to meet him personally, and his great regret that this was now impossible. Her words and manner implied an authorization that I should repeat these expressions to General Grant. She then spoke very freely and feelingly of the disturbances occasioned by the distress of the laboring class, declared her belief that a period of peace would be the best remedy, and finally said, "The Emperor knew that I should see you to-day. He has the peace of the world at heart, and he desires nothing so much as the establishment of friendship between nations. I ask you to make it your task to promote the existing friendship between your country and ours. You cannot do a better work, and we shall most heartily unite with you in doing it. This is the Emperor's message to you, and he asked me to give it to you in his name as well as my own." She bowed and left me. The deep, earnest, pathetic tones of her voice impressed me profoundly. I kept her words carefully in my memory, and have repeated them with only such changes as the translation makes necessary.

The same afternoon I accompanied General and Mrs. Grant to Potsdam. The fact that the dinner was given specially in their honor was evident on reaching the station. They were ushered into the imperial waiting-room, from which a carpet was spread to the state car. On reaching Potsdam, the first court equipage conveyed them, together with Mr. von Schlözer, German Minister at Washington, and myself, to the palace, the other guests following us. Before the dinner General Grant and Mrs. Grant and myself were received by the Crown Princess in private audience. The company numbered about fifty, including the Prince of Hohenzollern, Prince Augustus of Würtemberg, the members of the imperial ministry, and all the chief officials of the court. Mrs. Grant was seated beside the Crown Prince, and General Grant opposite, beside Mr. von Bülow, both being the places of honor. I did not consider it consistent with the dignity of the government I represent to make any stipulation concerning etiquette in advance, or even to ask any question, and I am consequently all the more gratified to find that it would have been unnecessary. During the return to another station, by a longer drive through the park, General Grant received every mark of respect from the people, who crowded the streets to see him pass. . . .

When Bayard Taylor returned that night from Potsdam he was in excellent humor, though really exhausted by the continued exertion which he was compelled to make, when he was far from well. "I am so happy!" he exclaimed. "I have won my first diplomatic battle. At the close of the dinner, Mr. von Bülow whispered to me, 'You shall have it all your own way.'" This was *à propos* of the Ganzenmüller case,[1] one of the many cases of contested citizenship which were constantly arising to perplex the legation.

TO A. R. MACDONOUGH.

FRIEDRICHRODA, IM THÜRINGERWALD, *July* 26, 1878.

I can't say that I am glad of the occasion [2] which has brought me a letter from you ; but I am very glad to get the letter, and will take it as a pledge that the two unwritten ones shall yet be written. Of course I'll do what is asked, and all the more because you will read my lines. I would scarcely trust any one else to do that. But I cannot undertake to have my "Epicedium" ready before September 1st. I am only just now getting into the writing mood again, having been physically and morally miserable for some weeks past. There was no chance of rest anywhere on the way to Berlin ; and when by the end of May I was beginning to get back my strength and spirits, there came the

---

[1] See *Foreign Relations of the United States*, 1878, pp. 216–231.
[2] The death of Mr. Bryant.

attack on the Emperor, the congress, General Grant's visit, and an unusual amount of legation business. By July 4th I was positively ill, and since then have spent more than half my time here, to get rest and mountain air. My great trouble has been gastric, — very painful and stubborn, — but it is now very nearly overcome, and I am entirely rid of the former mental and nervous fatigue. So I am gathering hope and courage again, and the future looks cheery.

My position in Berlin is much more agreeable than I anticipated. I was received there with quite unusual warmth and kindness. The Emperor, Empress, Crown Prince, and Bismarck were so markedly cordial that it gave the tone to all the court officials and affected the diplomatic circle. Then Lindau gave me a dinner to meet the authors and artists of Berlin, Rodenberg a journalistic dinner, and at George von Bunsen's I sat opposite Curtius, Mommsen, Lepsius, and Helmholz. Moreover, the legation secretaries turn out to be thorough gentlemen, intelligent, methodical, safe, and already on the most cordial and confiding terms with me. The first establishment in my office is thus most auspicious, and it will be easy to hold the ground already gained. Last week I received a stately diploma of my election as *Meister* in the *Freie Deutsche Hochstift*, a national literary guild, which has its headquarters in the *Goethehaus* at Frankfort. You will understand why I mention all these things, — to show you that the change of place is in all respects favorable and fortunate.

I made the acquaintance of all the members of the congress. After Gortchakoff, who greeted me as an old friend, I was most impressed by Beaconsfield. . . . Mehemet Ali Pasha interested me very much : he is amazingly strong, simple, and natural, for a man with his history. But Bismarck is still a head higher than all these. I walked alone with him in his garden for more than an hour, since then have dined with him, and now seem to have known him for years. . . .

TO HIS MOTHER.

FRIEDRICHRODA, *July* 31, 1878.

It's about time that I should write again. I have left the home letters to M. and L. for a month past, because I was so behindhand with all my correspondence. I don't know what M. has written about me, but I trust it was nothing to make you uneasy. The simple fact is, I didn't exactly know what the particular trouble was, and therefore ignorantly did what I should not have done. I was getting along finely until just before Grant came. There was a great quantity of fruit in the market, especially magnificent cherries, and I ate them twice a day. Besides, the weather was very hot and dry, we had much work in the legation, and I drank a good deal of ice-water. The trip to meet Grant, in the heat and dust, was very fatiguing, and I had considerable fever on the night of his arrival. I imagined I had a touch of malaria in my system; so I took a big dose of quinine and a hot lemonade on going to bed, and sweated furiously the whole night. In the morning I felt so wretched that I sent for the doctor, whose first question was, "Have you been eating fruit?" and the second, "Have you been drinking ice-water?" I had done just the wrong thing in taking quinine and sweating. I told him I must keep up during Grant's visit, so he gave me a stomach medicine and prescribed hunger. I went with Grant that afternoon to the Crown Prince, and had to stand nearly an hour. Next day we dined with the Prince at Potsdam, and I took nothing but soup and three stalks of asparagus. On Saturday we had the reception for the Grants, on Sunday they dined with us, and on Monday we dined with Bismarck. There I sat between the Princess and her daughter, the Countess Marie, and they were so charming that I forgot all about the doctor's orders, and ate of all the courses! Bismarck sat between Mrs. Grant and M., opposite. The whole thing was delightful.

Well, the Grants left on the 2d, but I was obliged to stay and preside at the American celebration on the 4th. I made two short speeches, started the toasts at supper, and then got away. We came here next day, and I improved so rapidly that in ten days I ventured to eat cucumber salad. This was a great mistake. It brought on an attack of what would be called "acute dyspepsia" in America. For four days I suffered tortures. I felt as if my stomach were in a coffee-mill, and slowly rasped and ground to pieces. It slowly passed away. I have since been to Berlin, — in fact, I left there yesterday, — and my chief trouble now is continual hunger. You must consider that I have been half starved for a month, have become quite thin (for me), and yet dare not eat a great deal at a time. I am forbidden to touch fruit, acids, or fat, must take a glass of mixed champagne and seltzer three or four times a day, sleep a great deal, and walk very little. My brain is entirely rested: I have no bleeding at the nose, I sleep like a log, do my official work easily, and am perfectly well, with the exception of a slight feeling of oppression in the stomach after meals. Two or three weeks more of this healthy mountain life will build me up completely. We have hired a carriage from Gotha, and drive out every day, rain or shine. M. and L. are quite robust, and Mrs. H. has improved wonderfully. There ! — you have the full report of my condition. The trouble is so different from what I supposed that I made it worse through ignorance. Now that I know exactly what it is I am determined to have it radically cured before I stop. But the dieting is rather hard on me.

Shortly after this letter was written, a remarkable improvement suddenly showed itself in Bayard Taylor's condition, giving him confidence of a speedy complete return to health.

TO JERVIS McENTEE.

AMERICAN LEGATION, BERLIN, *August* 23, 1878.

I have left your most welcome and delightful letter two or three weeks longer unanswered than I meant, but you gave me liberty to wait, and you won't object when you know the cause of my delay. I was thoroughly unwell, from sheer exhaustion, when I left home, but I did n't know how much nor exactly what was the matter with me, and it has taken me a long while to find out. Instead of getting some rest on reaching here, I was only plunged into new excitements. The attacks on the Emperor, the meeting of the European Congress, dinners and grand historic receptions, General Grant's visit, and finally a sudden deluge of official business, kept me in a state of constant tension ; and then, unfortunately, I did the two things which (the doctors say) were worst for my condition. I drank ice-water and ate much fruit ! When I went to the mountains, seven weeks ago, I was so wretched that all reading and writing was prohibited. I suffered from furious muscular cramps, pains in the stomach, spells of vomiting, and a persistent feeling of sea-sickness which made food repulsive. Until recently I have been nearly starved, and have surely lost twenty or thirty pounds of my weight. But complete rest, mountain air, and a rigorous diet have conquered the demon, and I now have my natural appetite and spirits, though I still live chiefly upon oatmeal, beef-tea, raw eggs, carp, and venison. All wine was disagreeable, and I still only take an occasional glass of the oldest and best.

In two respects I am most happily surprised. I like Berlin as a place of residence far better than I expected, and I find my diplomatic duties easier, more interesting, and more agreeable. . . . This place is very dear, but our knowledge of German life saves us much money, and we shall get along easily on the salary. We have taken an apartment of seventeen rooms (including four elegant *salons* and a ball-room fifty feet long and twenty high) for about $2,300 a year, but must furnish it ourselves, which will be a big outlay at the start. . . .

Well, what shall I say of all I have seen and learned, since that distracting evening off Sandy Hook? The time has been rich and rare in experience. Think of seeing and talking with Bismarck, Gortchakoff, Beaconsfield, Andrassy, Waddington, Mehemet Ali Pasha, Curtius, Mommsen, Lepsius, Helmholz, Grant, etc., etc., the same day! They are all pleasant and accessible people, but Bismarck is an amazing man. Beaconsfield was very friendly : he persisted in calling me *" Sans peur et sans reproche"! .* . . I shall not begin my literary work until we are settled in our own quarters ; but my brain is thoroughly rested, and I am anxious and eager to write. The proofs of " Prince Deukalion " are coming along. I have a little more than half the poem in type, and have also arranged for its simultaneous publication in London. I wrote a new short poem the other day, and have made four studies in oil while in the mountains. I have also met Anton von Werner, who is painting the congress, and shall meet Richter soon. But we have not yet been able to go to the gallery !

I must really close, in order to get to the opera (government invitation, with ticket for proscenium box !) given for the bridal couple. To-morrow I am invited to the high and mighty wedding at Potsdam, and when I tell you that I must stand up for five hours in a white choker you will understand that I am passably well again. M. has probably written to G. by this time, — she meant to. Love to G. and all friends.

TO HIS MOTHER.

AMERICAN LEGATION, BERLIN, *September* 3, 1878.

. . . I wish I had time to describe to you the royal wedding at Potsdam. I not only stood out the whole performance, but ate lobster salad at the supper. It was a superb sight, — seventy or eighty pages in scarlet and silver, giant grenadiers seven feet high, court officials in gorgeous uniforms, a blaze of jewelry, a dance with torches, illumination of the palaces and parks, etc., etc. I was the only one present in plain evening dress ; and part of my duty was to march across the grand hall, bow to the bridal couple, then to the King of Holland, and finally to the Crown Prince and Princess. I went out and back in a special train, and we were all provided with carriages. But I took my German man, Karl, along with me, and he looked out for my interests in the shrewdest way. I wasn't a bit fatigued the next day, but wrote a letter of eleven quarto pages to M., describing the whole matter. The same day I rescued a noted American manufacturer from prison by going there and threatening the police officials. The next day an officer came to report to me that the charge was a mistake. But we have no end of bother with unprotected American women, who are not fit to go a mile from home, they are so utterly helpless, and always come to the legation to shed their tears. I generally turn them over to Mr. C., upon whom falls the first shower, and then, if necessary, I see them when they dry up.

We find a great change in fruit and vegetables since we were in Germany before. Tomatoes are plenty at twenty-five cents a pound, and we have them sliced or stewed every day. Very large, excellent peaches cost six cents apiece, and plums and greengages are as cheap as blackberries at home. We only miss green corn, and must be satisfied with canned.

The carp here are specially good, and sea-fish come quite fresh from the coast. Partridges (our pheasants) are only thirty-seven cents apiece, and venison is about the same as beef. When we get into our new quarters, I think we shall live very pleasantly. The stately old door-keeper died there, two weeks ago, and his last words were, "*Frau* Excellency" (meaning M.), "the rooms are all cleaned."

Although the spirit in which Bayard wrote home to his mother and various friends throughout the summer was one of cheerfulness and hope, his actual condition was far from inspiring confidence in those about him. With his strong aversion from every form of sickness, he refused to admit to himself the low tone of his system, and the constant acute attacks which gave warning of his disordered condition were met and overcome successively without leaving him really aware of his danger. He was bidden to take rest in the country. Especially he was advised to take the waters at Karlsbad; but to do this he must go beyond the border, and he would not ask permission for this from his government so shortly after coming into office. He so far followed the advice of his physicians as to go with his family to Friedrichroda, but he could not be persuaded to remain there for any length of time. He was extremely conscientious about his official work. His efficient and considerate secretaries were entirely willing to relieve him of all burdens, but he insisted on making repeated visits to Berlin and staying there in the heat of summer, attending to the work of the legation. He had made a good beginning, and he had a pride in representing the United States with honor and thoroughly business faithfulness. Nor was he wanting in opportunity. There were many cases, especially of naturalized German citizens who had returned to Germany and fallen into difficulties, which called for delicate and wise management. Bayard Taylor's course in the Ganzenmüller and other cases did not save him from frequent abuse at the hands of intemperate German-American journals, but he had the satisfaction of knowing that he maintained the dignity of his country.

TO MRS. R. H. STODDARD.

AMERICAN LEGATION,
67 BEHRENSTRASSE, BERLIN, *September* 10, 1878.

Your most welcome and unexpected letter came yesterday. I had really almost given up the hope of hearing soon from either you or ——. How much you tell us ! The whole old life is more clearly revived by you than by any one else who has written to me, and both M. and I dipped into your twelve pages as into a refreshing bath.

You will have guessed, from all that has happened, that there was no rest for me until about two months ago. General Grant's visit came, the Fourth of July, the breaking-up of the congress, and my final break-down. . . . I went to the mountains near Gotha and vegetated, suffering horrible tortures from an affection of the nerves of the stomach, occasioned, the doctor said, by long-continued mental and nervous wear and tear. About the 15th of August the trouble left me, and since then I soar like a lark. I have not felt so bright and fresh for years. . . . I have mastered the whole routine of official business, and everything now runs easily and smoothly. Society has left Berlin until October ; the climate is delicious ; we have an excellent cook ; partridges are thirty-six cents apiece, large carp fifty cents, plenty of tomatoes, and Rhine wine of good quality thirty cents a bottle !

We have a job on hand, furnishing our residence, into which we move October 1st. We can't get furnished lodgings here, and must buy everything. . . . Our knowledge of German ways and prices is an immense advantage ; without it we could not live on the salary, big as it seems. There is a great rush of Americans here, and most of them expect some attention ; but so far I have only had pleasant experiences. Fiske has just left, after twelve days with us ; Boyesen and wife will be here a month yet. Governor Howard of Rhode Island (one of the two men who know all my poems !) left to-day, and others are coming and going all the time.

M. will agree with you about Beaconsfield. I introduced her to him, and she was greatly impressed by his personality. He was very complimentary to me, and made himself quite agreeable. He is what Goethe calls a " daimonic (not *demoniac !*) nature," — possessed with a strange, weird spirit. I never before saw a man in whom tact was inspiration. . . .

Poor Mehemet Ali Pasha! I had some long talks with him during the congress, liked him immensely, and now he is murdered in Albania. . . .

AMERICAN LEGATION,
67 BEHRENSTRASSE, BERLIN, *September* 15, 1878.

I wish all my friends at home were as considerate as you! I don't think they forget me, or grow the least indifferent through absence, but they don't recognize how rapidly the days go by, and how welcome all home news is to me. Since I last wrote I have entirely turned the corner of my physical troubles, and you would be surprised to see that twenty-five pounds taken off my weight makes me look almost graceful! I am really better than for two years past, and now mean to screw up my upper stories (as they did the houses in Chicago, by some hydraulic contrivance), and build a new basis under them. I can't eat quite enough yet, but my "misery" is a thing of the past, and my spirits are wholly of the future; which is as it should be. Somebody said the other day that I looked *distingué.* I should think so! One might as well be punched by a pugilist without getting a black eye as go through my experience for a year past without showing some signs thereof in the "thunder-scarred" visage!

If you were to see me now, as I drive down the Linden daily, in an equipage prescribed by the effete monarchies of Europe, I doubt whether you would recognize me. I usually wear a stovepipe hat of twice the usual height (which indicates a foreign minister), a black velvet coat embroidered with gold, blue satin vest, lemon-tinted pantaloons, pearly-gray gloves, patent-leather boots with gilded tips, and a white cravat fastened with a sapphire brooch. I carry a small ebony cane, have my mustache waxed into sharp points, and slightly powder my face to give me an aristocratic paleness. But I am not proud. When the guards at the Brandenburg Gate rush out to present arms, I slightly wave my hand, as to say, "I do not exact it!" and they retire abashed. Of course it is onerous to appear in this manner; but the dignity of our government does not allow me to depart from the established rules. (I protest: this will be taken as gospel fifty years hence, when autograph dealers get hold of it. M. T.)

You see how I am interrupted, and all my fine description snubbed. Such is the lot of all married men, as your own M. will admit. Well, to come down to the gross realism of life, we are over head and ears in preparations for completely furnishing our new residence, into which we must move in two weeks. (The address is already at the head of this letter.) We have to furnish seventeen rooms, five of them large state *salons ;* but I have economized carefully, and hope to carry the expense. By going ourselves and buying everything directly, instead of engaging the cormorant tribe of furnishers here, we have saved from fifty to seventy per cent., and I think we shall make as good a show as any legation in Berlin. I am very anxious to move, for I long to arrange my private library and go straight to work. I have just sent home an " Epicedium " on Bryant, for the coming Century Club commemoration, but have n't the slightest idea whether it 's good or not. I have also written another poem, half fable, which seems to me good.[1] The " Prince Deukalion " is all in type, proofs read, and everything ready for your vellum.[2] Type and general arrangement are lovely. Trübner will bring it out simultaneously in London. Since I wrote, I have attended the royal wedding in Potsdam, — a sight to see ! — and had to take part in the single-file official procession. I saw my Grand-Ducal Weimar friends, and had a most cordial greeting : something for the Goethe will come o' that ! The royal people also twice gave me tickets for the opera. But society has n't come back yet ; only there 's a great rush of traveling Americans, nearly all reputable people, good specimens, whom I am glad to see. Professor Fiske of Cornell was my guest for twelve days ; Boyesen and his wife are here ; and Governor Howard of Rhode Island, with family, have just left. The climate now is simply delightful ; I like Berlin more and more, — and I more than half like my official duties. When I fairly reach my literary task, I shall and *must* be happy. I can't write more now, and can't promise to write very regularly, but you 'll understand. We all join in love to you all.

[1] "The Village Stork."
[2] Mr. Bancroft manufactured the cloth used in binding the volume.

AMERICAN LEGATION,
67 BEHRENSTRASSE, BERLIN, *September* 24, 1878.

. . . Mr. R. called on Saturday with your letter. I remembered him, invited him to dinner last evening, and tried to do what I could to make his stay pleasant. It was very short, however ; he left to-day. I gave him a few hints of the trouble which I have with naturalized German-Americans, and the abuse which I expect to get from the German papers in the United States. In fact, the abuse has begun, as in the cases of Bancroft and Davis. Nineteen twentieths of the business of this legation is occasioned by that class of people. They make preposterous claims, write insulting letters, never thank me for aid, and yet are backed up at home by every German paper. I foresaw this result, and am not greatly surprised. In point of fact, I have gone farther to help the German-Americans than any one has done since the treaty of '68. My action is effectual in nine cases out of ten. I have taken a strong, clear, decided stand, as my dispatches to the State Department will show ; and almost every mail brings me a vile, outrageous article in an envelope, evidently sent by the editor ! Such is life.

I like Berlin more and more. We shall move into our own quarters in four or five days, and be finally at home here. The society is very intelligent and agreeable, and my official duties, though sometimes onerous, are not repellent to my taste. On the contrary, it is a kind of business which I like, because it deals with laws and principles ; and even the minor routine of legation work possesses a certain amount of interest. I am now sure of securing two to three hours a day for myself, which is all I need, and I have the most delightful and generous offers of assistance (in regard to the Life of Goethe) from all sides. Count Usedom the other day presented me with a cast taken from Goethe's living face, — a most rare and precious gift. . . .

67 BEHRENSTRASSE, BERLIN, *October* 1, 1878.

I ought to have written two days ago, when I had more time. We moved yesterday, and are still in a perfect chaos. None of the people keep their promises, the rooms are all upside down, and we have scarcely a place to receive a visitor.

But I must at least say how sorry we all are not to be present at the sixtieth anniversary. It is a wonderfully rare one, and we hope it will be made pleasant to you in every possible way. I am glad to hear that, except your rheumatic troubles, you keep so well and cheerful. Your lives have been laborious and eventful, but not unsatisfactory, and you may enjoy your years of rest with a clear conscience. We shall all remember you on the 15th, and shall be present in spirit.

The month of comparative restoration to health was followed by a sudden change for the worse, and the anxiety regarding Bayard Taylor's condition now led to a consultation of physicians on October 12th, and the result was a decision that the disease under which he was suffering was constipation of the liver. As a last chance of recovery he was ordered to go to Karlsbad at once. He was not, however, at first informed of the very critical condition in which the doctors found him, and wrote home with his usual cheerfulness and confidence.

TO HIS MOTHER.

AMERICAN LEGATION, BERLIN, *October* 15, 1878.

It is a lovely day here for your diamond wedding, and I hope it's as pleasant at Cedarcroft. We shall all be thinking of you, and wondering what is going on, and who all are there, etc., etc. I am very sorry we can't be present with the rest, but hope that we shall not be much missed in person, since we have sent representatives, and also mean to speak three words by telegraph, which I hope will reach you at breakfast or soon after.

M. tells me she has written to you about our going to Karlsbad. I am greatly relieved to know at last the exact cause of my trouble, and to have a certain cure for it. I have been drinking the water here for two days past, and feel already very differently. The two doctors say that if it were spring instead of fall I need not go ; but I shall get well so much more rapidly by going now that they advise it strongly. I don't suppose that I need stay longer than three weeks. I can now see that my trouble in the stomach came mostly from the liver. . . . The fact that I was so

much better until I took cold two weeks ago shows that the liver
is not seriously affected.

This was the last letter which Bayard Taylor was
to write to his mother. He was already in great pain
when writing it, and later, on the same day, another
consultation was held, when it was decided that it
would be useless for him to go to Karlsbad, and that
the removal would only hasten the progress of the
disease ; for dropsy had developed, and a week later
an operation was performed for the sufferer's relief.
From this time forward the fatal disease made steady
inroads upon his vitality. His indomitable will still
struggled against the inevitable. He rose and was
dressed each day, and went to his library. There were
the materials for the work to which he had looked forward so eagerly, but he could not touch them. Once
in the summer he had made a faint attempt, but
he was already too ill to make any real beginning.
Since so large part of his material was stored in his
memory alone, to work on the Life was not to make
an industrious compilation from published or written
papers, but to construct in a harmonious whole a
work which already lay in his mind. To do this,
however, was to bend all the energies of his nature
to a great task. This he could no longer do. He
had written two poems since coming to Germany.
When driving from Gotha to Friedrichroda he used
to pass through the little village of Wahlwinkel, where
he saw in the gable of a peasant's house a stork's nest
which had been there from time immemorial. Out of
that grew his poem " The Village Stork." The reader
who looks between the lines can easily follow the
thought which must have been dwelling in the poet's
mind, — his own wanderings in Egypt and Greece,

his long struggle with untoward fate, the slow recognition of his power, and even now the uncertain hold which he had upon the popular mind in his own most cherished vocation. The last verses which he wrote were those of his " Epicedium," written in September to be read at the Century Memorial to William Cullen Bryant.

From time to time in the early weeks of his last illness he drove out in pleasant weather, but for the most part he kept his room, seeing few people, but going through the necessary work of the legation. As the office was in his house, this duty was made easier for him; and his secretaries visited him for instruction or his signature, as circumstances might require.

It was after the disease had set in, but before its fatal nature had declared itself, that he had a visit from Mr. H. H. Boyesen, who has recorded in his " Reminiscences of Bayard Taylor "[1] a conversation which he had with him. The talk turned upon Goethe, and Bayard Taylor, recurring to a thought which always strongly affected him, said, —

" It is odd how deeply rooted the idea is among our people that because a man is a good novelist he must necessarily be a bad poet or dramatist, and if he is a good poet his novels or his dramas deserve only censure. A man like Goethe, whose rich nature demanded such manifold and various expression, would never be comprehended by our reviewers. They would damn 'Faust' because 'Werther' had been a success. ' Now you made such a hit with your novel,' they would say, ' why don't you stick to that in which you have excelled, instead of trying your unskilled hand on something which you don't understand?'

[1] *Lippincott's Magazine*, August, 1879.

Novel-writing, poetry, travels, the drama, are conceived to be each a separate trade, and to be a poet and a novelist at the same time is in the eyes of our critics about as anomalous as it would be to combine the practice of law and medicine, or to profess equal skill in carpentry and shoemaking. The Germans have a much nobler conception of the vocation of a man of letters. If he be an imaginative writer, no matter of what kind, they call him *Dichter*, and they leave the whole field of imaginative writing at his disposal. If Paul Heyse, who began as a novelist, writes a drama or a poem, it does not in the least disturb them. So also Gustav Freytag has gained an equal success on the stage and as a writer of romances. Goethe and Schiller would have been at a loss to define their proper specialty. Their vocation was that of *Dichter*, and they selected the form which suited best the idea they wished to develop. Their occasional hesitation between two literary forms thus becomes perfectly intelligible."

His own latest work, " Prince Deukalion," was published in November, and he held a copy of the book in his hands. He had not thought to receive much popular applause from a poem so serious in its plan, so weighty in its poetic thought, but he knew that there were some, the poets whom he knew and loved, who would share with him its high purpose. Two such wrote him from America, and their letters, among the last which he received, were witnesses to that steadfast purpose which he had kept through life, of reaching after the highest expression of his highest nature. "It is a great poem," writes Mr. Whittier, — "how great I hardly dare venture to say. To me it recalls the grand dramas of the immortal Greeks, not so much in resemblance as in its solemnity and power. I rejoice that such a poem is thine."

So strong was Bayard Taylor's own spirit of hope that those who were about him shared it so long as they dared. The disease had taken a fatal turn about the middle of November, and from that time on his sufferings were intense. They were borne with an heroic patience which called forth admiration from all around him, especially from his faithful attendant physician, Dr. Löwe. No word of complaint ever escaped the sufferer's lips. About the middle of December one of those delusive appearances of improvement which belong to the disease occurred, and seemed at the time to puzzle even the attendant physicians. On the 14th he felt so much better that he called for paper and pencil to draft a dispatch to the foreign office in reply to a message of sympathy which had been conveyed to him from the Emperor.

On the 17th a rapid change began, which was cruelly deceptive in its first form; for though his attendants knew the contrary, a sudden relief conveyed to Bayard Taylor the delusive hope that he had passed through a crisis and was now to get well. It was in reality a premonition of the immediate end. It was followed by extreme pain, which brought with it a bitter disappointment. On the 19th, after restlessness and wandering of mind, he was in his chair, where he now spent most of his time. His will flamed out in one final burst. "I want," — he began, and found it impossible to make his want known or guessed until suddenly he broke forth, "I want, oh, you know what I mean, that *stuff of life!*" It was like Goethe's cry, the despair of one groping for that which had always been his in large measure. At two in

the afternoon he fell asleep, and at four o'clock gently
breathed his last.

On the 22d of December the Americans then in
Berlin, representatives of literature, science, and art
in Germany, the diplomatic corps, and the Emperor's
special messengers gathered at the American Embassy
to pay the last honors to the dead poet. The Rev. J. P.
Thompson, D. D., addressed the assembly, using largely
the expressions of " Prince Deukalion." Then one of
Bayard Taylor's own fraternity, Berthold Auerbach,
spoke as a poet, turning to his friend and fellow-poet:

" Here, under flowers that grew in German soil,
lies the mortal frame tenanted for fifty-three years by
the richly-endowed genius whom men knew as Bayard
Taylor. Thy name will be spoken by coming genera-
tions, who never looked into thy kindly, winning face,
never grasped thy faithful hand, never heard a word
from thy eloquent lips. Yet no: the breath of the
mouth is exhaled and lost, but thy word, thy poet-
word, is abiding. On behalf of those whom thou
hast left behind, urged by my affection as thy oldest
friend in the Old World, as thou didst often call me,
and as a representative of German literature, I send
after thee loving words of farewell. What thou hast
become and shalt continue to be in the realms of
mind after ages will determine. To-day our hearts
are thrilled with grief and lamentation, and yet with
exaltation too. Thou wast born in the fatherland of
Benjamin Franklin; and, like him, thou didst work
thy way upward from a condition of lowly labor to
be an apostle of the spirit of purity and freedom, and

a representative of thy people among a foreign people. No, not among a foreign people : thou art as one of ourselves; thou hast died in the country of Goethe, to whose lofty spirit thou didst ever turn with devotion ; thou hast erected a monument to him before thy people, and wouldst erect before all peoples another, which, alas! is lost with thee. But thou thyself wast and art one of those whom he foretold, a disciple of a universal literature, in which, high above all bounds of nationality, in the free, limitless ether, the purely human soars on daring pinions sunwards in ever new poetic forms. As from one power to another, so wast thou the accredited envoy from one realm of mind to another; and even in thy latest work thou dost show that thou livedst in that religion which embraces all confessions, and takes not the name of one to the exclusion of the rest. Nature gave thee a form full of grace and power, a spirit full of clearness and chaste cheerfulness, and the grace of melodious speech to set forth the movements and emotions springing from the eternal and never-fathomed source of being, as well as from the fleeting and never-exhausted joys of wedded and paternal love, of friendship, of the inspiration of nature, of patriotism, and of the everascending revelations of human history. Born in the New World, ripened in the old, — and alas! severed so early from the tree of life! Thou didst teach thy people the history of the German people, that they, being brothers, should know one another ; we bear that in our memories. Thou didst put into words of song thy people's outburst of joy at their centennial festival ; when it returns again, and our own mortal frames lie motionless like thine here before us, then from millions of lips yet unborn will resound again

the name of BAYARD TAYLOR. Thy memory shall
be blessed!"

The sarcophagus was deposited in the Jerusalem
cemetery whence it was removed in March. It arrived
in America March 13, 1879. It was a Thursday, the
day on which he had died; and at the hour in the afternoon when he breathed his last in Germany, the
remains of Bayard Taylor were brought from the ship
to his native shore, as if no interval had elapsed.
Even here his second country followed him, for the
remains were escorted to the City Hall in New York
by members of German singing societies and by dele-
gations from other associations. At the City Hall the
coffin was taken from the funeral car and a dirge sung
over it by the German societies. Thousands of persons had gathered on news of the arrival, and stood
attendant upon the solemnities. It was Germany giving back to America in sorrow the son whom America
had sent forth with rejoicing. An oration was delivered by the Hon. Algernon S. Sullivan, and the remains were placed in state in the Governor's room of
the City Hall, where they were in the custody of a
guard of honor from the Koltes Post, Grand Army of
the Republic. The same guard escorted them to the
railway station the next day, when they were removed
to Cedarcroft.

The poet lay in the house which he had built until
the day following, when, after addresses by Rev. Dr.
Furness and Dr. Frank Taylor at the house, he
was borne by a funeral procession for three miles to
the cemetery at Longwood. The pall-bearers were selected from his literary associates and his earliest
friends. From all the country side his old friends and

neighbors, to the number of four thousand, stood and listened to the funeral service, which was read by the Rev. Dr. H. N. Powers, and to a few words from the Rev. Dr. W. H. Furness and Mr. E. C. Stedman. A burial ode was sung by a Kennett chorus.

Bayard Taylor lies buried in the country he loved so well, amongst his own kinsfolk to whom he had been so loyal. A wider fame and the meaning of his life are symbolized in the monument above him and in the plants which guard his grave. A Greek altar of the Doric order bears upon its frieze the words "He being dead yet speaketh." Upon the face of the circular stone is a bronze medallion of his head by Launt Thompson, surmounted by a carven wreath of oak leaves and bay,— emblematic of civic and poetic honors. Upon the reverse are the lines from " Prince Deukalion " : —

> For Life, whose source not here began,
> Must fill the utmost sphere of Man,
> And, so expanding, lifted be
> Along the line of God's decree,
> To find in endless growth all good, —
> In endless toil, beatitude.

When the sarcophagus was brought to the steamer at Hamburg, some evergreens in pots were found at its side. It was not known and never has been learned whence they came. They followed the body to its last resting-place, and there were set out in the sod. They came from unknown hands. They stand by the grave, witnessing to that affection and veneration which were paid to Bayard Taylor by numberless persons whom he never knew or saw ; their living green is a sign of that unfading memory which will be renewed with every fresh generation of lovers of poetry and honorers of noble aspiration.

INDEX.

goes to London, and then to Greece, 336; settles at Athens and studies modern Greek, 337; his interest in Grecian history and art, 338; makes excursions to Crete, Morea, and Thessaly, 339; returns to Gotha, leaves his wife, and visits Russia, 340; rejoices over the birth of a daughter, 341; attends the three hundredth anniversary of the University of Jena and returns to America, 342; abandons travel, in his mind, 343; resumes lecturing, 344; spends a rainy day in writing rhymes, 345; returns with enthusiasm to poetry, 348; is busy with building Cedarcroft, 349; makes a lecturing tour in California, 350; publishes "Travels in Greece and Russia," and "At Home and Abroad, First Series," 353; his Christmas, 354; takes up poetry with new ardor, 356; writes "The Poet's Journal," 366; is busy with Cedarcroft, 367; entertains the Buflebs, 367; has a house-warming, 368; takes part in the Presidential canvass, 369; proposes to translate Gustav Freytag's "Pictures of Life in Germany," 370; sends "The Poet's Journal" to press, 371; writes "The Confessions of a Medium," 372; his political views, 372, 373; his ballad of "Prayer-Meeting in a Storm," 373; his controversy with a Richmond lecture-committee, 374; his desire to write an American novel, 374; begins "Hannah Thurston," 374; gives up his New York house, 375; his exertions at the beginning of the war, 375–377; goes to Germany with his wife, child, and mother, 378; his literary activity there, 379; is received by the Duke of Saxe-Coburg-Gotha, 379; returns to America, 379; is invited to go to Russia as secretary of legation, 383; accepts the appointment, 384; his reasons for going to Russia, 386; his first experience of diplomatic life, 387; his opinion of the Czar, 389; resumes work on "Hannah Thurston," 389; is left in charge of the mission, 390; desires the appointment as minister, 390; performs important service in diplomacy, 394–403; intercepts Confederate dispatches, 408; communicates with Mr. Dayton and Mr. Adams, 409; resigns his position, 410; is offered a special appointment to Persia, 411; hears of the death of his brother Frederick, and returns to America, 413; publishes "Hannah Thurston," 415; writes a lecture on "Russia and her People," 417; prepares a Blue and Gold edition of his poems, 417; works at "Picture of St. John," and "Faust," 418; and begins "John Godfrey's Fortunes," 418; his work and hospitality, 419; his farm-life, 420; his enjoyment of the country, 421, 422; celebration of

his fortieth birthday, 427; his Sunday evenings at home, 427; his views upon the compensation of authors, 428–430; sets up "The Story of Kennett," 431; goes to Washington to see the grand review, 433; addresses the Progressive Friends, 435; is nearly killed by his brother's tombstone, 435; is irked by household cares, 436; his farm experiments, 437; finishes "The Picture of St. John," 439, 441; his reflections on it, 442, 443; makes a visit to Boston and neighborhood, 445, 446; goes into winter quarters in New York, 447; is consulted about a magazine, 448; his social entertainments, 449; takes a trip to Colorado, 459; the books he read, 460; takes up painting in oils, 461; plans for work abroad, 463; his ambition regarding "Faust," 464; his retrospect in view of "The Picture of St. John," 465; longs for rest, 469; goes to Europe, 470; visits Tennyson, 471; calls on Matthew Arnold, 473; breakfasts with Lord Houghton, 473; dines with Anne Thackeray, 474; at Gotha and Lausanne, 475; at the Exhibition in Paris, 477; in the Thüringian Forest, 479; in Venice, 480; is taken ill, 481; and dangerously sick in Florence, 482; goes to Naples, 487; has a narrow escape, 488; works at painting, 490; returns by Florence, 492; to Gotha, 493; returns to America, 494; plans of work at Cedarcroft, 497; labors on "Faust," 498; is asked to write the story of Abraham Lincoln, 499; celebrates the golden wedding of his parents by a masque of characters, 500–503; writes "Notus Ignoto," 504; and discusses it with Mr. Fields, 505; completes the first draft of Part I. of "Faust," 506; begins work on "Joseph and his Friend," 508; writes the Gettysburg Ode, 513; is invited to lecture at Cornell, 513; his work on "Putnam's" and "The Tribune," 514; reports country life in "Home Pastorals," 516; moves to New York for a while, 524; works at "Faust" and lectures on German literature, 525; goes to California on a lecturing trip, 527; his interest in the Franco-German war, and his literary work in connection with it, 531; carries "Faust" through the press, 533, 534; his dissatisfaction with country life, 535; is given a dinner upon the publication of "Faust," 542; engaged upon a Second Part, 547; publishes the completion, 554; his judgment of his own capacity, 555; the powers which he brings to the task, 556; his memory, 557; arranges to edit a "Library of Travel," 558; visits the Eastern shore, 561; visits Manitoba, 563; reviews "The Divine Tragedy," 567; determines to give up Cedarcroft, 571;

Poetical and Dramatic Works

OF

BAYARD TAYLOR.

———◆———

Poetical Works. Including all his poetical writings except those dramatic in form, embracing the Poet's Journal, Poems of the Orient, Home Pastorals, Ballads, Lyrics, the Picture of St. John, and Lars, besides those contained in earlier volumes, entitled simply "Poems." *Household Edition.* 12mo, $2.00; half calf, $4.00; morocco, or tree calf, $5.00.

In it the face and the soul of Bayard Taylor are reflected with perfect clearness and truth — for there is nothing to be concealed or softened; no stain is upon the memory of this man who, having set poetry before him as the means and end of his life, honored equally his art and himself. His natural speech was song; the passion, purity, and spontaneous flow of his verse are alike extraordinary. — *Portland Press.*

Many who are familiar with the productions of one period of his life, as presented in a single volume, have no proper conception of his power and scope as poet as shown in his work as a whole. — *Boston Transcript.*

Dramatic Works. Including all of his poems dramatic in form, namely: The Prophet, The Masque of the Gods, and Prince Deukalion. With Notes by MARIE HANSEN-TAYLOR. New Edition, uniform with the *Kennett Edition* of Taylor's "Translation of Faust." Crown 8vo, gilt top, $2.25; half calf, $4.50; morocco, $6.00.

"Prince Deukalion" and "The Masque of the Gods" are the works of a large, ripe mind in full command of all the resources of poetic writing. They represent years of patient and earnest thought, a large acquaintance with men and life in all its phases, as well as an individuality which, although it had come into contact with the thought and learning of many races, was strongly marked and harmoniously developed. No one who desires to know Mr. Taylor's genius at its best will fail to familiarize himself with these poems; they are an addition to our literature which we will do well to study. — *Christian Union* (New York).

Poems of the Orient. 16mo, $1.25.

"Poems of the Orient" bear the stamp throughout of vivid oriental experience. With the exception of two or three of the more elaborate pieces, it combines greater spontaneity of expression, a more intimate feeling of nature, and a more daring flight of the imagination, with a nicer artistic finish, than any of his former productions. — *New York Tribune.*

Poems of Home and Travel. 16mo, $1.25.

In certain particulars he is unequaled by any of our poets. In grace, in the power of producing clear, distinct, and lovely pictures of life and nature, in straightforwardness and felicity of expression, in an exquisite mingling of humor and tender pathos, in variety of sustained poetic power, and in vigor, naturalness, and manliness of thought and style, he has no equal among our home-bred poets. — *Christian Intelligencer* (New York).

The Masque of the Gods. 16mo, $1.25.

We can give but a faint idea of the sublimity of the conception which is wrought out in the drama. In some respects it approaches "Faust" in its tremendous power and suggestiveness. — *Troy Times.*

The Prophet: A Tragedy. 16mo, $2.00.

Mr. Taylor has drawn his prophet marvelously well. — *New York Tribune.*

This strikingly original poem. — *Philadelphia Bulletin.*

Prince Deukalion. A Lyrical Drama. 8vo, white vellum cloth, full gilt, $3.00.

This dramatic poem contains four acts, — the first representing the disappearance of Classic Faith, and the dawn of Christianity, — time, A. D. 300; the second, A. D. 1300, depicting the struggle of the Church of Rome with the human race; the third, the nineteenth century, with its conflicting Protestantism and Science; the fourth, the Future, with its larger faith and charity.

The appearance of this noble work is a notable event in the literature of our age; and is doubly important, — first, as the rich fruitage and experience of a life whose action makes no discount upon its aim and expression; and secondly, as the singularly complete and high representation of the most illuminated thought, hope, and belief of the age. . . . It is a work of which the very greatness awes, and even a little represses, the language of praise. It is a noble poem, which crowns the honorable head of Bayard Taylor as a master among poets. — *Portland Press.*

The Echo Club, and other Literary Diversions. "Little Classic" style, 18mo, $1.25.

A charming book of fresh and many-sided criticisms of poetry, with exceedingly skillful and good-humored travesties of the characteristic manner of the best known American and English poets, — Tennyson, Lowell, Whittier, Bryant, Longfellow, Holmes, Stedman, Aldrich, Emerson, Browning, Bret Harte, Poe, Mrs. Howe, Keats, Jean Ingelow, Joaquin Miller, Walt Whitman, and many others.

We know of nothing of their order of literature equal in merit to this series of papers. The geniality, humor, and rich fund of ability they display, no reader of taste can fail to appreciate. — *Boston Traveller*.

Home Ballads. With beautiful Illustrations, from designs by F. S. CHURCH, F. DIELMAN, G. W. EDWARDS, W. H. GIBSON, T. HOVENDEN, H. BOLTON JONES, J. N. MARBLE, F. D. MILLET, J. F. MURPHY, W. L. TAYLOR, and G. H. YEWELL; engraved by GEORGE T. ANDREW, W. B. CLOSSON, HENRY GRAY, E. HEINEMAN, W. J. LINTON, and ORR & CO. 8vo, full gilt, $3.00; morocco or tree calf, $7.50.

CONTENTS: The Quaker Widow; The Holly-Tree; John Reed; Jane Reed; The Old Pennsylvania Farmer.

We have no words except those of praise and commendation in respect to this beautiful book. Artist, engraver, and printer have combined to give an appropriate setting to a choice selection of Taylor's sweetest and tenderest poems, and the result is a holiday volume which to see is to awaken a desire to possess. The ballads are five in number, and are all redolent of rural life and scenery. . . . Each possesses a charm that makes it a well-spring of pleasure to the poetic soul. — *Chicago Journal*.

The gem of the season thus far is the beautiful holiday edition of Bayard Taylor's "Home Ballads." The illustrations are remarkably fine. The full-page figures have a life and expression rarely found in such illustrations. The smaller illustrations are all good, and the delicate half-titles are exquisite in design and execution. The bits of landscape, the grapes, the flowers, the holly, are admirable examples of drawing and engraving. — *Boston Advertiser*.

Bayard Taylor in poetry and in prose had a wonderful eye for the picturesque, and it is no surprise to find how fully these ballads lend themselves to illustration. The illustrations are enchanting.—*Christian Advocate* (New York).

Faust. By J. W. von Goethe. Translated into English Verse by Bayard Taylor. *One-Volume Edition.* 12mo, gilt top, $3.00; half calf, $5.00; morocco, $7.00.

Kennett Edition. In two volumes, 12mo, gilt top, $4.50; half calf, $8.00; morocco, $10.00.

The Same. Complete in two volumes. Each volume includes a Part. Royal 8vo, gilt top, $4.50; the two volumes, $9.00; half calf, $15.00; morocco, $20.00.

Mr. Bayard Taylor has rendered the whole poem in English wonderfully close and wonderfully free from strain and harshness. Line for line and metre for metre, he followed Goethe's way, flinching before no difficulties, and seldom otherwise than victorious, — a labor so great that no man could have hoped for success who had not in himself enough of the poetic spirit to undertake it as a labor of love. Bayard Taylor's "Faust" is altogether, to our mind, one of the most remarkable feats of translation achieved in any modern language. It can be safely maintained that the rich and varied music of "Faust" has never before been as faithfully presented to English ears. — *Saturday Review* (London).

Bayard Taylor's work is easily ahead of all others in respect of critical and laborious examination of all the sources of information touching upon the poem or its origin. His notes and comments are exhaustive, and *must* be consulted by any student of the subject who wishes to go to the bottom of disputed points. Although a half dozen translations have appeared since Taylor's was completed, we still pronounce his the "standard." — *Literary World* (Boston).

It is not only a success, in the common sense of the word; not only a faithful rendering of the sense of the original in pleasing English verse, but it is a transfer of the spirit and the form of that wonderful book into our own tongue to an extent which would have been thought impossible had it not been made. — *New York Evening Post.*

It combines the excellences of fidelity to the text and of poetic expression in so remarkable a degree that it is rightly considered a masterpiece of translation, and will be preferred to all previous English translations. — *Illustrirte Zeitung* (Leipsic).

*** *For sale by all Booksellers. Sent, post-paid, on receipt of price by the Publishers,*

HOUGHTON, MIFFLIN AND COMPANY,

4 Park St., Boston; 11 East 17th St., New York.

www.ingramcontent.com/pod-product-compliance
Lightning Source LLC
Chambersburg PA
CBHW021531110726
47902CB00004B/831